FREYA'S CHILD

By

P. J. Roscoe

Cover Art by
Loraine Von Tonder

Edited by
Veronica Castle

Published by
Crimson Cloak Publishing
All Rights Reserved

ISBN 13: 978-1-68160-344-5
ISBN 10: 1-68160-344-6

Publishers Publication in Data:

Roscoe, P. J.
Freya's Child
1. Fiction   2. Contemporary 3. Vikings 4.. Drama 5. Mystery 6. Fantasy

Acknowledgments

Jamie Lund, National Trust for your information on archaeological digs. The Grosvenor Museum, Chester for your helpful suggestions on archaeological digs

I'd like to thank Fiona for her honest feedback in the first edition. Paul for his wonderful artwork yet again. Karen for pointing out my mistakes. My friends and family who always support me, and last but definitely never least, my husband Martin, whose love and support keeps me going.

To all parents who love unconditionally ... but especially mine - Ken and Jacquie.

Prologue

*T*he dawn mist hung softly in the air, tinged with the promise of gold as the sun's fingers gently caressed the earth. The small group walked confidently but silently towards the house, their weapons hung loosely by their sides. They did not expect a fight. The decision made, the order given. What was the point of fighting it?

The small wooden door was shut. The animal skin hanging over it gently flapped in the cool breeze. The leader stopped and listened but there was no sound from within. Glancing upwards, he saw that no smoke rose from the small hole in the roof: something was wrong. He forced the door open, stepping into the gloom; the others swiftly followed.

His cry shattered the silence, followed by the smashing of pottery as he unleashed his fury at such blatant defiance. He had acted weak for the sake of friendship and battles won. A mistake he must rectify. The man charged out of the house and quickly scanned the surrounding area.

The others gathered around him. Hatred and fear burned on each man's face. Their weapons no longer remained idle. They gripped them tightly as the intensity of their emotion transferred to the wooden handles and along the shaft to the sharp, cold metal of their axes and swords.

Each man waited impatiently for their chief to give the order. They willed it, unable to keep their feet from moving. They had to go and they had to go now or may Odin forgive them if anyone else should step into their path. There would be no peace now until blood had been spilt.

Finally their chief gave the order and with it came their voices. They growled their consent and their bodies gave way to the roar of blood in their veins. They moved as one in the only direction their prey could have fled: the river, towards the sea.

***

The young girl watched the men disappear among the trees, and wiped away her tear. They did not see her and that would be in her favour, but she could not have stopped herself from watching even though her life may depend on it. Knowing the fate of the family and the reasons behind the decision did not lessen her grief: after all, she had known them all her twelve years and spoken with them almost every day.

She had sat beside the woman on untold occasions in the great hall whilst listening to stories, singing songs and praying to the gods. They had shared many meals, gossiping while she learned new skills for when she was married. Only yesterday she had shared a tearful moment with the woman Astrid over the death of yet another child. She had whispered her fear that the sickness was walking among them all and would soon choose another, and she was right.

She had heard the whispers of some who believed that this was a curse from the gods. They were angry because Halldor had allowed the priest to come into their village and talk of his God. She slammed her fist against the doorpost. She despised the new God that had brought so much unrest amongst her people. This one, true God who loved all of his children, yet the priest had said he had sacrificed his own son. Odin would triumph over such a cruel and weak god.

She closed her eyes for a moment, her head now resting against the wooden doorframe as a wave of dizziness swept over her. She felt hot against the cool morning air and knew that she had been cursed too. She had hours, perhaps a day before the sickness took a firm hold and then she would be fighting for her life. She felt the stirring of the world as it came awake and said a swift prayer to the God Odin and her favourite Goddess, Freya, before turning away back to her bed.

Chapter One

The rain had finally stopped sometime around four thirty. Getting out of bed for the sixth time Helen wandered around the house, their home for the last eleven years. Thoughts and memories of their lives ran at full speed through her head; it was beginning to hurt. Yawning, she made herself another cup of tea and climbed back into her cold bed, the mug resting warmly on her knee.

She sat that way for a very long time, trying to recall good memories. Most had centred around her daughter, but there had been others: though rare, they were there. She had woken abruptly with the early morning sun on her face and the cat purring loudly in her ear, the empty mug lying beside her.

Heaving another black bag out of the front door, Helen wiped her brow as the sweat trickled down the side of her face, tickling her neck. She glanced quickly inside the car to check that her daughter Charlotte was okay. She smiled as she watched Charlotte carefully comb her doll's long blonde hair. Her high-pitched voice spoke clearly and precisely to the doll about what was happening today.

"You all right, baby girl?" Her voice did not betray her inner turmoil.

Charlotte looked up, waved the comb and smiled, "We're okay Mummy. We are getting pretty for the journey. When are we going?"

Helen sighed loudly and pushed back a lock of hair, "Just getting the last bags now and then we're off on an adventure; five more minutes …" She hated pretending, hoping to keep Charlotte from getting upset. Although, if she really thought about it, her daughter hadn't got upset about the move when she'd been told. She had merely asked a few questions which had consisted of why, when and how and what would her new bedroom look like? Truth be told, she was the only one who felt negative about the move. She was the only one with doubts; but no one had cared if she would be upset.

Feeling miserable, exhausted and very lonely, she turned back towards the house and yanked out her large brown suitcase stuffed with clothes and knick-knacks. Jamming it into the last bit of space in the boot of the car, she ran back inside the house and picked up her large, multi-coloured shoulder bag that she'd had forever. It had so many patches on it she could barely remember the original pattern. Shifting it further up her shoulder, she scooped up a small handbag, a plastic bag full of sweets, crisps, fruit and sandwiches, a large bottle of water and a flask of hot coffee, all of which would be her life savers for the long trip.

Dropping them all onto their driveway she stopped. This was it; the moment she had dreaded for five months. From this instant her life was apparently supposed to change for the better! At least, that's what she'd been attempting to convince herself. Staring at her front door, a memory came rushing back and she swallowed hard to contain the growing emotion that was choking her.

He had wanted to paint it a bright red colour that she'd said reminded her of blood. She'd suggested a lovely forest green colour that he said looked like something you'd find in your nose. They continuously argued and bickered about it until finally she had given in for a bit of peace. He had painted it red. It did look hideous and after a few months he changed the colour again, to black. Only this time, he hadn't asked her opinion.

She thought of all the times he got his own way. Where they ate on the rare occasions he had taken her out on a date. The area they lived in, the holidays they had and when they could take them. It was always his friends from work that they met up with because he didn't like her friends, saying he hated all the girlie giggling.

Work had been another battle. When they had met and married, she'd been a full time nurse at the local hospital. A fact he'd used on numerous occasions to make some inappropriate joke to his work colleagues. However, once Charlotte was born, his attitude changed. She'd agreed in principal that she wanted to be a full time Mum for a while anyway, but once Charlotte reached a year old, she'd wanted to return to work on a part time basis. It was the cause of many disagreements on child-care, which was a joke as far as she was concerned, considering his lack of parenting.

Robert had not been happy about her pregnancy and had even hinted that the timing was bad. She'd known what that meant and withdrew from him even further. Robert played very little part in her pregnancy. Always too busy at work to come to birthing classes or meetings with doctors; he even missed the scans.

It was the morning her waters broke she caught him watching her in the kitchen, a slight smile on his face. "You're carrying a cherry pip. You look ready to burst ..."

She'd rounded on him, months of frustration unleashed, "Cherry pip! This is a baby, you idiot ... A BABY! You haven't shown one ounce of interest until now and that's the best you can come up with? You bastard!"

Robert had rushed to her side, taking her completely by surprise and held her tightly. She tried to fight him, but she was too big and too exhausted.

"I'll stay home today." It was as if he'd known. Later that morning, her waters broke and after nine hours of labour, Charlotte was born.

"My cherry pip." Was the first thing he'd said when the nurse handed him his child and it stuck. She became known as Cherry. He'd cared then. Taking the time off and spending hours with her at the hospital, staring down at his daughter, watching fascinated when she'd breast fed Cherry. Two days after coming home, he'd gone back to work.

Now he was getting his own way, yet again, they were moving house because he needed a new start. He needed to get away from the bad memories for which he was responsible. He needed to run and hide and pretend everything would be all right. He could go on pretending if he hid in his old town, returned to his roots and started again.

Robert had convinced himself that it could work, but not her. She was sick and tired of hearing about his damned needs. What he needed to survive, what he needed to get his life back on track, what he needed to save their marriage. 'Needs': it was a word she had begun to despise this last year.

He hadn't even had the decency to discuss the move before making a final decision. She vaguely remembered a brief conversation that went something like, "I need to get away from here, how about the Wirral? I have been offered a new job down there to start when I am ready. It's not the same amount of money, but we won't starve, so how about it? We leave as soon as we sell this place."

She had sat in stunned silence for a long time after he'd darted from the room in the hope of avoiding any arguments. A large part of her hadn't cared about moving. One house was just like another when your marriage is a joke, with no friends and no permanent job. The other part of her hated his every fibre and wanted to scream in his smug face to *go to hell! Go to bloody Wirral and never return.*

However, there was darling Cherry. How could she consider leaving her without a Dad? True, he hadn't been much of a Dad since her birth, except this last year. If his breakdown had accomplished nothing else, he had found his fatherhood and bonded with Cherry.

It sickened her that Robert finally decided to behave as though Cherry existed and it had hurt her deeply that their daughter warmed to him, accepting him without question and yes, she could admit that jealousy played a big part, but surely, she'd earned those feelings?

The day after his announcement, she'd cornered him in the kitchen and pointed out to him that Cherry had only just begun a new playgroup and would be starting school very soon. Had he considered Cherry's thoughts on the move? As it turned out he had: and Cherry was fine about moving.

She'd stared at him dumbfounded, looking for any sign of arrogance or smugness, but there'd been none. Merely a look of hope and expectancy; and she'd quickly left the kitchen feeling more like an outsider than ever before.

Shaking herself she tried to think of anything positive, but it was an extremely hard emotion to feel after the trauma of being married to a selfish bastard. She thought of all the times that she'd packed a bag, determined that enough was enough, only to cry and stay.

She was very aware that over the years she had become weak, allowing him to dictate her life; it wasn't something she was proud about. She cringed whenever she thought about it for too long. Robert had once been a man she could count on. A man who looked after her, loved her, wanted her, desired her, but that had been a long time ago. Now she had no idea what he felt for her and absolutely no idea what she felt for him.

The man in question had left yesterday in his car to follow the removal van and had hardly looked at her mumbling a goodbye and "see you around dinner time …?"

She'd closed the door without saying a word. Since his breakdown, she'd scrambled around for anything positive to cling onto, but her time had run out. They were moving away from everything she knew and she hadn't come up with any alternative plan. The sale of the house had been quicker than expected. Then the madness that followed, caring for Charlotte, packing, and sorting boxes in-between doing temporary work at the hospital; she hadn't given herself time to think about it.

She realised now that she'd welcomed the madness, allowing it to take over and pull her in. It meant she wasn't thinking, remembering or grieving for the man she'd lost. If she kept as busy as possible, she could pretend her life was fine and not shit. Now, she couldn't continue hiding from the awful truth; they were leaving today and her stomach clenched with fear at making a terrible mistake.

Her friends, who had once been many, had slowly dwindled over the last four years as she shied away from them, making excuses for not having nights out or morning coffee. She had withdrawn and they had not followed. The single goodbye card she received through the post yesterday had confirmed her loneliness. They had stopped coming to the house long ago, now they could not even come to say goodbye. The card soaked, by her tears, was stuffed into her shoulder bag, a reminder of what she had once had.

"Mummy! When can we go?"

Taking a deep breath, she quickly wiped her face and turned to smile at her daughter who was poking her head through the car window. "We're all set I think, or have we forgotten anything?" Pretending to search under the car, she heard Cherry tut.

"Mummy, you know Twinkle is already in the car with Emily and me."

"Is Twinkle all right?"

Right on cue Twinkle gave a loud meow. She plastered on a fake smile and pushed the bags onto the back seat next to Cherry and slammed the door. Twinkle meowed loudly again. The poor cat didn't sound too happy about the move either. She poked a finger through the cat basket and gave the cat a little tickle under the chin. Poor darling, she knew how she felt. After all, this had been Twinkle's territory all her three and a half years. She'd rescued Twinkle the day Charlotte had come home from the hospital, two days old. The kitten had been dumped in the bin outside the maternity ward; some person's idea of a sick joke.

Taking the kitten to the vet the next day, he'd told her that it was only five weeks old. Thrown away like rubbish: she'd decided there and then that she was keeping it, and paid for the treatments before gently carrying the tiny kitten home in a box, still with Charlotte happily sleeping against her chest in her baby carrier.

She must have looked a terrible sight to the young vet. Tired eyes she could barely open from only an hour's sleep. Her lady bits bruised and battered that had made walking a little difficult - and large round stains on her shirt from leaking nipples as her milk came in, which brought with it a wave of tears that sat on the surface ready to fall at every opportunity; she'd cried twice whilst with the poor vet. To top it all off, she stank of breast milk, baby puke and pooh! No wonder the vet always smiled whenever she returned for Twinkle's annual jabs, he was probably remembering the state she had been in.

Robert hadn't been enthusiastic at first, insisting that he much preferred a dog if they were going to have pets, but darling Cherry had taken one look at the tiny black kitten and gurgled with delight, following the little thing with her eyes around the room and following physically once she could crawl. Twinkle would curl up at the bottom of Cherry's cot, but people warned her it was not a good idea. Nevertheless, whenever they moved Twinkle, she'd go right back and immediately curl up and go to sleep. After watching the cat for a while, she'd decided Twinkle was harmless; quite cute really. When Cherry moved into her own bed, Twinkle moved with her.

Helen frowned. Perhaps she did have a comrade after all. Twinkle never went near Robert, sensing his attitude towards her. When he came into the room, Twinkle would either leave or change position so that her back was to him. She followed Helen and Cherry everywhere and if she wasn't sleeping on Cherry's bed she could be found on her side of the bed.

For a moment she stared around at her front lawn, immaculately mown; her flower beds, which were just beginning to come to life. The buds on the cherry blossoms were almost in full bloom. She would miss the scattering of the petals when the April winds came; she had always loved that. She would stand with Charlotte in her arms beneath the two trees and try to catch as many of the flowers as possible, loving the feel of them as they swirled around her. 'Fairyland', Cherry called it, a pink and white magic.

All of her potted herbs and flowers had already gone ahead. She worried about them surviving the long journey, as her garden had become her haven. It was her place to think and find some peace whilst potting a new herb or flower. She liked to experiment with different herbs and she already drank various teas using the herbs from her garden and knew she would need the calming, yet uplifting magic of a lemon balm tea later on today.

She looked down the road; the school run was over so it was quiet. The city lay just over two miles away and from her bedroom window, she could just see the top of York Minster. She could visualise the route she'd taken to work, the school she passed which would have been Cherry's school, 'The Golden Fleece', her favourite pub with its old beams and fine ales. She had been quite a regular there in the days before Cherry; so much so, they'd known her name. No one would know her in Wirral.

Would she find a new job in this new place? Enquiries had led her to a nearby hospital only a ten minute drive from Frankby. They had already received her C.V.; she hadn't told Robert. There were plenty of old pubs in the area and lots of history. Walks galore in all directions but nothing appealed to her yet, she hoped it changed once they'd settled in.

She glanced in the rear view mirror at her darling Cherry. Poor lamb, what was going on in her head? She had talked quite a lot about moving over the last few months, but Cherry hadn't shown any signs of trauma. Together they had looked up 'Wirral' on websites and had trawled through local parks, local interests and towns. Cherry was looking forward to visiting 'West Kirby' with its beach and boat lake but she wasn't convinced the 'beach' wouldn't be littered with rubbish and needles and dog muck and the 'boat lake' wouldn't have old trollies and fly-tipping peeping through the filthy water, but she kept her opinion and worries to herself.

A new school was waiting to accept Cherry in September and had sent details of a local playgroup, but it terrified her that the other children might not accept her. Nightmares plagued her of Cherry standing alone in a playground while other children mocked her, pulling at her clothes until she stood naked, cowering from the insults and laughter. She knew rationally that it was her own anxieties and fears projected onto Cherry, but it was a real concern. Perhaps it was time to call her by her real name until she knew how the other children would behave.

Another loud meow and a groan from Cherry brought her to her senses and she started the car. Out of the corner of her eye, she noticed across the street a curtain twitch.

"Be positive," the counsellor had said. "Find something good about the move and hold onto it."

Putting on her best smile, she waved to the old hag who had bitched about them for the past year. Her stories had become so ridiculous it beggared belief that people could be taken in by her lies. But they had and they had stared, pointed, and whispered. People were cruel. She certainly wouldn't miss that. The last straw for her had been the night Robert fell apart completely. Mrs Havers had come out onto her doorstep, arms folded and eyes full of scorn, to get a good view as their lives fell apart.

He had screamed and shouted obscenities, but only about himself. What Mrs Havers hadn't mentioned to those willing to listen was that he had then sat crying, heartbroken, cradling himself, refusing to allow Helen to comfort him until the police and ambulance had arrived. Who had phoned them she would never know for sure, but her gut told her Mrs Havers had had a hand in it.

Robert's breakdown had forced them both to confront their fears about life, their marriage and their jobs. They were quite rich, some might say, but it had cost them dear. Their marriage, if she could really call it one, had always come second to his job as an investment banker. Constant late nights, coming home stinking of alcohol and cigarettes, mumbling that he was going to bed with no explanation or apology.

"I'm working my arse off for you and Cherry," he'd shouted at her the last time she'd confronted him. "It's all for you. I want us to have a good house, a good life. I don't want us to be worrying about anything." Although Robert looked sincere enough, his story hadn't convinced her and she'd stormed off to their bedroom; he had slept in the spare room, again.

Not long afterwards, it had all fallen apart. He lost a huge amount of money in a bad investment and disappeared for a day. Having finally settled Cherry in bed she had jumped at the shouting coming from her front garden and had rushed out to find Robert kneeling on the grass, soaked to the skin as the February rain pelted down on his head, screaming obscenities at the night sky. She'd stared, frozen, unable to comprehend that this was her husband of eleven years. The arrogant man she barely saw anymore now knelt on their lawn crying like a baby. She would never get that image out of her head. Even the weekly counselling she had gone to could not erase that.

"Stop trying to erase it," the counsellor had said. "Accept it as something that has happened. The more you fight it, the more negative it becomes."

Therefore, here she was, over a year later, trying to accept it. She understood the need to leave the city and all its memories. Leave his job, his career and change his pace of life, it sounded good. They had enough money to survive until they got back on their feet. In theory, a move was a good idea, for him at least, if the marriage was still strong.

At least Mrs. Havers wasn't moving with them. She could not spy on their lives anymore and that was the first positive thought about the move, she clung onto that. Fighting back the tears, she slowly moved out onto the road, she would never give that dreadful woman the satisfaction of her tears.

Chapter Two

The drive from York to Wirral was never going to be pleasant, but even she hadn't expected such a nightmare. Motorways were not her favourite place to drive at the best of times, especially if Charlotte was in the car. The aggressive driving of the other drivers scared her and kept her speed to sixty miles an hour or less.

She planned to stop at least once, but she had had to stop four times to sort out Twinkle who was sick in her basket, which made Cherry cry. Hoping Twinkle would settle down while the basket dried, she allowed her to curl up on the passenger seat on top of her coat. However, half an hour later the cat did her toilet on the passenger side floor, making everyone feel ill. Thankfully, they had only been a couple of miles from the next service station and she'd cleaned it and the cat's basket as best as she could with wet wipes and bottled water.

The last hour of the journey had been awful as Twinkle meowed loudly wanting to get out of her wet basket, giving her a headache. Cherry had become even more upset, crying that she wanted to go home. The final straw had been when Twinkle managed to unhinge the lock on the basket and had leaped out onto Helen's shoulder, causing her to swerve and do an emergency stop. The start of her new life was not going well. They finally arrived on the Wirral disgruntled, exhausted and over two hours later than expected.

Frankby was exactly as she remembered it. A quiet tree lined road with large houses on either side, which meant lots of money and this made her nervous. What would she have in common with these people? Thankfully the houses were spaced out, which for her had been one of the highlights of moving, no neighbours. Fields surrounded their cottage and a little further along the road stood a large wood, a favourite for dog walkers and, she hoped, no junkies. It was pretty in its own way, but not home. Over the years they had visited the area whenever Robert had an urge to re-connect with his roots and she'd found the place okay in places, but she was a Yorkshire girl. Rugged, open moors, a sky that never ended and Heathcliff.

Robert had been brought up on the Wirral, but he'd left aged nineteen when his parents died in a motorway pile up. Choosing to take up an offer of a job from an old friend of his father's, he had moved down to London where he trained in the fine art of making money. Taking the job as manager of the York office, they'd met in a bar the night he was celebrating his success.

She'd reluctantly come with him four months before to view the two hundred year old sandstone cottage, their potential new home and thought it quaint, but found it difficult to feel any enthusiasm. Even when the estate agent had eagerly informed them that the cottage stood in the grounds of an old manor house, she still hadn't raised more than an eyebrow and that was just being polite.

Turning into the drive she smiled as Cherry gave a loud squeal, causing Twinkle to leap within her basket with fright, making it rock precariously on the front seat. "Mummy! This is a good place. Twinkle will love it. Wow! Look at all that grass! Mummy, is the sea over there? I love that tree, it's swishy …"

Her instant enthusiasm for the place was infectious as she stopped the car outside the front door. She was right of course. There was a lot of grass and this was only the front lawn, hidden from the road by a dense hedge that ended at a large gate that stood wide open. A long-standing willow tree sat cosily in the corner, its branches hanging lazily, swishing the grass beneath with every breath of air. Various plants and flowers dotted the borders of an immaculate front garden. The previous owners had obviously adored nature and had grown well established grounds.

The large back garden was twice the size of the front, most of that was also grass and borders but with a circular patio that nestled beside the large oblong conservatory. There had been a pond at the far end of the garden, but they'd insisted that it be filled before they move in. It was now a large sand pit complete with buckets and spades galore; a surprise for Cherry.

The gardens grasped her imagination. She had begun planning what to do almost immediately once the sale went through. There would be a lot of mowing, tending and digging up areas for her herbs and vegetables. She planned to grow apple and pear trees, raspberry and blackberry vines and possibly a grape vine. She'd already had success in growing a variety of vegetables and intended to expand into potatoes and pumpkins among others. All of this potential was for her, the house's selling point. She could hardly wait to get on her knees and dig in the dirt and claim the area as her own; she was glad Robert didn't like gardening.

She sat for a moment longer, watching Cherry run around the large garden showing her doll, Emily, every inch. She didn't notice the front door open until Cherry spun round and flung herself at the man standing within the doorway.

"Daddy!"

"Hello, my little Cherry pip, long journey?"

Although he hugged his daughter, he was watching her. She found that she could not look away. His green eyes held hers and for a brief moment she thought she saw a yearning. It was too much; she looked away first and climbed out of the car.

She yanked out the bags and suitcase before he could disentangle himself from Charlotte; needing to keep busy to delay the inevitable awkwardness. Twinkle flew

14

out of the car and stopped to sniff around the doorframe. Robert finally disengaged himself from his clinging daughter and picked her up. "Hello Twinkle and how was your journey?" The cat squirmed in his arms, unused to this show of affection, and he quickly released her.

"Oh Daddy, Twinkle can't speak, silly! But she did have a bad tummy and she did a smelly pooh!"

Robert laughed as Cherry pulled a funny face, "Oh dear, that bad eh?"

"Yes, Daddy, it was very bad. Where's my bedroom, Daddy?

He didn't answer straight away; he was watching Helen who had turned her back on them and was massaging her eyes. She looked tired and he knew the journey would have been very hard for her emotionally as well as physically. He wanted to go and hug her, kiss her, swing her round with joy that she'd come. He wanted to tell her how much he appreciated the chance she had given him. He wanted to help her with the bags and laugh about how much junk they had brought with them but he wasn't sure what icy response he would get, pure hostility or indifference.

"Daddy?"

"Sorry baby, I'll let you go and find it, I think there might be a treat on your new bed ..."

He watched her as she raced inside and smiled listening to her banging and crashing doors as she ran from one room to another, before climbing the stairs.

"Hello Robert, it took us longer than expected, but I don't suppose you were worried at all ...?"

He turned back to face his wife who was waiting expectantly for him to move, a bag in each hand and her old shoulder bag heaved onto her shoulder. The sarcastic tone was not lost on him and he felt his heart break yet again; would she ever forgive him?

His gaze moved from her belongings, to look at the cat who sat quietly cleaning herself, indifferent to the static that emanated between them. It seemed as if only Cherry and now Twinkle were unaffected by his breakdown. He knew even before he said it how feeble it sounded but he couldn't think of anything else to say. "Come in."

Chapter Three

The wind was picking up causing loose soil to swirl around. Kathryn cried out as some particles got into her eye. Rubbing them better she grabbed her anorak and quickly pulled it on, enjoying the warmth that wrapped itself around her chilled body. Glancing up at the sky, she reckoned they had another two hours perhaps of good light; but the possibility of rain was definitely increasing. Not for the first time that day she felt frustration and anger towards the thief who'd stolen their gazebo last night and angry at herself for being stupid enough to leave it behind.

She quickly turned back to the newly exposed area. She had just found another collection of broken pottery and she desperately wanted to see if any of these pieces were more intact than the last pile found. She muttered to herself and shook her shoulders. The weather was stressing her because of the lack of covering. Trevor had already told her it would take a day or two to get another.

Settling herself into a comfortable position, she carefully used her small trowel to move away the soil around what looked like three large pieces of pottery; or perhaps they were parts of the same large pot. Using her tiny brush, she very gently removed more and more soil, until almost an hour later she gasped with delight as it became obvious they were all part of the same large pot. What a find!

"Tony!"

A muffled response came from further along the trench where her colleague was digging; he had his back to her.

"Tony, can you come and help with this please?" She didn't bother to try to hide her excitement. Tony heard it and immediately lifted his head and wiped his brow with the back of his hand.

"Whatcha got?" he asked as he jumped up and came to stand above her. "Wow! Looks intact, I'll get a box." She didn't watch him but she could hear him collecting a sample box that might be big enough to hold their find. As she waited, she continued to brush more and more soil off the find, "Oh my God! Tony, it has an inscription … Look, do you see it?"

16

"Bloody hell yes, definitely rune. Can't make out anything specific ... unless ... is that an E or an F?"

"Never mind that now, I just felt a spot of rain. Let's get this into the box."

Carefully stepping into the trench Tony placed the large box beside the mound of earth that housed the brown pot. It looked like a large cooking pot made of clay, which they were able to confirm when together they managed to get it out of the ground without breaking it. With it safely resting in the box Kathryn could study it a bit better.

"It definitely had an inscription on it, but most of it has eroded away. So cooking pot is out of the question. I can't see the Norsemen inscribing their cooking ware, can you?"

Tony shook his head, "It looks like an F and is that an A? It could be the owner's name or the name of a god perhaps?"

Kathryn nodded and carefully wrapped the pot in bubble wrap and closed the lid. "We should mark the area and pull that tarpaulin over the trench, it's about to rain. Typical! First really good find and I can't take a good look and the area could be washed away."

Placing a grid over the trench she quickly marked out the pot's position while Tony called the two volunteers who were busy washing some finds in the large tent. Together they tidied away the chairs, tables, and sieved the bowls for anything small that might have passed them by. Satisfied the bowls held nothing more than mud and water, they carefully poured it away.

Placing the small finds of the day back in the bags, they put everything into a large box and carried it out to the van, along with the kettle, their cups, the brushes they used to clean finds, their equipment; even their cutlery came back into the van.

When Kathryn had finished the grid, together they secured the tarpaulin over the trench. Once they were all satisfied that it was secure they walked quickly back to the large tent, now almost empty, and watched the huge rain drops splatter against the windows of the truck and bounce off the muddy ground.

"I'm sure it will be fine."

Kathryn grinned, "Can you always read my thoughts?"

"Of course! Your face is pretty easy to read, especially when you frown like that."

"I'm not surprised I'm frowning, our first big find in four days and look at it, torrential rain, gale force winds, it'll all be lost if ..."

"Now, now, let's not go away with the fairies! It is the end of April. It is Britain. Of course there's going to be rain and wind and no doubt there will be a theft or two, but we knew this when we decided to be archaeologists. We have to deal with disappointment when we break our backs and still find nothing and we have to deal with bastards who steal anything that isn't stuck down."

Holding up his hand to stop her interrupting, he grinned, "The local police know to come past the site and check it out and once we find a huge silver hoard we can have all the guard dogs you want! Until then, chill out! Enjoy the fact that today we found a lovely intact pot and I also found some broken pieces of what look like pottery weights and an intact whetstone. I noticed you didn't ask about those ..." He put up his hand to silence her comments, "No, it's no use now, I'm hurt and in need of a warm drink followed by a large whisky, anyone join me?"

The two volunteers smiled but shook their heads, "No thanks, we have plans tonight. We'll be off now then, if we're finished for the day?"

Kathryn pulled her Jacket closer, "Yes, that's fine. We'll see you tomorrow. I think we'll try some test pits again and see what comes up. Thanks for today ..."

Tony and Kathryn watched in silence as the two women raced towards the old blue fiesta parked next to the van. Tony heaved a loud sigh as they drove away.

"You all right?"

Tony grinned, "Of course. I was just thinking what plans those two might have." Seeing Kathryn didn't understand he leant closer, "You know, woman on woman action!"

Kathryn slapped him playfully on his shoulder, "You dirty sod! Jenny and Pam aren't lesbians ... are they? I don't care who helps us as long as we get some help." She sighed loudly and massaged her neck, "I can't wait till the students start; and Trevor was talking to some more potential volunteers this week. We only have permission to dig for four weeks. It would have been nice to have the students start right away, but I guess I can't have everything go to plan. Proving we had something for them to dig was the first hurdle and thankfully geophysics proved that. I just want this to go well."

Tony shrugged, "It will go well. What could possibly happen that we haven't encountered before? If you're still worrying about that protester, Mr Merton ...? He's mental, but harmless I think."

"No, not really; although he is the most enthusiastic demonstrator we've ever had."

Tony shook his head, "Some people eh? What possible harm could we be doing here, in this place? Don't these people understand it's important to find out stuff? To know your history is so cool."

Kathryn shook her head in dismay, "Oh, that will do it; tell this Mr Merton that it's all okay, 'cause history is cool! Idiot!"

Tony pulled a face, and following Kathryn outside he quickly pulled the zip all the way to the floor of the tent. The museum held the finds and a zip wouldn't stop a thief from getting in, but they would only find a few plastic chairs, a long table and a couple of plastic basins for washing finds.

"Besides, in a few days, we'll have the wonderful company of students all willing to dig for you and crawl in the mud. In addition, if all goes well, a few more volunteers. We'll find loads of goodies, you'll see; and then Mr Merton will have to kiss your arse."

Kathryn slapped him again, "Oh, you'd like that wouldn't you, ya filthy pig!"

Tony gently pushed her and grinned, "Only if I can watch!"

With one last look around the small field, they reached the van and thankfully climbed in. Tony let the engine warm up a bit before he carefully drove out of the small clearing. Kathryn jumped out, closed the metal gate and padlocked it.

The health and safety officer had taken his job very seriously, instructing the workers as they erected the six-foot fence around the site. Kathryn and Tony remained silent, keeping their thoughts to themselves as they watched the area become cocooned in a metal palisade fence for the 'safety' of the public and to deter people from walking over the site. They knew from experience that it never stopped the enthusiastic thief. The theft of the gazebo had already proved that, and if people wanted to have a closer look at the site, they always found a way.

A dig in South Wales early on in Kathryn's career had shown her what some people would do. During the two-week dig, they lost half of their equipment, while they were digging. The thieves were brazen enough to steal from under their noses, literally. From the tooth brushes used to clean some artefacts to a couple of spades, trowels and even the majority of the grass turf, it was unbelievable. She'd shared that story with Steve, from the geophysics department, the other day when he'd come to the site. He'd laughed before telling her his own stories of past digs as he'd walked the length and breadth of the site.

Kathryn held the box on her lap to help cushion it from the bumpy ride. The drive to Liverpool didn't take long but she couldn't relax, this was always the most nerve racking time for her. The artefact was her responsibility once the earth had given it up and until she had it settled in its new home, the museum, she couldn't rest.

Nevertheless, her enthusiasm to investigate her find was battling with her sudden exhaustion and her need for food and warmth. She'd barely eaten all day and her bones felt chilled; she was desperate for a hot bath. In the end, she compromised and after taking the find to the museum, she had a quick meal with Tony before going home to a hot bath, and then crawled into bed in her favourite pyjamas hoping for a good night's sleep.

Sleep was not forthcoming straight away. Her head swam with questions about the find. Who would engrave a big pot like this? Her experience told her it was nothing more than a pot used to store ale or possibly oil, so there would be no reason to engrave it, unless the pot was used for a specific reason, a religious ceremony perhaps.

Sleep had been hard to come by lately anyway. An insomniac since her teenage years, she considered anything over four hours a good night. However, lately her sleep had been interrupted by nightmares that caused her to jump out of bed, convinced she wasn't alone; and she'd wake either crouched down in the corner of her bedroom or standing with a weapon of some sort in her hand, protecting herself - from what? Or whom? She had no idea. Nightmares and weird dreams weren't anything new, but something about these nightmares filled her with dread and they terrified her.

Her thoughts turned to Tony. They had been good friends for years. He was reliable, kind and always had her back. She loved working with him and missed his wit when they were on different projects. When she'd found out that they'd be working together at Thurstaston, her relief was profound.

She welcomed someone she could talk with. The arguments about digging the site had worn her out physically, but her determination had never faltered. The site was important, of that she had no doubt, but couldn't explain why; at least, not her personal beliefs. However, her evidence of a possible village had surprisingly been enough to warrant a four-week, fully funded investigation. Much to the disgust of the opposition led by Mr Merton.

He had tried his local MP, the local radio station and bombarded the museum with letters of complaint; addressing them to Trevor, the head of Archaeology. Twice he had organised a sit down outside the museum and both times he and his cronies had been escorted away. On one occasion Mr Merton had barged into one of Trevor's classes and ranted about archaeology being a rape on the earth and the students were nothing more than evil rapists.

She'd told Trevor to file charges, but he'd refused. Even the countless letters to the archaeology department, some of which had been rather personal, had not persuaded him to lock the crazy man away. Thankfully the press and locals were on Kathryn's side. If there was a lost village, they wanted to know about it. She felt under pressure to find it and stressed to do it quickly. She knew how public opinions worked. They wanted it now or they'd lose interest and start baying for blood - her blood to be precise.

Realising sleep was not forthcoming she fluffed her pillow and sat up with a huff. She went over the day in her head and remembered the feel of the pot in her hands. For the briefest moment, she'd felt something, a coldness that had made the hairs on her arms stand up and a wave of nausea. How could she have forgotten that? Until she recalled Tony had started singing along to an old tune on the radio and the moment had passed.

That was weird, but then, she'd had strange feelings before, with other finds. It was like a connection, a link to the past and sometimes, those finds had remnants of energy still attached to them. A friend of hers had told her she was sensitive, so maybe that was why she picked up these odd feelings.

Regardless of sleep, or lack of, she was looking forward to returning to the site tomorrow, the weather reports were good. She hoped the rain wouldn't cause too much damage as it had on a dig in Scotland a few years back. Overnight they had lost half the site to a small hurricane and high winds had covered the newly found burial chamber with debris, soil and turf. They'd had to abandon the dig until the weather had done its worst.

She did not have time to wait for good weather, time was ticking and the locals were hungry for news. She had a four-week window that seemed a long time, but in reality, four weeks might not do the site justice. All she could hope for was plenty of good finds to vindicate her claims. The first test pits and geophysics had provided enough evidence for a month; maybe she could find enough to make the site viable for a longer investigation?

What really frightened her and what she desperately wanted to tell Tony and Trevor was the real reason she'd asked to dig at Thurstaston. For as long as she could remember, she'd had images of a place in her head. They were almost constant, like a memory, but a memory she knew she hadn't had. Her parents had convinced her that it was nothing more than imagination, but not anymore. Over the last few years, the images had become stronger, compelling and clear; these images had led her to Thurstaston Common over a year ago.

The blue tarpaulin shuddered as the wind caught it, but it remained firmly rooted to the wet ground. The soil in the trench where the pot had rested shifted slightly. The small brass object hidden deep beneath the pot became visible for the first time in nearly a thousand years. The Gods were awakening.

Chapter Four

Four hours had passed since arriving at her new home and she was still on edge; jumping whenever he was near her. Robert mumbled something about making a cup of tea that she forgot in an instant in the frenzy of boxes and Cherry's excitement. Walking into the kitchen looking for a box containing screwdrivers and hammers, he'd pushed the lukewarm cup towards her. Feeling awkward, she thanked him, drank half of it before quickly retreating, the box of tools under her arm; he hadn't followed her.

She kept herself out of his way by starting on the mountain of boxes while he finished the beds and wardrobes upstairs. It annoyed her that he hadn't unpacked anything but she stopped herself from confronting him about it and instead considered the alternative. By doing the unpacking herself, she had a small chance to try and make this old house hers. Even so, it had been tempting to say what was on her mind; the words were always on the tip of her tongue.

As she organised the boxes, she began to wonder what would happen if she did confront him. It would be a perfect excuse to tell him exactly what she thought of him. The many scenarios that tumbled through her mind were always in her favour. She confronted him, he attempted to whine his way out of it, she called him something appropriate and left with Charlotte, to a new and wonderful life.

Would she ever do that so soon after arriving? Would she have endured that terrible journey from York if there were not some glimmer of love for him? On the other hand, was it purely for her daughter's sake? She shook her head as the never-ending questions continued.

Staring at the boxes of kitchenware and boxes labelled 'miscellaneous', she rolled her shoulders in an attempt to relieve the tension in them. She was exhausted physically, mentally and emotionally and she knew it, but couldn't make that decision to fix it. Maybe if she kept busy, the answer would come. She wasn't convinced but gingerly opened the box nearest to her and, taking a deep breath, dived in and kept busy.

***

Cherry lay on her small bed. Her teddies sat in a line along the pale yellow wall listening intently as she read them the story of the three bears from the small picture book. She giggled as a soft, cool caress touched her cheek. She looked up from her book and smiled, "That's tickly. Do you want to play?"

***

Helen stopped for a moment to listen. Cherry had been in her room for nearly an hour and it was very quiet. She hoped she hadn't fallen asleep or she'd never get her to bed at a decent hour. She stood at the bottom of the stairs and listened. Cherry's door was slightly ajar and she could hear her talking. She smiled to herself; she loved hearing her daughter play. At least one of them had settled into their new home.

She sat for a moment on the bottom stair and quickly rubbed her hands through her hair before massaging her neck; she ached and knew another headache was imminent. The low murmur of her child was soothing and she closed her eyes and relaxed her breathing. For now, she tried to stay within the moment and not think about the 'what ifs'. At this moment her baby was happy, content and obviously relaxed in her new surroundings. For now, she was all right sitting on the stair; nothing else mattered.

She didn't know how long she sat that way, but when she forced her eyes open, she saw movement in the doorway and realised he'd been watching her. With that knowledge came all the usual questions and she felt herself tense again. The questions were always the same and simple. Did she love him? Did she believe he loved her? Was it worth fighting for their marriage?

There was darling, innocent Cherry to consider and it was that small, perfect detail that it always boiled down to, their daughter. Could she even consider hurting her baby for her own happiness? Would leaving Robert make her happy? She'd forgotten what happiness truly felt like with a man. With Cherry, it was a constant happiness. A joy she could not quite put into words. Cherry was a gift they had made together. They should have been doing these jobs together; but they were not. Abruptly, suddenly angry, she stormed back into the dining room to finish the job.

Hours later, she stood back and surveyed the two rooms. All the familiar objects from the old house now sat in different places. It was an odd feeling seeing them in their new surroundings cleaned and free from the layer of dust that she'd packed them away in. The dust had felt like a comfortable blanket and it had brought tears to her eyes to wipe them clean, as if she was wiping away the very last residue of her old life.

Surprisingly, it had been a positive exercise to be able to put her stuff where she wanted and breathe her life into the bricks and mortar. She was feeling a lot calmer by the end of the day. She'd listened with half an ear to his own administrations upstairs and hadn't interfered when he'd come down to the kitchen to make Cherry something for tea. She'd kept herself to herself, within her own world, enjoying the therapeutic sorting of old memories. She'd stopped once to make herself a large mug of tea, and grabbed an apple before returning to her sanctum.

It was only when she'd finished and the empty boxes were stacked in the far corner, that she considered how different it might have been if he'd done this with her. Would they have circled each other carefully with guarded glances and awkward silences? Or perhaps it could have become the excuse they needed to break the tension, collapsing in a heap of tangled limbs, hungry mouths and exploring, yearning hands on the new carpet, or up against the bookshelf? She sighed loudly and licked her lips. Her body betrayed her longing whenever she thought about their lovemaking.

Sometimes, when they were dating, they would meet during their dinner hours and attempt to find somewhere private, just to touch each other; which was no easy task in the middle of a city but that had been part of the fun. He'd found any reason to touch her in those early years; sometimes pushing the boundaries of decency.

Some nights, she ached with a need so powerful it'd been too hard to ignore. Afterwards feeling dirty and ashamed she'd resent him all the more. Why should she do these things to herself just because her husband could not be bothered anymore? She wanted a man to desire her. The way he had looked at her when they'd arrived confused her. Robert hadn't looked at her like that for such a long time; what did it mean?

Married for eleven years, together for thirteen, and yet he felt like a stranger. The therapist had encouraged her to tell him about her needs, her wants and her hopes for their marriage. It had not gone as she'd expected. Instead of engaging in a conversation, Robert had fled the room and withdrawn further into himself, hardly speaking to her or making eye contact. Today, the way he'd looked at her had only made her feel uncomfortable.

Walking slowly upstairs, she went into her daughter's room, sat down on Cherry's bed, and listened to the howling wind outside. The rain that had kept her company last night had followed her down the country. It thrashed against the window that in a strange way made her feel comforted and snug.

Although this house didn't feel like her home - she looked down at Cherry, *their* home, she corrected herself - she hadn't really given it any chance. Maybe things would change here as he'd promised. She certainly hoped something would happen, but how long should she wait?

She leant forward listening to Cherry chatter away to her five teddies, which at that moment sat in a circle; each one had their own cup and saucer, and Cherry was passing around a plate of plastic chips and fake scrambled egg.

"Cherry, do I get any tea?"

"No, none left. Teddy Gerry ate it all up." Turning to the bear in question, she smacked its head, "Naughty Gerry."

"Oh dear, poor teddy, perhaps he was hungry after his long journey."

"Well, he is still a naughty teddy. Inga needs food ..."

"Inga? Which one is that?"

Charlotte giggled and shook her head, "Not telling."

"Not telling what?"

Helen jumped as Robert walked into the room. He'd become an expert on sneaking around the house during his recovery.

"Cherry has a friend." Her voice sounded strange, it shook slightly. She cleared her throat nervously

"Oh, I see. Does this friend have a name?" His voice shook too and he kept his gaze fixed firmly on teddy.

"Yes, Daddy, but I'm not to tell you." Cherry was looking up at Helen frowning crossly. "It was a secret Mummy."

"Oh, sorry baby, I didn't realise ..." Feeling her cheeks burn with embarrassment, she shrugged, "I'll leave you to it then, I'll feed Twinkle ..."

He looked across the room then and she saw a flicker of a smile before she quickly turned and left. Almost running down the stairs, she could hear them discussing what to have for their teddy bear picnic before bedtime and suddenly felt so alone.

Cherry had always tried to get Daddy's approval and attention. In a strange way, she had always been Daddy's girl, even if he hadn't known it. Cherry had stared open-mouthed at Robert the day he'd come home from hospital before flinging herself into her arms frightened. From that day, there had been a subtle shift in Cherry's behaviour and she couldn't deny that she loved it. Not that Cherry had ever rejected her. There were plenty of hugs and kisses, but Cherry had always been trying to get Daddy to notice her. Any crafts they did together, they were always "for Daddy."

When he was at home recovering, Cherry would stare with open eyes at this man sitting silently on the couch, before running away, clinging to Helen in fear. She'd welcomed the attention and she didn't want to lose all that now that he was getting better.

It upset her. She had given up work as a nurse and had become a full-time mum for eighteen months. She'd taken a few temporary jobs, mostly maternity cover but none of which had lasted more than a few months at a time, at the local hospitals and clinics. It was so cathartic going out to work and earning her own money, it helped her feel that she had achieved perfection, at least in that area. He had always given his opinion freely regarding her temporary work; he'd never liked it.

Cherry had been ill twice during that time and she'd had to give up work to be with her. Support from friends had been very thin on the ground by then as her friends dwindled down to embarrassing acquaintances met on the street. Her parents lived abroad and had shown no interest in behaving like 'grandparents', especially to any children that came from her marriage to 'him', as her mother had declared last time they'd come back to England. Robert never offered to help.

Cherry loved her, she knew that, but sometimes it felt like Robert and Cherry were a club of two who allowed her in on certain times. Irrational and absurd thoughts that just wouldn't go away: and that's why she had really taken those temporary jobs, to see if she would be missed - and she had been, much to her relief.

All thoughts of feeding the cat disappeared when she entered the kitchen, as a lovely aroma filled the room. Glancing at the oven, she noticed something cooking within it. A bottle of red wine sat on the breakfast bar with two glasses. Walking into the dining room, she saw the table set for two under the twinkling lights of three lit candles. Their best cutlery glistened in the light; their best napkins neatly folded beside two of their best china plates.

For a moment she couldn't think. Panic rose in her stomach as she walked slowly into the room and noticed the cat purring gently on one of the dining room chairs; a quick glance at her bowl told her Twinkle was fed.

"Cherry would like to wish you good-night and she wants a story off her Mummy."

Slowly she turned to face him, trying hard to keep her face neutral. She could feel herself shivering slightly and her heart seemed to be doing flip-flops inside her chest. "What's this ...?"

He took a deep breath himself before answering, "I know it's ... I just want to do something. Your daughter is waiting." As she moved to go he touched her arm, "And I'll be waiting for you here, when you're ready ..."

She felt the sting of tears behind her eyes as she heard the sincerity in his voice; she was not prepared for this. For nearly a year he'd barely acknowledged her presence if they were ever in the same room. Although both had become good at doing evasive manoeuvres so that didn't happen frequently.

Not trusting her voice, she merely nodded and headed for the stairs. Perhaps then, tonight was the night they would face their demons? As tired as she felt, she wondered if this was the moment she would know if their marriage was worth saving. She had no idea which one she would prefer.

Chapter Five

S he lay in the dark listening to the various new sounds that reached her. A horse whinnied nearby and she made a mental note to take Cherry to see them; she loved horses. She heard a car speed past and wondered who would be out at this time of the night. Glancing at her clock, she corrected herself, this time of the morning. It had been three hours since excusing herself and going up to bed pleading exhaustion, which in her defence, hadn't been a total lie.

Her body ached from lifting boxes and her shoulders felt stiff from the long drive. Within minutes of sitting down and enduring the awkward meal, all she had craved for was a hot bath and bed. Then, if she were honest, a cold bath of beans and a bed of wet fish would have been preferable to the unbearable silence that she had finally escaped.

Deciding sleep was not forthcoming she sat up and fluffed her pillow. Easing herself back onto the cool cotton she sighed heavily, her hand caressed the empty space next to her. Over the last year he'd slept in the spare room or on the couch depending on whether he'd sat up drinking or not. Occasionally, he'd crawled into bed beside her, always in the dark after she had settled down, and never said a word. He would remain with his back to her, balancing right on the edge of the king size bed. Never had she thanked the gods for his insistence that they buy a king sized bed until those moments.

She did not expect him. She hadn't expected him for such a long time so perhaps that was why tonight had been a huge shock; he'd given nothing away. He'd watched her silently, his face neutral as she excused herself from the dining room. She'd found it hard not to look at him, but she'd glanced across at him once, before bolting with as much dignity as she could muster.

They were at a stalemate, neither one would make the first move. Her fear of rejection kept her from making any moves. Had tonight been his attempt at making a first move and she'd rejected him? Part of her didn't like the thought of hurting anyone, but she had to allow herself a small pleasure in hurting him; see how he likes it! Childish, yes, but perhaps she could forgive herself this one indulgence.

She stiffened as a noise reached her ears. Cherry was talking in her sleep. She smiled, straining to grasp what she was saying but it was all gobbledegook and mumbles. Poor lamb must be exhausted. She hadn't even asked for another story, as was her usual routine, but had accepted a hug and a big kiss and snuggled down until only her head appeared above the covers.

She yearned to cuddle her. When Cherry slept, she could see the baby that she had been. Her soft breath, rosy, plump cheeks and her long dark eyelashes hiding those pale blue eyes. She still slept with one fist curled up near her mouth, a substitute for the breast. She dreaded the day Charlotte grew up, became a teenager and left home. Would she still see traces of her baby then? She hoped so more than anything, especially as it looked like she would be the only child.

She had stood far longer than usual watching her settle into sleep. Mostly enjoying the transformation of girl into sleeping baby, but if she were honest it'd been to compose herself for what she half expected to happen downstairs. Was he ready to begin a relationship now? Was she? Her earlier thoughts of passion in the living room came flooding back and she'd trembled with nervousness.

It had been over eighteen months since they'd been intimate and that had been a drunken fondle after he'd come home from a night out with his workmates celebrating something or other. It had quickly fizzled out when he'd fallen asleep kissing her neck. Pushing him off, feeling rejected, dirty and seething with fury, she'd have committed murder if he'd woken and tried again.

During that time, she had pined for the physical part of their marriage, but now, like this afternoon, it crept up on her. She was a sexual woman and loved sex and that was the hard fact. She'd stood in front of a mirror naked more than once checking her body hadn't completely gone south. She was still a good looking woman. Now, standing at the top of the stairs wondering if he was expecting something from her, she felt less than willing to give. However, if she rejected him now, their marriage wouldn't last.

He was waiting as promised, when after fifteen minutes of dithering, she'd finally gone downstairs to face him. Saying nothing, he poured a glass of red wine and handed it to her before switching off the oven and dishing out their meal. She'd stood like a statue, watching him, glass in hand, until finally taking a large gulp, feeling the glowing warmth trickle down her throat, melting some of her trepidation. She'd knocked back the rest, finishing the glass, before walking into the dining room, and sat down at one of the set places, her hand still firmly grasping the wine glass for courage.

Wordlessly he had carried in two plates of lasagne with a side salad, placing one in front of her. Seeing her empty glass, he quickly poured some more wine into it before sitting down opposite her and pouring a generous amount into his own glass. Not a word had been spoken.

She'd picked at her meal, surprisingly tasty, but her appetite had disappeared. She was almost through her second glass of wine before he quietly asked how her meal was. She muttered something positive and tried to eat a little more enthusiastically but he wasn't fooled. After a while, he'd sat back, his plate empty, and cradled his glass against his chest, watching her. It was all she could do to remain seated and outwardly look calm. Twice she'd glanced up and caught his eye. The look he'd given her was one she hadn't seen for so long she didn't really trust it.

Her stomach churned with nerves, as her pelvic region ached with the same longing she'd felt that afternoon while reminiscing about their past. It seemed her body remembered that look even if she didn't. She was sure that at any moment she would be violently sick, while inside her head she was screaming, "DO SOMETHING!" Draining her glass, she managed to look him straight in the eye and calmly thank him for the meal before easing herself out of her chair. She remained composed as she made her way to the stairs before taking them two at a time to her bedroom where she leant against the doorframe listening; he didn't follow her.

Now, curled up in bed alone, she needed to sleep, wanted oblivion from the torrent of questions that swirled around her head; but it wouldn't come. She heard a creak of a door along the landing and instinctively knew it was Robert. Shuffling down the bed, she closed her eyes as her own door opened. She knew he was looking at her and for a moment she had a sudden urge to smile and give herself away; she suppressed it. She could hear his breathing as he stood within the doorway, a faint aroma of soap reached her, he was clean and he was willing and wanting. She heard his soft footfall on the new carpet as he came closer, "Helen?"

Her own body surprised her again by answering as she felt the dull ache between her legs and a tickling inside her belly. She fought the urge, hated herself for it and hated him for throwing all of this at her. He'd given her no warning that he was considering saving their pathetic marriage or that he suddenly found her attractive again. Damn him! Turning her head, she opened her eyes to find the doorway empty. The moment had passed; both had lost.

***

Sitting bolt upright the scream died away to a groan as her body finally fought itself awake. With a trembling hand, Kathryn reached over, flicked on her bedside lamp and immediately felt better and safe as she hugged her knees to her chest. *It's only because my brain is working overtime over these new finds, that's all it is. It's stress. That's all folks!* She smiled at her own attempt to lighten her thoughts but the smile faded just as quickly as it had come.

She tried again to put a nice picture into her mind. Flowers, her favourite, daffodils, or was it sweet peas? Never mind, they are all beautiful ... just like that face of the girl ...*NO! NO! Damn it!* She could see them so clearly, their eyes staring in horror at what was coming ...Oh God! She flung herself face down in the pillow and shut her eyes tight. "Go away please! Please, go away ... go away ... go away ..."

The strange-sounding words pleading for mercy rattled around her head. The questions and confusion were all so clear. Why? She squeezed her eyes tighter; she didn't want to see any more blood and horror. She tried again, *flowers, cake,* yes, she liked cake, chocolate cake ... eating chocolate cake. Did Vikings eat chocolate cake?

She slowly sat up. She stared at the far wall of her room and thought about that. It was extremely doubtful, but it was a nice thought. She would hold onto that thought. The children had as much chocolate cake as they could eat before being slaughtered.

A large tear fell onto the back of her hand and she sniffed loudly. It was always Vikings. Throughout her life, her nightmares played out terrible scenes of slaughter and mayhem that had grown steadily stronger and clearer. It made sense lately because of her work. She was digging a possible village that in all likelihood was Norse, so it was logical that her dreams should be of Vikings. Right? Wrong! She had been dreaming of these people long before she had decided to dig at Thurstaston.

She sat forward and massaged her head, trying to relax. After so many years, it was all coming true, but how could she tell anyone? They'd think she was mad; her parents had considered it once or twice.

Vikings had grasped her interest from an early age. Her mother had a friend who worked in the local library. On a few occasions she'd been left to sit amongst the large cushions while her mother had gone shopping in peace or had got her nails done. The librarian had brought her many books ranging from fairy stories to poetry, but she'd refused all of them. Instead, she had found the books on history and the book on Vikings became her book of choice every time.

"She'll become an archaeologist one day," the librarian had smiled. "It's lovely to see a child interested in something other than beauty products and mobile phones."

Her mother had readily agreed, encouraging her reading, buying her books on every culture and era, that she'd study repeatedly. However, at night, it would be the book on Vikings that she'd peruse for hours and marvel at the pictures of the Valkyries, gods and goddesses, trying to make sense of her dreams and pictures in her head. The Vikings fascinated her, yet terrified her at the same time.

By the time she reached University and had endured years of nightmares and sleepless nights, she fought against her curiosity and had made the mediaeval period her speciality, but when she came to Liverpool, she'd met Trevor. His enthusiasm for the Vikings was contagious and he awakened a passion she could no longer ignore. However, the deep-rooted fear never left her and it was getting stronger; she reached for the telephone.

***

The phone rang for a long time before Tony finally managed to get himself out of bed and stumble downstairs to where he'd left his mobile. "This better be fucking good whoever you are!"

"Tony ... It's me."

"Kathryn? What the hell ...It's ten to five ..." He stopped rambling when he heard what sounded like a sob, "Hey, what's going on?" His fatigue and anger disappeared quickly as concern took their place and he sat down heavily in his armchair. "Come on; don't go all silent on me now, what's wrong?"

"I'm sorry, to wake you, I just ... I can't sleep and I'm worried and ... frightened and ..."

"Whoa there girl, you're not making sense. Frightened of what? Who?" Tony reached for a cigarette but stopped when he heard her explanation. "A nightmare! You woke me from a beautiful dream because of a fucking nightmare." He exploded, "What the hell is wrong with you Kathryn? No, in fact don't answer that, at this time of morning I don't give a shit! Get some more sleep. Dream of beautiful things like fairies and princesses! I thought you were in real trouble or something! Go back to sleep!"

***

She sat on the bed, hugging a cushion to her chest for the next hour, listening to the world slowly wake up. She switched off her lamp as the morning sun streamed into her room. She should have been excited for the day ahead. She should have been jumping up and getting dressed with enthusiasm.

The fantastic find from yesterday was sitting in the office waiting for her to clean it because she'd wanted to take charge over such an important find. She'd known it was wrong and no doubt she'd get a telling off, but she couldn't explain how hard it would have been to hand it over to someone else who wouldn't 'feel' the same way. She'd wanted to examine it, decipher its markings, and possibly get an idea of who had last touched it nearly a thousand years ago and yet she felt nothing but fear and dread, but of what?

Poor Tony, he would not forgive her in a hurry over lost sleep; she'd get him something as an apology. She did feel stupid telephoning him, but the need to hear another human being had been overwhelming. Now, she just felt deflated and embarrassed. The most frightening aspect of the dream was a knowing, a deep ache that came with these dreams that she had a connection of some kind with the victims of the massacre and yet, that just couldn't be possible ... could it?

Trevor spoke quite a bit of Swedish and Old Norse, but she'd never learnt more than the odd word. The language frightened her, which was irrational as it was just words and sounds, yet when she heard those words and sounds, it felt like her stomach was dropping and an anxiety within her subconscious rushed to the surface so quickly her head would spin and she'd shake with terror.

As Tony rightly asked, what was wrong with her? Perhaps she was too sensitive. Many times as a child she would hit out first before waiting for an explanation; it had got her into trouble more times than she cared to remember. It was a need to protect herself from painful words or possible beatings from potential bullies. Teachers and her parents had asked her why so many times, but she'd never been able to explain the need to protect herself, because, in truth, there was never any real threat, only perceived ones.

Heading for the shower, she tried to push the images of death out of her head. She couldn't dwell on it or she'd go mad; of that, she was certain. It was that knowledge that made her fight back and get on with her day. She had fought too long and too hard for this chance to give up because of nightmares.

Ten minutes later, wrapped in one of her big, cosy towels, she sighed; the hot water had helped a little, but the feeling of unease refused to go away. In frustration, she banged her hand down hard on the side of the sink. The images were just too clear.

Write it down. That was it, that was how you got dreams out of your head, wasn't it? Running into the bedroom, letting the towel fall, she grabbed a pen and paper and quickly scribbled down the landscape of the dream. The area looked familiar; the tree line and the rock formation with the land in the distance, across the sea ... Wales, it had to be. It was Thurstaston, it always was.

She sighed loudly, feeling irritated, and quickly rubbed her eyes. Of course, she had been dreaming about the dig site. Except this time, it'd been from a different angle. She had walked the length and breadth of Thurstaston Common and Royden Park, it was inevitable the landscape had made an impression, but her images were always slightly different. The scenery in general looked familiar, yet it was different. The trees, the village, but surely that was because she was expecting to find a village and her mind had placed one there? The only viable explanation was that she'd had some kind of psychic episode and she'd seen into her future: and that alone scared the hell out of her.

She grabbed the towel and began drying her hair: why couldn't she have a psychic dream of finding a Viking hoard or a boat or another big find, like Tony had said when they first dug some test pits, "Wouldn't it be great if we found a lost silver treasure?"

She stared at the piece of paper and read what she had written repeatedly.

'ASTRID.'

The name sounded loud in her head. Her hand trembled as she quickly wrote the name down. She forced herself to take a deep breath as she felt the rise of panic. Looking around her bedroom, she realised that it had become darker; the morning sun had disappeared and been replaced by a cool shadow. Throwing the pen and pad onto the table, she hastily grabbed her clothes and left, slamming her bedroom door behind her.

***

Tony didn't go back to sleep. He lay staring at the ceiling for a long time before returning downstairs in his dressing gown, and sat by the telephone. It wasn't like Kathryn to be like this, but ever since she had permission to dig, she had been as jumpy as a cat on pins! The stress of the last few months had been pretty bad with getting permission, then it being rejected, then having to present their case yet again with the changes demanded by the council.

He hated men in suits. He understood about conservation and needing to protect wildlife, but sometimes he was convinced men in suits just loved to play a power game. He'd voiced his thoughts on many occasions and during the fight to dig, he'd been convinced that they were going to say 'yes' eventually, they'd just wanted Kathryn to squirm for them just a little bit; it had been unbearable to watch at times.

Kathryn worked damned hard on her research, she didn't miss a thing as far as he could see. Many people had been very open to the idea of a dig and it was with great relief that the press got behind her and did a survey of local people. Eighty-one percent in her favour helped the battle. Kathryn persevered and her case of a possible settlement dating back to the Viking era had finally won. Kathryn's hard work had paid off, but sometimes he wondered at what price.

One of the main changes had been the area to dig. He'd expected that to become a major argument, but Kathryn had just smiled and nodded her consent. When he thought of that, he often contemplated if she'd played them, anticipating their move, because it seemed too good to be true that the site they had been allowed to dig was now producing finds, and the geophysics team had gone mental seeing the readings; had she known?

One day he'd ask her, but for now, he was happy with the finds, especially that pot from yesterday. The test pits had been a success with broken pieces of clay pots, a few whetstones, half an ivory comb, a fragile spoon made of wood and some amber beads. Some might say they didn't amount to much, but to Kathryn they had been gold.

They had adhered to every rule, smiled and bowed when necessary, kissed enough arse and shaken so many sweaty palms and still there had been one or two narrow-minded pricks on the committee. They both knew that they needed a good amount of evidence to keep the dig going and that pot might just be the start of it.

Deciding to jog, he quickly dressed and began stretching his body. If Kathryn had taken him up on his offer all those years ago, he could have been comforting her. His thoughts drifted to all the things he could be doing with her right now to work off his stress levels. He still pondered now and again how it would feel to make Kathryn scream his name in pleasure; perhaps the time was right to ask her again. Finishing his stretch, he glanced down at himself and grinned, perhaps he should take a cold shower when he returned instead of a hot one?

***

At some point during the night half the tarpaulin had come away and now lazily flapped against the sodden grass. Silently the man edged his way towards the trench; a quick glance around told him he was alone. Smiling to himself, he flung back the rest of the covering and peeped underneath. For a moment, he couldn't focus into the gloom as the sun was only just beginning to rise; inside the trench it was still dark. He could make out nothing and decided to step down. The soil felt soggy beneath his trainers but he ignored it as he bent down to examine the ground. He had a garden trowel pinched from a nearby shed and he began to scratch at the surface. Within a few seconds he heard a metallic sound.

"Perfect." He said to himself and without care or thought he started to scrape away the soil more quickly, desperate to reach the treasure he was sure he'd found.

A noise above him made him stop. He listened carefully before looking out. The sun's rays were slowly moving closer, he knew he didn't have much time before the early morning dog walkers came for a peep and for the second time that morning he chastised himself for being a lazy bastard.

He listened for a moment longer before deciding it had been nothing. He began to dig quicker. He could see a large section of something metallic. His excitement grew as he began to use his hands as well to move the clumps of soil. The smell of wet earth clung to his nostrils and he hastily wiped his running nose on his sleeve. Was it gold or bronze perhaps? He knew someone in a museum that would pay him good money and ask no questions. The noise was louder, more pronounced. He glanced up, trowel in hand, ready to fight off any other potential thieves or nosey old biddies.

Slowly rising from his knees, he held the trowel in front of him. The sun was just beginning to peek over the horizon and he could see that the field was empty. His hand dropped to his side. He looked left and right, shielding his eyes against the sudden glare of the sun. He began to turn around but he saw the shadow too late to react. The sword thrust into his stomach with such force that he was dead before his body fell.

The figure stood over him, watching as the life's blood ran out of the wound, mixing with the damp earth. Bending down, the figure dipped a finger into the warm, dark blood and inhaled the metallic scent before drawing a symbol in the air. Kicking the lifeless body aside, he pulled the bronze knife from the soil, wiping the excess mud off with a rag. Grunting, satisfied, the cloaked figure turned and holding the knife aloft, welcomed the sun with open arms.

***

The sun was just illuminating her bedroom when Cherry came bounding in clutching Emily. "Mummy! Mummy! Wake up!" Getting no response, she jumped up onto the bed and thrust Emily's face towards her mother's. "Emily says, get up Mummy, time for rice nice and we need a big cup of milk for our bones! Mummy?"

Cherry slowly edged her doll's face closer until her cotton nose was touching her mother's. "Nose to nose Mummy, don't you sneeze ..." She whispered as she sidled closer and lightly kissed Helen's nose.

"MUMMY!"

Helen gave a groan and snuggled down further into the warmth of her duvet. "What is it, Cherry?" The question was barely audible under the duvet as she fought to go back to oblivion. Hearing no response, her motherly concern won and she opened her eyes and pulled down the duvet so only her face was showing to focus on her grinning child.

"Everything all right?" Her voice was nothing more than a cracked whisper and she cleared her throat without much enthusiasm.

"Oh yes, Mummy, but Emily is hungry and wants some rice nice. Are you getting up now?"

Lifting her head slightly she moaned loudly realising how early it was, her body and brain quickly reminding her how little sleep she'd had last night. Her arms and lower back ached badly and her head felt mushy. "Baby, it's only half past six, Mummy and Emily need at least another hour, go back to bed."

"But Mummy, I can't go back to bed because they are in my room."

For a moment, Helen didn't respond and snuggled down under her cover. She could feel the pull of sleep but on hearing her daughter's steps, she frowned and peeked out. "Cherry, who is in your room, baby?"

"They are." Cherry stood by the bedroom door, one hand clutching her doll, with the little finger of the other hand planted firmly in her mouth. Seeing she had her mother's full attention, she ran back to the bed and climbed in on Helen's side. Helen reluctantly shuffled over away from her pocket of warmth and shivered slightly as her body settled into the cool cotton duvet; her daughter snuggled into her body and sighed loudly. Helen's irritation lasted seconds as she looked down at her child. Here was her baby wanting and needing her for comfort and it felt wonderful.

She watched Cherry's eyes slowly close and within a minute Cherry had dropped off to sleep with Emily hugged tightly against her chest. Settling herself into a more comfortable position, she gently laid a protective arm around her sleeping child but sleep refused to come back. Instead, she dozed; her head too busy playing out yesterday's scenarios to switch off properly. She opened her eyes and frowned as she watched her daughter's chest rise and fall; who were 'they'?

***

He listened, waiting to see where Cherry would go; he was glad when she went into Helen's bedroom, but felt sorry for Helen who would be woken at this unearthly hour. He thumped the pillow into a more comfortable position and flopped back with a loud huff. Sleep had barely come to him as he'd watched the clock's hands slowly move around, reaching each hour, tormenting his lack of ability to doze off properly. He had stood watching the night sky at one point, whilst listening to his daughter's murmurs in her sleep, lucky girl. He was glad that she had settled easily, one out of two was better than expected. Now all that remained was to win his wife back, start the new job and get on with their lives; simple really.

He was still staring up at the ceiling of the guest bedroom an hour later deciding it could do with a lick of paint. He was running through the variety of off whites that might suit the room and practising how he could suggest it to her over breakfast, at least it might prompt some kind of conversation? He recalled the evening's fiasco and cringed; he'd planned that for days and still she hadn't responded.

Not that he blamed her in any way. He'd made a complete mess of everything and now he'd uprooted his family and brought them here to his roots. A place he hoped would be a new start for all of them. He'd expected some argument, a fight, or worst-case scenario that she'd walk away and take Cherry with her; but none came. She'd barely looked interested, but had come nonetheless; and he dared to hope.

He knew that he didn't deserve his good fortune. He was well aware of what he could so easily have lost because of his voracious drive to earn more money. He saw it now for what it was, and without Helen and Cherry to enjoy it with him, money was nothing more than a tempting piece of paper that had lured him away from his real love. He cringed when he remembered all those awful clients and so-called friends who knew nothing of love or life beyond greed and power. He'd hated every one of them, but it hadn't stopped him playing the game.

He'd wined and dined them. Showered them with compliments and said all they wanted and expected to hear. He'd caught the disease of their success and before he'd known it, he'd become one of them. For what? To be lonely? Because, that is what he was, lonely. Money couldn't help that, could it?

A loud bang from downstairs made him jump out of bed and fling open the bedroom door. A second later, Helen opened the main bedroom door and stepped onto the landing, their eyes met briefly, before she looked away first towards the stairs. "What was that?"

He walked past her and stood at the top of the stairs and shrugged, "Not sure, I'll go and check." He noticed she was shivering, "You go back to bed." She didn't move.

He sighed loudly and slowly descended the stairs. Near the bottom, they curved slightly; he stopped here a moment and listened. Nothing.

Stepping into the hallway, he crept towards the lounge door and eased it open with his foot. He scanned the large room, but finding nothing amiss, he walked quickly to the back of the house to the kitchen and dining room. Nothing. All the windows were closed, the back door and the French windows secure. He opened these anyway and checked the conservatory that ran along the back of the house and that was secure too.

He quickly ran a hand through his black hair and rubbed his chin. He noticed Twinkle happily curled up on the dining room chair and smiled; there was no way an intruder would get in without her being disturbed. Twinkle hated strangers and men; he couldn't win. He was both of those. He would just have to make it up to her as well.

He reached out tentatively to gently stroke her fur but stopped midway as she slowly opened her eyes and surveyed him. She stretched quickly and sat up. She wasn't looking at him. Her attention was riveted on something behind him. Goose bumps ran along his arms and the back of his neck. He felt utterly stupid thinking it, but he was only wearing pyjama trousers and he would feel foolish and naked if he had to fight an intruder; he didn't even have a weapon.

He whirled around, half expecting to see the figure of someone in the shadows, but no one was there. Yet, he couldn't shake off the feeling that he wasn't alone, besides the cat of course. He watched her as she jumped down, walked quickly across the hallway into the kitchen and jumped up onto one of the kitchen stools. She seemed to be following something along the kitchen wall, moving her position so that she could survey whatever it was. He slowly followed and stood next to the cat, watching her behaviour and trying to see what she was looking at with such interest. Twinkle began to purr and rub against the breakfast bar. What the hell was it?

Suddenly, a cry from upstairs broke the spell for both of them, and he sprinted up the stairs, Twinkle getting between his feet and reaching the main bedroom first. She jumped onto the bed and immediately lay down, her eyes watching Cherry who was sitting upright, staring ahead. He instinctively looked behind him, to where Cherry was staring, but the goose bumps had gone. Helen looked worried; she didn't acknowledge the cat.

"Is she still asleep?" He knew this was a pointless question as it was obvious, but Helen nodded anyway, her gaze never leaving her daughter's face.

"Should we wake her?" He stepped into the room and gently sat on the end of the bed. Helen shrugged and slowly reached out and touched Cherry's arm, but she didn't respond. He did the same and quietly spoke her name. For a moment nothing happened, but then, Cherry turned to look him full in the face and smiled. "Good morning Daddy, I'm hungry."

Chapter Six

Tony walked quickly, the coffee he'd bought from the machine barely warm in his hand. He tasted it and grimaced, this wasn't coffee, it was warm mud and he carefully placed it inside a nearby bin. His eyes felt gritty and his head was stuffy. He was irritable and knew exactly who to blame. The jog hadn't worked off his frustrations or his sleepiness and the shower which he'd turned to cold half way through had only made him feel worse, switching it back to warm his chilled skin almost immediately.

Kathryn could be a pain in the arse sometimes and they weren't even shagging; never getting beyond a drunken kiss three years ago. He'd asked for more, but she'd declined, giggling about it at the time, but he'd realised that he had been deadly serious. He wouldn't have minded waking that early if she'd been in bed with him, but some stupid dream was too much.

Then again, she was gorgeous, only thirty and as far as he knew, she hadn't had a serious relationship for over a year with some idiot called Mark. Various people in the museum had told him that she only spoke with Mark every few days on the telephone and met infrequently for quick weekends before she'd found out he was seeing other women; what a loser! Perhaps it was time to show her how a real relationship felt.

He unlocked the small office he shared with her and another archaeologist, Susan: a dyke and proud of it. Waste of a good body as far as he was concerned, but some people just couldn't be convinced to try something! His relationship with Susan was a silent agreement to stay out of each other's way as much as possible. They tolerated each other's company on a short-term basis because they did respect each other's work.

He knew her thoughts on him consisted of a man with a huge ego, a small cock and a desperation to overcome that obstacle by sleeping with as many women as would let him. She knew that he considered her a waste to the female population and should try a good man before making any judgements on the male populace; it was a stalemate and one neither cared to waste time thinking about.

He switched on the light and closed his eyes against the sudden fluorescent glare. His desk was on the far right hand wall next to the one large window that overlooked the museum car park. The morning sun didn't touch this side of the building, making the room look gloomy until around mid-afternoon when it became ablaze with sunshine and then it could be too much to bear. They'd be diving for the blinds and opening the window before they cooked, especially in the summer.

Walking to his desk, he shook his head at the state of it. Every inch was littered with various research papers on Thurstaston Common and a pile of books about the area. They ranged from personal biographies, amateur booklets to myth. Beside these lay a thick folder of letters to the museum from people who lived or had lived near Thurstaston; he preferred these to the books.

They told tales of figures seen wandering the sandstone rock and misty, white ladies gliding along the road past Thurstaston Hall. They told of fairy lights seen dancing around the trees on full moons and dark shadows that terrified late night walkers; he loved them. Even if he couldn't substantiate the claim, he enjoyed reading them. He liked meeting the people from the area with stories to tell, though he was always aware that they liked to embellish their stories.

He could think of one elderly woman in particular who collared him in a supermarket one day. Her story waffled on about strange lights on the common when she was a young child that she'd watch from her bedroom window. "Whenever we had to walk that way to cut through, I'd cry and beg to go around, but my Dad would just pick me up and carry me till we reached our house. Mother was never that obliging. I'd get a clout from her and told to keep a tight hold of her hand and I'd arrive home shaking and soaked with sweat."

He'd listened politely and nodded in all the right places while he'd tried to judge her age. At least a hundred years, small and wrinkled, like an old raisin, with a distinct odour.

He'd finally managed to escape, saying he needed to find a pen quickly before he could forget her story and had run to his car, his shopping forgotten. He could count on one hand the people he'd met over the years who'd surprised him with their candour and he'd appreciated their conviction in what they told him. However, it didn't mean he believed, though sometimes, he wished he could.

He glanced towards Kathryn's desk on the opposite wall and bit the inside of his cheek; the mess on her desk was worse than his. The box they had brought back yesterday was sitting beside a pile of papers, along with the bags holding his finds. She'd get into trouble for that. Every item was supposed to be taken to the laboratory and logged properly. When they'd left last night, she'd assured him she would go and do it and meet him at the pub. *Serves her right if she does get into trouble and serve you right for being a lazy sod and not doing it yourself.*

Walking over to her desk, he ignored his own finds and glanced down at the closed box. He carefully opened it, looked inside and smiled. It was a good find, almost intact besides a few bits missing off the rim. It was definitely a vessel for holding large amounts of liquid, most likely ale.

He gently touched the pot and eased off a little of the mud that more or less covered it like a thick crust. It was very tempting to take it down to the lab himself, but he carefully replaced the lid and walked out of the office to the small kitchen at the other end of the long corridor that they shared with the rest of the offices on that floor. He'd make himself a decent cup of coffee and see what happened once he was a little more awake.

Ten minutes later, he wisely pushed a book out of the way to make room for his mug of hot coffee and a jam doughnut wrapped in a paper napkin: he sat down with a loud sigh. He ached with fatigue and his head still felt like mush. He would have his drink and then he would take his own finds to the lab and log them in. He regretted not having time to investigate them himself, but he'd catch up with them later, perhaps once they'd been cleaned. He had to get back to the site. Kathryn would most likely be there all day once she'd checked for messages and sorted out her find.

He would certainly be glad of more students, if they ever got them of course. Nevertheless, it would mean that any finds could be given his full attention and not just a passing glance before being passed onto the labs for a clean-up.

That was another thing he had in common with Kathryn, both of them liked to see a find all the way through, especially if it was a good one. He knew she would be feeling torn about the find, wanting to investigate it properly from start to finish knowing they only had a limited amount of time. He didn't particularly enjoy what he called 'the boring bits', where he'd have to catalogue a find and grid where it'd been found; it took him away from actually digging and exploring a site. He hated any paperwork that stopped him from getting out there and finding history; he knew Kathryn was the same. Where they differed was that she would work late into the night to get her paperwork complete: he would not.

He was a digger, an explorer, an Indiana Jones with a Liverpudlian accent and no silly hat and whip. He was a man who liked to find old treasures and understand what they meant to people from the past. It also gave him plenty of opportunity to cast an eye over the variety of bums and breasts, while the women bent down to their work. He always hoped one of them wouldn't wear a bra! He chuckled to himself, he really was a dirty old man; maybe Susan was right about him?

That thought brought him up sharp and he shook his head. No, that dyke would never be right about him. All he needed was a good woman and Kathryn would be his first choice. He wanted to wine and dine and ... He took a long swig of hot coffee and licked his lips, he wasn't going down that road this early in the morning; he had work to do!

***

Kathryn parked up onto the side of the road and turned off the engine. The sun was slowly edging its way into the grey sky. She stretched her arms above her head and took a deep breath to steady her breathing and her heartbeat. Why did she feel so scared? She quickly glanced around but she was alone as far as she could see, which bothered her. Another human being and a canine would come in handy if she needed it. What she needed them for exactly, she wasn't sure, but knowing someone was about might have helped her nerves.

Since her nightmare, she had barely kept still. After trying pointlessly to relax her body in meditation, she'd given up and exercised to an old DVD that she hadn't looked at for over four years. Her enthusiasm lasting all of ten minutes before she'd lost every ounce of interest and had showered again, dressed and left her flat before she could change her mind.

She'd made a decision whilst half-heartedly jumping around her lounge, that perhaps her sub-conscious was what was messing with her head. She'd been dreaming of the area ever since she could remember, which was freaky enough, but her nightmares had become worse in the last year; maybe on some level she agreed with the protesters, after all, Thurstaston was a beautiful site and she did not intend to destroy it, on the contrary, she wanted to preserve it; but what?

If she went down the road of believing that she'd dreamt of this exact site since childhood, that in itself was terrifying, but the how was something she couldn't contemplate. Had she truly believed all these years that there was a village and if so, how did she know? Moreover, if all that was true, then perhaps she needed to placate the area somehow, make peace with it.

It was never her intention to 'ruin' or 'destroy', words the protesters had used repeatedly; if anything, she was seeking answers to childhood dreams and adult nightmares. Maybe on some level, their words were adding to her sky-high stress levels, causing her already frazzled brain to inject a feeling of reality into her nightmare. Of course, it was all conjecture with answers that may never come, but now having made the decision, it felt right to ask for the earth's forgiveness and promise to return it to how she had found it.

She'd remembered an old friend from University who'd claimed to be a Pagan. She talked about connection with all things and that every living thing on the planet had energy. It got her thinking about the earth as a person and how it would feel if someone started exploring that person without his or her permission; it wouldn't be right. Her Pagan friend would say that her 'bad vibes and nightmares' could be the earth's way of retaliation. She'd never told her about her childhood dreams and she wondered what she'd have said about them now?

The silence hit her like a brick and she felt anxious and stupid. She'd tried not to think about it whilst driving, deciding it might be better to be spontaneous. But the truth was, she had no idea what she was doing. Should she do a ritual, an offering perhaps, to placate the earth's energies? Alternatively, was it all nonsense and she should drive to the museum, check her messages, catalogue the pot and take it down to the labs for cleaning?

It doesn't matter what you do so long as you believe it. Belief is what heals. She could almost hear her friend's voice as her phrase popped into her head.

She'd chuckled over that statement at the time, but she'd changed her mind over the years. She'd read of people who had strange encounters with aliens and ghosts:

weird dreams that came true or dreams that had been some kind of omen from the dead or caught ghosts on camera. She knew a few people who absolutely believed in all that and visited supposedly haunted places to 'talk' to these lost souls!

Zombies and voodoo, stigmata, astral projection, fairies. How could so many people be wrong? Yet how many people believed in God? What was real and what was fake? Who's to say that belief couldn't heal? She'd never believed in a god of any kind, especially a Christian one. She'd believed that she had power over her own destiny, but in the past year, she'd begun to doubt everything and knew that her old beliefs had been born from a 'need' to feel in control. The images in her head dictated another force at work and she hated that idea.

She couldn't deny unusual things did happen. Friends had joked about how people they hadn't heard from in a long time would suddenly phone them unexpectedly after they had spoken about them. One friend had told her about an incident where she had been on her way to someone's home hoping to arrive unexpectedly as a surprise, when she had met her friend coming in the opposite direction having had the same idea at exactly the same time! Coincidence?

Her old school friend, Veronica, would bring to school pictures of her 'ghost'. An elderly woman from the 19th century who had apparently loved the house so much, she still liked to wander the corridors of the old vicarage at night. 'She's harmless, but exciting', according to Veronica and her mother, who both claimed to have seen the 'lady' on numerous occasions. The pictures had never been anything other than, at best, fuzzy! She'd desperately wanted to 'see' this spirit.

They'd stayed awake in the hope of catching sight of the ghostly figure on many nights, feeling a mixture of hope, anxiety and fear. Wanting the thrill and enjoying the buzz in her stomach with every noise, they heard. She never did see anything and always left the next morning with a heavy disappointment.

Were these people so desperate to believe that they convinced themselves and those around them that it was 'real'? People were either freaks, desperate, or psychic perhaps? She was none of them: well possibly desperate, but not for anything spooky, only a man.

Her work meant too much and men always came second, and they found that out very quickly and left. Mark had begged her to move up to Scotland and move in with him. However, having only met him a dozen times during their ten-month romance that had consisted of long weekends of passion and walking, or both, to move to Glasgow permanently was not worth multiple orgasms, in her book. The idea of moving to a city repulsed her and he'd never understood why.

She had no idea why she'd told people that he'd cheated on her. She'd kept her private life with Mark very private. Playing him down and minimising their relationship. Perhaps she'd always known it couldn't last.

She rubbed her eyes and yawned, her brain was tired, stressed and overworked and she was thinking of past memories to delay something she wasn't a hundred per cent sure of. Anyway, a man would have to wait in line as a priority. Though there was a man who was constantly in her thoughts and not for nice reasons; that damned protester.

The dig was in jeopardy from the man whom she believed would do anything to ruin the excavation; she wouldn't have put it past him and his cronies to steal the gazebo knowing that rain can halt a dig without cover. She'd never met him personally, but had seen him in the distance, usually being escorted away by security. Something about the man gave her the creeps. Once, she had come out of her office and on hearing commotion from downstairs in the reception area, she'd frozen. A voice, for a split second had brought a fear so deep, she had almost wet herself. A moment later, the spell had been broken and she'd fled to the toilet shaking and confused.

Later, she'd found out it had been security escorting Mr Merton outside. He had attempted to force his way in to see Trevor again. Poor Trevor! Poor her! She was allowing this man to get under her skin and it was affecting her. She had to get a grip on herself, the dig was much too important.

She was anxious, it felt good to acknowledge that and she said it out loud, "I am anxious about this dig."

She smiled and repeated it another three times and took a long, deep breath. Yes, something could go wrong, but damned if she'd let it take over. The dig was too precious, especially after yesterday's find. She yawned again, not bothering to cover her mouth, the sooner she made peace with the site, the sooner she could get back to the office. Another hour and the two volunteers would be arriving, if they came on time today. Feeling the familiar tingle of excitement in her stomach, she climbed out of the car.

She shook her head and bit her lower lip as she quickly glanced around. "I am anxious, it is allowed ..." she repeated again. "I am anxious because I hate giving responsibility to others. These treasures are mine to look after and ..."

She stopped talking rubbish and chastised herself. Bottom line was Tony was going to kill her when he sees the find on her desk and Trevor would not be too pleased either. She had been unable to give it up to the people in the lab. Terrible as that sounded, it was her baby, her precious find and something about it had made her feel something she couldn't quite explain and hadn't attempted to.

So of course she was feeling apprehensive. Everything rode on the finds. Proof would help her case for digging and may help the protesters calm down. Finds meant funding and if she could prove there was a hidden village then perhaps she could get an extension on the dig.

She shut her eyes for a moment against the glare of the sun and remembered the first time she had come here, for real. She'd just finished a lecture about 'Medieval England' and was walking towards her office. She remembered feeling that horrible acid in her stomach due to hunger and then she was walking towards her car. No thought, except she had to drive. Half an hour later, she'd found herself parking up in a small car park. Climbing out, she'd stumbled up a well-worn path and found herself on a high brow of sandstone with views for miles in all directions.

She'd felt confused, bedraggled and questioning her insane action, but with all of that, there was a 'knowing', a sense of belonging and it terrified her. Walking slowly towards the highest point, she'd stared beyond the trees towards the spot they were now digging and cried. An elderly couple walking with their dog had watched her for a while before asking if she was okay. She'd reassured them saying that she was just having a bad day and they'd left her alone.

She'd staggered back towards the car, needing to get away. The smell of food wafted towards her and like a zombie, she'd followed the scent. The pub was her saviour; she'd never needed a drink so badly. Her first white wine was finished in three gulps, the second she asked for soda to be added and took it to a corner table by the window and tried to organise her head. She'd always meant to come walking in the area, but work commitments had always got in the way; she knew that was a lie. She'd avoided this place for reasons she couldn't, or didn't want to fathom. However, following her visit, the need to find out had escalated, so had the dreams. So much so, it had spurred her on to research the area and fight for a dig.

Glancing up at the sky, she knew that rain was inevitable, but she hoped that it wouldn't ruin a day's digging. Opening the gate, she quickly scrutinised the site but everything looked in order besides a few large puddles. Heading for the tent, she walked inside and saw that nothing had been touched; which made a nice change, perhaps the gazebo had been enough for the thieves?

A cold wind whipped up around her and she pulled her black fleece closer. She loved to dig and explore, but it was so much nicer when it was during the summer months. Zipping the tent again, she gripped her fleece collar with one hand and in the other hand she gripped her trowel as a weapon, just in case.

The tarpaulin had been flung back, revealing the eight foot long trench which now had an inch of water covering the bottom. She saw that the big stones they'd used to hold it down had been thrown in all directions; the wind must have been stronger than she'd thought? In the far corner of the site stood the portaloo and she quickly checked that before returning to the trench.

Stepping in, she surveyed the damage and was glad to see that it was minimal. The area where she'd found the pot had collapsed a little, but nothing that couldn't be fixed in minutes. Leaning forward, she placed her hand on the side to steady herself as she began using the trowel she carried to gently move the watery mud aside, gently patting it back to try and form a strong wall. She knew that it was pointless as the first drops of rain began to fall on her head.

Giving up, she straightened and started to wipe her hand on the wet grass when she froze. She brought her hand closer to her face to inspect it. Dropping the trowel, she gingerly touched her hand with the tip of her finger and felt nauseous; blood. Looking down to where her hand had rested, she could now see quite clearly a large pool of blood, mingling with the mud and the rain.

Glancing around quickly, she scrambled out of the trench, wiping her hands on the grass. She picked up her trowel and stared down at the pool. What should she do? Phone the police? She quickly searched the area, but couldn't find any evidence of foul play. No more blood and no body. It could easily be the blood of a rabbit or a fox. Any small animal could have died here at the jaws of a predator, its body taken away to be devoured ... so what was making her feel uneasy?

Running into the tent, she found one of the plastic bags used for finds, then using her trowel she scooped up the earth in the pool of blood and placed it inside the bag. She had a clean, but crumpled handkerchief in her pocket and she used it to mop up a little more of the water-soaked blood and placed that inside the bag. Maybe, she could determine for sure whether it was human.

Quickly placing the tarpaulin back over the trench, she secured it with pegs and a few large stones; then stood for a moment; the silence was overpowering. It was as if she had gone deaf as even the hum of traffic ceased and the busy road suddenly felt very far away. In a panic, she ran back to her car, slamming the door and locking it.

The panic attack hit her hard and quickly and she fought to catch her breath. Remembering the chant she'd learnt, she tried to focus on the words whilst slowing her breathing. "I am in control of my own body. It does not control me ..."

Realising she had blood on her hand she yanked open the glove compartment and snatched the wet-wipes, losing half of them as she pulled them out in her haste to clean herself. Her hands shook as she methodically wiped away every trace of blood. Ignoring the little voice in her head that said she had wiped away evidence of some terrible crime, she replaced the box and sat back, her hands resting on the steering wheel.

Her breathing became calmer and the shaking stopped, but the whirlwind of questions refused to slow down. The blood was human ... She couldn't know that. It could be an animal ... It wasn't. Why was she so sure?

She watched the rain as it gained momentum and knew the volunteers would have contacted the museum waiting for their orders. Without gazebos it would be impossible to dig in rain like this; they would have to wait until it eased off and that brought another anxiety of its own. Finally, she reversed the car out of the rough track, forgetting to close and lock the gate behind her, and sped away, ignoring a loud horn from the car she almost ran off the road.

***

The shadow among the trees shifted and the leaves swirled around its feet. The rain could not touch it. The sun could not warm it. The shadow stepped away from the shelter; its eyes surveyed what had once been home. Memories stirred, of fun, laughter, and merriment. Memories of the land flowed through the shadow. Recalling how it had once been, working the soil and watching as the crops ripened and knowing the people would not starve. The people. His people. They had shared so much sorrow. His family, long forgotten. Lost. Murdered. He felt the ache of separation and with it came the fury. The betrayal of one god brought sorrow and pain but both gods had betrayed him and that filled his heart with vengeance.

Chapter Seven

Nick trudged along the pavement, his head down, hidden within his hood; his cold hands thrust deeply into his track suit bottoms. He was soaked through and desperately needed a fag, but he'd smoked his last one an hour ago. Lee should have enough to share, he would scrounge one or two off him; besides, he owed him at least half a packet.

Finally reaching the block of flats, he climbed the stairs quickly to the fourth floor. The corridor was quiet, a string of clean, damp clothes hung limply across the passageway, he had to duck slightly so he didn't touch them. A split black bin bag littered the passageway, exposing the remnants of a Chinese take away and a multitude of cans. He kicked one carelessly as he neared Lee's door. He thumped the door loudly and listened, but he heard nothing from inside. He knocked again and lifted the letterbox to look.

He could see the narrow hallway littered with various take away boxes, some old newspapers and a car magazine lay where it had been thrown the other day; a jumper lay discarded on the dirty floor. He could smell the stale odours of cigarettes and beer and general dirt, but none of that bothered him. "Hey, Lee?" Getting no reply, he tried again louder, "Lee? Come on, open up ya' lazy bastard!"

He tried the door but he knew Lee wasn't in. The flat had an air of emptiness about it and he stepped away from the door. Where would he be at this time of day? The dole? No way. They'd got their money the other day. On a job? Not a chance, most likely trying to score something. They had smoked the last of the skunk last night and Lee did like to have some first thing in the morning. He glanced at his watch; it was nearly midday, perhaps he was at the pub?

He hated being messed about. Lee should have waited for him; they always went to the pub together. He slowly rubbed his hand through his stubble; he could smell the nicotine on his fingers and he inhaled deeply. God, he needed a fag! The local pub was a five-minute walk, he moved quickly, almost running down the staircase in his haste. He would feel better once he'd had his nicotine fix and then, he'd give Lee a good kickin' for making him run around after him.

***

After Cherry's strange behaviour, they had made breakfast, managing to dodge around each other with minimum dialogue. In fact, Cherry had made breakfast preparations quite easy by doing all the chattering. Firstly, she brought down to the dining table Emily, her favourite doll, as well as the majority of her teddies and dolls of various sizes. Lining them up, she had placed a plastic fork in front of each one and demanded that they join in with the first breakfast in the new house.

Next, she had decided on a bowl of Rice Nice, as she called them and a glass of juice. She then proceeded to give each doll and teddy one grain of rice for his or her own breakfast. Throughout the preparations, Cherry kept up a constant murmur that every now and then had included either Robert or Helen, prompting them to join in with the breakfast feast in their own way. Helen made herself a pot of tea and a slice of toast with margarine, Robert made himself a large, black coffee.

Seeing Robert without food Cherry piped up, "Daddy, why aren't you eating? You should eat breakfast. Mummy says food makes you strong."

Robert eased himself into the vacant chair next to her and gently stroked her cheek, "You're right, baby, but Daddy isn't hungry at this time of the morning; perhaps later, eh?"

Cherry shook her head furiously, "No, Daddy, you should eat now. I said so and so does Mummy". She folded her arms rebelliously and frowned, "Now, Daddy!"

Robert leant forward and glanced across at Helen who didn't move, but kept her gaze fixed on her child. "What is it, baby?" Robert touched Cherry's hand, but she quickly shook it off. Concerned by her obvious distress, he ignored the feeling of rejection that filtered into his brain and he shifted his position so that he was almost face to face with her. Cherry was looking at her half-eaten bowl of cereal. "Cherry baby, what's wrong? Tell Daddy ..."

Cherry violently shook her head and her bottom lip protruded; she was close to tears. "No! You have to do as I told you Daddy. Get stronger ... eat food!" Cherry reached out and pushed her bowl towards him with so much force, most of it slopped out onto the table.

Helen yearned to step closer and take charge of the situation as she always had, but she also felt a reluctance to interfere; she wanted to see how he handled it, for now. He'd never had to deal with a temper tantrum before, but she was on her guard, ready to step in if he didn't cope with whatever Cherry was feeling.

He hadn't moved but his gaze shifted between the mess and his daughter's face as she glared at him before abruptly turning her back, hugging her doll Emily to her chest. Even though her head was down as far as it would go, Helen could see tears beginning to fall down her cheeks as her lower lip began to tremble, but Cherry made no sound.

This last year had been a confusing time for Cherry as her father had actually begun to behave like one. Was this the beginning of a rebellion? She had never seen Cherry look so closed, not wanting Robert to touch her. Could she finally be retaliating against his behaviour towards her? She had been half expecting it.

If it really was her rebelling against everything, her need to boss Daddy into eating made sense. To make him join in with breakfast like a proper family was understandable, but she couldn't help feeling a bit sore that she wasn't making a fuss over her not being at the table. Granted, she was nibbling a piece of toast, but still ...

In the old house, he very rarely ate meals with them. Most of the time Helen had made her and Cherry a tray each and they had sat side by side watching some nonsense or other on the telly. Often having a chat and pinching from each other's plates, which was an on-going joke. Was Cherry trying to get her point across in her own way? She quickly glanced around at the dolls and teddies; yes, there was an element of 'family' about the table.

Robert sat back and was rubbing his chin; she could see that he felt out of his depth. She watched with interest and chastised herself mentally for feeling a tiny thrill of smugness. When no one said anything, she felt obliged to give the situation a nudge.

"Cherry, why are you getting upset? Daddy will eat breakfast when he wants to eat ..."

Cherry frowned and violently shook her head, "NO!" She shouted, "Daddy MUST eat NOW! He needs muscles."

Robert glanced up at Helen and shrugged, he looked embarrassed and he turned back to Cherry who was now getting very agitated; kicking her legs high enough to hit the underside of the dining table. "Cherry, darling, Daddy has ..."

"NO!" Cherry spat at him, the sudden anger in her face startled them both, "You don't have muscles, not like him. He must be eating all the time because he is stronger than you ... And bigger. He will beat you up!"

Before either of them could react, Cherry swiped at the table, her half eaten bowl of cereal, Robert's mug containing his warm coffee, a variety of plastic plates and forks, all swept onto the floor with a loud crash. Helen involuntarily stepped back as Robert jumped up from his seat in reflex. The coffee splattered down his pyjamas as the cereal splashed onto the dark wooden floor.

"Cherry!" Helen found her voice in the same instant, but the child was already jumping down from her chair and was running towards the stairs. Tears streamed down her daughter's face and she moved to go after her. Robert's hand grabbed her shoulder, pulling her back. "What the hell?" She turned to face him, "I have to go after her ..."

She could see he was trying very hard to control his facial expressions, but she wasn't fooled, she saw the anger and hurt in his eyes. A surge of triumph shot through her and she silently chastised herself for that too. It was hardly surprising though; Cherry had never behaved this way with either of them. Her concern for her daughter quickly outweighed any feelings she might have had for him and she yanked his hand off. "If you want to help," she waved her hand over the mess, "clean this up, will you; I'm going to check on Charlotte."

***

He slowly lowered his arm and stood motionless, watching as Helen ran up the stairs taking them two at a time in her haste to reach their child. In that moment he felt such a mixture of emotions, it was hard to choose which one felt acceptable. Anger, hurt, rejection, concern, all came, but as he watched his wife disappear, it was jealousy that won. Would she ever run after him that fast? He knew the answer and his shoulders slumped as a fresh wave of despair washed over him; his wife would never love him again.

He looked behind him at the mess and tried to think logically about the last five minutes. What had he done? Preparing breakfast had felt quite nice, although a little awkward. Cherry had been in a good mood, happily collecting her dolls and teddies. She had looked happy while dishing out a grain of rice to each toy; it was only when she saw that he wasn't eating that her behaviour changed. What was it about his not having any breakfast that had upset her so badly? She hadn't said anything to Helen and he felt ashamed for feeling such jealousy. He had no right to feel anything, not anymore. He should be grateful they were still living with him.

He recalled Cherry's tone, her face; he'd never seen such anger from her. To have that anger aimed at him hurt terribly, perhaps because it was mixed up with the enormous amount of guilt he carried. He really couldn't blame his little girl for being angry with him. No, after all his broken promises, his lack of attention, he deserved much worse.

He remembered what she had said: who was 'he'? Who had muscles? Who would beat him up? Misery overwhelmed him and he slowly sank down into the chair: a man, but who? Someone she knew? Someone she had seen recently?

He rapidly began to feel quite sick; it all made sense now. Helen hadn't wanted to move. For months she had moped about the house, avoiding him. Escaping outside, most days, saying she was going for a walk, or visiting old work friends. Some of those walks had lasted hours, usually as long as Cherry was in playgroup.

He had always thought it was because of what he had done to her over the years; his behaviour had become atrocious. He'd blamed himself, what else could he do? - he was to blame, for all of it. Work, putting their marriage second, his daughter third. In his arrogance, it'd never occurred to him that Helen might find another man. He couldn't blame her if she had found comfort in the arms of someone else. The very thought made his chest hurt and his stomach lurch. He hadn't offered her anything except loneliness and indifference. Slowly, he put his head in his hands and silently wept.

***

The figure stood and watched the man weep. For a brief moment, something stirred within him, but it had been too long since he had felt anything beyond fury, that he didn't recognise it and it vanished as quickly as it had come.

His eyes looked beyond the man, beyond the wall behind him and even beyond that. Out into the wood and the surrounding fields where he could sense the grass, the bark of the trees, the leaves, the scent of it all as the rain drops found each blade, every inch of the leaves, every rough surface of the tree and fed nature with its power. He closed his eyes and tried to remember how it felt ... but he couldn't. The pain of this knowing brought only a deep resentment; his gaze returned to the man, and he hated him.

Chapter Eight

It took a while to calm her daughter. By the time she reached Cherry's bedroom, she had thrown herself under her bed covers and Helen could hear her sobbing her little heart out. Any attempt to touch her was met with furious kicks and punches. Instead, she sat quietly and patiently on the bed, her hand gently resting on the edge of the covers. She knew Cherry would sense it was there once she calmed down and sure enough, after ten minutes of crying, she felt Cherry shift her weight and her small hand crept out from under the bedclothes, searching for her mother's comfort.

Helen waited as patiently as she could, allowing her daughter to calm down in her own time, but it was very hard. All she wanted to do was to fling back the bed covers and hold her daughter tightly. She was very worried, even though the counsellor had warned her that Cherry might display delayed shock at some of her father's behaviour and then the trauma of a move, but now it had come, she felt out of her depth.

"Mummy." Cherry's muffled voice broke into her thoughts.

"Yes, my darling." She hoped her own voice didn't betray her concern.

Cherry threw back the bed covers and looked up at her. "I've made Daddy angry, haven't I?"

Seeing the trembling lower lip, Helen leant forward and gently stroked Cherry's forehead with her hand. "Yes, I'm afraid you have. Can you tell Mummy why?"

Cherry shook her head and her gaze moved to look beyond Helen for a moment, before looking away. Helen glanced over her shoulder and shuddered, it felt cold in the room. Turning back to her daughter, she frowned, "Cherry, who were you talking about? Who has muscles, can I meet him?"

Cherry shook her head. "No silly. He only lets me see him. I don't like him very much, I like the woman ..." She suddenly clasped her hands over her mouth; her eyes grew wide for a moment, before she sat up quickly and threw herself into

Helen's arms. Her mouth tickled her ear as she whispered, "He gets angry if I say. Can I have some crisps?"

Helen clung to her daughter as a strong feeling of unease swept over her. The strange coldness eventually disappeared and the feeling of danger left with it. Every nerve in her body felt like it was on alert, but for what, it was only a cold draught? The reality was that the move had been traumatic for her. Surely it would be naive to think it hadn't been for her daughter?

The need to make up new friends was understandable. Cherry had always had a colourful imagination, but why did it have to be a man, with muscles? What was that about? Did she feel her father wasn't strong enough anymore that she needed a muscular father figure? That scenario would certainly make sense, but a three year old having thoughts like that made her feel such anger towards Robert, that if he'd entered the room at that moment, she wasn't sure if she'd have been able to contain it.

She quickly looked around the small colourful bedroom; it was a lovely room. She'd chosen the yellow herself once their offer had been accepted and the painters had done a very good job adding daisies randomly on the four walls. She had hoped the colour would help lift the mood; and it had, but she couldn't shake off the feeling something wasn't quite right here. She felt that there was something more to this sudden outburst and the uneasy feeling in the room just now.

She tried to slow her breath and calm herself as Cherry snuggled closer, Emily cocooned between them. Gently, she rubbed her daughter's back and started to rock backwards and forwards, hoping to bring some comfort to both of them. She quickly scanned the small room again to reassure herself, but about what? Could Cherry's reaction have caused some kind of hysteria? Perhaps in her weakened state, she was susceptible, overly sensitive to her daughter. Alternatively, the one explanation she was certainly leaning towards, the bloody house was haunted.

Needing to speak, to break the silence, she eased Cherry back a little so she could see Emily, "So, how is Emily feeling today? Does she like the new house?"

Cherry slowly shook her head, "No, she doesn't like it, she wants to go home."

Helen sighed, so she was right after all, Cherry was missing her old home. Holding her tightly, she spoke calmly, "I know she does, so do I, but isn't this a bit exciting, going somewhere new?"

Cherry suddenly squirmed to get off; she didn't look upset or angry now, but began rummaging in her toy box. Helen stood up, deciding to leave it there. It was no use pushing the child, she would give her a while to calm down and then they would explore Heswall and its shops together.

As she reached the door, she heard Cherry speak quietly, "Anyway Mummy, her name isn't Emily anymore; she changed it to Inga. My new friend."

Helen turned to look at her, but Cherry was busy setting up a hairdressing shop. She supposed that made sense too, change of address, change her favourite doll's name, but why Inga? It certainly wasn't a name she'd heard, so where had Cherry?

***

Einaar held out his tankard for more ale. The slave girl quickly filled it and slunk away. He found it very difficult to keep still and he began pacing the large room. His friends watched him through drunken eyes and shouted encouraging remarks before ordering more ale themselves. The air was thick with smoke and the smell of sweating bodies, ale, wine and roasted boar.

The celebration of Jol had only just begun when his wife Astrid had gone into labour. She had already lost a child in her seventh month, but this time, she had gone the full term. He felt that it was a blessing his child should be born now, on the first day of the feast of Jol. They had placed their hands on the sacred boar and asked the God Frey, to bring them a healthy birth and a strong child. They also asked the Goddess Freya, his twin sister, to be with Astrid and to help her stay alive. Then, as the boar was sacrificed, she had felt the first pangs of labour: it was a good omen.

He drank down his ale and quickly wiped his mouth with his hand. He glanced around the large hall at his comrades, his friends, his family. Nothing could go wrong tonight, how could the gods deny him a child. A son?

"Einaar, stop pacing, you're making me feel sick. Come, sit and drink with me."

"Haven't you had enough, old friend?" Einaar grinned mischievously as he listened to the bawls of laughter, coming from the group closest who had heard the jest. He deftly caught a piece of bread someone threw and chucked it over his shoulder without regard. Hearing a yelp, he turned to another roar of laughter as a woman clutched her eye, feigning injury. He quickly picked her up in his arms and twirled her around until she screamed to be put down. When he did so, she playfully slapped him across the head and waddled off, her cheeks burning with mirth.

Grabbing the half-empty pitcher she had left behind, he quickly refilled his tankard and pushed the pitcher along the table to his waiting friend.

Thorlak deftly caught it, raised it to his mouth, and drank, ignoring the liquid that ran down the sides of his face into his blond beard. The group nearest to him began shouting their encouragement and he continued swallowing, the muscles in his throat moved rhythmically until at last, he finished the last dregs and let the empty pitcher fall onto the floor. With a loud belch, he bowed, a little unsteadily, to his applauding audience and staggered away to relieve himself outside.

Einaar finished his drink and sat down. He used his knife to skewer a large piece of meat and an apple and began to eat, his thoughts only half on the merriment around him, the other half with his wife. He knew he could trust the bjargrygr; Dalla had been midwife to his village long before he had arrived from Dublin. All the babes under her care had lived, at least through the birth; after that, it wasn't her responsibility.

The few parents he knew who had chosen to allow their sickly child to die had been rewarded soon after with a child they could be proud of, a son. He prayed to the Goddess Freya that he would not have to make that decision. In addition, secretly, he prayed to the new Christian God for help. As Astrid had done as she'd turned away from the sacrifice. He'd seen her lips moving and a slight bow of her head told him her secret; he hoped no one else had noticed..

Chapter Nine

Scanning the half empty pub quickly, Nick realised Lee wasn't there. He chewed his lower lip then started on his fingernails, although they had long since been chewed off to the quick. His mind raced about where Lee might be, but besides his flat, the pub and the job centre he couldn't think where he would go. He wondered briefly if he might have gone elsewhere to score; Birkenhead perhaps? He wouldn't have gone as far as Liverpool, he was almost certain of that. Lee preferred to know who he was dealing with, especially after the last time they had gone to Liverpool on a mate's advice.

"It's cheaper and better quality over the water," he'd said. "If you're lucky, you might get a quick job doing them a favour, you know what I mean ...?"

They'd thought they knew what he'd meant but were wrong, when they found out it consisted of risking their necks to travel abroad with cocaine shoved up their arse. They'd expected a local job, selling to kids or hurting someone who'd pissed off the dealers, but not that. The dealers had not been happy and had made them suffer quite badly. No, Lee would not have gone over the water.

Nowadays, Lee never went further than the pub or the town. He'd sold his car over a year ago when he'd lost his job and it was doubtful he would have gone anywhere on a bus without telling him last night.

"You all right, Nick?"

He turned towards the voice and shrugged, the old man sitting at the bar was watching him intently; he didn't like it. "Fine," he mumbled: "Just looking for Lee."

"He hasn't been in today. Got a job perhaps, eh?"

The man's sarcastic tone was clear and Nick quickly stormed out. He stopped outside the door, uncertain what to do or where to go. His body shook and his head was beginning to hurt. His throat was dry and he needed to piss quite badly, but he wasn't going back inside. He knew that if he saw that bastard's smug face again he'd hit it and he couldn't afford to get arrested for grievous bodily harm again, not until his probation finished in four months, then he'd kick his head in, with no witnesses.

He curled his hands into fists and then slowly released them. He had to find Lee, he had to get some fags, he had to piss and he had to get a drink. Where the hell could he get all that, now?

***

Astrid grunted as another labour pain gripped her body. Kneeling down she tried to concentrate on her breathing as the midwife was showing her. Her breath came out in big, shallow puffs of air, her fingers dug into the large woman's arms as she supported her and then the contraction eased and she let out a long sigh.

Moving closer, Dalla, the midwife gently rubbed some oil onto her belly and then deftly moved between Astrid's legs and carefully with three moves, oiled her vagina. Astrid did not have time to complain as another contraction began to build, but its intensity was overwhelming and she let out a shout. The midwife watched her for a second before making a decision, quickly moved behind Astrid, and gently eased her onto all fours. "Just go with it Astrid ... Let the pain come ..."

The urge to push took Astrid by surprise and she caught her breath as the pain moved downwards, her pelvis felt like it would break, then it relaxed. She hardly had time to take a few breaths, before it came again, like a mounting wave of pressure, forcing downwards, moving her child closer to freedom. This thought alone made her ride the wave. She welcomed it, knowing that soon her child would be born and would be breathing in her arms.

Two women crouched in front of her supporting her arms and shoulders. She used them to push against as another force took hold. Everyone was sweating profusely as the heat from the fire mingled with the heat of exertion but no one took much notice. One woman wiped Astrid's brow every so often and another gave her sips of water between pushes. Abruptly, Dalla gave a low command and it was down to work. Astrid pushed hard and the child was free. She sagged against the two women who caught her and gently patted her arms and rubbed her back in congratulations before easing her back into a seated position. The midwife, who had expertly caught the baby, was now quickly cleaning its face of mucus with a clean cloth.

As she cleaned away the blood and slime, Dalla searched for signs of any disfigurements or weaknesses. She saw the obvious problem but kept her lips pressed firmly together as she gently wrapped the child in a warm blanket, all the while crooning and talking to the child in an attempt to keep her face as unreadable as possible.

Astrid watched Dalla carefully, barely noticing the clean sheet draped over her or the building contractions. She knew she had to ask the question, but there was some part of her that dreaded the answer because for now, her child was perfect, and hers.

The midwife saw her watching and carefully unfolded the blanket. She watched Astrid closely as she revealed the child was a girl. She saw the flicker of something that might have been dismay, but it was quickly hidden as Astrid reached for the girl. Whatever it had been was forever lost the moment Astrid held her child in her arms and the child looked back at her mother.

Dalla was pleased to see the love that flowed from the mother to her daughter. It did not happen often anymore, but occasionally parents were using her expertise for helping perfectly healthy babies into this world, only to discover the blessing of a daughter. Months later when she would be called again to the household, she would enquire about their daughter, only to be met with downturned eyes, unable to meet her gaze. Some would be blatant about it, informing her that having a daughter was unsatisfactory, and demand she bring them a son this time. Unable to have a child of her own, she had begged parents over the years to give the unwanted girls to her; none had.

She silently prayed to the Goddesses Freya and Frigga for this child's wellbeing as she slowly washed her blood soaked arms and hands in a nearby bowl. Leaving them wet, she turned back to Astrid who was quietly humming to her baby. Oiling her hands again, Dalla began rubbing Astrid's stomach, "Come along now, a little more work is needed here."

Dalla was relieved to see that the placenta came away without an immense amount of blood. She carefully inspected it before snipping the cord that held the child to it. "This should be offered to the goddesses Freya and Frigga as thanks for a safe delivery."

Astrid nodded and the other women who had moved away to stand in the doorway to give Astrid time alone with her child, now formed a circle around her. Dalla chanted quietly, the placenta on a round wooden plate before her. The women joined in quietly. Dalla drew a knife from her waist and cut the placenta in half. Throwing first one half and then the other into the roaring fire, they all remained quiet as they watched the flesh sizzle. Suddenly, one of the women screeched as half of the placenta rolled out of the fire, hardly singed from the flames. For a moment nobody moved, but all stared at the flesh.

"It is an omen," whispered one woman, then another joined in. Dalla quickly glanced across at Astrid who stared wide-eyed at the smoking placenta. She was clutching her child protectively against her bosom as if the gods themselves were going to come and claim her. Stepping forward, she blocked Astrid's view and swiftly picked up the placenta and threw it back into the fire. She remained that way until she was sure the flesh had completely gone.

***

Astrid watched Dalla standing in front of the fire. Her heart hammered against her chest as fear flooded her veins. Her child had hardly made any sound since being born. Even now, she lay quietly in her arms, fast asleep. Was it an omen? If so, it would mean that she did indeed have a sickly child and the goddess had decided not to allow her life. On the other hand, only one-half of the placenta had come out, so perhaps it meant only one goddess was pleased. She looked down at her sleeping daughter and knew that she would fight to the death to protect her child.

She was also aware of what that might mean; Einaar had not seen his child yet. Would he accept her or would she have to fight him too? She prayed silently to the Christian god that she would not have to fight her husband because if he denied their daughter, she knew beyond doubt that both she and her child would be leaving this night.

She silently watched as the women began clearing away the blankets and rags now covered in her mess. Everyone kept their eyes lowered and some whispered knowingly, but none looked at her or Dalla who had not moved from the fireplace. She remained silent, her back to the room.

Astrid hoped more than anything that she was praying to her goddess. They listened to the midwives, for they were the bringers of life. Were they not granted the knowledge of birth and all its mysteries? She stared hard at Dalla's back, willing her to beg her gods for mercy, and prayed with all her heart that today they would listen to her.

***

Einaar lifted his head off the long wooden table and stared drunkenly at the boar's head that sat in the middle of it. It was inches away, its snout almost touching his nose. He flinched backwards and felt the room spin slightly with the movement. He became aware that someone was standing next to him calling his name, and he slowly turned his head to look up.

"Aha! You are awake now!" His friend Thorlak playfully slapped him on the back. "We thought you had gone to the gods without us, old friend."

Before Einaar could reply, he was pulled roughly to his feet and turned towards the hall doorway. His vision cleared as he focused on the woman who stood there, Dalla. She stood motionless, waiting patiently for the cries and jeers to subside, which they did; and all eyes turned to Einaar. He shook his head to try to clear it and walked towards her, a little unsteadily, but he managed.

She watched his approach; her face remained blank, giving nothing away. Outwardly, he tried to look calm, but inside, his stomach was a knot of anxiety, how was Astrid faring? Did she still live? What about the child? Was it a boy? All of these questions were on the tip of his tongue, desperate to ask, but Dalla's presence, the air about her, told him to keep quiet for now.

Her eyes never wavered from his and the hint of a smile showed on her face as he neared, that lessened the fear in his heart; Astrid was safe. She turned away from him and reached out towards another woman whom he had not noticed. She stood in the shadows and carried a bundle in her arms. Dalla carefully took the bundle and turned back to him.

"Einaar, Son of Einaar the brave, I bring to you, your child." She held out the bundle which he noticed hadn't moved and fear stabbed at his heart again; was it dead?

Hesitantly, he reached out and took his child. His eyes searched hers, questioning, she gave a slight nod, yes, it was alive. He let out his breath, closed his eyes, and silently gave thanks to Odin. He flipped back the cloth that covered his child and froze. A girl. He glanced at Dalla, who was watching him intently and for the briefest moment, he didn't move, then he took a deep breath, nodded his thanks and exhaled loudly.

He glanced around the room at the large crowd, all waiting to hear his news. His decision made, he flipped back the blanket and carefully tucked it around his daughter's chin. She opened her eyes and looked up at him and in that second, every last uncertainty left him. He gripped her tiny hand and felt such an overwhelming feeling of joy as she gripped his finger tightly. He let out a shout and turned towards his people.

"My friends, I give to you, my daughter."

Shouts came from all directions with raised tankards and pitchers. Some clapped and some banged on the tables until Einaar raised his voice to be heard and they quietened down. "My daughter, born of Astrid: she will be blessed with the name given to Astrid's mother. I present to you, Inga, daughter of Einaar."

Chapter Ten

Tony sat back and stared at the shards of pottery scattered over the table. It had become obvious over the last hour that most of it was from the same large pot. What he stared at now, was a small but significant thumbprint. It had to be a woman's as it was quite small, too small for a man, but that was hardly surprising: as the women would have used the pots for cooking, it seemed likely that they also had a hand in making them.

The pot looked like one used for holding liquid, most likely ale or mead, possibly wine. He gently picked up a large piece and inspected it carefully, even sniffing it, which made him smile to himself; no residue, no discolouration, so perhaps it had been brand new when it was broken?

He looked across at the other remains found. More shards of pottery, some weights, and a small slice of a comb made from horn. If he were to make an assumption now, he would probably say that they had uncovered what remained of a home. The finds felt, 'homely' somehow, and so far, they hadn't found enough in the same area to suggest a dump of some kind or that they were digging in more than one home.

Of course, it was only a theory. Well, more of a feeling perhaps than a theory and it was really too early to say for sure but, if he was a 'betting man' he'd have to say that it would be very rare indeed to find just one house in a possible Viking area. They lived in small settlements or farms for protection; there had to be more.

He gently picked up his brush and carefully moved away more mud off another piece of pottery, another thumbprint came into view and he carefully sprayed it with water to clean it better. The two pieces fitted perfectly together so he was now certain that the same person owned the thumbprint; a woman? He felt the stirrings of interest and took another piece to clean. How interesting it would be to put together something made by a woman a thousand years ago who had left her own prints on it! How interesting indeed. It felt quite personal and he wanted to do this woman proud. She had carefully made this pot for whatever reason: now, he would fix it and her good work would not be lost forever.

***

Kathryn left the laboratory feeling quite ill. Simon had said that he would test her blood sample, off the record, but only when he wasn't busy. That generally meant he would do it if he remembered and she would owe him big time. No doubt, that would mean a terribly boring dinner whilst keeping him at arm's length. Then fighting him off on the way home and making a dash to her front door before he had time to get out and ask to come inside, again.

Their last 'date' had been an absolute nightmare. They had been introduced by a mutual friend from University: and she would never forgive Rebecca for doing it, either. She had quite liked Simon at first, his job sounded interesting. Within an hour, she had realised forensics was interesting, Simon was not. Once they got off the subject of their jobs, Simon had nothing else to talk about except ants; he liked them. She'd felt itchy the rest of the night, constantly touching herself in a way she hoped was inconspicuous, Simon had noticed and thought she was getting over excited.

The evening had not finished well, with her forcibly pushing him off her when she'd reluctantly allowed him in for coffee. He had made it very clear he didn't want coffee and had jumped on her the second she'd switched on the kettle. His glasses had snapped in what she could only describe as an assault on her body and she had had to slap him across the cheek. He staggered backwards clutching his face and made a grab at his glasses, sitting clumsily on her kitchen stool where her cat was idly licking herself. Simon's weight on her tail had not been welcome and Purdy had screeched loudly, scratching his thigh, before hissing and spitting with indignation as she ran off. Simon had left then with as much dignity as he could muster.

She couldn't help but giggle now whenever she thought about it, but there was no way he was coming into her flat again. For one thing, her cat Purdy would never forgive her. She hugged herself as she walked back to her car. Her smile quickly faded and she bit her lower lip as a niggling worry took over. What would it mean if it were human blood? What would happen to her dig? There hadn't been a body, but then again, she hadn't really looked, but she didn't want to think about that now.

It had looked like quite a lot, more than just a cut finger or something and the thought of finding a mutilated body was something she shied away from. On the other hand, maybe it was her imagination and the rain had made it seem like there was more blood? What the hell did she know anyway? There were too many questions that she was desperately trying to ignore. Why hadn't she gone to the police? Why did she have such a bad feeling? Why was she so sure it was human and not some poor animal?

The answer to the first question was of course her dig, what would happen to her dig? She knew the answer of course and felt sick, her knees felt like jelly and she leant against a tree. If it were human, there would be an investigation. The valuable time given to dig would be lost. She knew they wanted her dig more or less finished by the beginning of the summer so as to minimise tourist interactions, health and safety and of course, thefts. Investigations could go on for a long time. Crime scene would be cordoned off and that would be the last she saw of her finds. Not to mention her not coming forward with blood soaked evidence. Was her dig so important? More important than a human life?

Her fight to dig had become such an obsession. Taking every moment of the last year to argue her reasons, to justify to all concerned, even herself. She had never come to terms with that. She could justify to the council, the conservation bodies, the University, even the protesters that a dig in the area was worthwhile to see if there was evidence of Viking activity, but to herself? Her private reasons didn't make sense and it scared her beyond anything she'd known before: yet, here she was.

Thurstaston meant 'Thorstein's *Tun*': Old Norse which meant 'Farm or farmer near Torstein'. A large sandstone outcrop had been named 'Thor's Stone' but there was nothing Viking about that. It had a minimal connection to Norse compared to other places on the Wirral. Yet, there was never any other place for her, it had always been Thurstaston.

From childhood, it had been an obsession, a secret she'd kept hidden, but could never explain or understand why it had had to be a secret even from her parents. Who had done nothing but encourage her in her love of history. How could she tell them Vikings were her obsession and her worst fear? The Vikings who invaded Dublin were the ones who filled her head, but she'd never understood why specifically them? Throughout her life, she had tried in vain to stay away from names that sent a shiver of apprehension down her spine whenever she heard them, Ingimund and his invasion being one of them.

Queen Aethelflaed had granted him lands on the Wirral and they had lived in peace, farming the land and trading with neighbours until Ingimund became bored and wanted to conquer the city of Chester. Whenever she heard or read anything to do with this period in history she felt sick and had a knowing of something she couldn't quite place that terrified her. That feeling of helplessness had stayed with her throughout her childhood into adulthood. This dig was her way, her only way, of fighting back. Possibly finding answers and finding peace.

Reaching her car, she climbed in feeling a mixture of sickness and exhaustion; and she still had a long day ahead of her. Her decision had been made the moment she saw the blood by the trench; her trench, she wouldn't do anything to jeopardise her dig. She couldn't go to the police, she despised herself for it, and she would no doubt pay the price for it eventually. Later, if Simon kept his mouth shut just long enough to finish her dig. It couldn't be disrupted now and she pushed the thought away as to whose blood it was.

A new thought began to form in her head. She knew of a few people who would be very glad if the dig were to be postponed. Those conservationists and Mr Merton had all made protests about her digging around in Thurstaston Common. Could any of them have left it? Blood. It sounded a reasonable thing to do to try to stop her digging, didn't it? Would they really stoop so low? Could they? The way they had behaved these last few months, she wouldn't put anything past that group.

She did her bit against animal testing, buying animal free products, bought recycled goods where possible; buying fair-trade was something she had begun doing recently. She cared about the world, but knew there were extremists who would do anything for their cause.

She supported animal activists against animal cruelty, signed petitions and sent letters to her MPs, but violence was not something she condoned at all. If it was animal blood, that would be bad enough: but human?

If someone had indeed cut himself or herself, it would have to have been a big wound for the amount of blood left on the ground. It was a hard jump to believe that someone, even someone as passionate as Mr Merton could hurt themselves for a cause they believed in. Worse still, hurt someone else to make a point.

Starting the engine, she manoeuvred the car out of the large car park and headed back to the Museum. Regardless of blood and possible extremists, she had a site to dig and catalogue. All of these absences were extremely unprofessional and it wasn't like her at all. At other digs, she'd be there from sun up to sun down and work long into the night back at the labs with her findings. Her passion for archaeology had been commented on more than once. People watched her, learned from her, liked working with her. Her enthusiasm for the job infected others; or so she'd been told.

She knew damned well they were watching her with this dig and making notes of her lack of professionalism; it would go against her, she had to pull herself together and get on with it. However, the reality was that she didn't want to go back to the site alone. She was scared. From the moment she had first stepped on the site to map it out, she had felt eyes on her, watching her closely. The protesters were expected, but there was something else, something negative. God, she had to get a grip! She'd collect Tony, take the pot down to the labs for cleaning and hope that Tony would forgive her.

She pulled a face at the last two. The pot, because she had really wanted to clean it herself, but the reality was, she didn't have the time. As for Tony, well, she'd think of something. Regardless of her fear of what might had gone on there, she had to get back to the site. She hoped more than ever that the promised volunteers and students would be with them sooner rather than later, safety in numbers.

Chapter Eleven

Helen slowly dressed in an old pair of jeans and a jumper. Piling her blonde hair into a ponytail, she started on the nearest box that contained books they had collected over the years. She flipped through some of them, unsure why she was keeping them. Some had obvious sentimental attraction, like the box set of Beatrice Potter stories, which she was keeping until Cherry would really appreciate them. There were various books on 'how to' do things like decorating a home, easy sewing and computers for dummies; she put them to one side, thinking that they might come in handy. A few trashy books about love and romance she flung in the corner, the charity corner. Reading fictional characters getting more love and sex than she was, was not what she needed right now.

Opening another box, she found all of her historical books collected years ago. She decided to keep them and placed them in the walnut wood bookshelf that ran the length of the dining room. They looked so alone with the Beatrix Potter books at the far end. She found Robert's detective books he'd enjoyed reading in his spare time; she put them on the shelf also, he could decide on them.

Although her back was to the doorway, she knew that he had quietly passed by at least twice. What was he doing? Watching her or checking up on her? Picking up a large quantity of 'Mr Men' books, she dithered about putting them in Cherry's bedroom or here with all the others. Eventually deciding she didn't want to walk out into the hallway, in case he was still loitering there, she placed them down one end with the Beatrix Potter books; that would be Cherry's area.

At the bottom of the box she found a handful of leaflets of places she had visited over the years. She felt the sting of tears at the memories of wandering around a large house or castle, alone. Once Cherry was born, pushing her around the various parks and estates of grand houses, he had never come, saying he had too much work to do.

Sometimes he'd kissed her goodbye and had more or less pushed her out of the house to get some peace and quiet to work. Just another example of how he'd made her feel second place to everything; to work, his career, his business partners and associates, his clients, his secretary, to Cherry. Could she really believe that he truly wanted her to become first now?

"I'm making a cuppa, fancy one?"

She jumped and dropped the leaflets. He came into the room and bent down to help her to pick them up. He saw the tension and stopped, one leaflet hanging lifeless in his hand; she was remembering the past. He vaguely remembered the trips she would organise, first on her own and then with Cherry to various houses when she'd joined the National Trust. How many times had she asked him to come with them?

He couldn't remember any particular trip; he hadn't been interested. Sometimes he'd declined before she had even asked him to go, forgetting her almost immediately as his interest had moved onto something work related. Now though, he wondered if that was what she had expected and wanted after all. Is that when she met this man with muscles?

He stepped back, watched her as she collected the leaflets, and stood up; she didn't ask for the one he held and he placed it on the dining table instead. Bending down she picked up the empty box and began flattening it. She barely glanced at him, but did answer, "No, I'm fine, I'll make a coffee later."

Needing to say something, anything, he nodded towards the pile of leaflets, "What are you going to do with those?"

She finished with the box, picked up the pile, and placed them inside a large history book, "I'm keeping them. I intend to add to them, there must be something of interest around here."

The scorn in her voice was unmistakable, but he let it go. "There's lots of history around here. And we're very close to Wales, only half an hour to the border. When we've settled in perhaps we can take a drive around and explore … together?"

She glanced across at him and quickly hid her look of surprise with a shrug and turned back to the waiting pile of boxes. He thrust his hands into his pockets, the urge to help and continue a conversation was so strong, but he felt unsure how to proceed.

They hadn't sat down and spoken about anything; his fault of course. She'd tried hard in the beginning, to engage him in a discussion about his work, his breakdown, their pathetic marriage, the move. Eventually giving up, she would just sit, silently watching him, firstly in the hospital family room when she had visited him every day for the few weeks they'd kept him in to 'rest', and then at home.

Helen tried hard to support him once he'd come home, but not as a wife, but as a carer. Her job as a nurse really shone through, brisk and professionally done, like her job. That had hurt him more than he'd cared to admit. It was his own doing. Then he had realised how much he still loved her, desired her; and her coming with him to therapy had rewarded him.

He'd begun to believe that there was a chance of saving their marriage. She hadn't left him as he'd expected her to do. He wanted to believe so badly that it had nothing to do with Cherry, but now he wasn't so sure. Why was she still here if there was another man? Was he still around? Did she love him? Was she staying because he'd left her? What did that mean? He was desperate to find out, but in couple therapy, she had barely spoken, answering the counsellor's questions with a shrug or a "Don't know."

"You want any help with those?" Very lame, but he couldn't think of how to ask, "Do you still love me?" in a subtle way.

"No." She had her back to him as usual. He stepped to the side to see her face; she glanced up, "I thought you were making a drink."

The dismissal was clear as she didn't wait for his answer, but continued working through the boxes containing books, DVDs and some CDs. He knew he was hovering, but the urge to stay and be with her was tearing him apart. "I'll make a drink and come back and help … if you like?" He moved towards the door and looked behind at her to see any reaction; none came, she acted as if she hadn't heard him.

He also suspected that while he was making his cup of tea, she would be rushing to finish the job before he got back. He wasn't wanted, so what else could he do to make an impression? He glanced upstairs, perhaps he could make a start on the attic. The landing was stacked with boxes, but he had no idea what was in them. He had merely brought them down from the old attic, dutifully placed them in the van and forgotten about them. So perhaps it was about time he found out what memories had been hidden away. There might be something in there that could be a conversation starter? He cringed and slowly shook his head; what had he become? He glanced at himself in the hallway mirror and quickly walked past it, heading for the mountain of boxes and hours of hiding away from the truth.

***

"Where the hell have you been?" Tony sat back in his chair and stretched his hands behind his head. He was half way through a toasted teacake and shoved another piece into his mouth as he waited for Kathryn to take off her coat.

"Sorry, I had some things to do first."

She sounded a little out of breath and wouldn't look him in the eye as she moved towards the files and began flicking through them. It was obvious to him that she wasn't really sure what she was looking for, if anything at all, but merely doing something; he watched and waited. After five minutes of fruitlessly looking at the filing cabinet, she turned back towards him and slumped down in the opposite chair. Reaching across the wide desk, she grabbed the other half of the teacake and ate it quickly.

When she was finished, he offered her the last dregs of his lukewarm cappuccino. She accepted it with a smile. "So, when you're finished eating my food and drinking my coffee and rifling through old files, are you ready to tell me what the hell is going on?"

Kathryn glanced away, but he banged his hand down onto the table, making her jump. "You wake me up at some god-awful hour and now slope in hours late and leave me to enjoy doing all this work alone." He swept his hand over the desk and the container on it, which she saw contained fragments of pottery.

"Is that what you found yesterday?"

She sounded very tired but he couldn't shake off his annoyance. Even her question, feeble as it was, annoyed him, though he could see plainly that something was wrong.

He sighed loudly and sucked on his teeth. He tried to keep his voice calm, but it didn't work, "Yes, it is; well, some of it. I've taken the larger pieces down to the labs to be cleaned properly and fixed together. Some pieces were perfect." He nodded towards the box on her desk, "Don't suppose you've even looked at your own pot you found?" She looked up at him but quickly lowered her gaze. "Kathryn? Come on, we're supposed to be a team."

Her voice was barely audible and he had to lean closer to hear, "I ... I feel ... Oh God, Tony, I don't know." She threw her hands into the air in obvious frustration and exhaled loudly. "Never mind, we need to get a few hours' digging in if it ever stops bloody raining."

He came round from behind the desk and sat awkwardly on the edge of it. "Let's give it a few minutes, blue skies will follow, I assure you. So, start at the beginning, what was the dream?"

"Dream?" She shook her head slowly, "I don't really remember ... Vikings were in it."

"Oh well, of course they were, that makes sense doesn't it?"

Kathryn nodded, she licked her lips quickly. He could see she was trying to decide something and leant forward encouragingly.

"Yes, I suppose it does, but have you ever had a dream, but it didn't feel like one?" She looked up at him then, her face so full of hope. Could she explain it all to him?

He frowned trying to remember, "Well, I must have. Dreams can sometimes feel very real. You know, the ones where people say they are falling and come awake as the bed jolts, as if they've just fallen onto it, you mean like that? I've definitely had a few of those."

"Kind of, but more like the place you are, in the dream, feels like somewhere you know, you're someone you have been, that's impossible obviously, but it feels so real, more like a memory than a dream."

Tony rubbed his chin, "You're talking past lives and things?"

"I suppose I am … and it feels horrible."

Tony moved off the desk and walked around the small office. Finally he sat down in his chair and exhaled, "God, Kathryn, you never do things by half do you? So, if I'm hearing you correctly, you suddenly feel as if you have been a Viking before and you have remembered something from your past. In a dream? Because, in your dream you saw somewhere that looked familiar and I'll hazard a guess and say it looked like the dig site, hmm?"

His sarcasm stung her and she scowled at him, "Don't you take the piss! It was obviously a mistake telling you and I am sorry for waking you, but, I can't explain it, I just … feel something and I don't know why ..." She made herself stop, what on earth was she doing? This was pointless.

"Okay, so here's a theory. We are digging in an area known to have been overrun with Vikings at one point and we have found some finds; all very interesting I might add. It took a lot of fighting and negotiating with certain individuals to get this far." He held up his hand as she was about to but in, "And, there are still some individuals who are still dead against what we are doing, so, there is a high percentage of stress and tension, thus bringing with it bad nightmares which are understandable. Please don't go down that road of reading into things when there are obvious reasons. If you are having bad dreams, take a pill, do something good that makes you happy. Think logically for God's sake, Kathryn. Find some balance. It can't all be work. And, by the way, we should have been down at the site half an hour ago ... I told the volunteers to meet us down there rain or shine."

"You finished?"

He could see her fighting the urge to slap him, but her mood had lightened a little. "Yeah, I'm done. I'm going to grab a sandwich to take with me ..." Looking her up and down he added, "And you can pay while you get yourself something; you've lost weight, my girl. Then we'll get back to the site for the rest of this glorious day, okay?"

Kathryn grinned, "All right."

"I'll tell you something though, archaeology is much harder in the rain, I hope it stops by the time we arrive at the site. But if not ..." he pointed towards the back wall, "we have ourselves a new gazebo and Trevor left a message on the machine to say he was looking into getting another large tent to be permanently fixed at the site. Happy now?" He smiled warmly seeing her face light up and gently punched her arm, "And while we are driving to our destination I will tell you all about my hour with this amazing find."

Tony quickly put on his coat, "In a few days, God willing, we will get a bunch of students who will be full of enthusiasm. Who will constantly ask questions, usually lame ones and never leave us alone and by the end of the four weeks you will have lost all your hair with stress, not from some bloody dream, but because of the immense annoyance of students and good intentional volunteers; good hey? And you will beg me to take them away so you can have some peace, yes?"

Kathryn put her arm through his and tried to smile, "Yes, I can't wait. The place feels empty sometimes, you know, now the geophysics team has left."

"Empty!" Tony pulled a face, "Empty indeed! You shouldn't be feeling empty while I'm around!"

Kathryn slapped his shoulder, "Dirty boy! Come on then. I'll take the big pot down to the labs because I can't do it justice." She sighed loudly, "And it deserves someone's full attention and then you can tell me about the fragments you've been working on."

***

The dining room was finished. The large cabinet now housed every CD and DVD they owned on the top two shelves and on the bottom was packed every book she had decided to keep. In the far corner, Cherry's books sat slightly apart from their books with a large white porcelain 'A' between them. It was part of a gift given by Robert when Cherry had been two; a pair of bookends 'A' and 'Z', but the 'Z' had been damaged in the move so she had placed it in the bin. If he cared about it, he could retrieve it and fix it, but she doubted that would happen. She doubted if he even remembered that he had bought it. More likely that his secretary had bought it.

In the adjoining lounge the large lamps had been unpacked and stood proudly in two corners of the room. The black iron stand stood out against the cream walls. Their enormous settee sat along the opposite wall to the walnut cabinet; the large lone armchair beside it. She had bought a mulberry coloured throw a few months before and this now garnished the cream coloured chair, matching the mulberry cushions nicely.

A large rectangular Indian rug almost covered the cream carpet beneath leaving only a hint of the boring colour peeking out at each corner. The hi-fi stood in the opposite corner to the television system and she had managed to hang up four of her favourite pictures on one wall, each one depicting the 'Lady of the Lake', whilst on the opposite wall, she had hung a tapestry of assorted materials, all of different shades of green. She had seen it weeks ago hanging in a New Age shop and loved it instantly. The colours reminded her of nature, individual and beautiful, yet variants of the same colour. She stood at the doorway and sighed, the room looked like hers; she hadn't asked his opinion. The walls could be re-painted … depending on whether or not she was staying, she quickly reminded herself.

She didn't hear him come up behind her, but suddenly, he was there. He looked over her shoulder and whistled, "Wow! It looks great, are we allowed in it yet?"

Helen moved away from the door, moving away from him, "Of course, it's your home."

She turned to go but he stood in her way, "I was only joking. I was trying to compliment you, is that allowed?"

She shrugged, "I don't know."

He put his hand out against the wall to stop her moving past him; forcing her to look at him, which she eventually did and he flinched back at what he saw. So much pain, hurt and anger all directed at him. He was about to speak when Cherry came skipping down the stairs; the moment was broken and he reluctantly lowered his arm. She walked past him, but he noticed that she didn't touch him as he watched her meeting Cherry at the bottom of the stairs. "Hello darling, have you been busy?"

Cherry nodded and pointed at her tummy, "So busy, I need foods."

Helen laughed and taking Cherry's hand, they walked into the kitchen, neither one speaking to him as they focused on each other. He listened to their banter about making sandwiches for lunch and then Helen suggested a walk. He swallowed hard and felt knots in his stomach, should he go with them? He doubted Helen would want him anyway, and perhaps she wouldn't want him around for another reason. Would this be her first chance to meet this man with muscles? He heard Cherry ask the question, "Is Daddy coming?" He didn't make out Helen's mumbled reply, but he sensed it wasn't in the positive.

He had stayed out of her way long enough, believing that he was doing the right thing, giving her some space, giving himself time to think about what to say and do. Now, he was beginning to think he'd made the wrong decision. The attic boxes had yielded many memories from past Christmases and birthdays, the cot Cherry had used, with a box filled to the brim with old baby clothes. But most importantly for him was their wedding day. He'd found their wedding pictures, the album ripped and un-cared for which had torn his insides out; he had to change that.

Taking a deep breath, he marched into the kitchen, a forced smile plastered on his face and got involved with the lunch preparations. He giggled with Cherry over which jam to put onto her bread and laughed when she put some on his nose and he went cross-eyed trying to get it off. He forced himself to eat the ham salad sandwich he made just to be in the same room as them both and he forced himself to drink the orange juice Cherry poured for him. He was determined to be there when they made their plans for the afternoon. If they went out, he was going with them. He wouldn't give her the chance of meeting this other man. He would fight for his wife and daughter, whether she liked it or not. Sadly, he knew it would be the latter.

Chapter Twelve

T he rain that had come in short outbursts all morning had for the time being been driven away by the wind and though chilly, it was dry and fresh. They reached the site by late morning and she was grateful to see the two volunteers waiting in their car. Her adrenalin scurried through her veins as she got out of Tony's van to pull open the large metal gate and she clenched and un-clenched her fists to try and stop them from shaking.

She hoped he didn't notice that it hadn't been locked and she chastised herself for her stupidity earlier that morning. Blood or no blood, leaving the gate unlocked had been irresponsible. She was losing it. She would never have behaved so unprofessionally in any other dig, she had to pull it together or else.

It wasn't really much of a deterrent. Anyone with a bit of effort could climb over the fence or one quick yank on the chain would open the gate wide enough for a small or thin person to get through. But, it was all that she'd been offered in the way of security. Apart from the promise of the local police calling past the site on occasion, there was nothing stopping anyone coming in and vandalising the place; only the pool of blood.

It wasn't ideal, but she'd agreed readily at the time just to get the ball rolling, and they'd known it. She quickly looked around at the surrounding bushes; anyone could have been hiding within the tree line or crouched behind a bush.

"Morning, Kathryn."

The greeting pulled her attention back to the two women who were locking up their car. Wrapped in warm coats and waterproofs: she smiled back, hoping she looked convincing. She was still holding the gate open and she looked down at the cold, wet metal in her hand. Was it only hours before that she had run away in a panic from this place, her dig? It felt like a lifetime ago and she felt ashamed for behaving so feebly.

Everything looked the same as it had early that morning. The site looked empty, quiet and as it should. An archaeological site with the few ditches looking a bit waterlogged and the heaps of earth beside them, muddy and brown; no blood. Peaceful, nothing looked disturbed. She let out her breath that she realised she had been holding: what had she been expecting? A body drained of blood perhaps, or more pools of blood? The rain had waterlogged a lot of the area, but the pools of water looked clear and muddy, none looked red or sinister.

Tony headed for the large tent to check for any thefts, he came out smiling. He had the box containing the gazebo in one hand and his trowel in the other, "So, where to start? We could continue with your trench or continue what we were doing yesterday?"

She didn't answer him straight away. She was looking towards her trench with the tarpaulin. She swallowed hard, tried to take a breath, and felt herself quiver with apprehension.

"Hello, anyone home?"

His mocking tone forced her to smile briefly, "Sorry Tony, just thinking."

"Yeah well, don't think too hard, we need to get on with this!"

Pulling a face, she turned her back on him and walked slowly towards her trench. With a trembling hand she pulled back the tarpaulin and heaved a long sigh of relief. Tony had joined her. "Rain damage can be a bitch, but yours seems okay."

She let his mistake about her sigh go and nodded, "Yeah, seems intact, not much mud slide where I found the pot. I'll continue here if you'd be kind enough to erect the gazebo; and you carry on in your test pits when it stops raining. Until then, perhaps you could help me extend my trench?"

Looking across the small clearing, she could see where he had dug. He'd concentrated on a circular area where geophysics had found various marks indicating structure.

Tony nodded and began sorting out the new gazebo, glad of its cover as the heavens opened briefly. Everyone gathered beneath it and talked about this and that; but Kathryn wasn't really listening, she was thinking about her trench and the bloodstain.

She had a strong urge to extend it a few feet eastwards which would make it about ten feet long, but there was an inner battle going on inside her. Part of her wanted to dig and explore and find the evidence, but the other irrational part of her didn't want to be alone in the trench; she felt too vulnerable, but had no idea what the danger was. The blood had only helped strengthen her delusions.

Tony jumped down into her trench and peered intently at the soil. "It's discoloured around this area." He indicated the far corner where she had found the pot. "It looks charred, in fact ..." He bent down and quickly cleared away soil that had fallen from the sides and scraped away the near side. "It's all charred here too; there must have been a fire, but this doesn't look like a hearth. Would it be worth taking away all of this top soil and seeing how far it stretches?"

Using his trowel, he scraped away another area that showed more black and charred soil. "I think we have a burnt house here, see how it's just this layer and it seems to curve around in that direction ..."

Kathryn could plainly see the black soil curved to the left. "I'll extend this trench then and see if it continues, but the students would be handy right now, I won't be able to do this much justice in one afternoon. While it's raining, maybe you could extend the trench that way," she indicated east. "And get Pam and Jenny to help?"

"Okay sounds like a plan. And don't worry too much about scraping it all back, just get it started and that should give us an indication of whether it's a house or not. If it's just in that area alone, perhaps there was a small fire, but if it extends then maybe something significant happened here, an attack of some kind perhaps? Warring families or tribes?"

He glanced upwards, "With the possibility of more rain, I think it would be best if I carry on with my test pits in between showers. If I could verify a possible settlement, it would give our students something to aim for and I will dig down to that level to see if I find any charred soil. If I do, it could mean there was a big fire here, yes?"

She bit her lower lip, "I suppose it would."

Tony gently thumped her, "Don't sound so melancholy; this happened years ago."

She quickly changed the subject, "Do you think you might have one? A house or something I mean?"

"Yeah, I think I may have found a rectangular structure as the pits on either side of the circle show nothing, but on opposite sides, they show shards of pottery, those few household goods I found yesterday and in one I'm fairly certain was a post hole. So, I think I can say for certain, we aren't looking at Celtic, nothing as early, I think we are uncovering the Norse period, especially with the finds. Whether we actually have a burnt out village, is another matter, but wouldn't that be something?"

Kathryn nodded and licked her dry lips, his words made her stomach flip over with nerves. What if there was a village below their feet? A village burnt to the ground, its inhabitants helpless to stop it, their screams of agony and terror. Blinking away a wave of emotion, she busied herself with a bucket, a trowel and her kneepads. Kneeling down, she breathed deeply to try to compose herself and almost gagged as a strong smell of burning filled her nostrils and the screams of women echoed around her head. She stopped breathing and waited, but it was gone as quickly as it came, only the birds and the chatter of the volunteers remained.

***

Einaar closed his eyes as the axe crashed down, splitting the log. He felt the impact and quickly raised it again knowing this strike would finish the job; he was right. The large log splintered and separated; he bent down and picked up the smallest piece and threw it onto the growing pile. He liked this kind of work, he let his anger and frustrations find their target, imagining the log as an enemy to be defeated; it had been too long since a decent battle; all the men felt it, but only a handful had spoken out. They trained every so often to keep their wits and experience at their maximum, but it was different fighting a friend. Your aim is carefully placed and the swords are nothing more than wood so as not to maim your opponent too badly. However, Thorlak managed to knock out his opponent the other day!

So, for now his strength was used on the splitting of wood and on rebuilding his home as the roof had become weak during a particularly bad storm the week before. They had woken in the night shivering as the fire had gone out and a cold wind rushed into their home through a large hole. Inga had been particularly affected but Astrid assured him that her health was improving again. Those jobs were now finished, his roof was stronger than before, he had mended his door and carved out a new bed for Inga now that she was no longer a babe and replaced the bedding; it was time to prepare the ground for farming. The last of the frosts had finally gone and the ground was soft again.

He stood up straight and stretched his arms high above his head. His tunic and hat lay across a nearby branch. He closed his eyes enjoying the feel of the sun on his bare skin. It had been a long time wrapped up against the harsh cold winds, the snow and ice which some had feared would never melt, they had been proven wrong; it felt good to allow his skin to breathe.

"Einaar?"

He lowered his arms on hearing the voice and turned towards his wife who stood a few feet away. Inga stood half hidden within her mother's pinafore. He smiled and held out his arms. Inga pushed herself away from her mother's leg and walked quickly towards him; almost running, which was good. He was well aware of the comments regarding his daughter's lateness in walking and knew of the advice the women of the village had inflicted on Astrid. But what could he and Astrid do besides hope and pray to the gods that Inga would catch up; and she had - almost.

He picked her up and twirled her round, high above his head; she squealed, delighted. He brought her down and held her under his arm as he walked towards Astrid. It didn't go un-noticed to him that although nearing her third year, Inga weighed very little.

Astrid watched him carefully, she hadn't moved, but now smiled, relief written all over her face seeing his playfulness with their child. It hurt him to know that even now, she still didn't trust him completely where Inga was concerned. What else could he do? He had accepted her on the day of her birth, there was no going back. Not that it ever entered his mind. Nevertheless, he understood Astrid's uneasiness; after all, some parents still abandoned their sickly children to the elements. Leaning down, he gently kissed her on the nose, "My love?"

It wasn't like her to come and look for him, knowing how he preferred his own company when chopping wood. He saw her swallow, but she kept her chin high and looked him in the eyes. "Ingimund has sent word, he cannot go another spring without battle; his limbs grow bored of farming it seems."

Einaar sighed and gently put down his daughter who immediately sat abruptly near a small clump of early daisies. "It was inevitable. A fighter cannot become a farmer so easily. Where are the others?"

Astrid nodded her head towards the village, "They are gathering in the hall." Einaar moved to get his tunic, but she laid a hand on his arm to stop him, "Will you go? What about the planting? Food is scarce, the winter was too long."

He said nothing until he had finished dressing, and holding his hat in one hand, he rubbed a hand through his beard and reached out and touched her cheek, "Astrid, we have talked of this day many times. I know you hoped it would not, but I knew it would come. Ingimund is a fighter ... like all of us." Turning, he abruptly strode over to his daughter and picked her up. Inga giggled, delighted at the attention. "Your job is to look after this one." Putting Inga under his arm, he walked back to his waiting wife, reaching out he touched Astrid's belly, "And to bring me a son; I will deal with the rest."

***

Helen helped Cherry put on her blue wellington boots and quickly fastened her coat. Turning her back on him, she put on her own walking boots and a black fleece. The rain had stopped, but it hadn't gone for good. The clouds raced past, exposing a pale blue sky occasionally, perhaps just enough time to explore the immediate surroundings. Besides, Helen had promised Cherry she would take her to find the horses she had heard yesterday.

"Are we ready then?"

His light tone didn't fool her and she ignored it. Cherry didn't and ran towards the back door shouting, "YES! HORSES!"

Helen quickly followed, wanting to be ahead of him. If she was ahead, she didn't have to watch his pathetic attempt at joining in. Who the hell did he think he was fooling? She knew if she stopped to think reasonably that this was what she wanted, well, maybe. Moreover, that was what was niggling away at her; she hadn't made a decision.

Everything felt too late, the family man she was watching was a stranger. Now seeing him fooling around, laughing and joking with their daughter, it annoyed and hurt her terribly. Why couldn't he have done this years ago when it might have mattered? Taking a deep breath, she tried to calm herself; she had to get a grip on her anger. As the counsellor had reminded her several times, it wasn't healthy, she was only hurting herself.

Lunch had been awkward for her. Watching him from the corner of her eye she'd felt a strong urge to snatch Cherry away from him and tell her he was fake. That it was all a lie and he was nothing more than a selfish bastard! But how could she tell her that?

Another huge fear of hers was how long this newfound fatherly love would last. She knew the longer she left her decision the harder it would be, but a small, tiny voice kept stopping her from leaving; that 'What if' voice. What if he was sorry and he truly loved them both? What if it wasn't too late and she did love him? - leaving would be a huge mistake.

Her head hurt from all the questions racing around her brain, a nice walk in the cool air might help. She stepped out of the front door and breathed in the smell of mud and rain soaked grass and trees, no car fumes or bus fumes, no city crap to clog up her lungs here. It was a surprise, a nice one. It hadn't really occurred to her that the area might actually be a pleasant one. She watched Cherry jumping up and down at the gate, her excitement evident. Perhaps this was a better place for her baby. She gave him that possibility, reluctantly.

"Come on Mummy, I want to go over there." Cherry pointed across the narrow road to where she could see a wood. A stone wall with quite a few stones missing separated the trees from the lane and travelled along the side of the road, carrying on around a bend. Opposite their house was an adjoining field, which contained the three horses Cherry was so excited to see.

"I want to see them first. Please Mummy!"

Helen laughed; Cherry's enthusiasm was quite contagious as she felt a small thrill herself at exploring a new area. Taking a firm hold of Cherry's hand, she quickly crossed the empty road and headed for the gate. Cherry quickly climbed onto the first two bars and shouted, "Horses, come here ... come on!"

Robert leant against the gate, whistled and the nearest horse looked up, but bent its head back to the grass. Helen stood the other side of Cherry and clicked her tongue a few times. Two of the horses looked up this time and even better, they started to walk towards them. Cherry jumped down and pulled up bits of grass. Helen bent down and did the same, but when she looked up, the horses had stopped a few feet away. "Come on, here's some nice grass for you ..."

Cherry climbed back onto the gate and leant over, her arm outstretched, the clump of grass held loosely in her small hand. "Come on ... Come on. Here's your food."

The horses' ears twitched and they flared their nostrils at the offerings, but they remained watching. Suddenly, they both flinched as if stung by something and they turned and fled across the field to their companion. Cherry visibly jumped and dropped the grass. Helen instinctively made a grab for her and held onto her so she didn't fall. They all watched bewildered at the strange behaviour, until the horses stopped cantering and stood motionless in the farthest corner watching them back.

"What the hell was that about?" Robert sounded amused, which annoyed Helen.

"Who knows, perhaps they didn't like something." It was a cheap remark towards him, but she wasn't feeling generous. She saw the hurt look on his face but quickly cradled Cherry in her arms and turned her back on the horses and him.

Chapter Thirteen

Tony lay on his stomach and was digging carefully in his new test pit. He'd already found a shilling, a ten pence piece, a broken pipe which dated to around late 19th Century, now he was nearing what he hoped was the Viking era. All his other finds had been more or less at this depth, so he felt hopeful. He stood for a moment to stretch his back, before moving the waterproof rug lengthways and lay down again. His face was now inches from the small two feet by three feet pit that was just large enough for him to have a good scrape around.

He glanced across at Kathryn who was kneeling a few feet away. She'd barely said a word since they'd arrived and he was concerned; she was on edge, as if she was waiting for something. What was wrong with the woman? He'd never known anyone behave so irrationally over some dream and it un-nerved him a little. He wondered if the pressure was getting too much.

He certainly hoped she wasn't going to crack; it'd taken too long to get this opportunity. What would he do if she did? Take over the dig most likely, but he really hoped it wasn't heading in that direction. He rolled his eyes and chastised himself silently; he really must be tired, if he was already jumping the gun. Idiot!

His trowel scraped against something hard and he withdrew it. Putting it down, he picked up a soft brush instead and very carefully began brushing away at the muddy earth. He could just make out something small, with a tinge of green about it. Bronze?

His brush slowly cleared the soil, too slowly for his eagerness, but he knew how much damage could be done if he rushed it. Eventually more of the object came into sight; it was bronze. Something small and curved in an oval shape. Using a small trowel, he gently cut away at the surrounding mud and eased the object away from it. He held his breath as he carefully lifted it and placed it into the finds box beside him. It was a bronze oval brooch, intact and most definitely from the Norse period.

"Kathryn!" His excitement evident in his tone and he quickly cleared his throat as she jogged over to him.

"What is it?" She glanced down at the box. Her eyes grew wide and her mouth dropped open as she quickly dropped to her knees, "Is this bronze? It looks intact. A brooch?"

He nodded, grinning, he felt like a Cheshire cat, "Yeah, all of the above! It is definitely from the Norse period. Look, you can see the craftsmanship that has gone into this, even with all that mud." Bending down, he gingerly brushed more small clumps of earth off the object, "This is gorgeous, I can imagine this holding someone's cloak together, a woman's perhaps?"

He glanced across at Kathryn, who continued to stare at the find, He reached out and gently nudged her with the brush, "Hey, so, what are you thinking?"

She looked up at him then and gave him a brilliant smile, "What I think is that we have enough evidence here to keep our students very busy, that's what I think." Standing up, she moved to one side to allow Pam and Jenny a chance to look at the brooch.

She could see the seven test pits Tony had already dug. They ran opposite each other along a rough rectangle shape and the most recent was at the end, curving inward slightly following the lines from the geophysics which showed a possible wall of a house.

"I think we definitely have a house here Tony."

"I think you're right, my dear. I'm going to take a photo of this find and send it to Trevor, it'll make his day!"

Kathryn nodded, "I think we need to open this area up and see it all. The first job for those students who I'll bet will be here sooner rather than later once Trevor sees this."

She looked to where her trench lay. It was a good distance from this 'house'. She compared again the dark images on the geophysics sheet to where they had already dug. "I think I have another house or something similar where I am, perhaps some kind of storage over there next to it, but if we follow these lines here ..." Her finger followed the dark images, "If I am right, we should find more post holes over there ... and there ... which would mean that we have what might be a rather substantial settlement or village."

"Hang on." Tony raised his hand, "I'm going to play devil's advocate here: a 'possible' four houses and perhaps a shed or small barn does not a village make! Let's not jump to conclusions, yet."

Kathryn smiled meekly, "As you wish. Send that photograph to Trevor and we'll see." She turned away so he could not see the growing fear on her face. It was here, they were here; it was coming true.

Now, this wonderful find had brought with it a mixture of feelings. Her Archaeologist side was so pleased, knowing that it would help her cause, but finding the brooch with all the other finds confirmed that people had indeed lived on the site and if they did, then her nightmares were not fictional, irrational thoughts, they were real.

She shuddered and clutched her Jacket closer. From this angle, looking towards her trench, a flash of something crossed her mind, and it was gone. A picture, a scene of something terrible and she swallowed the nausea that suddenly choked her. It seemed important, something she had to remember, but her mind wouldn't allow it. She tried to force it forward, but Tony's voice interrupted her and she turned back to him. "What?"

"I was saying, I'll bag this and tag it now before I carry on with digging and then I'll lock it in my car for safety. Bloody hell, Kathryn, what is with you today? We find this treasure and you look like I've just presented you with a pile of ancient dog shit or something."

She cringed but attempted to smile, "Sorry, it is great, I mean it, wonderful, very pleased, it's just ... Oh, forget it, it's nothing."

She turned to walk away but stopped as she realised how close she was to where she had found the pool of blood. She edged around it and stepped into her trench, keeping her distance. She wouldn't blame Tony for getting annoyed with her, first she wakes him in the unspeakable hours of the morning, then leaves him waiting at the office with her find that she'd lied about taking to the laboratory and now she was freaking at the site; what must he be thinking?

She pondered telling him everything. Would he believe her or put her in the loony bin? Maybe she was going crazy, but if that was so, why did she know she was right about this place? It had been wonderful when Fred from Geophysics had confirmed her theory, showing lots of activity in this and the surrounding areas. It had been his findings that had swayed the council and the museum. She couldn't decide whether she was grateful for his findings or whether she'd secretly wished that he'd found nothing at all.

***

They slowly made their way into the wooded area. Cherry would occasionally make mad dashes after the numerous squirrels that seemed to manifest themselves everywhere. Helen laughed at her daughter's antics, but inwardly, her stomach was a knot, wondering what had spooked the horses like that. For the briefest moment, she felt unsafe and expected to turn around and see some maniac running towards them; of course, they'd been alone. Yet, the feeling of being watched had been overpowering until just as quickly, it had gone.

It hadn't escaped her notice either that Cherry looked back towards the house too before shrugging and turning to Robert to ask where they were going; had her daughter felt it? She was beginning to wonder if there really was something in the house.

She wasn't quite sure how she felt about that possibility, but it gave her a very good reason to leave. Her back up excuse, as if she needed one, but it was a possible plus. She couldn't stay in the house with Cherry until he'd got rid of the ghost! It sounded a plausible reason for staying away from him.

She'd gone to see a tarot reader once with an old friend years before meeting Robert. The woman had told her she would meet a man of her dreams and that there would be children. She'd also said that her life would change dramatically but it would make her a stronger woman. Did moving to a possible haunted house constitute a dramatic event or perhaps she'd meant the drama of the last year? Had that made her stronger?

She pulled her coat closer. The counsellor had told her she might feel apprehension about the move and they had discussed all the possibilities of what she might experience. Ghosts hadn't been one of them, but it was a possibility. Perhaps she was manifesting negative vibes in her aura, her mind was picking these up, and thinking it is someone else, when in fact, it is her own spirit projecting negativity? This had spooked the horses, which had reinforced her hoped belief that there was a ghost that would back her need to leave. It was a good theory and one that made perfect sense.

Robert barely reacted at the horses' behaviour, but then she wasn't surprised at that; he felt nothing. Now, here they were, walking within inches of each other. She was very aware of his presence, his lean body, his big hands so close to her own, and it made her feel very uncomfortable. Years ago, he would have reached out and held her hand, now he didn't bother.

Was she glad of that? She wasn't sure how she would react if he did reach for her, but she couldn't ignore that tiny part of her that yearned for him to grab her and twirl her around and show her he loved her. It also made her angry that he had caused this.

She risked a quick glance at him. She was a desirable woman; she had needs, which had not been met for a long time. She knew she was still attractive from the wolf-whistles she still got from workers she passed and the occasional times she had gone out with friends. Okay, granted, it was a given that builders whistled at anything with breasts and she had fine breasts, but it was rather nice sometimes, gave her a boost.

He cleared his throat, breaking into her thoughts, "Where would you like to go? Royden Park blends into Thurstaston Common. It climbs a bit and you can see for miles if I remember correctly. It has been a while since I played around here myself."

She shrugged; jumping slightly at hearing his voice; she'd been so deep in thought. It still took her by surprise when he spoke full sentences after months of silence or grunts when she had asked him questions. However, before his breakdown, conversations had been rare anyway and she wasn't sure how to feel about his efforts now. They always felt awkward, stilted, and fizzled out into long silences.

Resentment had built up after his breakdown as during those months of his recuperation he spoke only to his counsellor and his doctor. She'd felt shut out and it had hurt her deeply, more than she'd admit too. Now, it was hard to be bothered. Part of her wanted to make the effort but it battled with the part of her that resented him. She pushed aside the small warmth in her stomach that flickered whenever she caught him looking at her, even now, when he spoke to her, it betrayed her yearning for him and it was hard to keep her face blank.

He licked his lips and tried again, "Okay then, we'll head that way. There's a large sandstone formation called 'Thor's stone'. You might find that interesting."

His emphasis on the word 'that' wasn't lost on her, but she kept her gaze fixed firmly on Cherry who was running around a large tree trying to give it a big hug. She placed her hands into her pockets and slowed down so she was walking slightly behind him; he wouldn't try anything now for sure. She quickly blinked away the tear that threatened to spill down her cheek; she had won that round. There'd definitely be no loving gestures now, same as yesterday and so many days before that. She couldn't see his face, but doubted that he cared anyway.

***

Kathryn followed Tony into the large tent because seeing him leave had made her feel such fear, she'd felt compelled to follow, almost running to catch him up. She'd joked about being too excited about the find and he'd graciously allowed her to deal with it while he returned to the pit to log the exact location of the brooch.

She was busy writing out the information on the finds bag when she heard Tony shout a greeting. She didn't take much notice as they regularly had people passing by and the majority liked to ask questions. She liked this because it proved there was a lot of genuine interest in her work and they always wished them well in their search.

A few had known snippets of information that had been interesting about the area and one man, Bernard, had even brought a whetstone made of slate, he'd found years before. Since they'd begun to dig, he'd passed many times with his two dogs, a Rottweiler and a large German Shepherd and got into conversation with Tony two or three times a day. He always looked genuinely interested in the site and discussed Vikings at length.

"There would be four or five of us and we'd walk for miles," he'd begun the other day.

She'd nodded politely, wanting to get back to digging, but Tony had come up behind her, which had encouraged Bernard to tell them the tale. "We would come all the way up here from Hoylake and mess about as boys do." He'd winked at Kathryn then, making her smile, "We'd go and play at the dungeons."

"Dungeons?" Tony leant closer, his interest aroused; he loved caves.

Bernard had grinned, "Well, to us, they were caves, in our imagination of course, but really it's just an area with rocks and a small brook running through it." He'd pointed in the direction of Heswall. "We'd play for hours, there's lots of space for young boys to get into trouble!"

One or two people hadn't been so gracious and thrown a few insults her way. She'd kept her mouth firmly shut; she knew who they were and who they'd been sent by. Mr Merton had lots of friends, but thankfully, they hadn't given them too much grief verbally, but what if they were capable of doing something much worse? She thought about the trouble she'd be in if the police became involved over the blood and she shied away from it.

Tony sounded different though, something in the tone of his voice made her curious and she peeped out of the tent flap. Tony had his back to her and he was speaking enthusiastically to a man, a woman and a small girl who was staring at the excavation site with a strange expression on her face. Actually, as she watched, it became obvious Tony was only talking to the man, the woman seemed apart somehow, the way she was standing gave the impression she did not want to be there.

Curious, Kathryn stepped out of the tent and walked closer. The man was quite handsome, dark, slim and as tall as Tony, which meant she knew she would fit snugly in his chest. She blushed at the thought and turned her attention to the woman and the child. They had moved slightly away from the two men and were looking towards the long trench. The child in particular seemed fascinated and began tugging at her mother's hand. It had to be mother and child, they looked so similar, the man must be her husband.

"Hello," she called as she got nearer.

The woman looked awkward and pulled the child closer to her. Bending down she spoke sharply to the little girl and straightened up just as she approached, "Hello."

Before Kathryn could speak, Tony turned and clapped a hand on her shoulder, "And this is my colleague. Kathryn, may I introduce an old college friend, Robert." Turning back to the man, he indicated the woman and the child, "And these two I believe are his wife and daughter ...?"

Robert grinned, "Sorry, yes, very rude of me. Hello Kathryn, this is my wife, Helen and our daughter Charlotte."

"But, they call me Cherry," Cherry butted in quickly, and turned back towards the site.

***

Helen nodded and gave Kathryn and Tony brief smiles, but quickly knelt down so that she was level with Cherry. "What is it darling? You can't go in; there are lots of holes, what if you fell down one ... Hmm?"

Straightening up she held onto Cherry's hand and looked around, ignoring the conversation going on between Tony and Robert until she realised they were addressing her. "What?"

Robert stepped closer, "Tony has just found something interesting, fancy seeing it?" Tony and Kathryn were already moving towards the large tent. Robert turned to take Cherry's hand, but she giggled and ran ahead of him. Helen didn't look at him as she walked through the gate. Cherry ran towards the tent and caught up with the archaeologists.

"She's keen," said Robert, staying by her side. "Maybe this is her future, she likes history doesn't she?"

Helen nodded but did not want to get into any conversation with him. Who the hell was this Tony? Another part of his life Robert had never talked about. Another reminder of just how little he shared with her.

Reaching the tent, he stepped aside and let her go first. She didn't acknowledge it, but moved quickly past him to stand behind Cherry who was standing on tiptoe trying to see into the various boxes. Tony held a tray containing various parts of pottery, which was quite interesting. Then he smiled and held a small box. He was saying something about finding it a few minutes ago and something about it being a brooch, bronze perhaps, but she wasn't listening, she was watching Cherry. Her daughter had gone completely still.

Glancing upwards, she caught Kathryn's eye who was also watching Cherry very closely. Cherry made a strange noise, a deep growl that grew louder until she opened her mouth and screamed. The noise startled everyone and Helen instinctively reached for her child. Cherry was slowly backing away from the box; her eyes never wavered from the object. Helen caught her arm and pulled her daughter closer just as Robert reached out. Helen drew her to her chest protectively and finally the screaming stopped as Cherry began to sob uncontrollably, her face buried in Helen's coat.

"What the hell …?" Tony carefully replaced the box and glanced at everyone.

Pam and Jenny appeared at the tent opening, "Is everything OK?"

Robert frowned and shrugged, "Sorry about that, she has been behaving a bit weird lately, I think it's the move." Pam and Jenny retreated and he caught Helen glaring at him and shrugged again, "Well, what else is it then?"

Helen lifted Cherry who clung to her like a monkey, "I don't know either, but the move was the last straw wasn't it?"

Without waiting for him, she stormed out of the tent. Kathryn, Tony and Robert watched her go; no one said anything for a while. It was Kathryn who finally broke the silence, "Well, Robert, we have work to be getting on with. Perhaps you'll come again?" She knew she sounded patronising, but kids annoyed her with their strange ways and tantrums. She had better things to do than allow this one to get in the way of her work.

Picking up a trowel, she walked out of the tent. Tony clapped his hands together, "Robert, she's right mate; we do have a shit load to do, but hey, it's good to see you. Fancy a pint later?"

Robert dug his hands in his pocket, "Maybe, I'll have to see what's going on at home though." He looked out towards the far end of the site, he could see Helen struggling to carry Cherry, he desperately wanted to run after her and take the child.

"That was a bit strange."

He turned back to find Tony watching him closely,

"I mean, the way she reacted to this thing." Tony nodded towards the find box, "Any idea why?"

Robert shook his head slowly and exhaled loudly, "God bloody knows ... I don't. Things ... well, you've probably noticed that things between me and Helen aren't, brilliant."

Tony scratched his eyebrow, "Mate, it was like ice in here."

"I know. I had a great job with lots of money, but forgot about my wife and daughter. Lost it all. Had a breakdown and I think I've lost them too." He glanced outside, but Helen had gone. "I don't think she will ever forgive me, Tony ... but do I deserve it?"

Tony slapped him on the back, "Everyone deserves another chance, Robert, keep trying eh?" Moving towards the tent opening, he picked up a brush, "Fancy giving us a hand?"

Robert smiled and shook his head, "No thanks, I remember that dig you made me go on when we were in college. Fun, I believe you said it would be; back breaking is what I remember! I'll leave you to it." Walking outside he glanced up at the sky and back the way they had come; Helen was nowhere in sight, "Besides, I think I should catch her up and attempt to show her I do care."

"All right, I understand; don't lose this one, she's a cracker!" Digging in his jeans pocket, he pulled out a card with his name and mobile number on it and gave it to Robert. "See ya then ... and soon eh?"

Robert waved his agreement and broke into a run to catch Helen, his mind a whirl of questions. Cherry's behaviour, why? Tony, here after all these years and still doing his archaeology stuff? Helen. He had seen the venom. Why?

***

Einaar looked towards Halldor, his chief, who nodded his consent and Einaar stepped into the circle of men; each one stopped talking and waited to hear what he had to say. Einaar looked around at each man before exhaling loudly. "My brothers, Ingimund has declared war. He has broken the pact made with Aethelflaed and she will come to know of it, there is no doubt. He has declared his intentions to take the city of the Legions; it seems we have sat on our arses for too long ..."

"Speak for yourself you lazy sow!" a man from the back shouted.

Einaar waited for the laughter to subside before continuing. "We have crawled here having been defeated in battle but we saved our honour and we have become prosperous, the land rich and fruitful. Trade is good with our neighbours and have we not become content in our new world ...? However, Ingimund is not at peace here. He has sent word that he grows bored, and anger grows in him which cannot be quelled by farming this land. Only bloodshed will do for this chief. I wait to hear your answers, my friends."

The murmurs around him grew loud. Some shouted their disagreement, others merely sat and nodded. It was true, they had come here having fought and lost in Ireland and had met with hostility from the Welsh before being allowed to stay here only because of Aethelflaed's say. It hadn't sat well with many, but the land was good soil and their crops hadn't failed in the four years since arriving, though this winter had been hard and longer than usual.

Some, he knew, had settled well and were happy with their situation. Two men of the village had taken local girls as wives, while others still had the battle fire in their bellies. Did he? Could he fight once more knowing now what he had been told?

He glanced quickly around the room trying to determine the feelings of the village. Astrid sat in the far corner, her head bent to Inga who slept on her lap. Astrid was slowly rocking her, but instinct told him she wasn't singing to her daughter, she was silently praying the new words of the Christian God.

Odin, the god of death and battle, father of all the gods would understand man's need to fight, to gain land and power, but this new God, would not. They said he had compassion and such love for man that he sent his own son to die for man's sins. The priests had said that fighting was definitely a sin. The priest who'd dared to defy the gods and his chief had said so, and more.

Ingimund had rejected him, as had many others, but a few chiefs had allowed the priests to tell their tales; and some had listened to their stories. Many had simply walked away laughing at such fables, but others, like himself and Astrid, had felt a stirring within and had begun to quietly question and discuss in whispers this new God. He caught the eye of a few, before they hastily looked away. Those men, like him, attempted very hard to hide their emotions and thoughts, but failed as it read so clear on their faces; which god do we honour? The god of war, or this gentle loving God?

Chapter Fourteen

Trevor shook his head as he re-read the long letter. He'd been expecting it of course, but my god, the man could go on! '*Mr Adams, blah blah blah, I regret, blah blah, it is unthinkable ... blah blah ...*' He skipped to the end again, '*Since the allocated area has been widened without correct authority, I will be taking this matter further. It is inconceivable that this area should be desecrated for the sake of idle curiosity. I hope I can rely on your support ... blah blah ... Man of honour ... blah ... blah ... Head of the department ... blah ... blah ...*'

He carefully folded the letter and replaced it inside the envelope that also contained three photographs of Kathryn's site. He could plainly see a large trench running about eight feet, but the angle of the camera didn't show him how deep it was. A large blue tarpaulin lay near-by, near the portable toilet and next to this was stacked the grass turf to be replaced once the dig was over.

Another photograph showed him the large tent and a few test pits and the third showed the area as a whole. As far as he could see, Kathryn and Tony had not moved from the allocated area at all. He quickly scanned the photographs again to be sure and sighed loudly, that damned man had nothing; he could do nothing.

Reaching for his cup of tea, he sat back in his chair, what could he do? What did he want to do? He had mixed feelings about the dig at Thurstaston. His argument had always been that it was common knowledge that Norsemen came to the Wirral and settled in many areas, the amount of finds proved that beyond doubt. So why dig again? However, at the same time, the idea of unearthing new evidence of the Norsemen was a thrilling temptation, as they were his favourite characters in history.

Kathryn had put up a good fight though, he had to give her that, and she had managed to get her dig for four weeks, on the proviso that there was something worth digging for. Geophysics had quickly confirmed without any doubt that there was structure beneath the soil, and lots of it.

A meeting had finally confirmed that money would be found for a dig, but not the amount Kathryn had hoped for; which meant the help was not forthcoming immediately. The museum was short of funds and was sceptical, at best, but Trevor had persuaded them to let her try.

Therefore, what it came down to was that they had a week to prove there was a need for further investigation. By then, the students should be available as part of their studies. In the meantime, they could have volunteers; two women had come forward. As far as he knew, no one else was helping them.

Her enthusiasm had won everyone over, even he had been impressed by her argument and judging from what he'd already seen, she had been right to do so. Tony had backed her up every step of the way, even taking a large cut in pay while he was away digging. Enough to cover the cost of bringing in another lecturer, which had helped Kathryn's cause immensely. He wondered if she knew what Tony had done for her.

He wondered if all the pressure had got to her as reports of her absences from the site reached him. Late starts, leaving in the middle of the day for unexplained errands; and yesterday they'd left early. The weather wasn't helping and the theft had set them back, but still, her behaviour wasn't normal. It had only been a few days - if it carried on, Kathryn would never do the site justice in her four-week slot and that would look bad on her and the museum. Maybe he should consider delaying the interviews for volunteers?

He reached for another pile of photographs and looked through them. These were the copies of their finds, which to date were very impressive. The spread of the test pits did seem to indicate a possible house, maybe two, side by side, but that would need more than a trench; the whole area would need to be investigated.

The pottery was in some cases intact and some of the broken pieces looked fixable. He stared at the image of the brooch Tony had sent on his phone and licked his lips. If these were an indication of finds after only a few days' digging, what possibilities could be there? Kathryn had to get a grip or he'd have to put Tony in charge.

Kathryn talked of a possible village, he could see what she meant and he felt a stirring of excitement. He had been a field archaeologist for twenty-four years before the accident and the museum had offered him this job. Sometimes, like now, seeing photographs of the artefacts, he missed it.

He knew he'd never have taken the job as head of the Archaeology Department if he hadn't been confined to a wheelchair; he'd loved the dig too much. Finding a site that interested him and then having to fight for the right to excavate. Being given the go ahead, finding the students and volunteers and that first initial strike of the spade in the earth ... The beginning of an adventure into history-heaven.

He'd only accepted this job to be around when the finds came in; at least, he was still in touch with the digs in a small way. He saw everything that came into the museum, from the cleaning process, to the restoring of finds to having a say about the displays. He saw the artefacts come alive again after years of being hidden from the world; he couldn't complain really.

He undid the brake and wheeled his chair away from his desk. He'd already been down to the lab and their offices twice to see their progress, now he felt an urge to visit it again. The findings fascinated him and holding them brought a strange kind of thrill, especially once they were reconstructed. On occasion, he helped to clean and catalogue the finds. He found it all exhilarating watching the past come back to life and wondering who had last touched the object.

He grabbed the letter from the disgruntled Mr Merton, deciding to leave it on Kathryn's desk for her to see. After all, he should listen to her argument if indeed they had strayed from the area, though he didn't believe it for one second. One of the photographs fell out and he reached down to get it. As he picked it up, he frowned as he stared at it. Putting his glasses on, he stared hard at the small photograph and gently rubbed it.

It was the one of the eight-foot trench, with the tarpaulin beside it, but just behind that, he could plainly see what appeared to be the outline of a man. He looked closely, but he couldn't see any features and his legs seemed to disappear behind a small gorse bush, but surely, he was standing in front of it? He quickly replaced it with the others and headed for the elevator. He knew Mr Merton had formed a group against the excavation, no doubt, it was one of them spying on the excavation; he'd better warn Tony about that.

***

Robert caught her up quite quickly, but she'd refused to let him carry Cherry. Instead, Helen had marched on, ignoring him completely, refusing to acknowledge his questions about Cherry's wellbeing or the fact that he raced ahead and had the front door open ready for them. She strode past him as if he did not exist, straight upstairs, muddy boots and all and slammed Cherry's bedroom door behind her.

He stood at the bottom of the stairs for a long time, waiting to see if she would come back. Waiting to see if she would invite him up to help with their daughter. Waiting to see if he had the balls to go upstairs and find out the problem ... he did not. Eventually, he sloped off to the kitchen. Taking off his wellingtons, he took off his coat and shivered, he hadn't noticed just how cold the house was. Checking the kettle he clicked it on, if nothing else, he had an excuse to go upstairs and ask her if she wanted a cup of something. He'd better check the thermostat. He blew out his breath and raised his eyebrows as he saw its cloudy mist, bloody hell!

A movement from the dining room made him freeze. For a moment his breath stuck in his throat ... there it was again, a shadow moved across the back wall. He quickly looked around for a weapon and seeing the rolling pin Helen had out to make pastry with Cherry, he grabbed it and held it tightly as he slowly eased his way towards the door. At first glance, he saw nothing; the room was as they had left it. He looked towards the window, it was shut. He edged his way into the room, very aware of every nerve and every breath he was taking.

Every movement as he fought to breathe seemed as loud as to awaken the dead and give the intruder knowledge of where he was. He stepped further into the room, the rolling pin held in front of his body, slightly raised, ready to strike. He moved cautiously through the archway into the lounge, nothing had been rifled, nothing looked out of place, yet, something wasn't right. He knew he had seen something, someone, yet now, as he stood in the middle of the room, he knew he was alone. He lowered the rolling pin and looked around the room.

"What the hell ...?" He bit his top lip as his eyes rested on Twinkle. She lay curled in the corner of the couch, purring softly. She opened her eyes briefly, but quickly resumed her sleeping. He moved towards her and sat down, his legs felt wobbly and his chest felt tight as adrenalin pumped through it. He gently stroked the cat who didn't respond in any way, and he stopped. "Just like my wife ..." he said aloud, but he was alone.

***

Einaar already knew the decision of the chiefs and of the men. He sat staring into the flames of his fire pit and let his shoulders slouch. He was tense and heavy with fatigue, but he could not sleep. Astrid lay with her back to him, curling herself protectively around Inga. He had told her of the decision on his return to their home. She had barely responded, but had mumbled that she was tired and had curled up with Inga, not their bed, he noticed.

Astrid had left the meeting while it had been well under way, with arguments flying from all sides; no answers had been forthcoming. She had feigned weariness for leaving, but he knew the real reason; she had gone somewhere quiet to pray to the new god. To pray for a positive outcome to this new battle that Ingimund demanded.

If their chief Halldor found out, he would be very displeased, with all of them. The punishment would be, at best, banishment from the village; but he knew Halldor and that would never happen.

The acts of such cruelty he had done to the priest were degrading for any man, but this man of god had endured them all. Screaming only once and then praying loudly, his tears mixing with his sweat, his own piss and his blood. Halldor had continued his torture regardless until he had finally broken the man into pieces.

His penis and his scrotum, he had offered to Odin; as the man claimed to be celibate, they were pure and unused, a rare thing. Halldor had considered such an act a waste, "A man is Odin's instrument. His seed," he had declared to the village, the priest's bloody testicles in his hands. "It is a man's right, to spread his seed in those he has conquered ..." He glanced towards his pregnant wife, "And, to those who lie willingly with their Lord." He grinned as men shouted bawdy suggestions and some of the women giggled and blushed at the remarks.

He'd raised his hands before the large fire and everyone turned their faces to the sky, "Hail Odin, great father ..." Halldor's voice bellowed into the night sky.

"Hail Odin!" The multitude of voices was like a wave of power, he could feel the emotions that sent the words into the heavens.

"Hail Odin, Wise father, spear shaker, Master of the Runes, Master of fury, may your Valkyries find us worthy to sit in your hall." Halldor continued, "We, your people, loyal only to you. We are yours to command and obey. Receive this offering from one unworthy of your love and protection. Receive his manhood, which he allowed to rot. A man unworthy to sit amongst the warriors of ages and drink in your honour. A coward unworthy of your attention; may his death bring you some amusement." Halldor spat into the fire.

He stepped forward and threw the testicles and penis into the flames. A young girl held a bowl of water. He quickly washed his hands and walked away to his chair. The remains of the priest were flung in a near-by ditch for the wolves to devour; it would appease the god Fenrir, son of Loki and it might amuse Odin to know wolves would be getting what he did not want.

A great feast had already been prepared for the coming of the summer, Sumarmal, which was an important time of year. They celebrated that they had lived through another winter, the crops had been sown and were looking well for the coming harvest; the priest had been quickly forgotten ... but not by some.

There were seven villagers who had liked what the priest said and wanted to hear more about this god and his son. Astrid had enjoyed hearing about the son's mother, Mary.

Einaar stared at Astrid's back; her long yellow hair fell softly down the side of the trundle bed and he reached out to touch it. He knew she wasn't asleep, but she did not move, or acknowledge his touch.

He let go and reached for a mug instead. He had made three like it, all from cow horn. He looked across the fire to where Inga's little cup lay with various plates, bowls and other cooking utensils, she had been delighted last year when he'd made her very own cup with two handles either side. Soon she would be able to help Astrid with the household chores as all girls did. Time would move so quickly and then, she would be ready to wed. If he joined the war, would he be here to see it?

He silently berated himself for such foolish and cowardly thoughts. He was a Norseman, not a simpering fool. If he died in battle, then he would be honoured in Valhalla and would join his father and brother in merriment and feasting. Yet ... he drained the last of his ale, what if the priest had been right? What if fighting and killing were terrible acts and his soul would be damned? What if there was no honour in killing and no Valhalla?

He fought with his thoughts for many months now and still he had not found the answer he wanted. Years ago, he would never have questioned his faith. Odin was Lord of everything, chief of the gods. Thor, Freya, Frigga and Loki were all a part of his life from birth, but now the priest had muddled his head with the new God who he had insisted was the only god.

"So, he was the first God. Had Odin sprung from him and all the others followed?"

"No, my son, Odin does not exist, he is a false god." The priest had smiled patiently as the questions came thick and fast.

"How can you say such a thing? Odin is everything."

"There is only one true God, and he is everywhere, there cannot be two gods."

"This son of his, he only had one? No daughters?"

"That is true; he had one son, Jesus."

"So this god came down to earth and mated with a woman? Was she willing?"

"He sent an angel to tell Mary that she was with child; God's child. It was a miracle ..."

"So, he placed his seed inside her by magic, you say, did he have no other children? Did he kill his daughters? Were they not worthy of his love?"

"He had no daughters, only a son who died for our sins."

"What father sends his son to die?"

"A father who loves you."

"I have a father and a mother, I need no other ..."

The questioning had gone on into the early hours of the morning. The priest had not faltered in his stories. His answers were met with hostility by most in the hall, curiosity by some and indifference by the rest. Halldor found him amusing for a while; but soon his amusement had turned to fury as the priest pursued those who had shown interest; attempting to drown them in water, saying it would purify their soul and make them Christians. Halldor showed no mercy.

The priest had caused a rift in the village; that was certain. Tonight, men and women had argued about fighting when they had settled so well in this new land. He could remember not so long ago, those same men had wielded axe and sword and the women had readily followed. The priest had made them question and surely that wasn't a good thing?

His parents had never faltered, never questioned, but how were they to know? Had everything he'd been taught been a lie? How could it all be true? Alternatively, did he wish it so badly that he would believe anything?

The life they had made for themselves in this foreign land had worked well, he admitted that. He also knew he had blood on his hands. He had been involved in so many acts of barbarism, he couldn't comprehend how a kind, loving god would accept him; yet the priest had insisted that he would.

He had tried to forget by making amends and loving his family and honouring the gods. So what was he now? A sinner, so the priest said, but what else? A farmer? A warrior? If only he knew what he wanted to be then he might find some peace.

Astrid was not so confused. She had been barely sixteen when they had wed six years ago and she had already heard stories from her older sister who lived in the North. She had thought them then nothing more than beautiful stories, but since the priest, she had begun to question less and less. He feared for her and his child. She had kept her thoughts to herself for now, but he could see her wavering.

He had had to keep a firm hold on her arm as they watched the priest's torture, making sure she stayed silent, for fear of Halldor's fury. She said nothing, only stood and watched before finally turning away. Her lips moving silently in prayer, he knew to which god she was praying. Since that night, almost a year ago, she had changed towards him. A slight, subtle change, but a change nonetheless.

He heard a faint snore and smiled, Inga was asleep. He knew that he had a husband's right to lie with his wife, but he could not bring himself to do it without her consent. He reached out again to touch her hair, but still Astrid lay unmoving. "Astrid?"

For a moment he thought she was not going to speak, but eventually, she moved ever so slightly and turned her head, "Inga is hot to my touch, please, just let us rest ..."

He let his hand fall and moved silently to his own bed on the opposite side of the fire. It was too warm for rugs and he lay on his side staring towards his family. The decision made, they would march on Castra. The English called it 'Legacaestr' and some he had heard call it, 'Caerleon'.

But, whatever its name, within a month they would go into battle for it. Time enough to sow the fields again and prepare for the coming summer crops beforehand. Ingimund's arrogance that they would win was astounding and many men had laughed and made jokes, but each man knew what could happen if they failed. Failure was not an option if they were to survive here, so the crops had to be sown and plans made.

That would leave Astrid to defend their child alone. He glanced across the room to his family and sighed, a sick child was not what he needed right now. He knew, as did every man, that sick children could not be tolerated. Strong and healthy children made strong and healthy men and women; anything else was a strain on their supplies. Inga had never been a strong child, but not sick enough to be thrown aside; an act Astrid would never have contemplated anyway. Years ago, he possibly would have killed the child out of pity, but now, after the priest, he knew he could not. He would not.

He knew his perception had changed and also knew it could never change back. His head and his body wanted desperately to go back to what he had always known; the weak died, the strong survived. To die in battle was an honour. A man was all powerful; his seed must be sown wherever he had conquered for his essence to stay alive. He knew blood, sword, axe, earth, seasons, yearning, and lust and now he knew love and it complicated everything.

The love he felt for Astrid bordered on lust. The love he felt for his daughter was different to anything he had known. Could he truly kill again and look her in the eye? To fight to the death is to lose oneself in the battle. To lose all care for human beings. He'd seen men become like animals in a fight and everyone knew to stay away from them or lose your own life. They became so wild; they couldn't know who was the enemy or who was kinsman and he wondered again, which was he?

Chapter Fifteen

Helen eased off Cherry's coat and wellingtons, all the while speaking softly about silly things. Cherry clung to her, but she had stopped shaking which was a start. Helen gently pulled Cherry's arms from around her neck and sat down on her daughter's bed. Easing her into a comfortable position on her knee, she gently rocked her while she hummed any old tune; her mind was racing and she couldn't think of any of Cherry's favourite tunes.

After a while, she felt Cherry slowly relax and her limbs became heavy with sleep. Not wanting to lose the connection, but knowing her arm was losing every ounce of blood in it from the weight of Cherry's head; she carefully swivelled around and gently laid Cherry onto her bed. She made a small whimpering noise and Helen froze in her movements, keeping contact with her child, until she saw her daughter's face relax into sleep once more. She knelt by the bed, staring down at her and let the tears fall.

A slight movement out of the corner of her eye made her stiffen. Every muscle in her body immediately tensed, ready for fight because every ounce of her knew it was a man and Robert was downstairs. Her eyes looked to the side, but she could see nothing, she would have to jump up and spin around to face him, ready to scream and claw his eyes. Her heart thundered in her chest and seemed to vibrate up into her head, along her arms and for what seemed like forever, down to her legs, although, it couldn't have been more than a second or two.

She used her hands to push herself upwards and at the same time, she let out a yell and swung round to face the enemy. Her hands clenched into a fist and she stood prepared for battle. A small sound from behind her registered slightly, but she didn't acknowledge it as her eyes searched the small room. The wardrobe door hung slightly open and she focused on that. "Come out!"

When nothing happened, she took a small step closer. All the while thinking, he must not reach the bed and her child. She must, if necessary, kill. "Come out, I know you're in there …"

Every fibre of her being was on red alert. She knew she was being watched; she could 'feel' it, it was so tangible. Nevertheless, it was also becoming obvious that, besides Cherry who was still asleep, she was alone in the room. She slowly reached out and flipped the wardrobe door open further, it moved slightly, but enough to let her know the man was not hiding inside. Clothes, some boxes of toys and various cuddly bears and dolls packed the floor. No one could hide inside without breaking his or her neck or being a damned fine contortionist.

Her hands still clenched ready to fight, she slowly turned around and looked into every corner, there was nowhere anyone could hide. She glanced down at the bed, Cherry had curled up into a foetal position and her little finger clung to her bottom lip. Her gaze travelled down to the bottom of her bed and she stepped back. Cherry's bed had drawers underneath; no one could hide there either.

She froze as the icy breath prickled the back of her neck. She could feel the man's presence inches behind her. Where had he been hiding? was her first fleeting thought. Secondly, he felt quite big; he was a few inches taller than she was, judging from his breath on her neck, what damage could she do to him? His groin or his knees?

She whirled on her feet and aimed a blow downwards towards his knees. She briefly registered that she had her wellingtons on and wished for her walking boots that would cause more damage, before her aim sank into nothing. Staggering off balance, she whirled around, staring wildly around the silent bedroom.

***

Kathryn gently rubbed the back of her neck and yawned loudly. Every muscle ached and the drive back to the museum had taken longer owing to road works; she hated traffic jams, especially when she had finds she had to sort out before she could go home and try to sleep. Even as she thought it, she knew that was a pointless thing for her to think; sleep would, as ever, be a terrifying journey into another world, but her body craved the oblivion before the terror.

Carefully, she placed the broken pottery on the table of the laboratory along with the two whetstones she had found next to the remains of a small knife. All needed careful cleaning, especially the knife, as she had dug around it and lifted it out with a large amount of mud, not wanting to risk it.

Tony's test pits had also been lucrative in their treasures. Besides the brooch which was a fantastic find in itself, he'd un-earthed an iron fire starter in the shape of two horns locking together, one half of what could be scissors of some kind and three antler toggles inside half a broken jar, the rest of which she had placed on the table.

She stared along the narrow table at the hoard of finds. She could hardly believe it, the place was an archaeologist's dream, untouched and full of artefacts. Surely now she could prove beyond doubt that this had in fact been a village? Something many scholars disputed about the Vikings.

"They kept themselves in small groups so there was enough food. Too many people meant more work to feed everyone. One grinding stone was enough to make bread for so many people, we've never found more than one in any given area, so ..."

Her last attempt to debate this theory hadn't gone down too well. Thin theories and suppositions were never enough to win a debate; but now, what did she have? In the last hour of the afternoon, they had decided to do two test pits in the opposite area from where they were digging. Pam and Jenny had got quite excited at the prospect of doing their own test pits.

Geophysics showed that there was a possible wall in that area; within minutes, it was confirmed. Part of a wall could clearly be seen and both the volunteers had extended their test pits to make one five-foot trench. The finds on the table had all come from that trench which meant, they had at least three houses in the allocated area.

She couldn't wait to tell Trevor, she knew how pleased he'd be. Even though she hadn't known him out of his wheelchair, she'd heard from others about his love of archaeology and how much he missed digging; she hoped these Norse finds would bring him even a small amount of joy.

He'd helped to win her case and knowing that had brought with it a lot of stress; hating the idea of being wrong which would have looked bad on him. She also knew letters and e-mails by the protesters, which angered her greatly, were bombarding him. She could not abide people with no give. Like that old man, Merton, saying it was a place of beauty and it shouldn't be desecrated, well, what would his small committee wonder when they saw all of this history? Would it change their minds? Would it stop their harassment?

Soil can be put back, grass can continue to grow, but this history could have been lost forever if she hadn't fought to get the dig. She pushed aside the argument she had had with herself since taking the case to the museum that this history shouldn't be dug up. That it should be kept hidden. It was her inability to answer 'why' she'd felt this way that kept her continuing to fight and focus on the wonderful possibility. To find a village or a large settlement was a rare find for Norse. Small communities had been normal so they survived, anything larger was harder to maintain; or so they had thought.

Well, damn the man, she would get her students and she would dig up the whole bloody area and prove a Viking village lay on this common. Mr Merton and the old fogies could go and spit. She hadn't forgotten the pool of blood either. Throughout the day, she'd glanced at the area wondering if she'd done the right thing, but the more she considered it, the more she talked herself into believing that, yes, they probably would do something that extreme.

Perhaps they had left an animal there to be found and a predator had come along and taken it! She found that idea both repulsive and yet hilarious that nature could ruin their plan to frighten her off the dig. It seemed extreme for anyone to do such a wicked thing, too extreme for elderly people perhaps but not Mr Merton.

His fury at the public meeting had astounded everyone apparently, especially when he'd directed his anger towards her. The names he'd called her had shocked many and Tony, who had sneaked in the back to hear what was being said, had physically escorted the old man out of the building. She wished she'd gone and cursed her car again for breaking down on that particular night. Just to watch him being escorted outside by Tony would have been worth it. He was a big man, muscular and could hold his own in a fight. She'd witnessed that on more than one occasion whenever he'd met a thief or vandal on site.

She frowned; she should find out soon if the blood was human or animal and if it was and Merton was involved she wondered just how far this man really would go; bleed himself, or would he hurt someone else?

***

Nick sat hunched in the bus shelter as the rain pelted the pavement. He shivered as the cold seemed to find his emaciated body and he groaned with the dull ache that vibrated through his skin. He'd wandered around all day, finding cigarette butts in some pubs and begging two fags off an old man at the bus stop. He had considered mugging the old git, but a woman walking her dog passed by and he quickly walked away, now he regretted it.

No one had seen Lee all day. The usual dealers had not given him the time of day because he was skint and the regulars at the pub hadn't seen him for a few days. He'd broken into Lee's flat to keep warm; but he never returned from wherever he'd buggered off to. His neighbour was sure he'd heard him go out, but couldn't be positive.

Nick hadn't really been listening, the neighbour was a crack head anyway, he barely knew what day or month it was. It had crossed his mind that something bad might have happened to his mate. It wasn't like Lee to disappear without him; they went everywhere together, always had. Even in school, they'd bunked off and robbed together, even been sent to juvenile together; so where the fuck was he?

Deciding he'd had enough of being out, he walked towards the local supermarket. He'd wander around the aisles for a while and pinch something to eat and worst came to worst, he would get nicked and spend the night in a cell, at least he would be fed and he could always scrounge a fag off a copper.

***

The body twitched as the fox snuffled around it. The smell of decay and blood was strong on the wind and many predators had already tasted it. The fox's ear twitched as an owl silently flew down and landed on a nearby branch. The fox sniffed the air one last time before bending his head and beginning to eat.

98

Chapter Sixteen

H e heard movement upstairs and glanced at the mantelpiece clock, Helen had not left Cherry's bedroom for over an hour. He had been sitting on the couch all that time, the rolling pin lay across his knees. His mind fought to make sense of what he'd seen, but none of it made sense, unless he accepted that the house was haunted and ghosts really did exist; a notion he refused to contemplate. Yet, not every other scenario he considered had stood up to his scrutiny either, so every time he had come back to the only scenario that fitted; which was ludicrous.

His head hurt from the constant roundabout going on and on in his head. It could not be possible, yet he was sure he had seen a man's shadow moving across the wall, but ghosts did not exist. They were just stories that people needed to believe in so death didn't seem as frightening. He'd contemplated the idea that the muscled man had come to find Helen, but it still hadn't accounted for the fact that whoever or whatever it was had simply disappeared.

Surely, *IF* the house were haunted, he would feel something, like cold spots or doors opening by unseen hand; perhaps even blood on the walls? He grinned to himself, that was stupid, but people really believed this stuff! Fact was ghosts did NOT exist, so what had he seen? A trick of the light most likely and he was tired; his eyes felt gritty from lack of sleep. Cherry's outburst had caused anxiety and fear, on top of the stress he already felt; add the guilt and he was a walking lunatic!

He glanced down at the sleeping cat. Besides, Twinkle was fine. He'd read years ago about how animals reacted to strange phenomena. If it had been a ghost, surely the cat would have been scared. Raised hackles, hissing, spitting, the whole works; but Twinkle had done nothing. So, it couldn't have been a ghost ... unless it was a friendly ghost: or, he was seeing hallucinations again, and that bothered him the most.

He picked up the rolling pin, walked back to the kitchen, and replaced it. Whatever it had been, whatever he had seen, or thought he had seen, it was gone now. The only thing he knew for certain was that his fear had been real, the cat was still asleep and content and his wife who hated him was upstairs with his daughter whom he'd neglected all her life. What had happened to her today had unhinged him; that made sense; he'd stick with that theory, for now.

***

Helen stood up slowly and stretched her back. The room felt normal, it had done for a long time, but she had been reluctant to leave her vulnerable child to whatever it had been. She glanced down at Cherry, who had barely moved, she would have to wake her otherwise she wouldn't sleep tonight. Helen shuddered, what if it came back? Didn't ghosts walk at night? Except this one obviously, she quickly reminded herself.

An old work mate, Rachel, had told her once that she had seen a ghost in York. She had been in one of the old pubs, at the beginning of a pub-crawl, which didn't bode well for her tale, but she assured Helen, that she had barely touched her first drink. She had gone to the back of the pub looking to see if anyone else of the party had arrived before her and noticed a man standing with his hands in his pockets, leaning against the pub wall. Something about him had made her feel uncomfortable and she had quickly glanced around; seeing none of her friends were sitting among the empty tables, she went back to her boyfriend.

It was only as she walked away that she realised the man's clothes had been old fashioned, grubby looking and his face had been dirty. She'd mentioned this to her boyfriend, urging him to go and look at the man and guess why he was dressed that way. He'd agreed to check him out on his way to the men's toilet, but had returned quickly saying no one was there.

Rachel didn't believe him and had peeked into the room. Her boyfriend had already checked the toilets and there wasn't any other way out of the pub, she had asked the barmaid. On asking about any ghosts, the barmaid laughed and asked her which one? Apparently, women in the pub had seen a man frequently and a baby's cries had been heard. Rachel had been convinced that she had seen the man.

Helen loved the story. She believed in something after death, but what, she was not sure. She had been in a few old houses over the years and felt strange, as if she was being watched, but nothing like today. It didn't feel nice, she felt absolutely terrified for her child and for herself. Then she remembered Robert; should she say something to him? That would be a humiliating experience, but for the sake of Cherry, maybe she should?

The very idea of having a conversation with him right now, was a rainstorm of questions and emotions, but knowing his opinion on anything supernatural, the conversation would be ten times worse. She had her pride; after all, she knew exactly what he would say… "Don't be so pathetic, there are no such things and people who believe in them are just sad, lonely people who have a strong need to cling onto a belief. You don't believe in such nonsense …"

It hadn't been a question, he wasn't interested in her thoughts about the subject when she had relayed Rachel's story. It had been his usual way of belittling her and she had never had the fight to answer back. She would have loved to say, "Well, yes, actually I do believe, what are you going to do about it?" But, she never had … would she now?

She gently touched Cherry's cheek and stroked it lightly. "Come on my darling sleepy head, wake up baby. Come on, wake up …"

Charlotte stirred and opened her eyes and smiled, "Good morning Mummy, I'm hungry, can I have Rice nice …?"

Helen sighed with relief and collected her daughter up into a big hug. "Cherry baby, it's nearly tea-time." Sitting Cherry onto her lap, she made sure she kept eye contact, "Do you remember, baby; we went for a walk …?"

Cherry nodded and reached for her doll. "Yes, Mummy, we saw the horses. Mummy, I need a wee wee."

Helen let her go and watched her child open the bedroom door and go to the bathroom. A sudden panic engulfed her because she couldn't see her daughter and she moved quickly to the bathroom doorway and leant against the door frame. "Cherry baby, do you remember anything else?"

For a moment, Cherry didn't answer as she concentrated on her toilet. Wiping herself, she flushed the toilet and began washing her hands, "Yep, we met some nice people who had digged big holes." She suddenly frowned and stuck out her lower lip, "He was cross … not happy."

Helen flinched and quickly knelt down in front of her daughter, "Who wasn't happy, baby?"

Cherry shook her head, "Don't know …"

Helen gently towel dried Cherry's hands, "Can you see him now?"

Cherry shook her head and smiled, "No, silly Billy, only Inga here … see." She reached down and picked up her doll.

As Cherry was about to leave, Helen kept a hold of her hand, "Baby, do you see this man a lot in this house?"

Cherry nodded and withdrew her hand, "Yep, I see him all the time." Leaning closer Cherry whispered, "He brings a nice woman too, I like her better." Moving away, Cherry played with her doll, "They like Inga. They miss her."

Helen remained frozen to the spot, her heart doing somersaults in her chest as she watched her daughter walk downstairs. Finally, she found her voice again, "Cherry, is he angry?"

Cherry reached the bottom of the stairs and looked up. She raised her eyebrows and stuck out her chin as she thought, "No, not ALL the time."

***

Einaar woke to the sound and shot out of his bed into a crouched position, his knife poised for defence in his hand. His eyes adjusted to the faint light from the dying fire and he quickly looked around the small house. Astrid watched him with a blank expression, before she turned back to her child's bed. Einaar slowly straightened and shrugged, "What is happening?" He walked quickly to his wife and looked down at his daughter, "What is wrong here?"

Astrid sighed and wet her daughter's face, she did not need to answer; he could see the fever clearly and hear his child's moans. "What is it?"

"A fever that has come quickly." Astrid stood in front of him, watching his face for a moment before turning back to their child, all the while humming a tune and wiping Inga's face and neck with a cloth. She had a bowl of water next to her on the floor and he watched as she dipped the cloth into the bowl and rinsed it before placing it onto Inga's forehead.

Einaar moved slightly, "Let me see." He saw the way Astrid stiffened and her slight movement under her skirt. He stopped and watched her for a moment, "Do you honestly believe that I would harm our child, Astrid?"

She turned and looked at him, her gaze defiant and challenging. "I do not know, Einaar, would you? By our laws, Inga has the right to live. I have nursed her at my breast. You have announced her name and wet her forehead before witnesses. Yet, I do not know where your heart lies. But I know this, if you touch her, I will kill you."

He glanced down at her hand, half hidden among her pinafore, the gleam of metal. He sighed loudly and licked his lips. Holding up his hands he stepped closer to her, "I am changed, Astrid. I swear it. I do not know what has changed, but, I do not think that I can follow the old beliefs anymore ... I cannot. To kill someone I love," he turned to look down at his child, "just because of their weakness, feels an abomination. Now, we must help her get well. I believe that now. I was proud the day Inga was born and will be again someday. I am proud of my family and I will defend you both till the gods take my breath."

Dropping the knife, Astrid flung herself into his arms. He held her tightly, alarmed as she shook in his arms. That she could believe that he would feel disappointment at their child's sickness and not concern for her wellbeing appalled him beyond words and he clung tighter to her; needing to show her that she and the child were safe ... At least, from him.

Turning as one back to their child, they sat her up and removed her clothes. Einaar built up the fire again while Astrid sponged Inga with cold water. They both knew the danger from others in the village. Sickness was not accepted, especially if it was deemed life threatening to the people. Sickness was believed to be a weakness of the body and they needed strong, healthy children to become strong and healthy adults to fight and bring forth more healthy children.

No one expected to live to any old age; he was teased at having survived to reach his twenty-eighth year. Halldor was one of the oldest men, having achieved over forty years; he had been chief for five of those, having won the right in battle.

Rafarta was a true elder and honoured by the village. No one knew her true age, but her grey hair and wrinkled skin were evidence of many years. Her age brought wisdom, but it was her gift of second sight that had earned her the respect of the village because it had saved them from disasters more than once. She was considered by many to be closer to the gods themselves, and was given messages by them to save those who were worthy of the gods' favour. Her knowledge of all things living and dead was deemed useful and the women demanded her at every 'Thing'. The chiefs had not argued for she had a good reputation for truth.

She lived alone in a small house on the edge of the village. Each person would share their food with her to make sure they did not gain bad favour with the gods. Many consulted her to learn of the future; she had never been wrong. She had seen the battles that had brought them to this land. She had seen the Queen who would grant them this chance to live among the Saxons peacefully and she had seen who would become restless and ruin it all; of this, she had spoken at the meeting and many had read her unspoken words; their downfall was coming.

The priest had opened his eyes to their savage world. For centuries, their ancestors had explored new worlds and conquered those they found. Settling amongst many, as they had done here on the 'Wireal'; at least that is what the Anglo Saxons called it; he just wanted a home.

He knew all men were different; he had seen this in battle. Soldiers fought differently, dressed differently and their behaviour was different to his people as were their features, the colour of their hair, their skin. The one thing they all had in common was the colour of their blood. It glistened red and had the same metallic scent as anyone else, but did every man think the same? Feel the same? He had always considered men equal for the most part. Equal to die, to reign, to live, to become slave if conquered.

Why was that a bad thing? The priest had declared that the enslaving of the conquered and the selling of human beings was a great sin; yet the women slaves in his village looked happy enough. All the men slaves except two had died in Ireland during the fighting. They now served the village, under Halldor's protection and they looked content. They were fed, slept in a bed and had a woman slave if she was willing; their lives were good compared to others'.

This Queen allowed them to stay on her land, were they not slaves to her will? Never feeling as though the land was truly his, only borrowed. This Queen Aethelflaed was a follower of the Christian God. Was that why she had allowed them the land; accepting their differences?

Or was it all about greed like the priest had also said? Men just wanted more, never satisfied with what they had. He knew of Ingimund's need for more power, why else would he go back on his word? All knew the man's need for blood, yet the Queen had allowed him to stay. Was it compassion for their plight or was she waiting for a debt to be repaid?

A Queen had the right to use men in her kingdom. It would be of great benefit for a Saxon Queen to have Norsemen on her side; would he fight with Ingimund? Could he not? A while ago, he would never have questioned his intention, he would never have seen anything wrong with wanting to fight and conquer a city of great wealth, but now he saw it as tainted and evil ... A sin.

He met Astrid's gaze, reached out, and held her hand. How could he reassure her against the village? If Inga was still unwell come morning, people would talk and wonder and question and he would have to defend his right as her father to choose. He squeezed her hand and let go as the fire began to burn brighter. He carefully checked the cauldron that hung over the fire, the stew Astrid had prepared earlier was untouched. He found a wooden spoon and stirred the contents. Astrid offered him three bowls and smiled, "We will all need our strength for the fight ahead ..." It was going to be a long night, for all of them.

***

Kathryn was getting ready to leave for home when the phone rang. She dithered about whether or not to answer it as she had already stayed behind in the laboratory for over an hour, intrigued by the brooch. Tony had barely left. His yawning had become contagious and she'd ordered him to go home, declining a meal and a beer. She noticed that he was asking her out on what could be described by some as 'dates' a little more often lately; was she interested?

Her hand hovered on the doorknob, but in a huff, she marched back inside and picked up the receiver.

"Hello, Kathryn Bailey's office."

"Kathryn? It's Simon ... I have your results."

She eased herself into her chair and lowered her handbag off her shoulder. Her chest had tightened with fear; she knew what he was going to say. "Okay, so, tell me ..."

"Kathryn, firstly, where did you get this sample?"

Her head swam with lies, "I ... erm ... why?"

She heard him exhale loudly, "I don't appreciate jokes Kathryn. You already know the blood is human. What did you really want to know? Is it yours? Because if it is I can tell you that you aren't pregnant, you don't have any foul disease either."

"What!" She could feel herself tremble and clung onto the phone, "I don't know what you mean, it isn't mine, it, I ... found it and wondered about it. That's all."

"You found it?"

Kathryn heard the suspicion in his tone and hoped her own was light, "Yeah, you know, students' practical jokes and all that, little buggers! I just wondered, like I told you, if it was animal or human. Had they bled themselves or some poor chicken ..."

"A chicken! Jesus, Kathryn, your students can be so outrageous sometimes. That would be a very stupid joke to play on you. I hope you'll be reporting them? How much blood was there originally, because you gave me quite a lot, even diluted as it was with the rain and mud?"

"That was it, what I gave you. So, it was definitely human then?" She heard her voice tremor and hoped Simon wouldn't notice.

"Oh yes, definitely human, 'O' negative if you really want to know. Though I have to say, the student who did this to themselves is in serious need of therapy. I am a bit concerned about it; do you have any ideas who it was? Moreover, where the hell did they leave it?"

"Erm ... no, but I haven't really chased it up. You know what kids are like ... and besides I'm not with them full time, am I, so I don't feel able to chase it up. I'll chat to one of their tutors ..." She wasn't sure just how long she could keep her voice neutral and light as her whole body shook. "Well, thanks for that Simon ..."

"Not so fast Kathryn, I said you'd owe me. What are you doing tonight? You can tell me all about this trickster of yours."

She was shaking so badly she was having trouble holding the telephone to her ear. "I'm sorry Simon, I am so tired, and I need an early night, another time though eh?"

She heard him suck his breath through his teeth and he clicked his tongue a few times before answering, "Don't you want to know the rest?"

"Rest? What do you mean?" She slowly sat forward and leant her elbows on her desk.

"My dear, when I do tests, I do tests, not just to see if your sample was human, which was obvious, but all the other tests ..."

She sighed loudly, "I see and you won't tell me the rest unless I meet you tonight, is that right?"

"My dear, you make me sound so horrid. It's been ages since we've been out and perhaps, this time, we can visit my flat; I don't have cats ... Well?"

She shivered with revulsion, but she had to know more about this human blood. "All right Simon, you win, I'll meet you in an hour for a drink at the Golden Lion, but that's it."

"The Golden Lion it is and if memory serves me correctly, don't they serve a splendid steak with all the trimmings? I'll see you in an hour. *Ciao*."

She held the phone for a moment, listening to the purr of the line before replacing the receiver. Human blood. That sick and twisted man had done something; it had to be; and that scared her. If he could leave a pool of blood to be found, what else would he be prepared to do? Damn it!

She should tell the police her theory on Mr Merton; what if he was a psychopath or something? Maybe she should confide in Simon … No that was not an option; the less he knew, the better, for now. If she did involve the police, he would know soon enough. Then again, if she didn't tell him, he might get rid of the evidence and the police would need it. Oh God! Her head was spinning with questions, with no right answers.

Fatigue clung to her body while it shook with fear, loathing and revulsion. All she wanted to do was crawl under the bed covers and cry and shake; but she had to find out the awful truth and hoped she could keep herself together long enough to fight off Simon.

***

Tony sat in the warm pub, his pint half drunk, his eyes felt gritty from lack of sleep and he quickly rubbed them. He glanced down at the sample notes that lay on the seat next to him. He'd tried to read a little, but nothing was going into his brain tonight. Nothing but a pint and a chat with an old mate was on the cards tonight; then bed.

He'd been surprised to receive the phone call from Robert so quickly, but now that he was here waiting, he also felt a little apprehensive. They had known each other in school and bumped into each other again during a college party, hanging out together for two years, before Robert buggered off to the other side of the country; he'd never contacted him.

It hadn't exactly pissed him off, he wasn't some needy gay bloke, but he'd liked Robert, they'd got on well and had a laugh. When he hadn't heard from him, it hurt him a bit at the time, though he'd never have admitted it. Then the job at the museum had happened and Robert was forgotten. Now here they were again. What would he be like now, married and with a kid?

A strange kid, reacting the way she had and a very pretty wife too, but as Robert said, he'd messed that up and badly from the looks of it.

"Tony."

He looked up to see Robert walking towards him looking flustered and excitable.

"Hi, I can't stop long … Can I get you another?"

"No, I'm good thanks." He watched his old friend order and then sit opposite him on a stool, "So, how are you Robert?" Instead of answering, Robert picked up his glass and drank deeply; gasping for breath, he put down his empty glass. "Needed that, did you?"

Robert nodded and licked his lips, "I did. So, how are you?"

"I asked you first. How's your kid, feeling better?"

Robert breathed deeply to calm himself and leant forward, ignoring the question, "Tony … You've lived round here a while?" He didn't wait for a confirmation, but went on, "Have you … I mean, have there ever been any strange things happening around here recently?"

Tony frowned, "Strange things? Like what?"

"You know where I live, in Frankby, by Royden Park … Yes? Well, have there ever been stories of anything unusual …?"

Tony picked up his pint and shook his head, "I don't know what you mean, mate."

"I mean anything unusual?"

Tony licked his lips and leant forward, he could see Robert was becoming agitated, "Look, Robert, unless you tell me straight I can't …"

"I think our house might be haunted or I'm going insane and that alternative doesn't bear thinking about, yet…"

"You what?"

Robert's shoulders slumped; he looked deflated as he ran a hand through his hair, "Tony, I think I've just seen a fucking ghost."

Chapter Seventeen

Helen hid the small knife in her trouser pocket, feeling stupid and irresponsible. Knowing if it was a ghost, a knife would do absolutely nothing. If the stories were true, it would be nothing more than mist, thin air. Nevertheless, the feeling she'd had in Cherry's bedroom had felt too real, too solid, not a mist at all, so maybe the experts didn't know after all.

She had heard Robert go out while she'd been preparing something to eat for Cherry. He hadn't said a word, which irritated her; she deserved an acknowledgement surely? Would it hurt him to say he was going out and where to?

She knew the reason for her feeling; she was pissed off with him and his secrets and she had to admit, she was feeling afraid. As the night drew in, she was feeling more and more apprehensive about being alone. The house felt oppressive and lonely compared to their old home, which had streetlights and cars and neighbours. A Street full of Mrs Havers was possibly better than a dark lane of nothing. Nearest neighbours were a few hundred yards away and hadn't introduced themselves.

She stood in the lounge trying to think things through in a rational way. She had felt and seen this thing during the day; therefore, it was a threat at any time. This male presence had wanted to intimidate her; of that, she was certain. There was nothing nice or gliding-old-ladies-in-white about this ghost, she had sensed his anger in the very air and it had been directed at her, not Cherry.

Cherry didn't seem afraid of it at all. She was relieved to see that Cherry wasn't affected by the coldness or feel the uncomfortable atmosphere. She'd managed to get a few more bits of information as they had made beans on toast with cheese; Cherry's favourite meal.

Cherry finally confided in hushed tones that tickled her ear about seeing this man and a woman. Cherry told her that the woman was the man's wife and had long golden hair, like an angel. She was always smiling and had stroked Cherry's hair, which had apparently 'tickled'. They talked funny, but Cherry understood them and answered their questions, about her name, other children and Inga. This concept disturbed her greatly. They had been in the house two days and their child had been having secret conversations with ghosts, it seemed unreal and frightening.

Yet, here she was, a knife in her pocket, guarding her daughter against what? Ghostly intruders? Perhaps these spirits saw them as the intruders. Perhaps this house had been their home once and they hated their intrusion? The thought of doing the ghosts a favour and leaving flashed across her brain and she chastised herself for being a coward; a ghost should not be her excuse to leave the marriage.

She suddenly laughed out loud causing Cherry to glance up at her, the meal half eaten as she proceeded to cut up small squares of toast to give teddy before eating some beans. Helen bent down and gently kissed her daughter on her forehead, "I love you baby. You do know that?"

Cherry grinned, "Of course I do, silly."

Helen sat down heavily on the sofa, the whole thing was absurd. Here she was, knife in her pocket, going over the details of her own child talking to ghosts … in her own home! The very notion seemed out of this world and here she was, accepting it without a rational argument. *Think calmly*, she told herself and took a deep breath.

It was conceivable that her daughter would feel insecure with the move and with Robert's behaviour over the last year. It was also conceivable that she would conjure up new friends, also plausible that she would act out, have tantrums, test her and Robert and see the reactions.

It was also possible that Cherry could impose these feelings onto her. Wasn't she feeling insecure and alone and very sad right now? She was feeling vulnerable and in need of an excuse to move back to her comfort zone? That was what the counsellor had talked about, her comfort zone? Moving away from everything she knew and had known since childhood, for a man who hadn't shown her love or respect for years. Her anxiety levels would be very high; perhaps she was susceptible to suggestion? It made sense surely, as her daughter needed friends, someone to talk out her own anxiety in a child's way, and in her own vulnerability she had been drawn into Cherry's fantasy?

It would make perfect sense, because then she could talk herself into leaving this house and moving back to York. It wouldn't be betraying Robert, lowering herself down to his level when he had betrayed their marriage, it would be a perfectly good reason to leave; the house was haunted and their daughter was in danger. No, she quickly corrected herself, Cherry wasn't in danger; she was. Danger from what? might be the argument, but she was sure she could come up with something.

She'd read about people convincing themselves they were possessed or their house is haunted or their dead granny is visiting them from beyond the grave, when really, it was something else. Epilepsy, schizophrenia, water running under the house causing movement or just needing something so badly, you can make it happen. Did she fall into this category? If she was completely honest with herself, she fitted the criteria perfectly.

Feeling better, having almost convinced herself that the so called 'ghosts' were nothing more than some fabrication, she sighed loudly, but her feelings towards Robert hadn't improved. She walked back into the kitchen and reached for a pan; she would make herself scrambled eggs on toast. She had no idea where he had gone or how long he would be, but she'd be damned if she was going to make him anything to eat. She had come here to Wirral with him in some vain hope that he would make the effort to save their pathetic marriage; he hadn't tried hard enough.

She pushed aside the fact that it had only been two days and two nights and that he had made small attempts at connecting with her. If she accepted the idea that it was because of her vulnerability and anxiety that she had seen these 'ghosts', then it obviously wasn't working out quickly enough for her. The thought of uprooting Cherry again wasn't a nice one, but sooner rather than later would be a better option ... wouldn't it?

A noise behind her made her spin round. She froze as she stared into the eyes of a woman. She was barely three feet away, slightly smaller than she was, but this did not detract from the hostility in the woman's eyes. Helen recoiled and tried to look away to break the stare, her mind raced with fear. She could hear the television and knew Cherry was in the next room. How had the woman got in? She opened her mouth to try to warn her child, but nothing came out. She opened and closed her mouth, trying to grasp a word, a sound, but the air in her throat seemed to have been sucked out and she couldn't breathe.

Her body could not move. Her feet were rooted to the spot, her arms pressed to her sides. She was vaguely aware of the kitchen top pressing into her back, the pan inches away, a weapon. She wanted to reach up to her throat and move the unseen obstruction, but nothing moved; she was frozen. Only her eyes moved left and right, searching for a way to get past this woman whose hate and loathing flowed into her very being like liquid. It oozed from her and filled the kitchen. It enveloped her frozen body, filled every pore, muscle and bone. She felt it crawling over her skin and tried to shy away from it, but nothing moved, she was its prisoner.

She tried to focus on breathing; she had to stay alive for Charlotte. As the thoughts raced through her head, the inevitable knowledge that she could not save her child came racing after. The horror of it filled her heart and she could almost hear it break. She was lost, her darling baby was lost and there was nothing she could do about it as the woman reached out her hand and hissed one word, "Inga ..."

***

Kathryn flung herself off the couch and rolled onto all fours. Backing into a corner, she quickly scanned the dark room for the attacker; there was no one. She let out her breath, which came out as a sob and she let the tears fall as she manoeuvred her shaking body into a more comfortable position. She gently touched her cheek and wiped away the sweat and tears as the nightmare slowly dwindled and she was back in her lounge, safe and alone.

Reaching up, she flicked on the small lamp and heaved a sigh of relief as the orange glow banished the dark. She shivered as she realised the heating had gone off and she was wearing nothing except her knickers. She quickly glanced at the clock and groaned; it was barely midnight and she'd fallen asleep on the couch. Barely an hour had passed, now it would take forever to get back to sleep. Walking quickly into her kitchen, she flicked on the switch before entering. Feeling silly, but needing to be reassured, she gingerly checked behind the kitchen door and checked that the back door was locked. Satisfied, she filled the kettle and made herself herbal tea.

The nightmare was still vivid in her mind as she walked to her bedroom, leaving the kitchen light on, not caring about the expense. The light illuminated the hallway and she needed the reassurance. Her bedroom was the opposite end of her large flat, her bathroom next door; she flicked that on also. She glanced back towards her lounge, she dithered about whether or not to leave the lamp on and finally decided to do it, comfort was more important right now than the electric bill. Her sleeping had never been good but lately it had been terrible and it was some comfort to open her eyes and see a glow somewhere.

Her bedroom was chilly and she dived under the covers, her herbal tea held tightly against her chest. Switching on her small bedside lamp, she tried to breathe deeply and calm her mind. She did not want to remember the dream but it refused to go away. It lingered in her consciousness, stubbornly staying put however hard she tried to think of something nice.

She inevitably recalled her evening with Simon and recoiled from that experience. The man had more hands than an octopus. His constant questioning about the blood sample and her refusal to divulge any information about it had convinced Simon that she had sent him the sample on the pretext of getting him to see her again.

"A joke, indeed! Kathryn, that is the lamest excuse I have ever heard, darling. As if you needed one anyway. My door is always open to you, you know that. Are you going to tell me whose it was?"

"I'm afraid I can't, Simon, the joker ..."

"The joker ... of course. Well, this 'joker' has traces of illegal substances in their blood so please tell me it isn't yours; I'd hate it if you were some druggie!" He moved closer, "Like I said, you don't need excuses to get my attention, Kathryn. You may only be an archaeologist, but you have other assets I would love to explore ..."

Her being completely dumbstruck at his ludicrous suggestion convinced him beyond doubt that he was on the right track and he'd launched himself on her. They had been allocated a booth, even though she had said she would only stay for a drink. His insistence that they should eat had drowned out her refusal and she had felt obliged to follow the waiter, Simon steering her with his hand on her shoulder. They had been herded into a quiet booth near the back of the restaurant, her white wine placed before her, the menu placed in her hands and Simon breathing down her neck, his hand hovering near her thigh, the other arm leaning on the back of the couch as he'd explained about the blood.

She'd tolerated his closeness whilst listening to his theories, but once he finished, she tried to move away, to create space between them. Simon had had other ideas and placed his hand onto her knee, the other wrapped around her shoulder as he moved in. "Oh Kathryn, it is so good to feel you again. I'm glad you came around ..."

It was as far as he got before she grabbed her wine and poured it over his trousers. Some splashed onto her skirt, hence the reason it was now in the washing machine. He jumped up, knocking over his own brandy and coke, "What the …?" He'd exclaimed, his face like thunder, "Don't mess with me Kathryn, I don't like bitches who tease …"

Her emotions, already close to the edge, erupted before she could think logically and she had punched him squarely in the groin, which was fairly level to her face. Everyone nearest to the table, including the waiter who hurried over to find out the problem, heard his exclamation. Easing herself out of the other side of the booth, she'd smiled politely and informed the waiter, her friend needed some ice; before leaving as quickly as she could.

Her heart had been pounding against her chest as she ran to her car; expecting to see Simon coming after her. Her mind raced with images. Simon's expression when she'd hit him and the look on the waiter's face as he strove to stop himself from smiling. Simon's lecherous look when she'd arrived and the smug air when she'd given in and followed the waiter. What he had said about the blood sample; human. Drugs.

Climbing into her car, she'd driven around the corner and stopped because her legs were shaking so badly. She had behaved appallingly and no doubt it would come back on her ten- fold, if Simon had anything to do with it. That damned blood sample would be her downfall. Perhaps Mr Merton knew what he was doing after all, but worse still, perhaps he'd known what she would do or wouldn't do in this case and that frightened her.

She realised that she was clinging tightly to her mug and tried to relax her grip. The stress she was under was huge and now she'd only made it worse. The nightmares were so real; she felt as if she was falling apart and she bent her head and allowed the tears to fall. The images in her head refused to go away no matter how hard she tried; so much horror and bloodshed. So many deaths, so many murders; it compared to nothing she had ever witnessed on the news; perhaps because it felt so personal.

She closed her eyes and breathed deeply. She felt sick as the sword flashed before her eyes and the blade found its target. A woman defended her sick child who lay on a small, narrow bed, covered in sheepskin; the bloodied woman fell backwards and lay across the bed, almost crushing the dying child. The large man pushed the woman away and looked down at the unmoving child. He uttered a cry of despair as the sword fell. The girl's hand opened as death relaxed its grip and the object fell out onto the floor.

The brooch lay amongst the mud and the blood before it was crushed into the earth by the man's boot as he reached for a burning stick from the fire and set the house alight. The brooch that had been brought from their homeland; worn with pride and honour. The brooch that now sat in the museum.

Chapter Eighteen

Tony moaned and rubbed his chin, "Robert, we've been through this, you're just stressed, mate, nothing else." They had been sitting in the pub for over an hour, he was tired and starving, but he hadn't wanted to order anything while Robert had launched into his odd story. "Okay look, here's a theory; you say your daughter has changed her doll's name to ... Inga wasn't it? Well, that is a Viking name."

Robert leant forward, his second beer only half touched, he moved it away, "Oh yeah, do you know anything about it then?"

"Well ... I'm not an expert, Kathryn and our boss, Trevor are the ones to talk to about the Vikings, but I think it's Scandinavian and means 'Beautiful'. Do you know your name is Norse?"

"What: Robert?"

"No, your surname, Gunn, it means battle I think. Maybe you are a distant relation to the Vikings that lived here." Tony finished the last dregs of his pint and stretched his arms, "Fancy something to eat?"

Robert muttered something, but he was deep in thought. Tony watched him for a moment before reaching for the menu. Glancing through it, he handed it across the table to Robert who was staring off into space, "Robert? Fancy anything?"

Shaking his head, he quickly changed his mind, "Actually, yes, just some chips or something while we chat."

Tony nodded and went to the bar to order, coming back with half a lager. "Okay, food will be ten minutes, what else?"

Robert licked his lips, "Right, you say Vikings lived here, where do you mean? On land our house is built on? The estate agent said there'd been an old manor house there."

"Well, not necessarily. Frankby is an old Norse word, 'Frankis-byr' meaning something like a Frenchman's farm. It's possible the manor house belonged to that.

The village of Thingwall was their local meeting place where they made laws, passed judgements and all that and that's not far from you. The area we are digging we think was a small village, the finds have been amazing. But it's not known yet, so don't say anything."

Robert sat back in his chair, "Well, what else is Viking here?"

Tony sat back and stretched his legs, "Bloody hell, Robert, you are living in Viking central, mate. People are finding Norse stuff all the time. You have Meols where it is believed they landed. There is Bromborough where the bloodiest battle is supposed to have been fought, you've got ..."

"Yes, okay, thanks for the history lesson, but anything near my house?"

"Only our dig. Thurstaston means Tun farm or farmer and the name is Norse. Excavations in Irby years ago found Iron Age and Roman settlements, but that's it I think, I'd have to check our records."

"So, your dig is what ... just over half a mile from our house. Is it possible you might have disturbed something ...?"

"Disturbed something?"

"Yeah, you know, people say their house is suddenly haunted and it's because they have been messing around, doing renovations or something. You know, digging stuff up, it pisses off something, apparently?"

Tony laughed, "Jesus, Robert, are you serious! We haven't dug up any skeletons or a burial mounds or shit like that. If we had I could probably understand pissing some old Viking off, but so far, we haven't found anything like that. A possible village, that's all; it hardly constitutes messing about with someone's grave!"

Robert sighed loudly and sat back, "No, I suppose you're right, I'm sorry, I'm just trying to find an explanation for something that is obviously psychological. I need a solid explanation to explain what I thought I saw and felt, and I suppose you could call ghosts solid. Well, at least more solid than me, losing my mind ..."

He shook his head, "I need it to be anything other than what it is, I suppose. A ghost in our new home makes it more exciting. Something to take my mind off the fact that my marriage is in the toilet and my daughter is freaking out and who can blame the poor kid? I've fucked her head up so badly I'm surprised she even knows my name." He took a long drink and wiped his mouth, "My breakdown wasn't that long ago and that just about put the topping on my life. I'm still surprised every day that Helen and Cherry agreed to come with me and now, they have arrived and it's all happening and maybe, I can't take it. I only stopped taking the medication a couple of weeks ago and now, I just don't know if I did the right thing. You know, maybe I'm seeing things and hearing stuff again, but, Tony, I have to tell you, it was so real."

Tony didn't answer straight away as their food arrived. He sniffed his rump steak with satisfaction, picked up a chip, and devoured it. Robert barely noticed his own bowl. "Look, you've been through something I can't even imagine, but I do know women. Can you really blame your wife for feeling hurt? And maybe she is feeling a bit rejected? You just have to keep trying." He put a large forkful of steak into his mouth and chewed for a moment.

"As for your kid ...?" He shrugged, "Who knows what she's thinking, but seeing her react to the brooch like that was weird. Maybe she needs someone to talk to?" He swallowed and had a sip of beer, "But Robert, mate, you may have to come to terms with the possibility that it's over, maybe your wife has had enough?"

"Maybe ... but I couldn't bear that."

Tony felt uncomfortable; he wasn't used to this kind of talk, especially from an old friend he hadn't seen for years. He quickly glanced around the small pub checking that no one could hear them. He leant over, "Come on, eat up, you'll need your strength if you're prepared to fight for what you want ... Right?"

Robert looked up, "You're right. I know you are; it's just that feeling of something else in the room was so, real ..."

"Yeah, but like you said, the cat didn't react at all, did it?"

"Well, no, but ..."

"No buts. It's a new home, a new start and all that tension between you and your wife and kid ... It's a hot bed for feeling weird, I'd say. So, eat up and get back home. Did you tell her you were meeting me?"

The look on Robert's face answered that one and they fell into silence as each man ate, one with gusto the other barely noticing as he thought about how he was going to fix his marriage.

***

It took every ounce of strength she had to move her eyes, but eventually Helen managed to open them a crack. The light from the kitchen blinded her and she groaned, turning her head slowly. The effort to do just that was immense, but she tried again and managed to open her eyes fully; it took forever.

Moving her head slightly she could see the dark hallway through the open door; there was no light except the kitchen. The darkness felt solid. It surrounded everything, so did the silence; no sound, no Charlotte. The name brought a sudden wave of adrenalin forcing every muscle in her body to move. She tried to move her legs, but they had cramped and she groaned in pain and frustration as she attempted to lift herself off the cold kitchen floor.

Her arms were weak and wobbly as she tried to push herself up onto all fours. Cherry! My baby! Her need to get to her child spurred her on and she pushed herself harder, needing every ounce of strength to push forward. Forward ... forward ... towards the dining room, towards her baby. She had to fight the pain, fight the fatigue, the strange fuzziness in her head that made her think of being under water. She had to get to her daughter. How long had she been unconscious?

The dining room was empty. She crawled into the lounge and pushed herself onto her feet. She stumbled around the room, looking behind the sofa, the curtains. She felt sick, her chest was tight and her stomach clenched every time Cherry wasn't there. "Baby? Baby … please. Where are you? Please God, where's my baby …?"

She moved as quickly as her legs would carry her back towards the dark hallway. She pulled herself up the stairs and fell into her bedroom. Pushing herself up onto all fours again, she scrambled over to the bed, nothing. Pulling herself back onto her feet, she suddenly realised the noises she could hear, were coming from her. She wiped at her face as she tried to run to Cherry's bedroom, her cheeks were drenched with tears and snot, it blinded her vision as she quickly searched the wardrobe, the windowsill, she even flung off the bed covers, Cherry was nowhere.

A sob escalated into a scream as she realised she had already known her baby was not in the house. Her instincts had told her; now she might have wasted precious time searching when they could be anywhere. Doing anything. She retched and gasped for air as the realisation that her daughter was gone overwhelmed her and her body sagged against the bedroom wall. Cherry. Charlotte … her baby. She glanced down at her watch, she had been unconscious nearly an hour … Cherry was probably dead. Police? What was the point; they never found them alive or unharmed. She curled into herself and wept.

***

A few villagers asked about Astrid and Inga throughout the day and he had passed off their absence with an offhand comment about being busy. By the early evening, people were beginning to ask too many questions, passing his home with watchful eyes and whispered conversations. He kept the slave girl busy with other chores that had kept her outside for the best part of the day, but there had been moments when she had gone into the house and he had caught her staring at Inga with a knowing look.

He kept himself busy with odd jobs that needed to be done around the house. The land needed ploughing, but that could wait a day or two; he wanted to be near his daughter. He was sitting on his bench outside his home sharpening a knife, the sun was just beginning to set and the torches were being lit, when it occurred to him how quiet it was; it was too quiet. Something felt wrong.

Taking his sharpened knife, he slowly walked towards his neighbour's home; he was not working outside and he had not seen him since early that morning which was unusual. His wife was nowhere to be seen. He looked up and noticed that no smoke rose from the hole in the roof and the door was closed. He was about to knock when he heard a whispered comment and turned to the house opposite. A woman sat cutting vegetables into her pot, she saw Einaar had heard her and nodded with her head, "Not seen them all day, lazy pigs!"

He grinned and wished her a good evening. Children, that was it, there were not many children running around, doing their jobs, playing their games, making noise. People were talking in whispers and keeping their heads down. He called a greeting to one or two and got unenthusiastic responses. Only two men came to talk with him, but even they seemed on edge.

"What's going on here today?"

"Who knows, people are acting strangely. I think it's this coming battle; it's put everyone on edge."

"Halldor has ordered extra watch tonight in case the Saxons hear of our plans to attack the city."

Einaar nodded, "That could be it. I'll see you both tomorrow then ...?"

He was about to leave when one man stopped him, "There is something else, some are saying a sickness has come to our village. Do you know of it?"

Einaar shook his head, "No, but I will keep an eye out. Be well ..."

He turned away and hoped he was a better liar than Astrid gave him credit for. He heard the two men walk away after a moment's hesitation and heaved a sigh of relief. He was passing a friend's house when his wife Gudrid stepped out. On seeing him, she firmly closed the door and stood in front of it.

"Gudrid, evening to you, where's Gizur?"

"It is nothing ... really, a chill while he was out celebrating the coming battle. It will clear." Pushing him slightly, she quickly glanced around at the few people that were watching, "By Odin's grace, he will be on his feet tomorrow, you'll see. Come back then Einaar ..." Under her breath she added, "Please ..."

As he was walking back to his own home, he hadn't seen Sigrid as he was deep in thought, until she was upon him; she looked frightened, "Einaar, please, what is happening here today?"

"I don't know Sigrid. It seems a few people are sick, perhaps it is nothing more than food gone bad, or a slight chill." He looked back towards Gudrid who was collecting some water.

Sigrid edged closer, she glanced quickly around her to be sure they were not overheard, "Einaar, Ranulf is ill. Thorlak refuses to believe his son could be so, but it is true. He has had a fever since the dawn ... Einaar, I fear ... Swear to me you will talk to Thorlak. Don't let him hurt our son ..." Her voice broke and she quietly sobbed into her hands.

Einaar stood unmoving, unsure what to do, what to say. Finally, he reached over and gently touched her shoulder, "I'm sure it is nothing. Thorlak would never hurt his own son, Sigrid. As I would never hurt my own child, I swear it."

Sigrid shook her head, "I am not so sure. The fever is so strong ..." She swallowed hard and looked up at him then, "Your child? Is Inga unwell also?"

Einaar glanced around them before nodding, "Inga has been unwell, last night too. A touch of fever, nothing more." Feeling uncomfortable he quickly changed the subject, "Thorlak would never hurt his son over something so unimportant; that is folly ... I am sure you have nothing to fear."

Sigrid stopped crying and looked up at him, "She has been unwell? When did it begin?"

He frowned, "I'm not sure, sometime early evening, it is a chill, and nothing more ... You'll see." He was about to pat her reassuringly on her shoulder, but he let his hand fall to his side. Her expression had changed from worry to something else, she looked thoughtful and he was not sure that he liked it.

"Early evening? Yesterday?"

Einaar frowned, "I don't see the relevance, it is nothing, give my regards to Thorlak, I'm sure Ranulf will be well soon." He muttered a farewell and walked away, all the while knowing that Sigrid was watching his departure with that strange look on her face and it made him feel uneasy.

Reaching his own home, he walked in to find Astrid crying silently as Inga shook uncontrollably in her bed. A cloth lay limply across his child's forehead, but he could see that it hadn't made any difference to her fever; her cheeks were burning. He crossed to her quickly and knelt down by his wife. Gingerly he reached out and took Inga's hand in his own. Her burning skin warmed his chilled fingers almost immediately and he held them tighter.

He looked across at Astrid, she was gazing at Inga's face, tears streamed down her cheeks and she was mumbling a prayer to the Christian God for help. He felt torn; should he be doing the same? Would the Christian God listen and help his daughter more than the old gods?

Perhaps he should pray to Odin or Frigga, Goddess of children. Was it not she who helped in Inga's birth? On the other hand, perhaps Freya, the fairest of all the goddesses. Dalla would have called on her also during the birth, would she not protect her child now? She comes forward to comfort the dying, she is protector of the weak and a healer, was she not his best hope?

He clenched his fists and brought them down hard onto the mud floor, he didn't know what to do and it burned within him. In battle, he knew exactly what to do. His body trembled as he knelt down in the dirt and he felt shame at feeling so useless. He crossed himself as the priest had shown them, began with the Christian God, and slowly worked his way through the others. The gods could not have her. He could never live without her.

Chapter Nineteen

The drive home was barely five minutes, but he drove slowly and stopped once to try and organise his thoughts. Half of him didn't want to go back to the house, to see her, the way that she'd look at him, *if* she looked at him. He knew how much Helen despised him and wondered constantly why she had come at all when he knew that he was on a losing battle for her love. Her indifference hurt like hell. He deserved it, but that didn't make it any easier.

The other half wanted to race home, pull her to him and kiss her. Kiss her sweet lips until she believed how much he loved her. Kiss her until she stopped fighting him. Kiss her until she looked into his eyes and saw how deeply sorry he was for everything. Kiss her lips, her face, that lovely neck, take her to bed, and convince her with his body how much she meant to him. Last night had taken every ounce of courage to walk into their bedroom; he still wasn't convinced that she'd been asleep.

Cherry would be in bed by now, hopefully. It was late; surely the little terror would be fast asleep, especially after her strange little incident that afternoon. What did that mean, if anything? Maybe he shouldn't be thinking too much about that. The counsellor had warned him that Cherry might behave differently; well, screaming bloody murder was definitely different.

He moved his thoughts back to Helen and licked his dry lips. He could taste the beer on his breath; that wouldn't go down well. She'd say he was only having a go because he was drunk. If he was honest, he wasn't going to win whatever he did, but did he have the courage to hang in there and keep trying? He remembered the man with muscles and felt a wave of hatred towards him. Damned if he was getting his hands on his family without a fight.

He started the car and pulled out onto the road again. If nothing else, maybe he could talk to her about what he thought he'd seen tonight, get her perspective and find out how she felt? Had she seen or felt anything or would that frighten her? Would it add fuel to the fire and give her another reason to leave? He turned into the driveway unsure of what to say, how to behave.

The police car sitting outside the house completely threw him and he bolted out of the car the second he turned off the engine. "What's going on? What's happened?" He ran to the police officer standing near the front door.

"Sir, are you Robert Gunn?" Seeing Robert nod, he opened the door and escorted him inside, "It's all right Sir, there seems to have been a misunderstanding ..."

Walking into the lounge, he blinked at the amount of people in it. A policewoman stood nearby. A plain clothed woman was sitting next to Helen on the couch while a man was sitting in the armchair listening to the conversation. They both glanced up at his appearance, but went back to quietly talking to Helen, who hadn't acknowledged him, but sat on the couch, Cherry curled on her lap. His daughter was looking around silently at everyone, but she was clinging to Helen as tightly as Helen was clinging onto her. They both looked terrified and he moved quickly to their side. "What's happened?"

Helen buried her face in Cherry's long hair and he heard her crying. Cherry looked across at him, but clung to Helen even tighter, her doll hugged to her chest. It was the woman officer who answered, "They've had a bit of a scare, Mr Gunn. Your wife 'phoned in a panic, she couldn't find your daughter ..." In a lighter tone he guessed was for Cherry's sake, "But as you can plainly see, here she is, safe and sound."

She nodded towards the dining room and he rose to follow her. "It seems," she whispered, "that your daughter sleep-walked outside." She glanced back at Helen, who was now gently rocking Cherry. "It's really frightened her; she was in a real state when we arrived. She was convinced someone had taken your daughter, but within minutes of searching the garden, we found Charlotte, fast asleep in her little toy house. Poor lamb was cold, but the doctor has just left and given her the all clear. We weren't sure where to reach you ...?"

He was staring at his wife and child, he could barely take in the horror of what Helen must have gone through and yet again, he wasn't there for her. He barely heard the question, "What? Oh, I was with a friend, Tony Campbell, at the Anchor. Will they be all right? I mean, my wife looks terrible. Does she need something?"

The officer turned to look, "The doctor offered, but she refused. She's had a shock, a horrible thing for anyone." Turning back to him, she raised a questioning eyebrow, "You will take care of them ... Sir?"

"Of course, of course, I'll sort it out ... thanks."

They walked back to the sofa together and Robert quickly sat down and gently rubbed Cherry's back. He could see her fighting to keep her eyes open, Helen seemed completely oblivious to everyone around her. Her whole focus was on Charlotte. The officer knelt down in front of Helen and gently touched her arm. "Mrs Gunn ... Helen, we'll be off now. Don't worry about it, things like this happen sometimes, it's always nice when it's a false alarm. Take care, Okay?"

Helen nodded and fresh tears welled up in her eyes to cascade down her cheeks unchecked. Robert reached for the box of tissues and handed one to Helen, she didn't move, so he left it lying on her knee. He caught the eye of the woman officer and smiled, embarrassed. He could see that she was reading the home situation very well and it made him uncomfortable, as if he was to blame for not being home, but in the pub.

He showed the police out and watched them leave. He gently closed the front door, bolted it and chained it. If Cherry was prone to sleep walking, he would have to consider other, more secure means of keeping her safe. It didn't bear thinking about what might have happened if she'd gone out onto the road and been hit by a car or picked up by a passing paedophile He quickly rubbed his face to keep the tears at bay; no, it definitely wasn't worth thinking about.

Helen hadn't moved when he walked back into the lounge. Cherry was fast asleep in her arms. He hesitated, unsure whether to intrude and move Cherry to her bed. He eventually sat next to her on the couch and gently touched his child's face. He saw Helen pull Cherry closer and he sighed, "She's all right now. She's safe. Why don't we put her in her own bed? You look like you could do with some sleep …"

"She isn't safe."

Robert frowned, "What do you mean? She's fine … she's here?"

Helen shook her head slowly, "She isn't safe. They took her. They took my baby …" Helen looked around the room as if searching for someone, it made him uneasy.

"Helen, what are you talking about? You're frightening me, do you need something to help you calm down? I know this has …"

She turned and glared at him, her eyes wild with fear and anger, "You know nothing." She spat the words at him, accusing, "You weren't here. You're never here. They took her and I couldn't stop them …"

Her voice broke and her face crumpled and tears ran down her cheeks; she looked utterly destroyed and he knelt before her. Handing her the tissue, she quickly wiped at her face, but the sobs wouldn't stop, he could see that. "I can't protect her … I couldn't … they came … Oh God … my baby …"

Cherry snuffled in her sleep and squirmed on Helen's knee. Helen clung tightly in reaction to the movement and Cherry stopped and settled down again. Robert took the sodden tissue and gave her a fresh one. His chest felt tight with fear: someone had taken his daughter? It didn't make sense. "Helen, you have to tell me, who took Cherry? Who couldn't you stop? Did they break in? Did you see them? Did you tell the police?" Even as he asked, he knew the answer to that one, of course not or they would have behaved differently. They certainly would not have left so quickly. "Helen, tell me."

She looked up at him then, the fight had gone out of her. Her voice was barely a croak, but he understood clearly and a shiver ran through his body. "They're dead.

They came to our home and they took her … Our baby. They took her because they want their own child ... They want Inga."

***

Einaar stroked his wife's face as she lay sleeping, her head on his lap. He had dozed but for the most part, he'd sat all night watching and praying. Astrid had fallen asleep an hour before dawn. He let her rest, as Inga's fever seemed to be lessening and he felt a sense of hope. He looked over to his sleeping daughter and prayed one last time, a prayer of thanks to all the gods for her surviving against all odds.

Inga was a quiet child and for most of the time, she remained silent. She had barely cried since her birth and she never looked interested in the other children who came to play with her. She was a loner, who seemed to watch her surroundings with an odd expression. Many times a comment passed on her odd behaviour and some wondered if she too had the gift of second sight. He'd laughed it off, but something in her manner had always been different.

Inga was smaller than the other children her age and although she ate enough and drank milk, she was a pale and skinny child. Thorlak had teased him often that he had sired a pixie child, not a Viking girl. That said, she showed strength and courage in other ways. He had watched her determination to walk over the last few months and although she had fallen many times, she'd never cried, only looked more determined to get it right.

The other children may not interest her, but nature certainly did. Inga would stare for hours at any spiders or flies or insects of any kind. Her first proper giggle was when a ladybug landed on her knee last summer. Inga was captivated by it; her eyes never wavered from it. She'd sighed loudly when eventually it flew away, much to the amusement of Rafarta who had been watching her.

"A child of the earth, that one, Einaar, a child of the earth!" Rafarta had chuckled to herself as she had walked away.

He remembered now, the look she had given Inga, just once. Reaching her house Rafarta had looked back at Inga sitting in the grass and a strange expression had passed, before she ducked through her doorway and was gone. He wondered now if she had seen something.

Suddenly a cry broke the silence and he quickly pushed Astrid aside, grabbing his axe as he flew through the door. She woke with a start and jumped to her feet, immediately moving towards Inga's bed, but turned to watch him disappear through the doorway.

The morning sun dazzled him for a moment; it was barely touching the sky. He saw a commotion near Thorlack's house and gripping his axe, he ran towards the small crowd that was gathering. Pushing his way through, he found Sigrid kneeling in the dirt, her son, Ranulf lying limp in her arms; he was dead. Thorlack stood over his wife, his face pale; he held his own sword limply in his hand. Einaar walked forward quickly and touched his arm. "Thorlack?"

His friend slowly raised his face, his eyes met his own and his face crumpled, "My son .... my son. He is gone to Hel. He is lost ... We will never meet again for I will die in battle ... he is gone, Einaar, he is gone ..."

Einaar saw that Thorlack had not been responsible for Ranulf's death; the boy lay in his Mother's arms untouched. Sigrid was slowly rocking his lifeless body, refusing to allow anyone to help. Einaar touched his friend on the shoulder and Thorlak fell into his arms. He held him while he wept bitterly and silently cried himself, for the boy he had known since he had been born and the one he had secretly hoped would be a husband to his daughter.

He was not sure how long he stood holding his friend while they mourned his son, but he became aware of murmuring getting closer. Releasing Thorlak, they turned as one to the large group walking quickly towards them; Halldor was at the head of the group. He stopped a few feet away from Thorlack's house, took in Sigrid, Ranulf and finished his gaze on Thorlack.

He nodded silently, "You have my sympathy Thorlak ..." He looked back down at Sigrid who hadn't acknowledged his presence, "And you, Sigrid, you are not alone in your grief, two more children, babes, have died this night and Gizur is sick in his bed as is Gudrid, she is unable to tend her husband. I have sent some men to each house to ask who is sick. I have also sent out to near-by villages to ask if they have any sickness. It shall be dealt with."

He turned away and walked a few feet and stood, his hands on his hips surveying his village, "This will be a curse from that priest, no doubt." He spoke loud enough for those nearby to hear him. "This Christian god is weak and feeble, it will pass. It may take the weak and young or old, but it will not take the strong. His so-called god has no power over Norsemen, we will prevail here."

Taking one last look at Thorlak and his wife, he strode away. One of his slaves remained and bowed before them, "My Lord has asked that all men meet at the 'Thing' tomorrow morning as the sun meets the earth. He wishes to hear every man's thoughts on this sickness and its cause ... My Lords." He backed away and ran after the group of men who had stopped at another's house.

Einaar could see the couple standing near their doorway, he knew they had a six year old daughter and the wife was pregnant again, he said a silent prayer to Frigga for their children's safety. Without a second thought, he quickly added a silent prayer to the Mother Mary also, just in case.

Leaving Thorlak and his wife to prepare their son, he walked swiftly back to his own home. It was the last house in the large village as it was his responsibility to watch for intruders from the East. As he neared, he thought how lonely and quiet it looked compared to the commotion he had just left. Almost every one of the village had gathered there and now the nearest homes were empty, fires left untended as people had rushed out to see what had happened. Nevertheless, he felt a strange sensation of being completely alone for just a moment and he found he was clutching his axe tightly.

Astrid suddenly appeared at the doorway and smiled, "Where've you been? Come ..." Taking his hand, she pulled him into the house and stepped back so that he could see. Inga lay propped up and she smiled at him. Setting down his axe, he knelt beside her bed and grasped her hand, it was warm, but not of fever. He touched her cheeks and forehead and smiled, again, warm, but not feverish; his child would live. Astrid knelt beside him and he clasped her hand, "This is good." Turning to Inga he said, "My brave girl, such a fighter, yes ...?" He clasped her hand tighter and kissed it, "Nothing and no one will take my little girl. No one."

Astrid looked at him questioningly. He shook his head, kissed her hand too before bowing his head, and began to pray silently. For a moment, she watched him, something had happened, something terrible, she could see the strain in his face, the lines of grief but, for now, she did not press it. Her daughter was over the sickness, and she was sure that she was pregnant again. She had hoped for the last few days, but now the nausea could not be ignored any longer. At this moment, life felt good and she bowed her own head, prayed to the Virgin Mary, and gave thanks.

***

Kathryn woke shivering with cold. The blanket had fallen to the floor and she quickly reached down and pulled it back onto her bed. Sitting up, she pulled it tightly around her chin and waited for her body to warm before she allowed herself to relax. The nightmare was still fresh in her head, but in that moment before waking, she had had the frightening notion that someone was there with her. She listened intently, but no sound beside passing cars and her cat purring as she sat on her bedside table. She felt herself relax a little more, there was no way anyone was here or the cat wouldn't be behaving so friendly.

She reached out and gently stroked it. Purdy lifted her head and purred louder in glee. Kathryn sighed, it was nice having company, but when would she ever find a man decent enough to wake up to? Thinking of men, she tried to recall the man in her dreams. She had had a clearer picture of him tonight, definitely Norse, no doubt about that now.

He stood about five nine, muscular build with shoulder length, blond hair plaited on either side of his face. He had a moustache and a short beard. He wore a green tunic and brown hose with brown boots. She noticed his necklace, a Thor's hammer; considered lucky by Norsemen. He had been carrying an axe and a long dagger tucked into his belt; he looked very frightening. Yet, she didn't feel afraid of him; it was the other men in her dream that terrified her. Even though they had been only a blur their intense negative emotions had been felt and their appetite for destruction now filled her head.

She had never experienced anything so raw and powerful, and never expected to feel it in a dream, it was ridiculous. The anger and destruction displayed by these people was overwhelming. To her, it was extreme to contemplate murder, to do it without remorse was something she had never considered before. She had once watched a film where a Mother kills to save her child, and she'd wondered if she could ever do that?

She had been an easy going, reasonable woman in University, completely different to her teenage years. 'A fighter. Always getting into trouble, mixing with the wrong crowd; she won't amount to much at this rate,' was how one teacher described her. It pissed her off so much; she revised for her final exams and got the grades she needed to go to University.

She found that she was extremely happy when digging and researching history, which in turn helped her to become a happier woman. Sometimes she wondered if she had gone too far the other way. Nevertheless, she'd learnt over the years to be assertive in groups and had gained respect from the majority of people who mattered. Yet, she still felt so alone.

The man in her nightmare was alone. He'd felt alone, abandoned, yet he was an important member of the group. A man they listened to and followed in battle; but he wasn't the chief. She hugged herself, these dreams were becoming too vivid for her liking; it was impossible to know for sure about the man; yet she knew it was true without a doubt. It had to stop.

Stretching herself, she showered, dressed, and prepared a quick breakfast for herself and her cat. She didn't really have much of an appetite; the nightmare was still too vivid. There was also the problem of Simon. What was she going to do about him and the blood? What she needed now was logic and who better than Tony? Grabbing her car keys, she headed for her car. Yes, that's what she needed, logic and comfort and Tony was always good for both.

***

The walkers almost stood on the corpse's leg as their two dogs that had run ahead, had almost pulled it free from under the hedge. The woman gagged when she realised what it was; her companion stared at it for a long time before slowly backing away; the woman's retching finally bringing him to his senses. Calling the dogs to heel, the man deliberately turned the woman away, back the way they had come. He remembered the bungalow they passed not five minutes before and the owner had been gardening outside. He hoped that he had a working telephone, he didn't have his mobile with him today; he never took it out with him on his morning walks. For the first time, he wished that he had.

Chapter Twenty

*T*he next morning, just before dawn broke, Einaar wrapped his fur around his shoulders and kissed Astrid briefly but thoroughly before bending to kiss Inga on her forehead. Her head still felt warm, but she had managed a small bowl of broth and some goat's milk and that was a good sign. Leaving his house, he met other men coming out of theirs, many had weapons and all wore fur to keep out the early spring cold. It had rained overnight, and it threatened more.*

Einaar exchanged pleasantries with his friends as they walked to the meeting place. Thorlak walked alongside, but kept his eyes fixed on the ground, his weapon held tightly in his hand. Einaar attempted to talk with him, but Thorlak increased his pace and walked alone; Einaar shrugged and left him, for now.

They would be there before the sun rose too high in the sky if they hurried; and they did to keep themselves warm. Most did not wish to talk about the sickness, those that did, did so only in passing. He could sense their reluctance to say what was on their minds just in case it brought forth more illness. Any sickness was considered a curse from one or more of the gods, but which one? Could Loki cause such misery and grief for his own pleasure? Was this the wrath of Odin for listening to the Christian men? Could it be Freya, the fairest of all the goddesses, would she take the weak and the young for sport?

His stomach fluttered as he remembered how he himself had believed not so long ago without question. His loyalty was to his chief and to the gods, nothing else was important as a young man. When he took Astrid as his wife, he became beholden to her as he had with his parents, but it was not the same.

He had fought for the gods and sacrificed to the gods. Spoken to them as he would to his chief, he had been in awe of them. He quietly damned the priest for coming and immediately took it back. Whom had they displeased so badly that they would curse the entire village without judgement? He hoped someone at the 'Thing' would have an answer; they needed one.

His thoughts continued to trouble him as he walked. Another child, a baby, no more than three months old, a third son, had died in the early hours of the morning. His friend, Gizur was still alive, barely holding on apparently but his wife was not expected to live past the day. The speed that this sickness was killing frightened him terribly.

Gizur was a warrior, not weak or helpless. He was in his thirtieth year, had fought many battles and had many scars to prove it. The talk of the village had always been that Gizur was a favourite of the gods; no one could kill him. They had had many a night in jest, attempting to 'kill' Gizur in one way or another. The night eight men had pounced on him was a real test to see if he would survive; he had. Throwing them off like flies and downing a tankard of ale to prove he was well!

This sickness knew no bounds. Whatever Halldor might say, this sickness did not care if you were young, old, man or woman, weak or strong and he felt a slither of fear for his own safety and despised himself for it. They had to know where it had begun, and soon, or who knew how many it would take? Astrid's face lingered in his memory and he said a silent prayer to anyone who might be listening.

Arriving at the gathering, he nodded to men he knew by sight from other villages. In all, there were perhaps five hundred men and women. Some had brought their children; all were armed with small swords, daggers and shields.

Halldor stood in the centre greeting two chiefs who had come from the other side of the hill. Both had their own men standing nearby but they kept their distance. Polite niceties and honours were shown, but an unspoken agreement was understood; keep your distance, or else.

Men, armed and watchful, stood around the perimeter of the clearing, keeping an eye out for any Saxons who might want a fight. They looked fairly relaxed, and to the average man nothing looked amiss; but he noticed how they watched the men from his village. Their body language was subtle; it would not do to kill them before any ruling had been decided, but they would protect their own from this disease.

Halldor had already warned them not to mix with the other villagers until they had talked. Ingimund would not tolerate a village being obliterated unless completely necessary; it would not help his battle strategies by half his army being murdered before they could spread disease. So the quicker they found the cause of this blight on his village, the better for everyone.

He was on a slight rise from where he could see everybody. Fires were being lit and many moved towards them. His men built their own and sat down around it. They had brought provisions for the short journey and shared them amongst themselves; their party looked solemn compared to the others he could see.

Women began preparing food while they waited for more people to arrive. Einaar had seen this many times, of course. A large 'Thing' was held three times a year and could be requested for any other important event. They had held a small gathering only the other week to discuss trading further afield and there had been whispers of the coming raid on Castra; he wondered if that would still happen?

He hoped not for many reasons. He did not consider himself a coward, he could and would fight and kill if necessary, but it angered him that Ingimund should break his word. He had shown himself to be a man who could not be trusted. Trusted men seemed very few and far between these days. He had hoped his fighting days were over and he could enjoy his life as a farmer now. Fighting had been such a large part of his life since a boy, but, now, he was not so sure. Not his ability, he knew he could still wield a sword and axe, but what of his conscience?

He answered a shout from a farmer he had met twice on previous Things, but he did not speak as the man quickly moved away to the safety of his own fire. Einaar shrugged and walked towards the circle of men of his own village and warmed his hands, glancing quickly at the other men huddled around it. He had fought with some and if, or perhaps when, the battle came, he would no doubt fight amongst them again. Another chieftain arrived and with him came thirty men, armed and ready for a fight. He felt for them; they were warriors, they fought, they died, but how could they fight a sickness?

With his old beliefs, there had been a fear behind it, in that it was better to die in battle and therefore go straight to Valhalla, a place of ale and women and song. It was hard not to stop believing, that in death, there was a place for him where his father waited for him. He had never feared the place, only waited for it. Now, he could not deny that he liked working the earth. Growing his own food and having his own animals, a quieter, simpler life.

In his world, that meant dying from sickness or old age and going to Hel. A place he feared twice over now that he had heard the priest speak of something similar. But if what the priest said was true, then it was a better thing for his soul to live as a farmer and stop fighting and killing and learn to love his neighbours; but for what? A place in Heaven? A place similar to Valhalla. Which should he choose?

Going into battle for Castra seemed unnecessary for him, it was all for Ingimund. What would he get from killing the English? The city was said to be a good stronghold with many riches, but would it bring him a sense of honour or loyalty to his Lord? Would it renew and strengthen the old feelings he'd felt as a youth, all-powerful and dominant?

He shied away from those memories of bloodlust and acts of such savagery, there could not possibly be any honour in them. His heart beat faster as he remembered so vividly those moments before the battles and raids. The adrenalin, the roar of blood in his ears, the shouts, the noise, the screams for mercy, the clash of metal, the dull thuds as his weapon found solid bone and flesh all seemed to melt into one; until the silence.

He had never looked any of the women in the eye; he often wondered why that had been? He had taken his pleasure only once with a slave, drunk and covered in blood and gore. He had raped her without conscience, until the day after, remembering her cries for pity; he never touched another woman in anger again.

He left the other men to do as they would; enslaving some, killing others, but he would take no part in it.

He had a clear recollection of the men he had fought and slaughtered over the years. Some faces he remembered better than others. They had given him a good fight, or they had played a coward, begging for their lives. One man had offered his own twelve-year-old daughter as a slave if he had spared him. He cut off his head and took his daughter into his own household; where she remained until last year when he granted her freedom when she became the wife of Eric, a young warrior, now a farmer, like them all.

He heard a horn and looked up, Halldor had stepped forward, his arms outstretched. He called on the gods to be with them and then called on the other chieftains to step forward and all three stood before the large crowd. "Come forth all who have witnessed this sickness." Einaar stepped forward as did the other men from his own village, but no one moved from the other settlements dotted along the coast.

He heard the low murmurings from the men standing near him and he saw subtle shifting of their positions so that they formed a rough circle, their backs to each other. Only Thorlak stood apart, his axe held firmly in his hands. He glared at anyone, willing them to fight him. Einaar moved closer to his friend, his own axe swung loosely by his side. He could feel his hunting knife that he always kept in his belt and with good reason; it reassured him.

If Halldor was over-ruled by the others, then they could be slaughtered to keep the sickness contained and he felt the stirrings of readiness to do battle as his blood pumped around his body; his hand gripped the axe tighter. His eyes searched the crowd, gauging the feeling and if an attack did come, where it would begin.

Halldor stood motionless, waiting for the other chieftains to make their move; nothing happened. Halldor was considered the strongest of all of them and he had earned his right to rule the village. Besides, he was a close friend to Ingimund. He said nothing, but Einaar knew that Ingimund's failure to attend the Thing had insulted Halldor deeply.

No one moved for what seemed like a long time, but every man was judging the other. Weighing up his options and the other man's ability, but something had to happen soon. It would take but one shout, a slight movement, a noise, to begin carnage. Eventually Halldor nodded towards his own men, he looked proud, his authority had won out, and grunting his satisfaction, he turned to the other chieftains who stood beside him.

They had a long conversation in low voices, though the others still kept a distance. Ale was brought and meat was shared, but not from the same plate. Einaar had no appetite, but drank a horn of ale while keeping an eye on Thorlak, who looked like he would happily kill anyone who looked at him badly. He was quaffing ale as if it were water and did not acknowledge his chief when Halldor turned back to the waiting crowd. "It is decided then. This sickness is a curse on my village and mine alone. I will not allow some pitiful god to take my people. Odin will triumph and we will be strong again. I will find where the sickness has begun and destroy it. In seven days, we will return here, the course of it gone or I shall forfeit my land."

Einaar saw the men around him relax slightly, but they still kept a firm grip on their weapons as they walked away; constantly alert for any sign of betrayal. Einaar noticed many people stepped away from them as they approached, fear of catching the sickness evident on their faces. He was glad of it as it meant they had a better chance of leaving unharmed. On the road back to their village, Halldor called a meeting for tonight, they had to find the source of the sickness ... or else.

Chapter Twenty-One

R obert slowly stirred three teaspoons of sugar into the mug of tea. Helen didn't take sugar, never had as far as he could remember, but he'd heard that it was good for shock; and Helen was most definitely a woman in shock if ever he saw one. She had refused to tell him anything else and after twenty minutes of trying to coax it out of her, he'd given up and gone into the kitchen. He saw two pieces of bread ready to be popped down in the toaster, and the box of eggs sat open on the counter. She had been making herself something to eat. What had stopped her?

He walked quickly back into the lounge and offered her the mug of hot tea; when she didn't acknowledge it, he put it down on the small table. Sitting in the armchair opposite his wife and child, he watched her as inconspicuously as he could over his own mug of strong black coffee. She didn't seem to notice anything. She sat staring into space, as if she was reliving something in her head. Her eyes and nose were red from crying; these were the only colours on her face; she was dead pale. Wisps of hair had escaped her plait, her shirt looked crumpled and he could see stains on her knees, but where had she been crawling around?

He could not begin to know what it must have been like for her, to find that Cherry had gone; how long had she searched? The terror of it made his chest tighten with emotion and he felt a small relief that he had been none the wiser; quickly followed by intense guilt that he hadn't been here yet again when she needed him. He should have been here protecting his family, his child, but from what? Sleepwalking?

Cherry had been acting rather strangely since they moved in and he couldn't blame anyone but himself. His family had always come second to work, which had caused his breakdown, resulting in his need to move back to old familiar surroundings, and he had moved them without asking, he was nothing more than a cruel, insensitive, selfish bastard. Cherry had never given an inkling that she was upset about it, but it was obviously affecting her, and badly, if she was now sleepwalking as well as having screaming fits at nothing.

There was another niggling question going round in his head, that he did not want to dwell on: was this the other man? He'd convinced himself that he'd fight this muscle man for his family, but if it came down to it, did they want him to? In addition, if the answer was no, as he suspected, would he give them up for the sake of Cherry's behaviour?

Then he remembered Helen's exact words, "They took her", she'd said, not *him*; so who were *they*? If he was to believe Helen, someone had come into his home and taken his child … into the garden, which was preposterous. If they were snatching her, why didn't they take her completely away? Was it to frighten Helen? A threat perhaps? Maybe Helen had told this other man it was over and he had taken Cherry?

He shook his head and sipped his coffee; whatever had happened, all the scenarios in his head sounded daft, over the top, incredible. Even the one that kept pushing itself forward, that Helen was telling the truth and *they* had stolen his daughter. He knew he wouldn't want to know who *they* were because his gut told him it would have something to do with his own conversation with Tony this very evening; and that would be the most incredible and terrifying scenario of all.

"Helen? Helen? Come on, you have to talk to me. I have a right to know, don't I?"

At this, she looked up at him, her face full of scorn, "Right!" She spat the word at him in contempt, "Right, what right do you have? You haven't been here with us for years. Damn your right!"

He leant forward regardless, ignoring the venom, "Helen, I know I've messed up, but tonight I couldn't know, could I?" When she didn't answer, he gently nudged the mug, "Look, it's nearly two in the morning, drink some of this and try to rest, you look shattered. If it will make you feel better, I'll stay with Cherry and …"

She was no longer looking at him, but beyond him, at something behind him. The growing look of horror on her face made his skin prickle and his stomach clenched with fear. He'd noticed the room getting cold, but put it down to the early hour and tiredness, but now, the room had a distinct chill, one he had felt before. Every hair on the back of his head sprang to attention, as did his fight reflex.

She moved slowly, her eyes locked on whatever was behind him as she closed an arm protectively around Cherry. He seemed to move in slow motion as he moved his hand forward and closed around his empty mug.

He whirled round and in that second, he lunged the cup in the direction of the lounge door. Cherry jumped slightly and muttered in her sleep before snuggling closer into Helen, who wrapped her arms around her, trying to protect her with her own body.

He quickly looked between them and the doorway, before staring at the black mass that filled it. He could vaguely see the hallway light through it, but it gave no illumination. Suddenly, the mass split in two and he was able to make out two figures; instinct told him it was a man and woman. He heard a groan behind him and knew Helen had seen these before.

He took a step backwards as the two figures moved closer. He wasn't aware of feet, they seemed to glide. They were perhaps twenty feet away and he was finding it difficult to breathe. His mind raced with possibilities of weapons, what would work? A bible. A crucifix. Holy water. They had none.

He had not seen her move, but suddenly Helen was by his side, her hands clenched, legs wide ready to fight, "Come on then you bastards. You're not taking her this time. You are not sneaking up on me from behind now. Fight me! Fight a Mother …"

He stepped closer to her and clenched his own fists, "All right, let's see if you can fight us both. You're dead, we're alive. Come on then, 'cause you're not taking my Charlotte!"

He heard a cry and for a second, he thought Cherry had woken, but just as quickly realised, it was from the woman. The noise seemed to emanate from her like a low howl, which then changed into a wail, and abruptly, they were gone. He could see the kitchen light and the hallway clearly and the room did not have a deathly chill anymore.

He glanced across at Helen, who was breathing hard. Her hands clenched ready for them to come back; but nothing happened. He knew his legs were going to give way from beneath him and quickly sat down. A moment later, Helen did the same and he could see for the same reason. Both of them were shaking quite badly and Helen was quietly crying, with relief or shock, he couldn't tell.

He gingerly reached out and touched her cold fingers, she quickly met his gaze before looking away at Cherry who now lay curled up onto her knees, her hands hidden beneath her stomach, her small, round buttocks pointing to the sky; she looked peaceful and angelic. Robert swallowed hard the rising emotion and bit his lower lip. Looking down, he also noticed that she hadn't moved her hand away. "I … believe you and I'm sorry I wasn't here to protect you before."

Helen nodded and wiped her face with the back of her other hand. "So, what are we going to do now?"

Robert shrugged, "I don't know. The most obvious thing right now, is to move, but where to and for how long …" His voice trailed off.

"Move?" She looked down at their sleeping daughter, "I'd move right now, this very second, but …" She frowned, "I have a terrible suspicion that they will find us anywhere."

"How do you know that?"

Helen sighed loudly, "I … felt their pain and their sorrow. They want their child … and I don't think anything is going to stop them. You heard that cry. That is every mother's nightmare. I felt that pain when I couldn't find Charlotte; my heart broke. I heard the same thing in that woman. Dead, or alive, it doesn't matter, her heart, her soul, is breaking for her child."

***

Kathryn was in the office early. Trevor came in a few minutes later startling her as she was sipping a cup of coffee. He declined her offer of fetching him a cup and she sat down and waited for the reason for his visit. She guessed that it would have something to do with her dig. Trevor grinned at her, seeing her expression of defiance, ready to argue with him.

"Okay, no lectures, I can see for myself that your argument was right, it seems to be working out for you." He indicated a box nearby which held shards of pottery, "I've looked at some of your finds, they do indicate a possible settlement. Are you thinking along the same lines?"

Kathryn nodded, "I am. At first, I can't really explain why I just knew it was a good site for archaeology, but now I am convinced it is. Have you seen the brooch?"

"Yes, it was being cleaned when I saw it, but it is a perfectly preserved specimen, I don't think I've ever seen one so good. Except for the small dent, it's unblemished."

Kathryn swallowed. She suddenly felt hot and wiped her hair out of her eyes, "Yes, the dent. What could have caused that do you think?"

Trevor grinned, "I am honoured that you believe me to be such a good archaeologist that I can say what has caused dints and breakages! How the hell should I know, Kathryn! It could have been the weight of the soil, it could have been dented when the wearer was using it, there's no real way of knowing … Why?"

Kathryn flapped her hand, "Oh, I don't know, it's nothing really; you know how I like to know everything …"

Trevor watched her carefully for a moment before easing his chair towards the door, "All right then, keep me up to date as I have to have a meeting with Merton later. I have to explain to him what finds we have found to try to keep him, how shall I say … compliant with our dig. If I can persuade him that we, I mean you, are finding worthwhile archaeology, then he might back off with his constant letters."

"Letters?" Kathryn smiled, "Is he still that bad!"

Trevor returned the smile, "You should see the stack of complaints and the petition which thirteen people signed! His gang of pensioners no doubt. I left his latest letter on your desk yesterday." He rummaged around under some new mail. "Here it is, got some pictures too. I'll leave it here for you to look at. He talks about you digging where you shouldn't, moving the goal posts and so on and so on. So, please make sure you stay a good girl and dig where they authorised!"

Kathryn opened her mouth to protest when she saw him smirking, "Am I ever anything else Trevor?"

"I'm not answering that one, just be aware of his latest whinge. Well, I promised I would keep them updated and that I would talk to you. I have, so now I'll pass on my findings and who knows, they might relent and save a couple of trees in paper!"

He was just manoeuvring himself out of the door when Kathryn called after him, "Trevor ..."

"Yes?"

"Do you think ... I mean, is this Mr Merton dangerous in any way?"

"Dangerous? How? He's a sixty something with nothing better to do." He thought for a moment, "He's lived in the area all of his sad little life, which means he must know the area well. Have you considered that he may have already known there was a settlement and that is his reason for not wanting you to dig? Perhaps he had his own agenda for the area. Who knows, I certainly can't fathom the man. But dangerous? I can't see how, unless you mean is he a dangerous influence, is that it?"

Kathryn bit her lower lip as she tried to think what to say; but at that moment, Tony wandered in. "Good morning campers, in early? Trevor, how's things?"

"Oh, you know ... pretty good, you'll get your students. I believe there are seven slaves for you and we've checked out another three volunteers, so I guess you'll have a few to boss around, eh Kathryn?"

"Erm ... yeah, I guess so ..." She tried to smile back and reached for her coffee to hide her face, as she knew she wasn't very good at hiding how she felt, and at that moment, she could have screamed with frustration. She had been so close to talking about the pool of blood, it had felt right to divulge this horrible find to Trevor somehow, but she still wasn't sure whether or not to tell Tony. Trevor would be bad enough, but telling Tony what a stupid thing she'd done was more than she could bear right now.

She attempted another reassuring smile at Trevor who was watching her closely. "Right, well, it's a good day, we should get going and prepare for our enthusiastic students." Grabbing her coat, she left her coffee and walked out of the office.

Trevor quickly followed her, "If there's something you want to tell me Kathryn, I'm here, I'll back you, especially if it's about Merton."

"It's nothing really. I just like to know my enemies, you know?"

Tony caught them up, "Are we ready then, I'm excited about what we'll find today, are you?"

135

Kathryn grinned, "Yes, as always." Walking away, she turned back to Trevor who was watching them go, "I'll talk to you again."

Trevor sat unmoving until he couldn't hear Tony's loud voice anymore. Going back into their office, he casually picked up various objects from the site. Most of it was down in the labs, but he picked up a large piece of pottery and looked closely; it had various rune markings from the Elder Futhark.

He peered through his magnifying glass; that was definitely an E and an I, some was missing, but he was sure there was an R and an A. What was intriguing was that Vikings didn't decorate their pottery, or, at least, the farmers, the average villagers wouldn't have bothered. So why were these? It had some significance, he could feel it.

Replacing the pottery, he looked around Kathryn's office. What had made her ask about Merton? She'd looked uncomfortable about it, whatever it was. Had he threatened her? He didn't think that was his style, but he'd learned that people never behaved how you expected them to when they were enthusiastic about something. With one last look, he closed the door behind him and headed back to his own office. He would find out one way or the other and if Merton were responsible for any bad behaviour, he would have him locked up, regardless of his age.

Chapter Twenty-Two

They barely moved away from the lounge and if they did, they moved as one. At one point in the early hours of the morning, he noticed Helen's fidgeting and guessed its meaning, knowing he needed to use the bathroom too. He voiced his own need and was rewarded with a sincere look of gratitude, with the hint of a smile; the first positive look he'd had from his wife for such a long time, he almost wept.

He bent down to pick up Cherry and noticed her hesitation; he tried to smile reassuringly, aware of how hard it must be for her to relinquish her baby after almost losing her; especially to a man who didn't deserve a chance.

He gently carried Cherry to the top of the stairs and sat with her on his knee. She murmured and twitched, but didn't wake as he wrapped the blanket tight around her; poor darling was exhausted. He watched Helen cautiously walk into the bathroom. All the while, listening, but nothing happened. He heard her rinse her mouth with mouthwash and wash her face, before they swapped over. Once he was feeling refreshed, he ran into Cherry's bedroom and brought down her duvet. Taking her back into the lounge, they wrapped her up warm and snug and used the blanket to keep themselves warm.

Then they had sat together on the couch; their feet up on the coffee table, Charlotte curled up between them, protected by their very presence. At least, as protected as she could be against ghosts. They remained silent, each on full alert, waiting to see what would happen next.

Robert's head felt like it was going to explode. His mind raced as it went over and over the events of the last few days. Those loud bangs, the shadow, the brooch, Tony's dig, their conversation, the cat's reaction. That felt important somehow but he could not think why? It hadn't acted scared in any way, only curious perhaps, almost indifferent; as it behaved with him.

They were evil, surely? No, that wasn't a question, they were evil; they took his little girl. Good spirits did not do that, did they? Oh, what the hell did he know anyway? This wasn't an episode of Casper the friendly ghost; this was poltergeist from hell! He glanced at the television in the far corner of the room and made a mental note to keep it switched off, for now.

He quickly peeked at Helen; she hadn't moved, except one hand was softly stroking Cherry's cheek; he felt a pang of jealously and despised himself for it. They had barely touched since his break down and if he was completely honest with himself, barely before that. Work and money had always come first, that was what had excited him, then. Since the confrontation with *it*, they had held hands for a moment, and he longed to touch her again.

They were still sitting together unmoving when hours later Cherry woke demanding the toilet and breakfast. He could see how Helen fought to stay awake and insisted she lie on the couch. She'd finally given in, insisting though that Cherry remain sitting on the couch once she'd relieved herself. He silently watched her for a while as Cherry curled up on his knee, her doll clutched to her chest, the remnants of sleep lingering a little longer. She did not seem in any way traumatised by last night's events. She sat sleepily, giggling now and then at the cartoons on the television which he'd put on reluctantly, the volume low.

"What's wrong with Mummy?" Cherry whispered into his ear, her lips tickled. He said a silent prayer that the abduction hadn't been successful and choked back his emotion on what could have happened to his baby.

"Mummy couldn't sleep last night ... bad dreams. Did you have any bad dreams, Cherry?" He asked the question as lightly as possible, but she didn't act differently.

"No, I had a dream about fairies and policemen and ... I can't remember. Did you have nice dreams, Daddy?"

He felt his heart miss a beat when she mentioned police, but she had turned back to the television, it was obvious that she hadn't associated last night's police with a real event. "Yes darling, Daddy had a lovely dream, I got a lovely cuddle from my beautiful girl and here she is; it's come true!"

Cherry giggled and snuggled closer into his chest, "Silly Daddy. Can I have some Rice Nice for brekkie, Daddy?"

"Okay: you stay here all snuggled with Mummy, I won't be long ..." As he stood up, it occurred to him that he would be out of their sight for a few minutes and panic overwhelmed him. He didn't want to wake Helen, yet he couldn't leave Cherry unprotected. He stood unsure, torn as to what to do, he looked down and saw Cherry looking up at him strangely, "Right, I'm going. You'll stay here ... with Mummy OK?"

"Daddy ..."

She sounded unsure; he quickly came back and knelt beside her. "What is it, baby?"

"It is diff-er-ent, isn't it?"

He swallowed hard. Her eyes stared into his, innocent, questioning; did she know something? "Different?"

She nodded slowly, "Yes, house is, diff-er-ent, isn't it …?"

He opened his mouth to answer, but quickly closed it again, what could he say? *Yes, it is, it has two ghosts who stole you! Two ghosts who hurt Mummy. Two ghosts that don't fuckin' exist.* The sentences screamed in his head, but he managed a weak smile, "Yes, I suppose this house is, different. That's a big word …" He waited to see if she would elaborate, but instead, she thought for a moment, shrugged and turned back to a new cartoon.

He slowly rose and walked into the kitchen. He rushed around getting what she had asked for; his need to get back into the lounge was overwhelming. He listened to the sounds from the television and checked the lounge twice while the kettle boiled. He made juice, her cereal and two cups of coffee and almost ran back with the full tray.

He felt his chest lighten when he saw all was well. He quickly glanced around the room, but he knew there was no real need except to satisfy his own fear. The room felt warm and homely. Cherry lay on her stomach, her head in her hands watching some cartoon he could barely hear. Helen, lay curled on the couch, her head resting on her arm, the blanket had slipped onto the floor and she stirred as he came in and put the heavy tray onto the coffee table. He busied himself pouring Cherry her cereal and milk and sat back with his cup of strong coffee. He glanced back and forth between his women. His two beautiful ladies; how could he ever have put them second? He pretended to sip his drink to hide a tear; he never would again.

***

Tony noticed Kathryn was quiet on the drive to the site and he wasn't blind either when they arrived; she became tense as they neared the place and made a terrible mess of trying to hide it. He'd always thought she was just overly excited, but now he was beginning to think she'd never been happy at the dig and had always made some excuse never to be alone there.

He bit the inside of his cheek as he contemplated the past few weeks, with geophysics, the council, the museum. She'd never stood on the site alone as far as he knew; which for Kathryn, was very odd. For all the years he'd known her, she'd turn up early just to stand amongst the trenches, the heaps of mud, the grass turves, the stones and 'feel' the place and ask its forgiveness for the disruption, promising to put it right. He knew without asking that that hadn't happened here.

She was nervous, jumpy, glancing up from her work and stopping every so often to listen, but he had no idea to what. The only explanation was that Mr Merton had got to her more than he'd realised. He'd have to get to the bottom of it one way or the other; this wasn't fair on Kathryn. She was one of the most enthusiastic and resilient women he had ever known and he didn't like the idea of someone diminishing that.

He didn't notice the police car until he'd locked up the van and walked towards the site. Kathryn had stopped and was watching the two police officers approaching. Something in her manner made him quicken his step to get to her side, she looked terrified. She didn't ask them any questions, inviting them to follow her into the big tent; he found that odd. It was as if she had been expecting them.

He quickly followed and unlocked the stack of plastic chairs in the corner, offering them to the police; he remained leaning against the long table.

"We've found the body of a young man nearby; a local man. We're asking people in the area if they've seen or heard anything unusual. Perhaps you've seen someone hanging around?"

When Kathryn didn't answer, he cleared his throat and answered the questions. No, he hadn't seen anyone hanging around acting suspiciously. No, besides the gazebo nothing else had been stolen. No, they hadn't heard anything unusual, or seen anything strange.

The questioning went on about their movements; times they arrived on site and left over the last few days. Their details and where they could be contacted. Kathryn joined in where necessary, but she was detached; her behaviour was completely out of character.

She answered their questions as he did, but something wasn't right, he knew her better than that. She visibly paled when they told her about the body of the man and how long they thought he had been dead. Anyone who didn't know her would have thought that quite normal; who wanted to hear about dead bodies? In fact, one of the officers leant forward to ask if she wanted some water; Kathryn refused. Dead bodies, skeletons, sacrifice victims had never bothered her before. Okay, they were usually hundreds or thousands of years old, but still …

Perhaps the nightmares she was having were making her jumpy. Even as he thought it, he didn't really believe that. Nightmares came from anxiety, stress and fear. What did Kathryn have to fear? He watched her closely and hated himself for what he was thinking. He couldn't possibly believe or contemplate that Kathryn knew something about this man's death? Could she? Could he?

***

Einaar grasped Astrid's hand beneath her skirts, he could feel himself getting hot, Astrid noticed and was passing him tankards of watered down ale. Halldor had been speaking for a long time until finally he moved to sit down and allowed the others to argue their points. Since that morning, three more had gone to their beds, Gudrid had died, and four children were not expected to survive the night.

"We are cursed!" The shout was loud enough to silence everyone in the hall. The old woman took her time walking into the Great Hall; she knew she did not have to rush, she had everyone's attention. Halldor allowed her to stay, as he believed she

had the gift of magic and wisdom. Her years walking the earth meant she was closer to death, could only mean that she was closer to the gods, a good combination as long as they were useful. When she spoke, people listened.

"We are doomed to wither and die, because we are torn in two." Rafarta looked around the room, staring at each man and woman's face. She turned her head and spat in the nearest fire, "Our souls have become torn in two and so we allow our bodies to become weak. Weak enough for this plague to take over and our souls be dragged away to an unknown place. Not to Valhalla; but to a place where warriors are never welcomed. We know its name though we dare not speak it ..."

The audible gasp and sobbing from her mesmerised crowd gave her the courage to step further into the room and she began to move around the villagers, looking at each person in turn. The room fell silent as they watched to see what she would do next.

Halldor sat on his chair observing her very closely, the goblet of mead forgotten in his hand. He had to find where this curse had come from and destroy it. His land, his title, even his life depended on it. His own wife lay sick in her bed; she had fallen victim to the illness this very day. His heart was heavy with fear as she was with child. His eldest son sat nearby and next to him his three brothers and a sister. He had arranged for them to be moved to another house tonight. To be cared for by one of his slaves in the hope that they would be safe.

He would kill any man to save his wife and children, but this darkness that crept silently around his people could not be slain unless he found the source. Perhaps if he could find how this sickness came to his people, perhaps then, it could be stopped and his family spared. He leant forward as Rafarta slowly made her journey around the room. If anyone could find the answer, he believed it was she.

Einaar gulped down his ale. It seemed to stick in his throat as Rafarta came closer and closer. He knew she was coming to him. He knew it without any doubt and he wondered how he was going to get Astrid out alive to reach Inga, whom they had left sleeping in her bed. The fever had gone, but it had made her tired, so she slept most of the time. Astrid had been appalled to contemplate leaving their child, but Halldor's orders were clear, everyone, who was without sickness must attend the meeting. The slave girl Bridgette had been warned to remain to watch over her.

He felt for his knife; it would not be a decent weapon against his people if they turned on them, which he was expecting. Their loved ones had died, many were sick. He looked around at their faces and saw despair, they needed something to fight, to blame. Inga had been the first to be sick. She would be blamed and he knew her fate.

Astrid covered her mouth to stifle her moan as she realised the danger their child was in. Einaar clasped her other hand tightly then abruptly let go as Rafarta stopped before him. She quietly looked him up and down before turning her attention to Astrid who was hugging herself; she did not look up. She was with child, she had told him the great news only hours before. The very thought of losing any of his children turned his stomach to ice. He gripped the small knife, willing her to speak or move on.

Rafarta continued to stare at him. He stared back, knowing the longer she stayed, the more the villagers would become suspicious and they would come to the right conclusion, but he couldn't form any words. He could not think what to say that would make the old crone move on without causing attention. The longer she stood before them, the worse it would be. She was reading him. He could almost feel her claw-like fingers searching his head, reading his thoughts; suddenly, Rafarta moved on.

She slowly made her way back to the doorway and bowed to Halldor, "My Lord Halldor, sickness is everywhere, in everybody that I see. Be it in their body or their mind, it is a sickness that cannot be stopped. Some will live and some will die. Stay in your village Halldor, do not venture far from your door, your need will be great before the sun's rays warm our soil. This curse has run its course. It has infected every soul ... I bid thee farewell my lord, for my body is weak ..." Her eyes met Einaar's, "And I will be dead before the waning moon rises".

There was complete silence as the old woman shuffled out into the dark. For a moment, no one said anything as all eyes rested on the empty doorway. Finally, Halldor called the gathering to end and people fled, grateful to be able to leave and go back to their own hearths behind closed doors.

Einaar pulled Astrid to her feet; her legs gave way beneath her and he had to hold her up as they quickly made their way to the door, when Thorlak barred the way. His hair was matted, his face dirty and lined with grief and his clothes stunk of filth, vomit and earth; a jug of ale hung loosely in one hand. "What did she mean, Einaar? What do you believe her words meant? Was my son torn in two? Am I weak?"

He could barely stand and his speech was slurred. His eyes were bloodshot from lack of sleep and weeping. Einaar reached out to him, but Thorlak slapped his hand away and drank from the jug while staggering backwards. He righted himself just in time before he fell over, and stared at Einaar.

Einaar firmly pushed Astrid outside where she turned, unsure what to do. "Go, check on Inga ..." He knew they were the wrong words to say as Thorlak's face crumpled for an instant as large tears fell down his cheeks but just as quickly, he turned and with a roar, he pulled out the small axe he held in his belt and swung it with a yell of despair and let it fly. It missed Einaar by an inch and embedded into the wooden door.

"Your child!" he roared, "Your child is safe and well, while mine lies cold and alone in the dark, lost to me forever!" He spat the words out, "Gone. Forever. While your girl child sleeps and dreams mine is ... Where is mine?" He took a step towards Einaar, his fury barely contained, "Where is my son?"

Einaar pushed Astrid away and watched her run towards their home before turning back to his friend. He swallowed hard and took a deep breath; he wasn't sure what his friend was thinking. Did he suspect Inga had been the first to be sick or was this purely grief for his son?

The only thing he knew for sure was that Rafarta saw and understood what it meant for Inga; in everyone's eyes, that meant she was responsible, the cause of all this death. She had said nothing, knowing she would be among the dead perhaps, but she had given him time. Time to leave; to escape the villagers who would kill Inga and anyone who got in their way: but first he had to get past Thorlak.

"Thorlak ... friend. Let us walk back to your house. Your wife ... "

"My wife needs me. Is that what you were going to say?" Thorlak staggered slightly as he moved to the nearest table and finished the half-empty jug of ale. He abruptly wiped his mouth and sneered, "My wife does not want me ... she wants her son." Tears came again, he let the empty jug fall to the floor, "Our son, she doesn't want me ... or anyone. She wants to die now to be with Ranulf so that he is not alone in Hel. And I ... "

He stared at Einaar with such hatred, breathing hard, his hand went to his dagger in his belt, "I want to know the truth of it. Rafarta knew the truth ... I saw it on her face. She knew that you, my own friend, are the cause of all this death. Where is Inga? No one has seen her. Is she sick, Einaar? Is that pixie child of yours sick? You listened to that priest ... you and Astrid. I saw her praying when she thought she was alone, I saw and said nothing. You are my oldest friend. I thought you would forget such nonsense once he was dead, but you haven't, have you?"

Einaar raised his hands, "Thorlak, please, you don't know what you are saying. Go home, rest and we will talk in the morning ... " He was aware of a few people drifting in and out the opposite end of the Great Hall and Halldor had not moved from his seat. He was watching the confrontation very carefully and it was making Einaar very nervous.

He barely saw the move. As drunk as Thorlak was, he was still quick, but his aim was off by a foot as the knife swung across open air. Einaar flinched backwards, "Thorlak ... Stop this. Remember, I am your friend ... "

"No friend of mine would kill my son," Thorlak roared as he made another attempt with his dagger, barely missing Einaar's shoulder.

Einaar gripped his own knife and crouched ready to fight, but a shout from Halldor brought men from outside who surrounded Thorlak to remove him from the hall. Thorlak was big and muscular and fought hard, but eventually it took six men to subdue him enough to be half led, half carried outside where Einaar heard a loud thump and knew they had hit him, hopefully hard enough to let him sleep until morning.

He was about to check he was all right, when a large hand on his shoulder stopped him. He turned, knife at the ready expecting to fight, but was alarmed to turn and face his chief; he lowered his arm. "My Lord ...?"

"Say nothing, Einaar."

The order was kindly said, but an order none the less. Halldor walked away to the far table in the hall and picked up a full goblet of mead left behind in the haste to leave. "Where is your daughter, I have not seen her these past few days?"

"She is asleep in her bed. Astrid did not want to wake her for the gathering." He tried to keep his voice steady.

"I see." Halldor quickly glanced around the hall. There were people watching and he turned his back on them, he spoke quietly, "I believe Thorlak is right, no one has seen Inga; is she ill, Einaar?"

"No ... My Lord, she is well."

Halldor watched him carefully and nodded, "I see, she is well ... now. She was the first, wasn't she?"

"My Lord ... I ... no, she ..." Einaar hung his head, "But, she is not the cause of all this. I beg you, do not ... I will fight for her ... I would die for her ..."

Halldor watched him for a long time before he nodded, "I would expect nothing less from you, old friend, but I agree, the child is not to blame for this, you are. You heard what Rafarta said, torn souls; you cannot worship two Gods, but you listened, didn't you Einaar. You listened and I know you prayed to this God and it has angered ours. Perhaps it is my fault for not stopping this sooner, but out of respect for years of fighting side by side, I did not. I hoped you would see how false this Christian God is." He sighed loudly and drank some mead. "This is my punishment; my own wife is sick and carries our unborn child ..."

He drained the goblet in four swallows and gasped, wiping his mouth with the back of his hand. "You let a sick child live? Inga has been a strange and weak child since her birth. Many believed she came from the fairies as her behaviour was always inward, one with nature, never with people and that saved her. I would not anger the gods for giving us the child, I hoped she was a gift and would bring luck to our village; she is not, she has not, therefore, she must die; send her back to the gods and hope it pleases them."

Seeing Einaar shake his head, he slammed down the goblet, his eyes never leaving Einaar's face, "Who do you love and serve, Einaar?"

Einaar felt his stomach clench with fear, "I serve Odin, I serve Frigga and Freya, I beg for their help every day. I believed we were blessed also and I acknowledged my child on the day of her birth and Astrid suckled her from her breast; that is our way. I have followed our laws, I will not turn my back on my child now, My Lord ..."

Halldor stepped back and surveyed him, "Then, you will ask for their mercy. Tomorrow, at dawn, I will come for the child. If you wish to do Odin's bidding, then so be it. It is right that a father should do his duty to spare his child any pain and suffering, though, under my hand I swear it would be quick also."

Einaar stared at him, fear clenched his stomach and he could smell his own sweat, his mind raced with options, anything to save his family, "My Lord, she is a girl. What shame is there to harm a female? My wife, she is with child, how can I ...? Is it not dishonourable to touch her wickedly? for she will fight to save Inga and rightly so. To kill without surety of their blame ...? It is wrong and you know it ..."

Halldor let his head fall forward and stared at the ground for a moment before inhaling deeply, "Yes, Einaar, your words ring true; to harm any woman other than a slave is dishonourable." He reached out and gripped Einaar's shoulder, "But, hear me Einaar and hear me well, I give you this chance to serve a father's justice in honour of battles done. But do not take me for a fool, I will serve justice on you all, man or woman or child, to cleanse my people of this curse. I have given my word to the council. If you betray me and our gods, I swear my vengeance will be great. This is my ruling; you will obey me ... or die."

Chapter Twenty-Three

It had been over an hour since the police had driven away. Tony hadn't had a chance to talk with Kathryn as she'd fled to her trench the second they'd left. He'd been about to go after her, when a bunch of students turned up and he'd spent the time filling them in about the site. He had now set them to various tasks. Kathryn had stopped digging for a few minutes to introduce herself and set out what she expected from them, before disappearing back to her trench, taking two students with her.

He'd watched the students and the volunteers disappear to various parts of the site; but now he stood watching the back of Kathryn's head as she bent to her work. If he was completely honest, he was too scared to talk to her. He didn't like the myriad of thoughts running through his head. He caught the eye of a student called Carolyn, nice girl, she smiled and he smiled back. Grabbing his spade, he tried to pull himself together; he had a new trench to dig. He glanced across at Kathryn's trench; he let it go, for now.

It hadn't been too long before he began to find shards of pottery. The student's genuine exclamations helped his mood slightly; it was refreshing to hear genuine excitement at a find. He didn't feel anything until he found a lovely jet bead. He sat on the edge of the trench and held it in the palm of his hand. Looking down to where he'd found it, he smiled when he saw another exactly the same. Placing them in a finds bag, he sat down again and wiped his brow; it was getting warmer. He looked at the box almost full of shards of pottery and the bag containing the jet beads; he should have been feeling elated, but he wasn't.

The police officer had been quite open about what they had found and it sounded like something from a zombie film. The animals had had quite a banquet off the corpse after he'd been skewered by something very sharp and long that had gone right through him. "A long dagger, a knife, a sword or a spear perhaps? Soil was found in the wound, we'll take some samples from the area if you don't mind ... see if we can narrow it down."

"Yes, of course officer, take what you need, just be careful where you stand ..."

"I don't suppose you've found anything like that?"

"What, a spear? A dagger? A sword? We should be so lucky. No, only pottery and other household items; they're all logged at the museum if you need an inventory?"

Tony swallowed hard and fought the nausea that threatened to take over. The body had been found in the woods nearby; it was not a comforting thought. He carefully picked up bits of pottery and a piece of bone that had been whittled into a very thin, sharp point for using as a needle most likely, though it was missing the end. He was trying to keep his mind occupied because a dark cloud hung over the site now and it annoyed him. He should be feeling some sympathy towards the victim, but all he could think was, what next? What else could happen to make the experience less fun?

Standing up, he stretched his back and glanced over to Kathryn's trench. She was kneeling with her back to him, and from the way she was going at it, he thought she was taking out her own emotions on the soil. At this rate, any finds would be ripped to shreds; he'd better talk to her now before they lost any good finds.

He was about to move when he noticed a man standing just within the tree line. He was barely twenty feet away, but he couldn't quite focus on him. His instincts told him it was a man, but there was something odd about him that he could not quite place. What caught his attention was the way he was watching Kathryn. His curiosity was evident, yet, he was watching her with such a sad look on his face, almost wistful. Tony moved slowly so as not to get his attention.

He would swear he never turned away, but the man had gone. One second he was standing in full sight, the next, he was not there. Tony rubbed his eyes and walked quickly towards the trees, but nothing, no man, no footprints in the mud, nothing. He turned towards Kathryn who was now kneeling up and watching him closely. Their eyes locked and he saw that she had seen him too and in seconds, he was by her side, holding her hand tightly as he led her to the big tent.

"Are you sure it was a ghost?" Tony poured them both strong coffees from his flask and wished he had some whisky to add to it.

"Well, you saw him, did you look away?

"No. One minute he was there, watching, then … Jesus!"

They were sitting amongst the bags of finds, which they had dug over the last hour. Pieces of bone, broken bits of horn, an iron needle and a small antler that looked like it had been made into a toggle for a cloak perhaps or a tunic, as well as more bits of pottery and the two jet beads.

They looked at the finds and shook their heads. Both fell into silence as they tried to find the words. Everything before them was tenth century; the time of the Vikings settling on the Wirral. It couldn't be argued anymore, they had a settlement here. How large a settlement was yet to be seen, but the finds did not lie; and neither did their eyes.

"Maybe, just maybe, it was a figment of our imagination. I mean, look." Tony waved his hand around the tent, "We are surrounded by Norse findings and it is fairly obvious now that this was a settlement of some kind. What if we somehow want to believe it so badly, we created this figure from our unconsciousness to bring life to the site?"

"What, both of us at the same time?"

"Well, yeah, why not? Stranger things have happened, I mean, Christ, everyone is seeing ghosts these days. What if I somehow projected a Viking thought? They say that people can do this type of thing, especially after some kind of ordeal. Those walkers finding that body so close can be classed as an ordeal, I mean, I don't know about you, but I'm spooked ..."

Kathryn remained quiet. Taking the mug of steaming black coffee, she inhaled, closing her eyes for a second, enjoying the smell. It was real and it smelt of comfortable things, good old ground coffee. She opened her eyes to find Tony waiting for her to speak. She took a deep breath and let it out slowly, she was so scared she was shaking; where was she supposed to begin? "Tony ... something happened to me a few days ago ... here, at the site. I mean, if I'm honest, it's been happening long before we started digging ..."

"You're not making any sense Kathryn, what happened to you?"

"Yes, sorry. I've been trying to make sense of it all myself, and I'm still confused even after all of these years ..."

She saw Tony's confusion and stopped, "Yeah, sorry, I'm not sure where to start; I'm jumping ahead ... but I will begin with when I came here early, the other day, to, well, it doesn't matter why, only that I was here, alone and I found ... something, next to the first trench." She swallowed hard and took a steadying breath, "Blood. Quite a lot of it. I had it checked and it was human. I think it might have been this man's blood. I think he was killed here and for whatever reason, he was moved."

Tony stared open-mouthed before shaking himself slightly, "Fuckin' hell Kathryn, you have to tell the police."

"I can't! Don't you see, if the police get involved, they will tear this site apart and any evidence will be destroyed? God knows what will happen to me for withholding evidence. I fought tooth and nail to get this chance; I will not have it taken from me. It's too important." She stood abruptly and began pacing, "Tony, we have an important site here, its story has to be told. I ... think that is why he is watching me, watching us, to make sure it is told."

"I don't know what to say. Let me think a moment ..." Tony clung to his mug. He needed the warmth as he felt chilled to the bone. She was right of course; the police would probably tear the site to shreds looking for evidence, and for what? This guy sounded like a real loser, drugs, suspected robbery, put an old lady in hospital after mugging her; would anyone miss him? "Who tested the blood for you? Was it that Simon prick?"

Seeing Kathryn nod, he shook his head, "That slimy git will tell someone sooner or later, Kathryn; if you don't, it might look, well, you know ..."

"Do you think I could have killed a man, Tony?"

He barely heard the question as she spoke so quietly. He stared at her for a moment before he shook his head, "No, but, I have to be honest, it fleetingly crossed my mind but only because you were behaving so weird around that policeman, but no, you aren't capable of killing, you're only capable of covering it up."

She flinched at his sarcastic tone, but said nothing; she was waiting for him to continue. He walked away from her, needing a second as he fought to control his emotions.

"As for that ... whatever we saw, be it a ghost or a figment of our troubled minds, I don't have an answer. What is it with people and ghosts lately anyway? I had Robert telling me last night that he thought his home was haunted and I ..."

"What!" Kathryn moved towards him, "Robert, that friend of yours who came yesterday with that screaming kid? Didn't you say he'd moved back here?"

He swallowed hard and scratched his head, "Now hang on, you don't think he has anything to do with all this, do you? He's a good man, or at least, he used to be."

Kathryn slowly sank into the nearest chair, "I don't know, but it is a bit of a coincidence don't you think? He moves in, someone is murdered, most likely on this site and we start to see ghosts and he says he is experiencing stuff?"

Tony shrugged, "Yeah, I see what you mean, but Robert isn't involved, I'm sure, besides, he has his own problems. Marriage problems." He quickly added seeing her curious look, "But, if I'm to take on board that we are all seeing ghosts from this settlement, why Robert? He isn't involved with this dig and he lives, what, about half a mile away? Ghosts don't travel, do they?"

They were quiet for a while, each contemplating the questions and possible answers. Tony spoke first. "You said it started before we began digging, what did you mean?"

Kathryn drained her coffee and set down the mug purposefully, she kept her eyes fixed on his as she took a deep breath, "I mean that I am more convinced than ever that I was meant to find this village. I believe that I once lived here, in a past life." She held up her hand to stop him, "Over the years I have had terrible dreams, nightmares really, of a place, of people that feel so real. Since last year, they have become much worse, much more real and much more frightening. I remember everything and everyone I have seen in my dreams, and now ... I have seen him here, in the flesh so to speak and now so have you. I recognise him, from my dreams, from my past."

Tony shivered, he felt goose bumps up his spine and the hairs on his arms tingled. He clung to the last remnants of warmth from his coffee. "If you say you know him, give me a name?"

149

Kathryn stood up and walked to the tent's opening; she looked out at the site and said a silent prayer that the students were out there; they weren't alone. She didn't turn back to him, but stood still, looking at the site, but for a fleeting moment, she saw it as it had always been in her dreams. Her heart pounded in her chest, "Einaar. His name is Einaar."

***

Robert sat on the toilet seat and tried to keep his eyes on the bathroom door. He'd already showered while Helen kept watch from the hallway; he had refused to leave the room. Cherry sat on the floor wrapped in a large towel, playing with her doll. He was trying to listen just in case, but every pore in his body was fighting the urge to watch his wife. It had been a long time since he had felt aroused, *damned fine time to feel it now*, he thought; and quickly stood up and vigorously brushed his teeth.

Helen turned off the water and hid herself behind her own large towel before stepping out of the shower. She smiled down at Cherry before sitting on the vacant toilet seat and drying herself, which was difficult considering the confined space and her attempts to hide her nakedness. She was all too aware of his presence, his side-glances, and it tore her in two.

One part of her desired him and was only too aware of how her own body was responding and hated herself for it after all that had happened, while the other shied away, needing to keep a distance, and felt disgusted that she should feel anything after last night's nightmare. She tried to believe it was because of the situation, the adrenalin rush of fear, anger and frustration, but was it?

"Cherry, are you dry sweetie?"

"Yep, and Inga is too." She stood up and showed Helen that her doll's hair was indeed quite dry.

"Good girl, now, go with Daddy and get dressed, as quickly as you can, okay?"

Cherry frowned, "Why?"

Helen glanced up at Robert who was waiting by the open door, "Because, we are going on a little trip, will that be nice?"

Cherry flung off her towel and dashed past Robert before he could grab her, "NO! NO! NO! I don't want to go on a trip!" She dodged past him and ran into her room.

Robert and Helen quickly followed and found her under the bedcovers. "Come on baby girl, it will be a nice trip, just for a few days ..." Helen looked across at Robert for confirmation of this, but he shrugged.

Cherry flung back the duvet so her face was showing. "Why? I like it here, why can't I stay? You go!" She hid her face again beneath the duvet and continued to shout, "NO! NO! I won't go!"

Helen sighed loudly and sat back on her heels, "Well? What the hell do we do now? We can't stay here ... Robert, where are we going to go?"

"How the hell should I know?" He was irritated by Cherry's behaviour and that made him feel angry with himself. How could he be anything but joyful that she was still here? Everything just seemed so unreal. Last night felt like it had happened to someone else. He knew it was probably down to tiredness, but still, his family needed him, perhaps, wanted him and he damned well could not let them down now.

He rubbed his hands through his hair trying to think, "Sorry, I'm tired ..." Changing the subject, he quickly looked around the room, "Are they always here? I mean," He quickly added seeing Helen's reaction, "Have you seen them during the day, before yesterday?"

Seeing her nod slowly, he quickly rubbed his neck. Helen reached out and gently stroked the outline of Cherry's head. She had become quiet. "Cherry sees them all the time." She mouthed.

"Okay, so, we need to leave. Pack a few things while I stay here with Cherry. You'll be all right?"

Helen raised her eyebrows, "I suppose so." Turning to the unmoving duvet, she bent down and tickled it; the duvet giggled, "As for you, young lady, get dressed while Mummy does the same and then you can help me pack a bag." Silence. She shrugged and quickly turned away to her own room.

Robert watched her go, he didn't like the idea of not seeing her to check if she was safe, but he had to stay with his daughter. She seemed to be the one they were after for whatever reason. She was the one he had to protect, and would do with his life.

He sighed and quickly rubbed his eyes, the hot shower had only made him sleepy. He abruptly moved to the small wardrobe and chose some denim dungarees, an orange tie-dyed long-sleeved top and underwear for Cherry.

None of it felt real. If someone could say to him, it had all been a terrible hallucination, then he would gladly believe it; but it hadn't. Cherry's disappearance had been all too real, at least for Helen, he quickly corrected himself; he hadn't been here, as usual. Whatever had happened, he couldn't let that happen again, regardless of what he wanted to continue believing.

Ghosts! Evil spirits who kidnapped small children; it was like a Grimm fairy story. It was a joke. A terrifying, gut-wrenching joke; and who would believe them? The police? He couldn't contemplate what might have happened if the policeman hadn't found Cherry in the garden. What would Helen have told them? *A ghost took her.* Social services and the local loony bin would have been called. They would be locked away and labelled 'mad child killing parents' and doped with drugs until they confessed.

Who would ever believe that some Vikings had taken her? He froze: Viking. What was it that made him think that? All that he'd been able to make out was darkness. Two distinct shapes in a mass of pure blackness, yet when he'd thought 'Viking' he'd known without doubt that he was right; why? Tony would know something about it all, even though he denied it last night. He was digging up some village from that time. Had he dug up some pissed-off corpse and he hadn't told him?

Pulling a giggling Cherry out from under her duvet, he quickly dressed her. Helen came rushing in just as he was finishing.

"Everything O.K. baby?" She knelt down in front of Cherry.

Cherry shook her head quickly, "Nope. Inga not happy." She held up her doll, "Inga not happy at all, she wants me to stay."

"Well, Inga will have to get used to it, won't she." Robert picked her up and held her tightly as they moved quickly into the main bedroom. Helen was behind him carrying some of Cherry's clothes; she was trying to ignore the feeling of being watched and the terrible fear that crept into her stomach. The sooner they left, the safer her baby would be.

***

Einaar gently pushed Astrid ahead of him. The dawn was not far off and he was not nearly as far as he had hoped to be. Inga had cried silently for a short time, sensing the urgency and tension as Einaar and Astrid quickly got together a few supplies, wrapped her in her sheepskin and quietly left through the opening in the back of their home Einaar had created using his large hunting knife.

She'd watched him, asking only once what he was doing as he carefully cut through the wall, checking all the time for anyone close by. Twice he had stopped and had quickly covered the hole with a basket as people passed close by. He had stood at the doorway, nodding acknowledgment to those passing and returned inside muttering to himself.

He was no fool. He knew Halldor had ordered his men to watch him and his family. What had he told them? Probably not the truth or Inga would be dead by now. He was keeping his word, allowing him to slaughter his child mercifully. How could he even contemplate such an act? Was Halldor so blind to love? Could he truly kill his own child if the gods demanded it?

"Why, Dada?" She was still weak from the fever and could barely do more than raise herself before flopping back onto her bed.

He'd stopped and looked at her briefly before resuming his task, "It is necessary ... Now, let me work."

Astrid gently sang to her until she fell asleep. It had been full dark when Inga had woken as Einaar gently picked her up and carried her wrapped in her bedding to the opening. Astrid was waiting the other side and he carefully passed her through. Astrid had placed her finger over her mouth showing she had to be silent, Inga nodded once, but tears had fallen down her cheeks, she was scared, she sensed her parents were scared and that in itself was terrifying; her father was afraid of nothing.

Einaar stopped a moment to get his bearings. He knew the direction of the sea, but he had gone a long way round to keep away from the other villages. He did not know if Halldor had sent word as to who was to blame, but he could not take that chance. He quickly glanced down at Inga. As if she could be blamed for such a thing. It was no use thinking such things. The decision had been made, Inga and now his wife would die alongside himself if they were caught. They had to keep moving.

He shifted Inga's weight to his other arm and continued, Astrid stumbling ahead of him. He knew she was crying, from the way she kept lifting her apron to her eyes, but he heard no noise. 'Silently', he had said and silent his women were. He felt a stab of pride for them both and grief struck his heart at the thought of losing them. He reached out and gently touched his wife's hair; she half turned in acknowledgement and picked up the pace. He smiled at her courage and followed her, all the while looking behind him, knowing that soon they would be missed and all of Halldor's revenge would swiftly follow.

***

"I think we have to speak with Tony first." Robert pulled on a jumper and tried to keep hold of Cherry at the same time as she wriggled to get out of his grasp. Since they had told her about the trip, she had done everything to hinder them leaving.

Helen made a grab for her daughter as Robert lost his hold and caught Cherry as she made a dash for her bedroom again. Cherry screamed and pulled away. "Come on now love, please stop that ... We have to go."

"NO!NO!NO!" Cherry shouted and pulled her tongue, "I don't want to go, I want to stay here with Inga."

Helen exhaled loudly, she could feel herself getting angry, the urge to leave was overwhelming, "Right, I've had enough, you're coming, right now and that's that!"

Picking her daughter up round the waist, she heaved her over her shoulder and walked out of the house. Robert watched stunned for a moment at his wife's determination, and he felt proud that she was his. Picking up the suitcase, he quickly followed and locked the door before getting into the car. All the while Cherry was crying and howling which he was aware to anyone watching looked bad. He glanced around, but he saw no one, yet knew without doubt they WERE being watched.

He started the car and looked at Helen who was staying in the backseat with Cherry, "So, shall I go and see Tony first? He might have some answers?"

Helen shrugged, "At the moment, I don't care, just get away from here." She had to shout over the din Cherry was making and she grimaced at the noise; this was such unusual behaviour, it frightened her.

The drive to the site took less than five minutes and he pulled up between a small van and an old Ford Fiesta. He could see a few people moving around the site and he suddenly felt safe. This was reality, life was continuing and there were other people doing their jobs, with no knowledge of what had happened to them. He stepped out and walked up to the nearest young man. He wore camouflage trousers and had the longest dreadlocked hair he'd ever seen; the blond tresses passed his backside. He was drawing something and didn't notice Robert until he stood before him. "Hi, I'm looking for Tony ...?"

The young man looked him up and down for a moment before nodding his head in the direction of the large tent, "He's in there."

At that moment, Helen got out of the car and he became aware that everyone was looking towards his car as Cherry continued to shout and scream. He quickly glanced at the young man and rolled his eyes, "Kids eh?"

The man, a student most likely, looked back at him and grinned, "Yeah, kids, who needs them." And resumed his work.

Robert flushed with embarrassment and anger. He had such a strong urge to slap the man that he quickly turned on his heels and walked to the tent. He glanced behind him and saw Helen was following him with Cherry who had now stopped screaming and was making small whimpering sounds; perhaps she'd tired herself out; her screaming had struck every nerve in his body. He was on tenterhooks and took a deep breath.

Tony stood at a long table, a brush in one hand and some kind of pottery in the other. He looked up as Robert came in, quickly followed by Helen and Cherry who was now silently staring at the ground. "Hey you, how's it go ..." He stopped in mid-sentence and slowly lowered the artefact, "What the hell ...?"

Robert hadn't really taken much notice of how he might look, but a quick glance at Helen told him he couldn't look much worse. A night of stress, fear, heartache, lack of sleep could not have done wonders for them and judging from Tony's and the young student's reaction, they must have looked worse than he imagined.

"Tony, I don't have much time, we are leaving." He said the last word very quietly and nodded in the direction of Cherry who stood silently next to Helen; a frown on her face and her bottom lip protruding. Helen had her arm protectively around her. "We need you to tell us about this site. Is it a village of some kind? Have you found bodies? Tony, have you messed with something ... you know, a curse or something? I don't bloody know what I'm saying ..." He slowly moved to the nearest seat and almost fell into it. Helen moved to another chair and slowly sat down, Cherry climbed onto her knee.

Tony watched them silently. He took in their pale faces, the black eyes from lack of sleep with a redness about them that told him they had cried. Helen looked the worst but his glance stopped at the little girl, something wasn't right and he felt a sense of fear creep into his stomach. "What's going on? I mean, Robert, you look terrible. Curses? Last night it was a friggin' ghost, now what?"

Robert just shook his head slowly. Now that he was away from the house, every last ounce of energy had left him; he was utterly exhausted. Helen seemed to feel this and straightened herself, letting out a long breath. She looked up at Tony and gave him a half smile, "I suppose we do look terrible, as you put it, but we have good reason."

Taking another deep breath to steady her quivering voice, she continued, "There is something, in our house. Something that took our baby girl ..." At this, her voice broke and tears cascaded down her cheeks, but she angrily wiped them away, "You may not believe in such things and frankly, I don't care: it happened and it was pure luck we got her back. What we want to know is, has there been anything, strange here? Any bodies dug up. Anything, unusual ... anything that could help us understand *why*?"

Tony leant heavily against the table and stared at her. He regarded Robert who sat with his head bowed, rubbing his eyes trying to stay awake. Eventually he licked his lips, "You need to speak with Kathryn. She told me a strange thing this morning too." He quickly went to the tent opening and called her name before returning to the table grabbing the large flask as he passed. Pouring two large cups, he passed the hot coffee to Robert and Helen, "You look like you need this, sorry it isn't stronger."

Kathryn entered the tent and took in the small group, "What's happened?"

Tony waved his hand in the direction of his friend, "I think you need to talk." He glanced down at Cherry who was now fiddling with Helen's bracelet, "Why don't I take the little one to visit the trenches, eh?" He saw Helen recoil and hold her daughter tightly. He knelt down and looked Helen in the eye, "Your angel doesn't need to hear this, I promise I'll watch her."

Reluctantly, she nodded and relinquished Cherry who was wriggling to get down once she heard Tony's offer. She held Tony's hand and promised to stay with him. Helen watched the pair walk outside and felt a sudden rush of panic. She stood as if to chase them, but Kathryn stopped her, "We need to talk? So, tell me everything ..."

Chapter Twenty-Four

Jonah stood before the small group and met each person's stare; daring them to speak; no-one did. He knew they were all feeling deflated, but he hadn't given up, not yet. "I know that they have been granted students as well as volunteers, I saw them myself, but that doesn't mean we should give up. We can still fight."

The small group grumbled and murmured and he sighed loudly; it had been a long fight and it would be the easiest thing to do, but he couldn't give up, not yet, they were too close. Not for the first time he wished he'd gathered a more substantial army; hired a few local thugs perhaps, but he'd argued that point with himself for a long time and his reasons for not doing so still stood. He needed to control the outcome and with thugs, it was too unreliable.

His neighbour, Linda, stood up and pulled her coat closer as they hadn't put the heating on in the small community centre they used for their meetings. "I just don't see how we can stop them now, Jonah. They have already dug a few trenches and today they are extending them. I've seen the holes that Tony Campbell has been digging. They have had results, apparently some really decent finds: and I've seen Time Team; they will make them bigger and find more finds and get overexcited and before you know it, they'll have dug up the whole site if necessary to find the village; if they haven't already."

Jonah shook his head, "They haven't been given permission to bring in any diggers and I doubt very much that will happen. To reach the site they would have to trample conservation ground and I know that would not be permissible. If anything, they have to dig by hand."

"Yes, that's true, Jonah, but they still have weeks left and if they are already finding stuff ..."

"I hear your worries there, Linda, but we can still do a lot of damage to, shall we say, hinder their efforts?"

Linda slowly sat down and glanced nervously at her friend, who gently shook her head and patted her hand reassuringly. They were both nervous, but after consideration, they had decided to go to the meeting in the hope of finding out the truth. They could sense the others felt the same and knew that each person was willing another to ask the question burning on everyone's lips.

In the end, it was Harry, a retired teacher living in Heswall, who finally cleared his throat and stood. "Jonah, we started this campaign over a year ago to stop them digging up the beautiful Thurstaston Common because it's a place for walkers and wildlife to live in harmony, right?" Seeing a few nods he continued, "Now, in just a short space of time, they have found the village, and frankly, I am beginning to believe it is time that we shared our knowledge ..." He held up his hands as Jonah's colour changed to a dark red, he quickly added loudly, "Now, please hear me out, I have a right to my opinion ..."

He heard many positive murmurs at this which encouraged him to continue. "We have followed the old Norse ways for years in secret and have held our gatherings in and around Thurstaston because of the old parchment you found. It reinforced our Pagan beliefs, knowing the land had once felt the tremor of Viking feet. How you came across that small book Jonah, well, that's your secret and I won't press you, but I am beginning to wonder if we were wrong to have kept the information to ourselves."

Seeing he had everyone's attention, he quickly continued. "It was agreed that such information would bring archaeologists to tear up our precious site, but they came anyway didn't they?" He looked around at the faces of his friends and noticed a few nodding their heads in agreement; Jonah remained perfectly still.

"Perhaps, if we tell them about the lost village, maybe they won't need to dig it all up? Maybe our information will be enough? They have found lots of finds; maybe with that parchment, they can establish that there was indeed a village on that site and be done with it?"

He glanced at Linda and smiled, "Time Team don't dig up the whole area, just enough to prove their point. Maybe, this Kathryn Bailey will be happy to do the same and besides, her boss may not allow a dig to carry on once the evidence has been brought to light? Money is scarce, it may be that proof is all that is needed; and we have it and they have found a lot of it, so ...? And..." He swallowed nervously, "Of course, there is the matter of that murdered druggie who was found nearby. The police don't seem to have any answers yet, but I've heard that the body was moved, he wasn't murdered there. The police have questioned the archaeologists, but they haven't stopped the dig."

All eyes slowly turned to Jonah who stood motionless at the front of the group. Everyone could see he was fighting to keep his temper and Harry quickly sat down with some relief. Those around him gently patted him on the shoulders, giving him their support and no doubt, their relief that someone had voiced the murder. He did not believe that Jonah could have been responsible for the murder, but he couldn't deny that Jonah was very passionate about keeping the site of the village secret and sacred; others thought differently and had voiced their fears and it frightened him.

"I see..." Jonah managed to say after a few moments, "Do you all feel like this? That we should abandon everything we have fought for over this last year and give in? Let them tear up our secret, tear up the earth for all to see and gawp at? Perhaps we should also tell them that we are a Pagan group who follow the Old Norse gods and tell them all our secrets ...?"

Maud raised her stick slightly, "Jonah, I'm too old to be scared of you, so here it is, the question everyone here is unable to ask you outright is this: did you have anything to do with that man's death? We all know your passion for keeping this village a secret and everything kept as it should be, so did you?"

Jonah slowly lowered himself into his chair and stared back at the group. He knew without counting there were seventeen of them. Including him that made eighteen, two nines, a sacred number. It had taken him years to find the right people to join his group. People he could manipulate, frighten and coerce into doing the rituals needed to keep the energy contained. None of them knew the true meanings or the real sacrifices he had had to make, but now, it seemed some of them were getting a backbone and he could not have that.

He noticed a few people looked uncomfortable now that the question was out in the open and he felt satisfaction at their discomfort. Licking his dry lips, he addressed them, "I don't really know what to say to that question, except that, yes, I am passionate about this village and what we do and I believe without doubt that it should stay hidden and untouched. Did I kill some drug addict to stop the digging? No, I did not and frankly, I am disgusted. If I was going to try and stop the dig, surely I would have made sure the body was found on the site, not a good distance away, am I right?"

He watched as each person thought about it logically and smiled to himself. He still had them. His puppets would do whatever he asked because they felt embarrassed at their ridiculous assumptions, if only they knew. Now, they would feel embarrassed at voicing such allegations, thinking they had hurt his feelings; now, they would owe him their allegiance.

As the meeting broke up, he let each person come up to him and apologise. He took the offered cup of tea and congratulated Jackie on her delicious Victoria sponge. He shook hands and nodded graciously at their clumsy attempts to make it better. Tomorrow, he would tell them his plans to sabotage the dig, and they would do it, because they were old, bored people with nothing in their lives, except him and their secret group, which made them feel alive.

It felt good being in charge, knowing people would follow without question. He was the boss, the man with all the power to decide life or death. Yet, there was a niggling energy that had resurfaced. It had taken him by surprise at first, then he'd felt amused. Now, he wasn't sure how he felt, only that he had to confront it. It was weakening his hold on his people; another sacrifice would be in order and that would be a pleasure.

***

Kathryn smiled nervously, "You want to know about the site, the village?"

Helen glanced at Robert before answering, "Yes, you see, as we tried to explain, something bad happened last night. Something has been happening since we moved into that house." She lowered her eyes and quickly wiped them, "Something took my baby girl and I couldn't fight them. They took her."

Kathryn stared at Helen as if she had gone mad, Helen looked up and saw it, "I know what I sound like but, Cherry has been acting strange. From the moment we moved in she had been seeing them, talking to them. She has even changed her doll's name, which I think has something to do with them. And then, last night, they took her and she was gone ... for hours, the police found her in the garden." She quickly glanced behind her before continuing, "She doesn't remember it, I think anyway. Damn it! Can you help or not? because I don't know what is going on and it seems a very big coincidence that you start digging this place and we have horrible things happen and we only live the other side of those trees and ..." Helen slowly stood, "You said, a village ... This," She swept her hand around, "This, was a village?"

Robert stood and moved to Helen's side, "Is that true, this place was a village? From when? How old is it?"

Kathryn took a step backwards and leant against the finds table, she was trying to slow her breathing as she looked from Helen to Robert, trying to take in their story. Her heart was beating fast as she considered the possibilities of what they were saying. She believed them. That was without doubt, but with the knowledge came a terrifying feeling that was threatening to overwhelm her very being. She was trying to recall every detail of every dream she had had over the years and knew it was all connected, it was important somehow, but she couldn't find the words to speak, what to say, to explain, to find the connection between them all ... if there was one?

She quickly rubbed her cold hands together and took a long, deep breath. The variety of emotions that coursed through her body made her shake; the police, the ghost of Einaar, the students constantly asking questions and now this; it was too much.

"This village as we have discovered, was Norse, Viking." She saw the look that passed between Helen and Robert and nodded, "I see you suspected that? We, I mean, some of us didn't really know what we would find here, it just seemed a likely site for an archaeological dig."

Helen leant forward, "Is that true? You didn't really know what to expect when you dug here? You see, Kathryn, I know bullshit when I hear it, I've become a bit of an expert over the years so, you knew this was a village, right? Otherwise, why dig here, why not somewhere else?"

Kathryn glanced at Robert; he looked a little flushed and embarrassed on hearing Helen's words and she felt uncomfortable. "You're right. I knew we would find, something significant, but I didn't really believe it would be a village, until later on ... I guess I didn't want to believe that all these years had been real. You see, strange things have happened to me since I was a little girl, but these last few months, it has become worse, more pronounced, specific, if you like." Seeing their uncertainty she quickly added, "Dreams, nightmares, about a place, people, death and, I think I was there. No, I mean, I'm sure I was there, here, in this village."

"Are you talking about past life?"

Kathryn grimaced hearing Robert's scepticism, "After all you say you've been through, you can't ponder the possibility of past life? You do surprise me!"

Robert shook his head, "Hey, there's being haunted and then there's fairy tales. We haven't lived before, that's just wishful thinking. It's a need to believe that this shit life isn't our last chance, that we can come back as something or someone else. Christ, I mean, if you had a choice, why can't you come back as a prince or the pope or fuckin' Elvis for God's sake, that's crap ... No offence," he quickly added.

Seeing Helen staring at him open mouthed, he quickly cleared his throat of an imaginary obstruction, "Oh come on! You can't really believe in that?"

"How do you explain what we saw? Ghosts! You didn't believe in them yesterday did you and look what happened. They have come from somewhere; so, what are they, Robert? Spirit? If they are spirit, where have they been all these years? Why hang around? You've witnessed spirit, so you can agree that after we die, we have a spirit or a soul, so where does it go? What happens to it? Or are you saying we all die and then hang around for an eternity 'cause there isn't anywhere to go?"

"How the fuck should I know!" He began to pace feeling his emotions hover between anger, frustration, and fear, "All I do know is that I bought that house and now what? We are here, in a cold tent having some freaky conversation about past lives and I can't even protect my own family against ... against what? Ghosts? Spirits? Echoes? Call them whatever you like, the facts are, we are here when we should be at home, having a nice lunch and getting our marriage back on track ..."

"What the hell is this for you? An inconvenience to getting our pathetic marriage back on track? They took Charlotte! Was that just inconvenient?"

For a long time they stared at each other, both breathing hard, searching the other for acceptance, acknowledgment of the pain, the blame. He looked away first and sat down deflated, "Kathryn, tell us about these people, who were they?"

Kathryn glanced between the two of them, unsure as to what conversation was really going on between the couple. Whatever it was, it was electric. "Well, this was a village, that's a fact because we can tell that from the distribution of finds. What it doesn't tell us yet, is that this was a large village. It had a chief and around a hundred people lived here." She coughed nervously, "I mean, that is what I know, not what I can prove yet." She quickly rubbed a hand through her hair, "In my dreams, I mostly see one family, over and over. I know some kind of illness begins to kill the villagers and I remember other things too."

Her voice was barely a whisper now. She really did not want to remember the other terrible things she had seen. The torture of a man she knew was a priest and the slaughter of the village, seen up close as if she were standing alongside the killers. Too frightened to give them proper burials, they were burnt en masse and if she concentrated, she could smell the cloying stench of burnt flesh; she swallowed the rising bile.

"Do you remember any names, in your dreams?"

Kathryn met Helen's stare and nodded, "Yes. The family, who I mainly see, I know them. His name, is Einaar, his wife is Astrid and they have a young child, a daughter, her name was Inga."

***

Tony watched as Cherry peered into one trench after another. She seemed much happier and content since she was last here and had calmed down considerably since her arrival. He wondered if perhaps she was playing up over her parents. His own, younger sister had caused a right ruckus after their parents' divorce. She had been seven; he was three years older than she was and although it had affected him, he hadn't begun drawing on the walls or having screaming tantrums whenever anyone said "No" to her. He hadn't argued over everything and cried all the time.

He'd withdrawn into himself mostly. Allowed Rachel to have all the attention and silently listened to his parents fighting over who got what and where the children should live. Children did the strangest things when faced with horrible circumstances; he admired how children were so resilient; carrying on with life regardless; maybe adults could learn a thing or two? Watching Cherry now, away from her parents, it certainly mirrored his own experiences.

Cherry wandered over to the longest trench and knelt down ignoring the wet grass. Carolyn, a mature student, was busy scraping away and didn't notice the child at first until she spoke. "What's in there?"

Carolyn sat back on her heels and wiped her brow, "I'm looking for any signs of a house or wall. I think it's a house 'cause look ..." She pulled across a large box filled to the brim with broken pottery and some grooming objects, Tony bent down to examine them. "See," Carolyn continued, "They used these to eat off, like your plates at home, and this ..." She picked up a comb made from horn, "They combed their hair with this, can you see?"

Cherry peered closely at the comb, "Yes, I remember ... what's that?" She was pointing at a small square object lying half hidden in the box.

Carolyn smiled and gently picked it up. It was about two inches long and very smooth, she handed it to Tony whose face lit up, "That is what's called a rune stone." Looking up at Tony, "So, what do you think?"

He gently rubbed it with his thumb to clean it better and grinned, "This is fantastic! Look Cherry, it has a marking on it." He leant forward and showed her the stone. It did not pass his attention that she didn't touch it, but kept her hands by her side. He looked at Carolyn and met her eyes, they both shrugged in unison, obviously a stone wasn't as exciting as a large hole?

He placed it carefully back in the finds box and stood up, Cherry was still kneeling, her attention on the large trench. "I have to get a plastic bag to put that into, Cherry." When she didn't acknowledge him, he quickly added, "We'll be making this trench bigger once I've catalogued the finds, would you like to see that? Maybe your parents will let you have a dig around in the soil?"

As he walked away to look for a plastic bag to put the rune into, he quickly glanced back at the little girl who remained unmoving, staring into the trench. Stolen, Robert had said. Who would steal a child? He didn't want to think of the answer. He didn't feel comfortable leaving her even for a second, but the rune find was indescribable, he had to put it somewhere safe; besides, Carolyn was right there; he'd only be a minute.

As he neared the tent, he heard a cry behind him and knew instantly, it was about Cherry. Within a heartbeat, Helen flew out of the tent and quickly scanned the area. Seeing Carolyn bending over something, she pushed past him even as he was moving towards the trench and reached her daughter in seconds.

"Baby? Cherry darling ...?" She looked up at Carolyn who was frantically shaking her head watching Cherry who now lay unconscious in her mother's arms.

"I don't know ..." She answered to the unasked question, "She was leaning over the trench one second, she reached out and then, she just collapsed ... I don't know ..."

Tony quickly looked around and noticed various students on their mobile phones; he knew they were calling for help and tried to feel reassured. "An ambulance is on its way. Don't worry, she'll be all right ..."

Helen didn't answer. She was checking all her daughter's vital signs, Robert was now kneeling next to her holding his child's hand in his own.

"Did she bump her head or something?" Kathryn finally asked the question. She was hovering beside Tony; he glanced at her and noticed how pale she looked.

Helen shook her head, "I can't see any bump." She looked across at Carolyn for confirmation and she shook her head.

"No, she didn't fall; she just reached down and picked this up from the soil." Kneeling down, Carolyn carefully picked up the small, square object and held it up for everyone to see; it was another rune stone.

***

Einaar paced while Astrid gave Inga some more water. They both knew travelling was not good for her after such a terrible fever, it was a risk, but one they'd had no choice but to take. He walked a little, back the way they had come and double-checked for signs of their pursuers. There was none, but that did not stop the clenching fear in his stomach that made it hard to breathe. He knew without doubt they were coming and theirs would be an easy trail to follow.

He looked up and judged it to be mid-morning. They had been up since it was full dark and the stars had been their guide. He wished more than ever it could still be so, they might have a better chance at their escape; as it was, he was running for running's sake instead of waiting for the inevitable. Astrid knew it too, but he suspected her reasons ran far deeper; she would do anything to protect her child, as he would also do, now. A few years ago, would it have been the same, or would he have taken Inga's life to spare her the pain of the fever? He knew the answer and it repulsed him.

Movement among the clump of trees caught his eye and every muscle became alive and alert, tiredness and fear gone in an instant. He backed away from them and moved silently, but quickly to where he had left his family. Astrid turned at his appearance, saw his face and quickly gathered up Inga into her arms and moved fast. They were on a slight ridge, if they could get to lower ground where it was flat, he would see them coming and have a better chance of fighting them off while Astrid and Inga escaped.

They did not bother to be quiet anymore; they knew Halldor and the others were not far behind. Knowing how many others would have been helpful, but Einaar could guess to around nine; Halldor's most faithful group. He had stood in battle surrounded by men and survived, could he take on nine on his own? If he could kill Halldor, he could survive; but he forced that thought away; no one had beaten Halldor in battle. He silently prayed to the Christian God that he could give Astrid and Inga enough time to escape, to reach the sea where they could find a ship to travel back to Ireland. 'Please Lord, let them be free.'

Inga felt the change and began to cry, Astrid quietly soothed her, all the while half running down the embankment. Her mind raced with possibilities and none of them were favourable. They were going to die. What had to be asked now was, should it be by others' hands, or her own? She held her child closer and whispered something about it being all right and hating herself for lying. Inga was no fool. She could see and feel the danger, she only wished with all her heart that the child did not understand that it meant death.

She screamed as a man loomed up before her. Giermund, she knew him. He lived opposite them with his wife and four children. Two of his children had fallen sick; she had not known whether they still lived when they had left. All of this flew through her mind in an instant as he stood motionless blocking her path. His expression was blank, almost as if he was not alive, but looking closer into his eyes, she could see the pain mingled with frustrated anger and knew that his children had perished.

Yanking Inga behind her back to shield her, she heard a cry and the clashing of steel; Einaar was fighting for their lives. She dived for her knife she kept on her belt and in one motion swung it upwards in a wide arc hoping to catch Giermund across the chest or better

163

still, his neck. He was quick though and flinched backwards; she missed. He grabbed at her wrist and twisted. She cried out as the pain ripped up her arm and she fell to her knees; he let go and quickly wiped his hand on his trousers.

So, they thought they were contagious, that might be in her favour. Jumping up, ignoring the pain in her arm, she dived on him, clawing at his face and hair, anything that might slow him down. He shouted and tore at her, trying to pull her off, but she felt overwhelmingly powerful as she fought for her child's life. Her nails ripped at his skin, his eyes, she pulled clumps of hair, her legs wrapped around his waist to stop him from throwing her off. All the while, she shouted at Inga to 'run', to 'get away from here' knowing that it was pointless, where would she go? How would she live?

Giermund was yelling, she was shouting, she did not hear or see the other man who came and pulled her from behind. The first she knew of him was when she landed on the ground with an earth-shattering thud that made her eyes water and forced the breath from her lungs. She doubled up and fought to get to her knees, seeing her child kneeling only a few feet away. Tears streamed down her cheeks as she crawled to Inga; the two men watched her; keeping their distance now they had her under control. She was vaguely aware that she couldn't hear any other fighting and wondered if Einaar was already dead.

Then, in one short moment, it did not matter, as Giermund raised his sword. He hesitated, it was a dishonour to harm a woman, especially one of their village, but the other man she knew as Hakon moved quickly to stand behind Inga and from the corner of her eye she saw the glint of a knife. Before she could react, he had yanked Inga from her tight grasp and slit Inga's small throat. Her child barely made a sound as her head rolled forward onto her mother's chest, her innocent blood splashing onto her tunic.

Astrid held her tightly until she could not feel her daughter's heartbeat and then looked up again at Giermund. Her eyes met his and she gently nodded her permission. She closed her eyes as the sword came down. She did not hear or care as the noise of its descent was like the breath of the wind.

Chapter Twenty-Five

Robert felt quite detached from the scene playing out before him. The paramedics were superb with both Charlotte and his wife who clung to their child with all the force she could, as if willing her to open her eyes with her mother's power. It was Kathryn and the woman paramedic who eventually managed to calmly take hold of Helen's arms and ease them off Cherry while at the same time, the other paramedic, a male, got stuck in, checking for vital signs and calling Cherry's name.

He stood watching it all as if it were happening on television. He heard the man call her 'Charlotte' and Tony quietly corrected him and said she was known as 'Cherry'. He watched as the man carefully but quickly checked her breathing, her pulse and called her 'Sweetheart'.

He looked up as the woman relinquished Helen into Kathryn's arms and quickly came to help him. They both spoke nonsense, calling her name, asking questions about what had happened. Helen didn't answer. She wasn't noticing any of it, her whole focus was on Cherry. Helen's reaction scared him. She was a trained nurse, yet at this moment, she looked so vulnerable and helpless, it made him feel ten times worse.

After fitting Cherry with a small neck brace, they carried her into the ambulance. She looked so small on the stretcher, it broke his heart. Silently, Helen climbed in after them and he watched as they closed the ambulance doors and took his wife and child away; he had barely moved. Tony gently touched his arm and manoeuvred him towards their car.

Tony got into the driver's seat and held his hand out for the keys; he gave them without comment. The drive to the hospital seemed to take forever, but it was only ten minutes in reality. On arriving, Robert rushed into A&E and searched for signs of Helen; seeing none, he marched up to the desk. The receptionist told him where to find them and he ran to the room.

He found his daughter on a big bed that made her appear even smaller than her three years. Doctors and nurses surrounded her. Poking and prodding, and asking Helen question after question, but she was not responding. He stood by her side, before a nurse turned them around and walked with them outside the room. "We will need you to fill out a form ..." He was about to argue when she quickly added, "It will help us help your daughter. She's in good hands, I promise ..."

Like two robots, they shuffled towards the receptionist who gave them a regrettable smile, "It won't take long and it will help to focus on this, just for a moment. Now, your child's name?"

It was Robert who answered her questions about their daughter, her age, any allergies, any diseases, had they been on holiday recently? What was she doing when this happened? It was this question that Helen seemed to hear. She had her back to the receptionist, her gaze never left the closed door to Charlotte's room, but at this she slowly turned and at the same time, she put her hand into her pocket and froze. Robert watched her for a moment, before he stepped closer. Her eyes met his own as she slowly pulled out the small square object. Her gaze travelled downward to look at her hand and she screamed and screamed at the rune stone that she held.

***

Kathryn stood motionless for a long time after the ambulance left quickly followed by Tony and Robert. Carolyn had come to stand next to her. Kathryn eventually turned to her and let out the breath she had been holding. She was visibly shaken. "What happened, Carolyn?"

Carolyn licked her lips and wiped her hair away from her eyes, "I have no idea. One minute she was interested in the trench, and then she just, collapsed. She did lean over, but I'm sure she didn't bang her head or anything. I think she picked something up, but ..." She quickly walked back to the trench and jumped down into it. She scoured the area, before shrugging, "Whatever it was isn't here now. Maybe her Mum took it, or her Dad, for the hospital to see?"

Kathryn knelt down, "What did this thing look like?"

Carolyn reached for her finds tray and handed it to Kathryn. "See that?"

Kathryn did and carefully picked up the small object. "Bloody hell! This is a rune stone with an inscription from the Elder Futhark. Are you telling me the child picked up another one? Did she swallow it or something?"

"No nothing like that. It never went near her mouth, I'm pretty sure of that. Jesus! It happened so fast, but I think it looked like that shape, so maybe it was another rune? Yes, I remember now, I think it had the same markings on it ... which is weird eh? If, they are original, surely the markings wouldn't be so, I don't know, obvious maybe?"

Carolyn waited for a response. Getting none, she frowned trying to remember, "She bent down, and flicked away some soil, almost as if she knew it was there sort of thing, you know ... and then, she leant forward, her fingers touched it and this may sound a bit lame, but I thought for just a few seconds that time kind of, well, stood still. Like, I knew where I was, but seemed to freeze. God, that does sound silly doesn't it? It's probably shock or something. I do feel a bit shaky, I just don't know ..." Her voice trailed off and she sat back on her heels. "I hope the kid's all right?"

Kathryn nodded, glancing between Carolyn, the trench and the rune stone in her hand. She had been half listening to what Carolyn had said, but all the while she'd felt nothing but revulsion at what she held in her hand and had been fighting the urge to be sick. The rune stone throbbed against her skin as if it had life. It felt warm and alive and every ounce of her being wanted to throw it away, or better yet, burn it or bury it, anything to keep it away from people. It oozed evil, pain, and suffering. As if hatred and anger had been sucked into this small stone and now flowed from it.

Replacing the stone in the finds box, she wiped her hand against her jeans as discreetly as she could, trying to eradicate the feel of it. Reaching into her pocket, she brought out a wad of small plastic bags she kept for special pieces. Opening one, she nodded to Carolyn to place the stone inside; which she did without any expression of relief; perhaps Carolyn couldn't feel the rune stone's energy?

"I'll keep this safe." Kathryn held the bag by the top so as not to feel the stone inside, "If you could map everything in the trench, noting where this was found, thanks."

"You think we should carry on after ..." Seeing Kathryn shrug, Carolyn continued, "Will there be a health and safety issue then? You know, we're supposed to have cordoned off the site ...?" She waited for a response, but Kathryn was staring at the bag. "Okay I'll concentrate on that area then? See if there are more of these runes?"

That got Kathryn's attention and she wanted to scream 'NO! Leave it alone', but instead, she merely nodded and turned away, back to the tent, away from the students who watched her. Away from all prying eyes where she could crumble and fall apart as the vision of people dying filled her head. It was all too much. Since that morning she'd experienced so many traumatic and frightening experiences, it didn't feel real and all she wanted to do was curl up in a ball and forget everything.

She knew who had cast these runes. The memory was suddenly so clear. As children, they had been in awe of her and had whispered together whenever she had passed them. Always silent, always alone. The other elders lived with their families, but they were few. Many had not survived the crossing from Ireland and some had sacrificed themselves to the water, not wanting to be a burden on the village. They were remembered and honoured; Rafarta was feared.

Rafarta was a woman who shared nothing with anyone, unless the gods demanded it; and this annoyed Halldor. He wanted the power to command her visions, which he hoped would bring him more dominance over his people and those in the new land; but it had not happened that way. Rafarta was cunning, telling him enough, but never telling him everything; it is what kept her alive. That and the belief that Rafarta was connected to the gods and she had used runes stones to communicate with them; and these runes were hers.

She had spent days finding the right, smooth stones from the riverbed and cutting marks into them. Then, only when she was satisfied, had she uncovered a small vial that held some of the priest's blood. She had collected it the night he had been killed; no one had questioned her motives. Now, she mixed it with her own and she had marked them; the blood filled the grooves. The blood of a Christian man; a holy man of one God and she, Rafarta, a believer of another God … a heathen.

Kathryn wiped her face and realised it was wet with her tears. She couldn't fight it anymore; it was all real, her nightmares, her memories, all of it and it terrified her. Images of Rafarta, Astrid, Einaar flashed before her eyes, but how could they hurt this child? Why would they? Unless, she was involved somehow and going on what she now had to believe, the kid must have lived here before too. She had to talk to someone before she went mad.

***

"We cannot find anything to make sense of Charlotte's condition." The doctor stood before them looking utterly perplexed. Helen had been given a mild sedative and was lying propped up with cushions on a bed, Robert stood next to her. "I'm sorry, there isn't anything more I can tell you, other than, we will continue to keep an eye on Charlotte, and any change, we will let you know immediately. For now, by all means, you can sit with her, we will organise for a bed to be placed in her room …"

"Is she very sick?" Robert swallowed hard to stifle the rising tears, "I mean this ... this, condition, is it like a coma?"

The doctor sighed and ran a hand through his hair. "I can honestly say, I don't know. It's like she's in a deep sleep judging from the brain waves and the pupil reactions, but, as you said, she hadn't taken anything to cause such a drugged sleep ..."

The implication wasn't lost on Robert and he frowned, "You've tested her for drugs, alcohol, anything that she 'might' have taken, so putting that aside, why has this happened?"

The doctor smiled uncomfortably, "As I said, we don't know. It could be a form of epilepsy, but her brain wave patterns don't agree with this theory. What we do know is that she is breathing on her own, which is a good sign. She seems to be in deep REM sleep, as if she's dreaming," he added, seeing Robert's confusion, "We will test her for a condition known as narcolepsy." Seeing his blank face he quickly continued, "It's when the patient suddenly falls asleep, but it usually lasts a short amount of time. Charlotte has been like this for nearly four hours, and I have never heard of a person with this disorder being so young. It is believed to be a genetic disorder, quite common really, but this is only a vague guess, so ..." He shrugged and turned to look at Helen, who was watching him but hadn't moved. "We'll keep an eye on your wife too, she's had a shock."

Robert mumbled his thanks and sat down heavily in the armchair next to Helen's bed. Seeing this as a chance to escape, the doctor quickly left. Robert barely noticed; his head was fighting all sorts of thoughts and scenarios. Playing repeatedly the days leading up to the previous night's hell and now today. He saw again and again Helen's face as she pulled that stone out of her pocket. What did she know?

He wanted to reach for Helen's hand but knew she still held the stone tightly. He had no desire to touch it himself and hated that his wife held onto something that he had no courage to do. He was a coward. He had been a coward in their marriage and he was a coward now. It was too much of a coincidence to think the ghosts had no part in this latest nightmare, but how, he couldn't fathom. He just knew in his heart, they were to blame for this and he was to blame for the rest of it.

He should have fought the ghosts in their home; then none of this would be happening now, surely? Cherry would be playing happily in her new back garden or upstairs in her room before teatime. Helen would be happily ignoring him by keeping herself busy and he would be watching her, plucking up the courage to speak to her every so often to try to connect with her as he had tried their first night.

Instead, they were here, in a hospital and his darling child had something unknown. His wife was in shock and drugged and he was doing nothing. What could he do, a mere man against something dead? God, he wanted to hit something and hurt those responsible and every ounce of his being told him he was right. It was too much of a coincidence that yesterday evening, Cherry had been taken out of the house by something unnatural and now she was unconscious. None of it made sense. He had no idea what to do; he was useless.

**

Tony paced the hospital corridor, his head a whirl of possibilities. He saw the doctor leave Helen's room, but for now, he couldn't bring himself to go inside and talk to Robert. His world had been secure, knowledgeable. He found old things people had forgotten or discarded and he worked out what their lives had possibly been like. What they ate, where they lived, slept, crapped. The objects he found had substance, solidity, they had been made and used and he understood that.

He looked down at the polystyrene cup that held the remnants of his coffee. Who would find this in the future? Someone might find it and wonder at the stupidity of using such an object when it's bad for the environment. That made sense to him. It was real. However, this stuff about ghosts stealing children and terrorising a family was inconceivable.

He drained the lukewarm liquid and carefully placed the cup in the bin. He leant against the wall, watched the patients, the nurses and the people he presumed were visitors, and thought how good life can be when all things are explainable and solid. He looked towards the door to Helen's room and walked over to it. Looking through

169

the small window, he sighed loudly, Robert sat hunched forward in a chair while Helen lay inert on a bed, a blanket thrown over her legs.

He was about to knock when Robert looked up and saw him; he moved towards the door slowly so as not to alarm Helen, but she didn't move. "How's it going?" He knew it was a stupid question but he couldn't think of anything else.

Robert shook his head, "Helen's in a bad way, they've given her something to keep her calm for now. Cherry is ..." His face crumpled and he looked away. After a few minutes, he sniffed loudly, "They don't know about Cherry. The doctor mentioned some sleeping thing, he also mentioned epilepsy ..."

Tony nodded, "Was it Narcolepsy?" Not waiting for a reply he continued, "I think we both know it isn't that, right? For a start, I think she's too young, and ..."

"Yes, damn it, I know it isn't that!" Robert pushed himself away from the door. "I have to check on my baby but how can I save her from them?

Tony fell into step with him, "I don't know mate, I really don't know."

Chapter Twenty-Six

Kathryn was staring down at the finds box idly picking up objects from the latest trench, when she became aware of someone standing at the tent's entrance. She looked up at the elderly man and her heart missed a beat. She didn't move for a moment as she tried to catch her breath; she knew him, that much she did know, but not here, not this time and she suddenly felt dizzy with fear.

He watched her face, his own remaining blank, not moving from the entrance until he was sure she did know him, as he knew her. Only when he saw the knowledge in her eyes, did he move slowly into the tent and take a seat opposite her. He quickly glanced around at the finds boxes and his gaze fell on the box containing the rune stones kept separately in a small bag. Carolyn had found five more in the past two hours; each grey stone carved; the markings on them clear as the day they were done.

She said nothing as he reached inside the bag, picking one out between his thick fingers. He held it up in the light between his finger and thumb, gently rubbing it before carefully replacing it with the others. He looked into the next box and picked up a comb made of horn, part of a horn bugle. A broken piece of an iron brooch that looked like the back end of a horse and a whetstone made of slate. He held this tightly before reluctantly putting it back. He sighed loudly before turning his attention to her. He tried to smile reassuringly, but he didn't really manage it, it looked more like a grimace and he quickly gave up seeing the look on her face. "I didn't mean to frighten you, Kathryn Bailey, I thought it was about time we met again ..."

She paled as he spoke and quickly folded her arms across her chest. He bit his lower lip and clicked his tongue while he thought for a moment, his eyes never leaving hers. "I see that you know what I'm talking about ..." When she didn't reply, he shrugged, "Very well, I'll do all the talking, shall I? So, you didn't listen to the warnings and dug anyway and, I presume from the ambulance this morning that something bad has happened?"

He peered into another finds box and picked out what looked like an iron needle, still caked in mud. He replaced this and picked up a piece of a bowl, "Touching these brings back memories ... shreds of memory anyway, a bit like these broken pots." He replaced the bowl and picked up the rim of a cup, "I can almost smell the ale and mead that this would have held; can you?"

She slowly shook her head and he grinned, "I guess it's different for everyone. Besides, you were very young."

"Young?" Her voice came out strangled, no more than a whisper and she tried to clear her throat.

He didn't react to her obvious discomfort, but averted his gaze to offer her time to compose herself. He stood slowly and went over to the long table, picking up various pieces found that day. Most of it was Chester ware pots, which made sense, being that the city was not far away. It was obvious that they had been wheel thrown and kiln fired; it fitted the Chester ware theory. Besides, she knew the villagers had traded with the locals.

"What do you remember, then?" His question made her jump, as she had been engrossed in her own frantic thoughts of where she knew him.

"I ... I don't really know what you mean. Who, are you?"

He laughed softly before replacing a broken piece of ivory comb and turned back to face her. "Are we really going to do this?" When she didn't answer, he sighed and returned to his seat. "Very well then, my name is Jonah Merton." He saw her eyes widen, she knew his name at least. "I see you do know me and yes, I'm the one who's fought against this dig of yours."

"You're Mr Merton? The one who sent all those letters of complaint? I don't understand." She quickly licked her dry lips.

He shrugged quickly and leant forward, "I think you understand more than you're willing to say right now which is fine, but don't you see why this village should never have been dug up?"

"I ... no ..." She couldn't think and she was feeling more and more uncomfortable under his scrutiny. The students felt a long way away, would they hear her if she screamed?

He sat back in his chair, crossed his legs and folded his arms, watching her with interest, "I see. So, you are playing the innocent card? I could have sworn you knew me. Was I really mistaken, Kathryn?"

She hated the way he spoke her name. He was mocking her because he knew only too well that she'd recognised him; his eyes filled her nightmares. "I ... was only a child ... I, it wasn't ..." She gave up. Her whole body sagged and she leant forward, her head in her hands. "I don't really remember ... but, you ..." She was crying openly and quickly wiped away the tears. "I remember you now ... what you did. What he did?" She corrected herself and wiped a sleeve across her eyes, "I was so young. A child, you said. We didn't have a chance ... did we?"

He suddenly stood and she quickly stood too, making her chair fall backwards. For the briefest moment, she saw the man she remembered in her dreams. The man she had once loved as her chief. The man who had protected her family and her village from all enemies, and they had trusted him with their lives. But an invisible enemy had come and he had not fought it and won; instead, he had murdered those he felt were responsible and the rest, for the sake of his own life; he had sacrificed to the gods. He had them all burnt.

She searched his face for any sign of remorse. Even a small amount of acknowledgement for his wicked deed or shame; there was nothing. He merely watched her and she hated that she was crying. Crying for the people she had loved and had lost. Her village, his village and he had killed them all.

Without another word, he walked to the tent opening and looked out. He turned once and regarded her again, a slight smile played on his lips before he nodded his farewell and was gone. She stared after him, feeling the fury rise within her, her body shook with it and she felt her teeth chatter. The shock of seeing him and knowing him was too much to bear after so many events that day. Why had he come? To gloat, to challenge her or to reminisce? The tent opening flapped gently in the breeze, she turned and vomited.

***

Nick crouched down as the old man passed him. He'd hung around over the past hour idly checking out the site, looking for something to swipe if an opportunity came. He'd managed to cadge a fag off the policeman who'd interviewed him over Lee's murder, but that had been ages ago; now he had nothing. He'd broken into a car yesterday and stolen the CD player and loose change, which he'd exchanged for a bit of weed, some tobacco and two cans of lager. He was kicking himself now; he should have argued a better deal.

He eyed up a young woman kneeling in a trench on his right. She had a nice round arse, but with her back to him, he couldn't see her tits. He looked around for a coat or purse; seeing none, he edged around to the other side of the site nearer to the large tent. He'd seen a couple of 'Time Teams': he knew they kept finds in a tent, maybe that's also where they kept their handbags; he could nick something to sell?

He knelt down behind a thick gorse bush; he could see five student types, and they were all busy digging. He watched the old man stand amongst the trenches, he had an odd smile on his face as he turned around in a circle, looking at each trench in turn; odd bastard! As if hearing his thoughts, he abruptly stopped smiling and walked to the gate. Turning, he looked towards the bushes he was hiding behind. Nick ducked down further as his gaze fell on him; but the old man carried on towards the gate and out onto the road.

He shivered; he was sure he'd seen him, but obviously his eye-sight wasn't as good as he thought. He slowly edged his way closer to the tent and listened; someone was crying; he'd have to wait until they left. Minutes passed and he became aware of how quiet it had become. He could see the students digging and scraping, he knew the road wasn't far off, but, it was as if he'd suddenly gone deaf. Putting a finger into his ear, he wiggled it around, but it didn't make a difference; he couldn't even hear the birds that only moments ago had been chirping and singing in the trees overhead.

He became aware of a strange sensation of being watched. His body seemed to prickle all along his spine and the hairs on the back of his grimy neck stood on end. He could suddenly smell his own acrid sweat, his greasy hair and unwashed body; every sense was alive, more alive than they had ever been. He didn't need to turn around to know that a man stood behind him. He did not need to look to know the man was not of this earth. But he looked anyway and a small sound escaped his dry lips as he met the eyes of a dead man.

***

Robert slumped in the armchair and quickly glanced out of the large hospital window. Tony stood leaning on the windowsill looking out at the darkening sky. Robert rubbed his hands vigorously over his face, trying to wake himself, but the bone-deep fatigue would not go away. He was sick of this place. Sick of hearing the doctors say the same nonsense and the consultants arguing their opinions; he knew none of them had a clue what was happening. A child who showed every sign of being asleep, but wasn't? A child who did not respond to any stimuli, any drug that 'should' have woken her; but didn't. His head was full of their possibilities, their theories, and their proposed actions and knew it all to be pointless.

He had sat for hours staring at Cherry, willing her to wake up; but in his heart, he knew that was not going to happen. He'd become aware of passing people, nurses, doctors, some had had that look on their face. Not experienced enough or not caring enough to hide their thoughts; 'bad parent syndrome' he'd decided to call it. They had made up their minds that he, Helen or both of them were responsible in some way for Cherry's condition. What or how, they obviously hadn't worked out or he would be talking to police by now; he expected that soon regardless and he dreaded it.

After Helen's frantic phone call about Cherry being taken, and now this unexplainable event, he was surprised they weren't arresting him and Helen already on some abuse charge. What was he supposed to tell them? "Yes, officer, don't worry, our daughter has had some kind of supernatural episode because she touched something on a dig: Oh, and there's a couple of pissed off Viking spirits hanging around my house which I think have something to do with this, please go and arrest them!"

He must have made a noise because Tony turned to look at him, "All right?"

"Do I fuckin' look all right?" He suddenly couldn't sit anymore and began walking around the small room; flattening the end of the blanket on the bed, gently touching Cherry's toes, staring into space, straightening a picture of a vase of roses on the wall when all he wanted to do with it was throw it through the window.

Tony watched him pacing around the room. He could see that Robert was close to losing it; the police hadn't helped the situation, acting as if Robert was responsible in some way. They hadn't said anything, but their body language had been very clear and one of them had said they wanted to question them again later. He had no idea what they would say. What could they say about the little girl? He wasn't sure he believed Robert's theory, but what he did know for sure was that a little girl was lying in a hospital bed and something had happened to put her there.

He'd stood at the end of her bed with Robert, watching her little chest rise and fall. The monitors around the bed, gently beeping; the heart monitor was a satisfying noise, letting them know, her little heart was working perfectly. "A steady and strong heart," the doctors had tried to reassure Robert; he hadn't really listened to them.

He'd gone over and over that moment of walking away. Had tried to recall whether Cherry had looked ill in any way; but no, if anything, she'd looked healthy. He could remember a slight pink to her cheeks, whether that was from the previous tantrum, he didn't know, but, from what he could recall, he had considered her a normal four year old. He had said as much to the doctor.

"You need to get out of here Robert." He waited until his friend turned to look at him before continuing, "Just for a little while, you know, clear your head a bit. I could stay here if you like, in case Helen wakes up ...?" He didn't mention Cherry's waking up; he knew that neither of them expected that.

Robert looked unsure. He looked towards the door and then outside the window. He ran a hand through his hair and licked his lips. "But, what if ... shit! I just don't know what to do Tony. If I leave, will they let me go, do you think?"

Tony glanced towards the closed door and shrugged, "You haven't done anything wrong, have you? The police have spoken with us and we told them what we could; which wasn't much. I know I have nothing to add, do you?"

Robert shook his head slowly, "No, what could I tell them anyway? My daughter touched some old stone and this happened? As if they'd believe that! I'd be an inpatient in seconds and then what?" He walked to the door and quickly looked out into the corridor, "Come on then. I need to go back to the dig site. Helen will be all right for now ..."

"And Cherry?"

"I can't protect her, Tony. I need answers to do that and I'm not going to get them here; will you help me?"

They walked fast. Tony didn't remind Robert that it was now full dark or that he'd left the keys with Kathryn to lock up; he just let him walk for now. He was walking fast and it occurred to him that they looked conspicuous, as if they really 'did' have something to hide, but he understood Robert's need to do something; anything.

He understood that feeling of uselessness. He'd felt that as he'd watched his mother slowly die of cancer six years ago. He understood that terrible feeling of helplessness when you can't fight the invisible killer; in her case, within her breast. His father had sat opposite him at the hospitable bed and he knew he'd felt the same thing. His sister had withdrawn; that feeling of helplessness too much to bear. Being there for his old friend felt useful. He wasn't sure how yet, but he knew that he wouldn't leave him.

No one stopped them. In fact, no one took any notice of either of them. They reached the car and Tony got into the driver's seat. He was shaking with adrenalin and noticed Robert was the same. Taking a deep breath to try to calm himself, he started the car, put it into gear and turned to his friend, "So, it's no use going to the site, it'll all be locked up. Besides, the finds will be at the museum."

"Yeah, okay, it's a start. Helen has the stone Cherry touched clasped in her hand, but there might be something else ..." He shrugged; what else could he say? It felt like he was falling into a huge chasm that had opened up beneath his feet and it terrified him. He'd fought long and hard to get out of that black hole last year and he'd done it with the knowledge that he had a wife and a child. Maybe not a loving wife, but who could blame her for that? He'd been given a second chance with his daughter and now he sensed he was losing her. Well, damn that! He was not losing his child without a fight.

Chapter Twenty-Seven

Helen stood a little shakily at the end of the small bed. Charlotte looked so peaceful; she could almost believe everything was all right. She eased herself down into the armchair nearest the bed and reached out to hold her child's hand. An electric shock ran between them and she jerked her hand away. She sat back stunned, staring down at her own hand and then towards Charlotte's; she saw nothing unusual. She reached out again and gently touched her daughter's fingers; it was like pins and needles running along her own fingers into the palm of her hand.

Refusing to stop the touch, she walked her fingers further along Charlotte's hand and gently clasped it. The pain that shot up her arm made her gasp and she let go. "What ...?"

She stared down at her child who was totally oblivious to the strange and painful sensations and wondered what was happening. She sat back in the chair and her hand went involuntarily to her cardigan pocket. She could feel the small round lump of the rune inside and she slowly drew it out. She stared down at the red marking on it and knew it was blood. How it had remained so intact after all these years, she couldn't contemplate, but of two things she was absolutely positive, it was some kind of evil magic and it was genuinely old.

She gently placed the rune on the floor, fighting the urge to throw it out of the window because she knew it was important somehow. She shook her hand hard, trying to rid the feeling of its coldness and reached out for her daughter again. Nothing. No electric current, in fact, no painful sensations of any kind. She looked down at the small rune; how could something so insignificant be the cause of all this? She bent to retrieve it, but quickly changed her mind and instead, eased herself onto the narrow bed and cradled her child's head.

She contemplated the meaning of the rune as she let her tears fall. If it had caused such a shock to her, then to Cherry, it must have been much worse. The thought of her child experiencing such pain made her feel sick and she held her daughter even tighter, hoping to alleviate some of that pain. The possibility of losing Charlotte was

177

inconceivable, yet the doctors were confused and unsure, the police accusing and cautious, especially as Robert seemed to have disappeared; it didn't look good. She let the tears fall untouched, mingling with the golden tresses of her baby as her heart broke completely.

***

Trevor did not move when Kathryn had finished her story. He watched her face, unblinking, before he slowly sat back in his chair. He said nothing as she bent down, plucked a tissue from the box, wiped her face, and blew her nose. He said nothing as she sat down opposite him, her eyes watching him, searching his face for reassurance as he stared back.

"Well?" Kathryn broke the long silence first; she couldn't stand it any longer.

He cleared his throat, "Well indeed." He nervously scratched his neck, "Kathryn, I have to ask, are you feeling, stress? Feeling overworked? Anything, to explain what you've just told me?" He didn't wait for a reply, "Because, I mean, really? You want me to believe this story of yours? I can barely begin to find words ..."

"I know, I know!" She leant forward and placed her face in her hands, "I hear myself telling you and seeing your expressions and I know." She threw her hands down, "I bloody know what it sounds like, but what can I say? It's the truth."

Trevor exhaled loudly and rubbed his chin, "Bloody hell, girl, you've told me some whoppers over the years, but this ... this is incredible." He moved his chair round to the side of the desk so he was closer to her. "You remember all of it, vividly?"

"Yes, I do now. Over the years it came to me in bits, mixed with dreams I couldn't quite remember, you know the feeling?" Not expecting a reply, she continued, "But lately like I said, for the most part, I remember him, Halldor and some of the families he murdered, but it's Einaar and his wife Astrid I remember best of all ..."

"Yes, you said, and their daughter, Inga was it? He, this Halldor, had them killed because he thought they were responsible for this plague type thing that was suddenly wiping out his village, this village; your village that you have dug up. Kathryn, do you hear what I am hearing, love? You're absolutely sure, you aren't somehow projecting yourself into a possible scenario or something ...?"

She shook her head, "No, Trevor, I'm not!" She could hear her voice getting louder and stopped to take a breath. "All I know for sure is that all of this is linked to this poor child. The rune stones, me, the village, even the spirits of Einaar and his wife. We have all been drawn here ... even Halldor who has been fighting us all this time ..."

"Who you say is this Mr Merton?"

"Yes. Why is that, do you think? Why would he try to stop the dig? His crime was nearly a thousand years ago, I doubt the police would be interested now!" Kathryn grimaced at her own joke and continued, "We've already seen burn marks in the soil, that wouldn't prove anything other than there was a fire, his killing spree wouldn't be detected, unless ..."

"Unless there were bodies ..." Trevor finished her sentence and took a steadying breath. "But why would that matter now?"

"I have to find the answer." Kathryn gently reached out and touched his hand, they were both shaking.

Trevor looked down at his feet for a moment before moving his chair a little closer. "Kathryn." He fought to keep his voice soft, "All I'm hearing is a stressed out woman. A woman who is so involved in everything that she is having wild dreams which feel real: I mean, who wouldn't want to feel like they weren't a Viking or a Roman or someone from history, who perhaps made history? It seems only logical that you should become so involved as to feel that you are a part of this lost village, it is after all, a huge find. I haven't been able to find anything in our papers to suggest there was a large village here."

He reached out and held one of her hands and squeezed, "Kathryn, darling, you're tired. You said yourself that lack of sleep has been a big issue for you lately. You're getting too involved in it all, and I really think this is your mind making dreams feel real. Hell, even I've had dreams where I wake believing I can walk again and I've stood up and fallen flat on my arse, but in that short moment in time I believed it wholeheartedly ... do you see?"

Kathryn slowly removed her hand from his and stood up, "Yes, I do see. I'm sorry to have bothered you Trevor."

"Hey come on, don't be like that. What else can I say to the story you've just told me?"

She shrugged and walked to the office door, "I guess I hoped you of all people would accept what I said and help me find the answers."

"Why, because it's a Norse mystery?"

"Yes." Without waiting for a response, she softly closed the office door.

***

Helen splashed cold water over her hot cheeks and angrily wiped them with a cloth. The policewoman had barely left and she couldn't stop shaking. How could Robert leave her and Charlotte? That fucking coward! After everything he'd put them through, the first sign of shit and he's off with his old mate! She slammed her fist down onto the basin and flinched as the pain shot up her arm; *damn the bastard!*

She glanced out into the small room to check Cherry, seeing that nothing had changed she withdrew back into the bathroom to finish her ablutions. Seeing her daughter like this was agonising, gut wrenchingly painful, but why would he run away? She thought he might have gone back to the cottage for Cherry's things, but then remembered they were in her little teddy bag in the back of the car, along with her doll; and the tears came again.

Wiping her face again, she stared at her reflection and felt utterly wretched and alone. She couldn't tell the doctors about the rune stone and she couldn't tell the police that ghosts had taken her baby; who would believe her? The doctors and police already looked at her in such a way as to imply she knew more than she was telling them; and of course, they were right, but what could she say?

A noise caught her attention and she went to the bathroom doorway. She watched as the morning sun shone through the large window; its golden rays filled the small room and for a moment, Cherry was bathed in a golden glow; it looked beautiful. The feeling of wonder abruptly turned to panic and she rushed into the room, flinging herself protectively over Charlotte. "NO! You can't take her, you can't! She isn't dead, damn it! SHE ISN'T DEAD!"

She wrapped her arms tightly around her baby, as if holding onto Cherry would stop her spirit leaving; she knew this was pointless, but she couldn't let go. Then, she saw her, almost hidden behind the rays of light. Her breath stuck in her throat as she thought it was her baby coming to say goodbye and a moan escaped her dry lips. Then the apparition stepped forward very gently, or perhaps she glided? Helen had no notion, only that the girl was closer and she could see it was not Cherry, it wasn't her baby and she felt sick with relief.

The child was perhaps a little younger than Cherry. She didn't speak, but Helen stared into the girl's blue eyes and knew that this was Inga and she meant nobody any harm. She was a child, nothing more.

Helen slowly eased herself off Cherry, glancing down to check for vital signs; seeing the rise and fall of her small chest, she looked back up into the face of Inga. She quickly licked her dry lips and cleared her throat. Her heart thrashed against her chest as she leant forward, "How can I help you? Why are you here? Are you here to help my baby …? Are you lost?" Her voice sounded strange, alien, but she swallowed and cleared her throat again, her eyes never leaving the unmoving spirit. "Do you know how I can save my daughter?"

For what seemed a long time, the child did not respond; Helen repeated the questions. The child's gaze moved downwards until it rested on the hospital floor. Slowly she raised her hand and pointed. Helen looked and her stomach clenched with fear and revulsion. The grey rune stone with its blood red marking lay where she had placed it. She looked back at the child; the room was empty.

Slowly she walked to where the child had stood and felt a slight chill, nothing more. She looked down at the stone and forced herself to bend down and wrap it in a bit of tissue before putting it into her pocket. The child had given her a starting point; a confirmation that the rune was the key, it had been the cause, now perhaps someone knew the cure.

She gently kissed Cherry on the forehead and walked to the door. Every ounce of her being wanted to stay, needed to stay, but the hard, cold stone in her pocket was a reminder that others might have the answers she needed to get her baby back, and if she had to fight a horde of Vikings or the devil for her baby's soul, then so be it. Walking out of the room with one last look at her daughter, she walked fast and with purpose.

***

Rafarta sat huddled before her own fire. She knew what was coming. She had known for some time that death was nearby, but had prayed hard to Odin that an answer would be forthcoming; it seemed that the great God had not listened. She heard the cries, the screams and the shouts of fear and disbelief coming from outside; they were getting closer as the men moved from home to home. She huddled closer to her fire to try to feel some warmth in her old bones, some comfort before the end; she felt nothing.

She opened her right hand and stared down at the runes she had made out of necessity. She'd known the man of God was coming and he would bring anger and hatred. He would separate the village and man would turn against his brother. She had screamed her curses at him for bringing this death upon the innocent and she had watched with satisfaction when they had slaughtered him like a pig.

She had silently stepped forward as they had gutted him and filled her bowl with his blood. No one had questioned her. Halldor had watched and nodded his approval. She knew that he hoped for some magical providence, such a stupid man.

Now as she held the stones in her hand, it felt as if every one of the runes was home to a hundred ants. Her skin crawled holding them, but she refused to let them go yet. Within the firelight, it seemed as if the markings had come alive. The blood as dark and red as the day she had made them to see death.

Death was here. She had known Halldor would find Einaar and his family and she had heard the whispers that all would be well once the bringer had been sent back to the gods. The villagers trusted their chief to save them from the sickness. The fools! She had looked into Halldor's eyes in the Great Hall and seen his mind. She had observed his treachery that he would commit out of fear and said nothing. Now, it was too late.

Too late to change his mind. Too late to warn the villagers. Too late to save herself. She became aware that the smell of smoke was stronger. Another cry shattered her reverie and she dived onto all fours and began scrambling at the dirt floor. They were close now; she could sense them. Digging quicker, her nails clawing at the damp earth, she made a deep small hole and threw the runes into it. She had barely managed to replace the earth when her small, wooden door was pulled aside. She stared up at the man she had known and served. Her eyes never left his even as the blade swung across her neck.

Chapter Twenty-Eight

Robert collapsed onto a chair while Tony looked along the table where the finds from yesterday's excavation lay. He picked up one or two items without taking them out of their bags and quickly replaced them; he had no idea what he was looking for anyway. "So now what? These are bits and pieces of pottery with fragments of decoration and markings. I've already looked through most of these and there was so much of it I wouldn't know where to begin."

Robert rubbed his eyes, "I don't know ... I just don't know! I had to get out of that hospital, I felt so useless. I still feel useless here, surrounded by all this." He vaguely waved his hand around the room, "I don't know or understand what is happening to my Charlotte and less of an idea on how to save her. All I know for sure, is the doctors can't ..."

His voice cracked with emotion and he bent his head. To say it aloud made it all too real. His darling baby was gone. If he was to believe Kathryn and Helen, she was possibly with ghosts, for God's sake! Maybe that was it? They'd tried to take her body and that hadn't worked, so now they'd somehow taken her mind and soul. It was impossible to contemplate. How was he supposed to bring her back?

Did other parents of sick children conjure stories? Was it a coping mechanism to help through the trauma? He could make sense of that however twisted it might sound. Was that what they were doing, some kind of mass hypnosis? Alternatively, was he losing his mind again? Seeing strange things, feeling paranoid, they were all symptoms of his previous breakdown. He'd stopped taking his medication a month ago and hadn't made any new appointments with a counsellor as promised. His psychiatrist would have a field day with this story and he had no doubts as to where he would end up.

A noise in the doorway made them both jump, "Hello gentlemen, you're in early Tony ...?" Trevor wheeled his chair further into the room and stared at both of them, "You both look terrible. I had a very interesting conversation with Kathryn last night. Would that mean anything to you ...?"

He watched their reactions before continuing, "From your silence, I take it you know what I'm talking about. Past lives and Vikings etc. Is it true? Are you as concerned as I am?"

Tony glanced across at Robert who shifted uncomfortably in his chair. Tony picked up a stapler before quickly replacing it, "Erm, yeah, I mean, I don't know what she told you, but ..."

Robert jumped in, "Look, I don't know who you are and frankly, I don't have time to care, sorry ..." he quickly added, "But, my daughter is lying in a hospital bed. The doctors don't know what's wrong with her; some kind of coma; the point is, it happened after touching something found on the dig and the other night, she was abducted by ghosts ..."

Seeing Trevor's reaction, he bit his lower lip to stop himself from telling him exactly what he thought of his opinion, but a quick glance at Tony stopped him and he quickly continued. "Viking ghosts to be exact and we think there might be some kind of connection. From what Kathryn told me yesterday; they belonged at the site, it was their village or something and for whatever reason, they have interacted with my daughter and now ... This has happened. I don't believe in coincidences ..." He glanced at Tony, "So there it is."

Trevor took a deep breath, he was shaking. He could see the emotions playing across the man's face and knew how hard that had been for him. He'd gone home but had been unable to sleep, so he'd come back to his office; he always found being around the artefacts comforting. Kathryn's story plagued his head and by the early hours of the morning, he found himself believing it the more he looked at it objectively.

As an archaeologist, he had come across ghost stories before. Tombs and burial mounds mostly, guarded by the dead. He had a catalogue of stories he'd picked up throughout the years; Wales seemed to be the most active, with Egypt being a close second; so why not Vikings? He'd heard of black dogs flying through the night as part of the wild hunt taking those unfortunate souls who meet them, to white ladies terrifying any man who dared venture too close.

One of his favourite stories had been the golden man, seen in the nineteenth century in a town called 'Mold' in North Wales. Many years later workmen digging up a road had come across a burial mound with a giant of a man clad in golden armour; the breastplate now sat in the British museum. He believed in spirits so long as there was documentation to prove it, but past lives and ghosts stealing children was one step beyond.

He was sure he'd seen a ghost once when he was a student; a young girl. He had stayed behind in university to finish an essay and it had been quite late when he'd finally left. The corridors were empty and it'd felt quite eerie when he'd opened a door and a young girl was standing there. Apologising, he'd stepped around her to walk down some steps but it hadn't been until he'd reached the bottom step when it occurred to him that firstly it was a bit late for such a young girl, she'd looked about eight or nine and secondly, her clothing had been a bit odd. Looking back up the five steps, she wasn't there. Running back up to the door he'd flung it open and looked down the corridor: nobody.

He'd asked one of the professors the next day if anyone had had a child with them last night, but she'd not heard of anyone bringing children to the University late at night. A few weeks later, they were doing some research on the grounds of the University when his friend had come across an old newspaper article about a terrible accident. In the early nineteenth century, cottages had stood on the site before the new university had been built. A child, a young girl, had been trampled to death by a coach and horses; the man responsible took it badly and shot himself.

The librarian had told them, "I've heard people have seen their ghosts wandering around the place. The old man is begging forgiveness but the little girl won't give it ...!"

Trevor had laughed with the rest of them as they had messed about making ghostly noises, but he hadn't felt completely sure and to this day, he hadn't really made up his mind about it, until this very moment. He glanced across at Tony and then back at Robert, "I didn't believe Kathryn, but, now, I'm not so sure. The things she told me are remarkable to say the least and now, your daughter ... I can barely take it all in."

"You think it's easy for me?" Robert said gruffly, "It's a nightmare and I have no idea how to wake from it."

Trevor nodded, "I'm sure of that, I have no doubt it must be terrible for you. Will you tell me what has happened?"

Robert sat back and rubbed his hands through his hair, "Yeah, why not?"

Trevor shook his head, "Robert, I understand your scepticism, but it won't help, I need to know the facts if I am to help you ..."

"Help me?" Robert leant forward, "Can you help my daughter?"

"Perhaps. Please tell me everything about these Vikings, everything you can remember about them."

Tony had pinched the kitchen kettle on their way in, along with sachets of coffee, sugar and powered milk; he would deal with the complaints from the staff another time. He switched on the kettle and began making three strong coffees as he listened to Robert describing in detail everything that had happened to them since moving into the cottage. Although Robert had already told him most of it, the part about the black shadows sent shivers up his spine and he silently sent a prayer to any angels listening that the little girl wasn't with them.

***

Helen cautiously opened the front door and peered into the dark hallway; it felt normal. Stepping inside she gently closed the door behind her. The house still felt new to her and she felt like an intruder as she stepped further into the hall, all the while listening for any noise. The house was quiet. She heard nothing except the low hum of the fridge in the kitchen and her breath, short and trembling with fear.

She'd asked the taxi to drop her off on the main road and had made her way over the field behind the cottage, all the while looking out for police cars. She felt like a criminal sneaking towards her own home, but she couldn't afford to be stopped and questioned even more. She'd dived behind a bush when a white car had driven past and hid behind the stone wall when a cyclist rode by; no one saw her.

Although the morning sun illuminated the house, she reached for the light switch and held her breath as the hallway was flooded with light. She quickly glanced into the lounge, one of Cherry's books lay on the sofa and her throat constricted with grief. Fighting back tears, she headed for the stairs and looked up; the landing was gloomy and had an air of malevolence about it. Pressing the light switch, she bit her lower lip nervously when the light didn't come on. She tried again, knowing even as she did it, that there was no point.

She swallowed and licked her dry lips; she could sense the house listening, waiting. "Cherry?" Her voice sounded strange as it echoed around the empty home. She listened intently; all her senses were on alert; it felt like the house was listening, waiting, so she began to climb the stairs slowly, "Cherry darling ... It's Mummy?" Only silence as the house seemed to be holding its breath waiting to see what would happen.

***

Kathryn sat in her car in the lay-by for a long time. She'd finally stopped crying but her head ached and she couldn't think straight anymore. At one point, she dozed off from sheer exhaustion and woke with a stiff, cold neck, hands like ice and bursting for the toilet. She'd hurriedly relieved herself behind her car before running back inside, locking the door and turning on the engine to warm up.

She felt responsible for that little girl somehow. She'd followed her curiosity and instincts to dig in that area, all the while fighting her bone-gnawing fear; was that wrong or was she a victim in all this too? Halldor's betrayal had left a stain so deep, it had haunted her whole life and she despised him for that. Her childhood lost because of dreams of another childhood cut short; it wasn't fair.

She knew now why she had followed her dreams without reason or proof, she had needed answers to the questions that had tormented her mind for as long as she could remember. Perhaps there'd been an element of revenge? Like a posthumous trial? Finding the answers, the evidence of Halldor's crime, her murder, though what it would achieve in the end would be questionable. A murderous moment in history uncovered for the world to see and question and judge; perhaps that was enough for now?

Moreover, what of Rafarta and her runes? She knew they would have significance otherwise Rafarta would never have made them, but she could not fathom the connection between her runes and this child? Unless ... the child had a connection to the village? Rafarta was powerful. Her connection to the energies of the earth, air, fire and water and the gods and the goddesses was uncanny. Could Rafarta's power still be so strong after so many centuries hidden beneath the soil?

She wiped her nose with her sleeve. So many questions rattled at full pelt around her head. Reincarnation. Ghosts. Einaar, Astrid, stealing Cherry ... Why? Cherry in some kind of coma because she touched a rune stone of Rafarta's. The rune stone was in the trench next to where she'd found the pool of blood. The drug addict ... why was he killed? It must have been his blood, so why move his body? To kill him on site was one thing, but for his body to be found on site was quite another; it would have stopped the dig for sure, so why move it - unless his blood was necessary on site, but the dig had to continue to find the runes. She was beginning to feel as if she'd been set up somehow and it wasn't a nice feeling.

Starting her car, she thought for a moment where to go first. Back to the hospital or back to the museum for the rest of the rune stones? Deciding on the hospital, she would make a short detour to Robert's house first; she wanted to see it for herself and perhaps re-connect with Einaar and Astrid; maybe they would help her save the little girl?

***

Robert felt like his whole body ached. His head throbbed and his eyes felt gritty; he hadn't slept for such a long time it felt like he was stoned. He looked across at Tony who was staring down into his empty cup, he did not look much better. He had a rush of gratitude towards his old friend and then felt a rush of guilt and remorse, for here again was someone else he had left behind in his search for power and wealth.

He hated himself more than he ever thought possible at this point. During his breakdown, he'd retreated into his own little world for most of the time. He'd ignored Helen, his family, his friends, but worse for him was that he had ignored darling Cherry; his precious daughter. He could vaguely remember hearing Helen asking if he wanted to come with them to a park, feed the ducks, visit some place or other; he had always said no. Preferring to be alone in the quiet house, the curtains drawn where he would lie on the bed or the sofa and stare into space ... remembering.

He would go over and over his carefree days as a student; when he'd had a large circle of friends and he'd be out most weekends. He could recall the night he first saw Helen and the moment he knew he'd fallen in love with her. Their perfect wedding day and the two weeks in Greece; not as much sightseeing had gone on as planned; instead they'd curled up for hours in bed, just staring at each other, touching, exploring and making plans together.

Then he'd remember how cold, selfish and cruel he'd become. At the time, he'd shied away from the truth, telling himself that he was doing it for her. To give her a good life, a life free of worries; but the day she'd told him she was pregnant, he'd felt nothing but betrayal; it hadn't been part of the plan for another few years and he'd been so angry, he'd dared to tell her it wasn't a good time, perhaps in a few years …? When he remembered that day, he felt physically sick. He hadn't even been at the birth, a meeting had run over; that had been much more important. He didn't deserve his daughter.

Now she was gone. Helen was lost to him, of that, he was fairly certain. He felt physically sick. He didn't deserve his daughter. He'd let her down, he deserved pain and suffering, but Charlotte did not. His baby deserved life, a good life. He had to fight, and he had to keep going, the alternative didn't bear thinking about.

Abruptly he stood up, "Right, what are we doing 'cause I'll go mental if I stay here with no answers."

Tony looked him up and down and smirked, "You fancy a fight then Rob?"

"I'll fight every damn' ghost in this fuckin' world if I have to; I want my baby girl back!" Turning to Trevor who had been reading through the finds list, he raised his eyebrows questioningly, "Well? Find anything useful in all that?"

Trevor slowly took off his glasses and shrugged, "It would seem a lot of the finds were centred on one area, which would suggest it was one dwelling. The rune stones Carolyn found also came from that area. The way they were found tells me that they were all placed there together, not scattered, do you see?" He glanced at each man before continuing, "So, that would say that a person hid them, buried them, so why do that? From where they were found it would suggest they were buried at the same time as the fire which swept through the village, which Kathryn has already told me about." Seeing Tony's expression, he stopped, "Has she said something to you?"

"Yeah, she did say something about it."

Robert shook his head, "Yeah, when she told me and Helen I thought she was nuts, now I don't know. But if she is telling the truth then, maybe she can remember something that will help us?"

Trevor shook his head, "I find all this too hard to contemplate, but Kathryn said she was a child when she died. Runes were not for children to play with; they were sacred to a wise woman perhaps or the chief if he was spiritual." He gingerly picked up the bag containing the five rune stones and placed them on the table.

"These were specially made for some long lost reason. Our analysis shows the markings are coloured by human blood."

Tony leant forward, but kept his hands behind his back, "But these look fresh. If it had been blood surely it would have dissolved away, I mean, for Christ's sake, they have been under the soil for hundreds of years ..."

"I know, I know, it is impossible to fathom how they have remained so perfect, but they are as fresh today as they would have been when made." Trevor turned to one of his books, "It says here that rune stones made with human blood were used for some diabolical purpose, the secrets of which have never been found. They can only guess that the blood may have come from some victim, an enemy perhaps. The runes would have been made whilst chanting long lost words to invoke the intent. Perhaps this person was punished. And, if we are to believe Kathryn, then this person may have been murdered along with the rest of the village."

"Do you think these rune stones have anything to do with my daughter?" Robert stood in front of the table but like Tony, felt no inclination to touch the runes.

Trevor nodded, "I think so, though how or why, I have no idea, but Carolyn and Kathryn both told me your child touched another one of these and collapsed into her state, is that true?"

"Yes, Carolyn said she was kneeling down and reached for it and ..." Robert frowned, "Helen has it, the other one, the rune Cherry touched, and I saw it in her hand. I think she knows ..."

"Knows what, mate?"

Robert turned to look at Tony, "I think she knows it all lies with this rune. The way Helen looked at it when Cherry collapsed; it is the only thing that makes sense, I think she understands."

Trevor nodded, "Most mothers do. Is she still at the hospital?"

Robert shrugged, "I have no idea, but I doubt she would leave Cherry alone, besides, the doctor gave her a mild sedative to calm her, although that should have worn off by now." He glanced at his watch, "It is almost ten in the morning."

"I think we need that other rune stone. If memory serves me well, we will need the whole set to bargain for your daughter's life. And, I think we should find your wife and Kathryn, they play a part in all of this."

"Why?"

"Because, Robert, I have, shall we say, dabbled over the years. As an archaeologist, I have witnessed many strange and unexplainable things and followed my curiosity, which has taken me to depths of depravity I would not care to explain. I had hoped to leave all of that behind me, but, it seems that is not to be the case."

He tried to smile reassuringly, but failed. "I know someone who might help, but I don't trust him. I don't think at this point we have much choice if I'm to believe everything I've heard. We need to be prepared for a battle and the best way to be prepared is to have knowledge. It's too much of a coincidence, past lives with Kathryn and Mr Merton and God knows who else. That murder, this dig, those runes, everything has a reason and I can't think of anything else to try. If what Kathryn and yourselves are saying is true, the police can't find Charlotte, she's not anywhere they can go; we need to go a different route. They say, go with your instincts, so, I'm going with mine ..."

Robert moved quickly towards the door. He put the bag of rune stones in his jacket pocket and fought the urge to be sick. He began dialling Helen's phone number on his mobile and was already walking away. He turned to see that Tony and Trevor were hastily grabbing their coats and switching off lights ready to follow him. For the first time in a long time, he felt he had a purpose, and damned if anyone was stopping him, dead or not.

Chapter Twenty-Nine

"**S**he's not here! She's not here!"

Kathryn had found Helen sitting in the middle of what she presumed to be Charlotte's bedroom sobbing uncontrollably and shouting those words over and over. She'd stood frozen in the doorway, unsure what to do. Helen needed to get it out of her system and perhaps this was the best thing for her? Something broke inside her and she ran to the woman who was almost a stranger and held her tightly, feeling her own tears run down her cheeks.

It took a long time for Helen to become calmer, her sobbing subsided into occasional sniffs and muffled groans, and Kathryn felt able to release her. Part of her missed that contact and she stood up awkwardly, her legs were stiff from kneeling so long. She quickly found the bathroom, pulled a wad of toilet paper off the roll, and brought it back. Helen didn't acknowledge her at all, so she left it beside her, wiping her own tears with the back of her hand.

She glanced around the pretty room and swallowed the rising emotion for the poor child. Teddies and dolls littered the small bed. On the small wooden dressing table sat a lamp in the shape of a flower, a pair of discarded socks next to it and a drawing of what looked like a beach scene. On the window ledge she saw various pictures of the family in a variety of flower shaped frames, the largest one was a picture of a cat. The single wardrobe and a large toy chest completed the furniture in the large room. She knew the child hadn't been in the house for very long, yet the room was Charlotte's completely, and that was the awfulness of it.

She turned back to Helen who was watching her. She sat on the bed, "You OK? Stupid question, I know, but ..." She shrugged. What else could she say?

"Yeah ... I just thought she might ... God!" Helen banged her fist down on the carpet, "I feel so useless against this ... this, thing! Whatever they are. Where is she? Do you know?"

Kathryn shrugged, "I'm not sure. In the past, perhaps? In their own world, another dimension, I don't know, but I think the runes are something to do with it.

Charlotte touched it and that is what led to all this, so, in theory, I think that is what might bring her back?"

Helen searched her face before reaching into her pocket and bringing out a tissue. She placed it on the floor and looked up at Kathryn, "This is the one she touched. In the hospital, I saw a child, a young girl and don't ask me how I know, but, I am convinced it was Inga, their own daughter."

"Wow, that's amazing! How do you know, though? I mean, it could have been a trick of the light, your emotional state."

Helen blew her nose on the wad of tissue paper before answering, she looked annoyed, "Yeah, my emotional state is hanging on by a thread right now but I know when I see a fuckin' ghost all right! And how the hell can you question me after your revelation yesterday?"

Kathryn held up her hands, "Hey, I'm sorry, I know I have no right to question you, it's just, I can't understand; if it was Inga, then why take your Charlotte? What has separated them in the spirit world?"

"I don't know. I always presumed we would be with our loved ones when we die."

"So did I. Puts a different spin on everything I've always believed." Both women were silent for a few minutes as they thought about the implications of being separated from everyone you loved in heaven, or would that be hell?

Kathryn spoke first, "So, did this ghost do or say anything?"

"Yes actually, she did, she pointed at the rune stone."

Kathryn looked down at the stone wrapped in tissue and shuddered, "What do you mean?"

Helen quickly explained how it felt in her hand and the electric shocks and how she'd dropped it on the hospital floor. "It makes my skin crawl and it makes me feel like I am in the presence of something very wrong, I can't explain it better than that."

Kathryn sighed loudly, "Thank God, I thought I was the only one. When Carolyn found the others, no ounce of my being wanted to touch them. They ooze evil and I feel dirty just being in their presence."

"How did Carolyn react to them?"

Kathryn frowned, "Actually, she didn't seem bothered by them. Excited at having found something unique, that's all, I didn't see her look uncomfortable."

"Don't you think that's a bit strange? I mean, here we are, we don't really know each other, but we're both feeling the same thing when other people aren't. The only other connection is the ghosts in this house are people you can remember from your other life. Then Charlotte touches something from your village and now, she is gone ... somewhere ..." Her voice broke with emotion again and she swallowed hard, "Do you think I lived here before? Did Charlotte? Do you know me? That might explain why I feel revulsion and shock when touching the stones and others haven't?"

Kathryn thought for a minute, "I suppose that would make sense. Any spirit connected to that time might feel some residue off these stones ... I don't know, it's a theory, but why did it affect Charlotte in that way and no one else?"

"I don't know. Maybe it's because she's a child. The electric shock was quite strong, even for me ...?" She thought for a moment, "Do you think there are others? Robert and Tony? I read somewhere years ago about past life theories, that you meet the same souls in every lifetime to learn something. Not necessarily related, but they will have a significant reason for being in your life. They knew each other as children ..."

Kathryn stood up and licked her dry lips. Seeing how she suddenly looked agitated Helen stood too and looked around nervously, "What is it?"

"I know another person connected to the site, a man who has been against the dig since it was first announced, a Jonah Merton, he came to see me, to see if I knew him."

"And you did?

"Yeah, I knew him. While we were talking, the images of him as my chief Halldor came flooding back."

"Bloody hell!" Helen gasped in disbelief, "So, what did he do?"

Kathryn bit her lower lip and shrugged, "What could he do? He seemed pleased with himself and glad that I recognised him. He still had many of Halldor's traits, it was scary. I didn't feel safe with him and I think he knew it, and liked it."

"Could he be significant in getting my baby back do you think? If he's really lived before and, as you say, he was your chief?"

"I wish I knew. I have my suspicions about him for other things, I wouldn't trust him."

"I don't need to trust him; I don't care if he's the devil. If he can help bring my Cherry back, I'd do anything." Helen walked to the top of the stairs and looked back, "Where does he live?"

Kathryn groaned loudly, "I don't have his address, but Trevor might. Merton has sent my boss lots of letters complaining about the dig, they should have his address on. However, I really don't think this is a good idea ..." Seeing Helen's determined look, she took out her phone, "Hang on, I'll call Trevor, he's probably going to fire me anyway after the story I told him last night and then have me locked away dribbling in my tea." Her attempt at lightening the mood was ignored. She shrugged and dialled the number.

***

They were in the car heading for the hospital when Trevor answered his phone. Hearing his end of the conversation, Robert slammed on his brakes and pulled into the side of the road. "Is that Helen and Kathryn? Where are they? Is Charlotte okay? Has she woken up?"

Trevor raised his hand to silence him as he listened to whoever was speaking, "No, don't do that, we'll meet you at the site, he lives somewhere nearby, if we need him we'll find him. See you soon, and be careful, both of you." Putting his phone away he smiled, "It would seem we are all on the same page in terms of having ideas to get your child back. Head for the site Robert, the girls will meet us there. I believe that is where we should start."

Robert moved out onto the road, "Any news of Charlotte?"

Trevor shook his head sadly, "I'm afraid not, but let's not give up yet eh?"

Robert drove as fast as he dared, he didn't want to catch anyone's attention; but it was difficult to stop his foot from pressing fully onto the accelerator. His mind was a whirl of questions with impossible answers. Was his little Cherry pip dead and that was just her body lying in the hospital? Would Helen forgive him for leaving the hospital? Would she understand now that she had, too? Could they do this together? Would it work whatever Trevor was thinking? Were they all insane?

He wished more than anything that this was a bad nightmare and soon he would wake up and hear Cherry asking for her 'Rice nice'... It would never happen again if they failed and he quickly wiped a stray tear from his cheek.

***

It was deathly silent as Kathryn got out of her car again, the gate swinging gently behind her. She turned and wedged it into the grass verge so the others could drive straight in. The students had been told to have the day off, using Charlotte's condition as an excuse. They'd barely argued; nothing worse than digging with a hangover.

She stopped, standing with the door open, feeling uneasy and vulnerable. She listened intently, for what, she wasn't sure, but listened anyway. Helen seemed to feel the same, as she stood motionless on the other side of the car. Kathryn glanced across at her and met her stare. "What are you thinking?" she asked in a whisper.

Helen was biting the inside of her cheek as she quickly glanced around, "I'm not sure, but it feels, different. It looks spooky with all those bushes, anyone could be hiding there, you know?"

Kathryn glanced nervously towards where Helen nodded, it was too easy to imagine someone standing, watching them unseen. The bushes that surrounded most of the site had never bothered her before now. She felt a strong urge to get back into the car and wait until the others came, but Helen had already closed her door and was moving slowly towards her. "Shall we wait here? They shouldn't be too long."

Helen wasn't listening. She was staring intently towards the area of the long trench where Charlotte had collapsed, a slight frown on her face. She started to walk towards it, but stopped when Kathryn gently placed a hand on her arm, "What is it?"

"I'm not sure, but I feel ... I don't know, I can't explain it, I just, feel ..." She continued to look in the direction of the trench. It seemed to Kathryn that she had become unaware of her presence and shuddered.

At that moment, a car drew up next to hers and she sighed with relief as Tony climbed out, quickly followed by Robert. Tony helped Trevor with his wheelchair while Robert hastily jogged to Helen's side, barely acknowledging Kathryn as he passed. She walked back towards Trevor and Tony and smiled weakly, "Good to see you."

Tony smiled and quickly glanced around. Trevor looked sheepish as he looked up at her, she playfully punched his arm, "See, I never lie to you, do I?"

"I guess not, at least, about this." He wheeled his chair forward a little, though it was difficult on the uneven terrain, "So, this is it, is it, the village site. This isn't quite what I had in mind when I said I would come and observe your work. I would have preferred a busy site, full of students, volunteers and interested onlookers and not looking out for the police or supernatural beings, but, it would seem fate has other ideas ..."

Tony managed to push him a little further past the cars. The going was bumpy and slow. All three stopped as they neared Robert who was standing a little behind Helen; she had not moved. Tony left Trevor and went to Robert's side, "What's wrong with Helen? Is she still a bit woozy from the sedative?"

"I don't think so, that should have passed by now surely. She's just staring over there. I can't see anything, can you?"

Tony shook his head, "No, but, the place feels a bit weird?"

Kathryn joined them, "What's going on? She was doing that before you came." She pointed towards Helen, "It's freaking me out."

Suddenly, it was there. It changed so abruptly, no one had time to breathe. The air felt heavy and oppressive and Helen took a step back as a large black mass formed before her. The trench was ten feet away and the blackness filled it within seconds.

Robert froze for a second, before reaching out and pulling Helen to his side; she didn't notice, her whole focus was on the growing blackness. Tears streamed down her ashen face and her body shook, as did his. He became aware of nothingness, no sound, no air, no light, only the darkness as it reached out to them. He felt the pain, the horror, the suffering and agonies of that blackness and his stomach clenched in terror as it gained strength. He knew it was using their energies; as it grew, he became weaker, light-headed, an easier victim.

He couldn't remember reaching for her hand, but suddenly there it was and he clamped onto it. He could feel the slick sweat of each other's palms, but he held on tighter. The blackness looked solid, but then he could see people within it, reaching out, begging, moulding into one form after another; there were so many men and women. Trapped and frightened, their screams silent, yet their mouths open wide in a never-ending agony of eternity.

The blackness wanted them. The energy had awakened and it was not complete, not whole without them. He could see the eyes, beseeching him and the hands, reaching, begging and he almost gave in. He felt his body sag and his will to live diminish and in that second, he began to move forward, his hand outstretched. Charlotte was gone; perhaps she was within the dark. It was his duty as her father to bring her back.

A sound beside him made him turn his head as Helen opened her mouth and shouted, "NO!" over and over again. Her voice brought him back to reality and gave him courage and he took up the chant and as one, they stood before the blackness and took back their right to live.

Chapter Thirty

K athryn sank to her knees as every ounce of strength she had left her, she could barely keep her head upright. Tony fell down beside her and put his head in his hands. She managed to twist around slightly so that she could see Trevor. He was sitting rigid, staring at the trench. His hands were white as they clung to his chair's arms. It seemed as if she could see every white blood cell in his face; he started to shake, crossed his arms as if he was hugging himself for comfort and bent his head.

She knew how he felt. She wanted nothing more than to turn inward, go foetal and never come out of that safe position. She glanced at Tony, but he was staring down at the ground and trying to steady his breathing. He looked like he was about to vomit and she wanted to tell him it was all right; but her mouth wouldn't work. It felt like her brain and her body were no longer working together.

She managed to lift her head and look towards the trench, where only seconds ago, death had stared back at them; there was no sign of anything amiss and she fleetingly questioned whether it had been real, but another quick glance around at the others answered that stupid question.

She had felt the breath of death and decay. Felt the fingers of those long gone, dust and bone within that blackness and heard their cries of outrage and despair. A tiny part of her had welcomed the familiarity of some of the energies that she could almost put names to. However, the larger part of her soul had shrunk away in terror from it and it was this that had won overall. She couldn't help but wonder what could have happened if she'd let her old soul reach out for those remembered? Would she have become a part of that death? The answer came immediately inside her head, 'yes' and she let the tears fall as relief swept through her; she was alive, here and now and that was what her soul wanted.

***

Helen became aware of her body after what seemed like hours, but could not have been more than a few minutes. The sounds of the countryside reached her first. Birds twittered in the branches nearby and a dog was barking in the distance, followed by the answer of an angry owner. She could hear the low hum of cars from the nearby road, which meant people, going about their lives only hundreds of yards away; they might as well have been a hundred miles away for what use they were.

A plane high in the sky overhead, she managed to look up and saw the familiar white line against the cloudy blue sky and wept with relief. They had all stepped into something that did not belong in their world. It had broken free and pulled them all in, just for a moment, but a moment was long enough to feel and understand that it was torment.

She'd felt a yearning for freedom so strong, it clung to her skin, her cells, her very being. She'd become a part of it, touched its very essence. She began to cry uncontrollably for the poor souls trapped within its darkness, for herself and her own loss, but also for gratitude; Charlotte was not there, she was not a part of that blackness.

Slowly, she became aware of the others behind her. Of Robert who still clung to her hand and was watching her with such love and concern it unnerved her; she quickly let go and wiped her hand on her jeans. She saw him about to speak, but stop himself and sink back onto the grass. She kept her eyes averted; she didn't know what to say to him as every emotion was whirling around her body. Grief, fear, revulsion, anger, frustration and something else she hadn't felt for such a long time with him - love. It made her too angry to even admit it, so she forced it aside and let the anger come instead.

Robert reached out, she saw his need for comfort, reassurance and she flinched away, stumbled and sat down heavily on the wet grass. She looked up at him briefly and turned away when she saw him rejected and hurt. She couldn't think about him and his needs right now.

Their baby was lost. Why should she think about him? Had he ever thought about her or darling Cherry? When had he put them first? The full extent of her mistake filled her very being, what were they doing here? She should be at the hospital with her baby, protecting her, talking to her, reassuring her that she wasn't alone; instead, she'd left on some crazy notion that she could find the answers … She was wrong. The thought made her find the strength to stand.

Her body was heavy; every movement was an extreme effort. Managing to stand a little unsteadily, her stomach clenched, she turned to the side and vomited bile; she hadn't eaten for such a long time. Wiping her mouth, she noticed Tony and Kathryn sitting on the floor near the cars looking shocked and scared and felt a wave of gratitude; a man in a wheelchair sat behind them looking dazed; that must be Trevor, Kathryn had mentioned.

Somehow, she managed to stumble towards the cars and rest with her back against one, catching her breath. Her energy drained, which did not surprise her. She'd read that ghosts needed energy to do what they did. Whatever she had just witnessed had obviously needed everyone's energy judging, from their behaviour.

"Where are you going?" Robert had followed her; he reached out and touched her arm.

She pulled her arm away ignoring his hurt expression, "I'm going back to the hospital of course! Whatever that was ..." she vaguely waved her arm in the direction of the trenches, "It might be able to reach Charlotte, I have to protect her, I made a mistake leaving her alone, I should be with her, not here, with you." She spat out the last two words and turned to go.

Robert moved to stand in her way, a huge effort considering he was having trouble staying upright. "No, we should stay here, this is where they are; can't you feel them?"

She glared at him, her breath quickening as she fought her emotions, but did not answer.

He stepped a little closer, "I know you hate me and I deserve that, but tell me, honestly, didn't you feel them, here, within this place? They're stuck here ... I think they were scared. Something made them retreat or we'd be dead."

"I think you're right." Trevor's voice sounded odd and he quickly cleared his throat, "As soon as you stood together as man and wife, mother and father, united, it retreated, I saw that and felt that."

Helen looked unsure. Robert nodded his head, "I think that's true. When they came, in the house, we stood together, they retreated, didn't they?"

"Yes, but, if that's true about having power as husband and wife, that would mean nothing coming from us, we're a joke. I think it's just coincidence."

She held his stare, but he didn't look away, "Maybe that's true Helen, but I still love you, more now than I ever have ... fool that I am, I didn't realise how much until you backed away." He took hold of both her arms, "I deserve that. I deserve to lose you and maybe I deserve to lose Cherry too ..." His voice cracked with emotion, but he carried on, "But whatever I deserve, our daughter does not deserve this and I will fight to get her back. Let me fight by your side. We might not be husband and wife anymore, but we are still father and mother. I believe the answer is here; I'm sure of it; please Helen."

The indecision was overwhelming. The need to get back to her baby was extremely powerful, but if the answer to saving her daughter lay here ...? She silently asked for guidance; was her child safe at the hospital? A small voice answered, "Yes" and she broke down and sank to her knees.

The blackness had filled her every pore with fear, there had been no room for hope within that darkness. Now, she understood. That was it. Whoever they had been, had no hope. There was so much pain and misery without hope of being at peace. Little wonder then that they were pissed off. What little hope she had for Cherry was the only thing keeping her upright and moving. She knew how important hope was and silently prayed that it was enough.

It was a long time before she was able to speak. By that time, everyone had regained some of their strength and had moved inside the cars for some warmth. She sat in the passenger seat of Kathryn's car, Robert stood leaning against the car, facing her, while Trevor sat in the passenger seat of Robert's car, the door wide open, Tony sat in the driver's seat and Kathryn sat in the back.

"Don't ask me how I know this, but I think these people need help. They aren't evil, just without hope."

"What do you mean, Helen?" Trevor leant closer; the bag of runes he had retrieved from Robert sat on his lap and clattered slightly with the movement that made Helen shudder.

"I mean, they have no hope. I felt their pain and suffering, so, imagine all of that with no hope of ever having peace; I guess it would make me feel nothing but negative which in turn would turn inward and bring anger, frustration, hate ..."

"If that's so, is it the same for the Viking ghosts that came to your home"

"You mean Einaar and Astrid," Kathryn chimed in. "I didn't feel them in that ... thing."

Helen shook her head, "No, I didn't get a sense of any one particular person. When they came to our home, they stepped from blackness. They seemed to be one whole, which then parted and formed them."

"I see, so Einaar and Astrid are separate from the others. From what you've told me, Kathryn, that would make sense, wouldn't it." Trevor pulled his Jacket closer, "If this Halldor murdered his villagers, that is one thing, but he went out and murdered this family separately. You said he hunted them down. Do you know what he did with their bodies?"

Kathryn shook her head, "No, I don't think I ever knew. I think he murdered the village as soon as he returned from killing Einaar and Astrid and of course little Inga."

Tony shook his head, "What drives a man to commit such an evil act, do you think?"

"I don't know, Tony." Kathryn turned to look at him, "Fear maybe? He was scared of becoming sick. A chief shouldn't die like that. He should die in battle, with honour."

"Jesus, Kathryn! Where did that come from? You sounded sorry for the bastard! He was a killer, nothing more. There's no honour in killing a child."

"Sorry. I guess it's residue from my Norse soul. They truly believed that a dishonourable death would send them to Hell"

Trevor nodded, "Yes, that's right. Valhalla was the place they strived to reach. Christians know it as heaven; same thing but with different names and if I remember rightly, different pleasures awaited them." He quickly added seeing Robert frown.

"I read somewhere that time has no meaning when we die. Imagine nearly a thousand years of torment, would that feel like a thousand years or not? Is what we saw proof that there isn't a heaven or Valhalla, that there is only death?"

"Maybe." Kathryn looked out at the site of her village where the black energy had formed, "But, what if you believe that every soul has a journey over many lifetimes, like I have journeyed? I died here, but I'm not stuck here, I have been reborn into this life. Maybe, they are stuck? Maybe, the others haven't been able to continue on their journey, wouldn't that make them angry? I know I would be."

"OK, if that's the case, and we are to believe that you lived in this village before, why aren't you stuck? Why aren't you a part of whatever that was?" Tony waved his hand vaguely in the direction of the trench.

Kathryn shrugged, "I'm not sure, but perhaps it has something to do with the idea that I was a child when I died. I read a book about spirit and past life when I was starting to have these dreams and memories and it said that children are such pure spirit, they go immediately to heaven, or whatever you want to call it. They are innocent."

Kathryn thought for a second, "That would make sense though wouldn't it? I mean, Inga, their child!" She quickly glanced around at each person before settling on Helen, "You know, you told me, in the hospital, she was alone ..."

"You're right!" Helen licked her dry lips, "You're right." She repeated, "She came and she felt, okay."

"What do you mean OK?" Robert was studying her face.

"I mean she wasn't scary, well, not in the same sense as her parents were, you know, but she had an almost, serene feel about her, calm, nice, I wasn't really scared. I don't think she is trapped, I think Kathryn's right, she's free."

Robert crouched down, "So she's free, to do what?"

Helen was getting excited, it felt like this was important and glancing at Trevor; she could see he was thinking something too. "Well, I was in the bathroom, in Charlotte's room and I heard a noise or something. I just felt a change, I guess. When I looked, a young girl was standing beside Charlotte's bed and I just knew it was Inga. I'd dropped the rune stone Charlotte had touched and she pointed at it and disappeared."

Trevor suddenly leant forward, "Are you sure this spirit, pointed at the stone?"

"Well, yes, it looked like it, there wasn't anything else on the floor; I'm sure, why?"

Trevor glanced up at the growing clouds and sighed, "I know a man who lives nearby, he knows more about rituals from different cultures than anyone. We knew each other many years ago but I haven't seen Bernard for a long, long time, but if it's rituals and supernatural weird stuff, which I can safely say that this is what we have, then he's the man to talk to ..."

Seeing he had everyone's attention he continued, "I'm not an expert, but I do know a thing or two, you get to learn things in this archaeology business. How people died, sacrifices and all that. The Vikings worshipped many gods and goddesses, but the one for children and childbirth was the goddess Freya, among others anyway. I was looking at some of these stones and three are slightly different to the others. I think the markings were something silver first, before the blood which was added later."

Tony sat forward interested, "So, what runes were different?"

Trevor held them out for everyone to see, "These three, Kaunaz, Fehu, and Tiwaz, three of the runes that represent the goddess Freya." He looked directly at Helen. Without saying a word, she reached into her pocket and pulled out the rune stone still wrapped in her tissue. She uncovered it and held out her hand. "And that," continued Trevor, "Is Uruz, the fourth rune."

***

The nurse stood in the open doorway. The child's condition hadn't changed in any way. All her vital signs were normal as if she was sleeping; but of course, she wasn't. She'd stroked the little girl's hair and talked to her about silly things, favourite cartoons and teddy bears, but only silence and the constant beeping of the heart monitor was her answer.

She had been about to leave and finish her rounds when she sensed a change behind her. Now, standing in the doorway, she was afraid to turn around and look back into the room. Afraid to turn her back and walk away and afraid to leave the child alone and vulnerable.

There had already been talk. Vicious gossip about the child's parents leaving her alone. How could they, unless they were somehow responsible for their daughter's condition? Even though every test had been done to check for every possible drug, nothing had been found; but that hadn't stopped the talk, it never did. She'd stood up for the parents, at first. She'd seen the state the mother had been in, no one could have convinced her she was guilty of anything; then, they had gone.

The police had questioned them briefly, focusing on any actual cause or blame, but both parents had been in shock. When the parents disappeared, the police had become very interested in their whereabouts; to leave their sick child without informing the hospital of their intentions was odd and set the tongues wagging even more.

The last she had seen of the mother had been late last night when she'd attempted to get her to eat something or at least drink the cups of sweet tea she had brought her; they'd remained untouched. Coming in for her shift, she had been greeted with more questions, gossip and accusations; it saddened her. It crossed her mind that the mother had done herself some harm, her grief over her daughter being so evident, but the police hadn't found them, yet.

The sense of dread left as quickly as it had come and she stepped into the room. Checking the girl's pulse, she noted that it was a little quicker, but soon returned to the slow, weak pulse she had come to know. She wrote down the change and time and left the room; she would be back in fifteen minutes anyway.

The child stood silently in the corner of the small room and watched the woman in white look after the sleeping girl. Once she left, she stepped closer and peered down at her. She was pretty, like an angel and she looked warm and snug in her bed. She would have liked this girl to be her friend but she knew that was never to be. Their time would come one day, but not today. She felt a stab of bone deep sadness for her mother and father and hoped that this girl's mother would be successful or all hope would be lost.

Chapter Thirty-One

Nick felt the rope around his neck tighten as he tried to move his hands. He stopped and the panic rose again as he realised if he moved he would strangle himself; there was no hope. Slowly, he let his arms relax and felt the rope loosen slightly and he breathed as deeply as he could. It was a hard thing to do as he lay on his stomach, his hands behind his back and the only way to release the tension on his neck was to move his arms a little further away from his body, which hurt, but he had no choice.

He had no idea how long he'd been unconscious, but his body throbbed everywhere. He could taste dried blood from a wound on his head that stung painfully. It couldn't have been for more than a few hours or so. He'd long since wet himself and he could smell his urine along with the damp earth beneath his face. The small, dark room smelt dank and musty, an old cellar perhaps? He had listened hard for any sounds that might tell him where he was, but beyond the occasional sound of cars in the distance, he heard nothing.

It took him a while, but he eventually managed to sit up, although it was very painful, and when he'd finished he was covered in sweat, blood, and tears. He sank back against the cold stone wall and gasped for breath. It wasn't much better sitting up, but he tried to relax his body enough so that the rope loosened ever so slightly. Someone had placed a chain around his ankle and it chafed his skin whenever he moved. His hands dug into his back and he had to keep his head tilted slightly backwards; but it was better than being on the floor.

His eyes searched the darkness and up towards where he was guessing a door might be and he could just make out a vague outline of what looked like a small door above him, perhaps seven or eight feet. He couldn't see stairs, but liked to believe he could 'feel' them there in the darkness. A possible way out; or a way in ...

The man hadn't said a word when he'd brought him here. He'd felt so groggy from whatever drug he'd been given that he couldn't put up a fight, but he must have protested at some point because he'd been hit with something heavy and everything went black.

He didn't know if he'd been thrown down or dragged; his head was so foggy from the wound and the drugs. All he did remember was that he'd been at the dig site; he remembered a girl with a nice arse, hearing someone crying and then he was here, in the dark, sore, terrified and terribly thirsty; he let the tears fall. Would he ever see a girl with a nice arse again? He suspected the answer to that was extremely doubtful, and he felt his bowels loosen and he cried with shame and for the horror that awaited him.

***

Trevor directed Tony and within minutes, both cars were parked outside a small, plain looking bungalow at the end of a long, narrow lane the other side of Thurstaston Common. Kathryn looked at her watch and sighed, it was nearly midday; her body was beginning to remember that it hadn't slept properly and her bed had never seemed so far away or so inviting. As if reading her mind, Tony came to stand beside her and gave her a brief hug, "Not to worry," he whispered, "it'll be over soon and then you can sleep for a week after a long hot bath."

She gave him a fleeting nod and attempted a smile, "I doubt it Tony; we still have a dig to finish ..." She wasn't sure whether she even believed it, but thankfully Tony let it go.

She glanced across at Helen and Robert who'd travelled with Trevor, they didn't look any better. Helen was fidgety and was close to losing it; the urge to get back to her daughter must be overwhelming. Robert didn't look any better, but he also looked like he'd kill anyone who made the mistake of saying the wrong thing; like a predator waiting to be set free. The only time that persona dropped was when he was watching Helen. He loved that woman, anyone could see that; except Helen.

She tried to pull herself together; how could she ever have known that her nightmares would lead to this madness? It couldn't possibly be true, in the real, factual world; yet here she was, outside some poor man's house, looking bedraggled, to ask him about some bloody Goddess! She quickly rubbed her eyes vigorously to wake up: it was all surreal!

She followed the others through the garden gate and up the path to the porch. She thought about all the people going about their daily lives unaware of such evil and darkness so near to their homes. The dig site was less than half a mile away through the trees. Did any of the other people living nearby have ghosts? It would be strange if it were only Helen and Robert's cottage, surely.

The bell sounded very loud to their tired ears. She watched as two women strode purposefully into Royden Park; they were talking quietly whilst walking their dogs. One woman didn't stop her chatter as she bent down and picked up her dog's ball and threw it. She barely stopped midstride while both dogs, a brown and white spaniel and a golden Labrador, tore after the ball barking excitedly; It felt peculiar seeing other people doing 'normal' things.

She should have been digging on the site; feeling the adrenalin rush when she found another small item. She should have been working with students, explaining, lecturing, sharing the joy of a find; assuming any students did turn up on a Sunday. Instead, she was here, waiting to see if some person knew anything about the hell they had witnessed.

She turned back to the door and gasped when she saw the elderly man appear in his doorway; his two dogs silently standing guard on either side of him. He looked at everyone in turn, giving them a slight nod before his gaze fell on Trevor and his face broke into a smile. "Well, well, my old friend, what on earth brings you here, to my door?"

He opened the door and the dogs ran out to sniff the uninvited intruders. They barked briefly, but a sharp command from their owner stopped them at once. He moved aside to let them in and she waited while Robert and Tony carefully lifted Trevor's chair into the hallway. Helen followed the men, Kathryn came last, and smiled awkwardly, "Well, this is a turn of events, no wonder you showed interest in my dig, you should have told me you knew Trevor ..."

The man bowed slightly, "My apologies, I didn't want to, shall we say, scare you away; I've enjoyed our little chats."

"I guess I can forgive you, we could say we are even now that we're invading your home ..."

He smiled slightly and turned to close the door, "I think we can do that, Miss Bailey."

She followed the others into the small sitting room and sat on the large, dark green sofa with Helen and Robert. It was very comfortable and deep seated, so much so, she had to sit forward so that her feet rested on the floor. She looked around the rectangular room, the midday light streamed in, showing books of all shapes and sizes filling every spare space. A stack of magazines and newspapers filled the farthest corner and a smaller pile had already reached half way up the wall behind the door.

Various statues, ranging from Celtic gods to African goddesses with huge breasts lined one shelf and cheap porcelain figurines of ladies in flowing gowns filled another. Amongst them all were shoddy looking fairies, and squashed in-between all of these were crystals; Amethyst, Citrine and Haematite being the majority, though there were many other small pieces thrown around the room which occasionally caught the sunlight and sparkled like tiny jewels.

All of these oddities intermingled with the ordinary; the small television, the stereo and speakers, the gas fireplace and the two lamps on either side of the window, as well as the green settee and two armchairs; the room was very full.

The room held an odd feeling. A study, a place of learning, yet, someone's home; she couldn't decide if the two mixed. They'd liked Bernard and his regular visits whilst walking the two dogs who were sitting calmly by the door. He had been a welcome face amongst those who fought against the dig. It'd been encouraging to know there were people out there who cared. An amateur historian he'd called himself; and she'd believed him; but looking at him now, seeing him in his own environment, something felt wrong and she was beginning to feel uneasy.

"I wasn't sure if you still lived here. Still like your reading I see …" Trevor nodded towards a stack of books.

Bernard shrugged, "I've been out with the dogs already. Did a little gardening, read a little; I have other hobbies now … I get a lot done …" Bernard sat back in his armchair and waited.

"Oh yes of course, perhaps I should introduce everyone …"

"I know who I need to know, for now …"

Trevor coughed nervously, "You want to know why we're here?" Trevor glanced quickly around the room but everyone was watching and waiting for him. Kathryn looked uncomfortable; she was glancing across at Bernard every so often and fidgeting. Helen and Robert looked hopeful and he took a deep breath. "We're here because we need your advice, your expertise on Viking laws and rituals."

Bernard's expression didn't change, but he sat back in his chair, "I see ... All of you?"

"I am sorry about that, it couldn't be helped, you see, we're all involved. Haven't even been to bed yet."

Bernard looked closer at Trevor and around the room, "Yes, I can see that." His gaze rested on Helen a moment longer than the others and she sat forward expectantly; when he didn't say anything she spoke up.

"Can you help us?" The pleading in her voice wasn't lost on anyone. "It's my daughter …" Fresh tears rolled down her face, "Something has happened to her. She touched a rune stone that was dug up and now she's lying in a hospital bed and the doctors don't know what to do and then we all saw … Oh God! I don't know what we saw, but I think she's been cursed or something … or taken by Vikings."

She thought he wasn't going to answer as he watched her for a few minutes. He absentmindedly stroked one of his dogs' ears as he looked at her, she could see he was thinking. She knew she wasn't making any sense and was about to try again, but the words wouldn't come out, her throat constricted with emotion and she gave up.

Robert reached out and held her hand tightly as she sobbed quietly; she did not pull away. Trevor jumped in, "You see, these people have been seeing the ghosts of two Vikings; so has their daughter, Charlotte, or Cherry as she's known. We believe their names are Einaar and Astrid, parents of a child called Inga, they were murdered. Yesterday morning, their daughter touched a rune stone and collapsed. Her body is in the hospital, but we believe she isn't there, her soul I mean. This morning, at the site, we all saw a black mass of negative energy. We believe they were the lost souls of these villagers who were murdered by their chief and all of them angry and without hope. We believe there is some link between them and what has happened to the little girl, it's too much of a coincidence. I believe we can get the child back using the runes somehow. I also believe the ritual to invoke the goddess Freya would help."

"I see, and why would that be?"

Trevor frowned, Bernard seemed a bit too calm for his comfort. "Well, some of the runes are Freya's rune stones. The child touched one and at the hospital Helen saw Inga, the Viking child, who pointed at the stone."

Bernard didn't move, but watched him carefully, "So, with all this, you have deduced Freya would help bring back the child from another dimension. For what purpose and why was she taken in the first place?"

Robert jumped in, "Because we think that somehow, the parents have been separated from their child, this Inga and maybe they have taken our baby instead."

Bernard slowly turned his head towards Robert, his face impassive, "I see: and why do you think they were separated?"

Robert shrugged and turned to look at Tony who in turn looked at Kathryn. "I think that they got confused, at the point of death. A priest had come to their village spreading stories about the Christian God. I think that at the moment of death, they didn't know where to go; unsure which god would accept them. Inga was a child, pure and innocent. She wouldn't have understood different gods and beliefs. Her spirit would have gone to the light. The other villagers might have become confused and become stuck in their anger and betrayal; we have to help them ..."

They were all watching Kathryn now and she attempted a weak smile. The emotion she felt was over-powering and she fought to control her tears. She was surprised at the intensity of her grief for her villagers. These were her people, they had once been her family; she felt that strongly now.

Bernard was watching her more intently than the others and his scrutiny made her feel very uncomfortable. The room was silent for a long time, but finally Bernard broke the uneasy stillness. "Well, I have to say, Trevor, I have heard some stories in my time, but this is a whopper."

"You don't believe us, after everything you know?" Trevor sounded gutted.

"Oh no, don't get me wrong, I believe you about the Viking spirits, I have felt them for a long time, long before you, young lady, started digging."

He pointed at Kathryn and she felt her fear increase, something about his look, his voice, so familiar. She glanced across at Tony and tried to tell him telepathically something was wrong, but he just smiled at her reassuringly and held her hand. She squeezed it and he squeezed it back. She dug her nails into his flesh and held on when he tried to let go, "Hey, come on ...!" Tony whispered to her. She stood up, half pulling Tony up with her, "Well, I'm exhausted, we don't have time to make him believe us. Sorry to have bothered you Bernard ..."

"Oh no, you don't want to go yet." Bernard's voice was ice cold, which caught everyone's attention, "Please take your seat and let's have a conversation."

Trevor glanced quickly between Bernard and Kathryn before he moved his chair forward, "I think perhaps ..." He got no further before Bernard barked an order and the two dogs which before had looked quite placid, now stood in front of the door and growled.

"What the fuck ...?" Tony and Robert said in unison as both stood up, Robert pulling Helen to her feet behind him, Tony moved to stand in front of Kathryn.

"Now gentlemen, no need to be alarmed." Bernard leant back in his seat as calm as if he were having a pleasant conversation. "We have some important matters to discuss." He looked up at Helen, "You have seen them, Einaar and Astrid?"

"Yes I have, we both have, but my daughter ...?" Helen looked puzzled at the sudden change, but stepped forward, a look of determination on her face. "Look, I don't know what this is about, but I need to get back to my child ..."

"You said she wasn't at the hospital, only her body, so why go there?" He leant forward, "Sit down and I might be able to help you."

Robert stepped towards him but stopped when the growling of the dogs increased. "Help us? Do you know something that can wake our daughter up? Because if that is true, I'll tell you now, I couldn't give a shit how many fuckin' dogs you have, I'll rip your throat out myself if you don't tell us. Is that plain enough for you, you smug looking bastard!"

Bernard sniggered, "Well, we can't have that now, can we. Please, be seated and I'll explain."

He waited patiently while they all slowly sat, Trevor reached out and nudged Bernard's knee, "If you know something, Bernard, stop this bullshit and tell us."

"Very well; I'm surprised little Kathryn over there hasn't recognised me, but she was just a child." He ignored the small gasp from her and carried on. "I have a big interest in what happens to Einaar and his woman, Astrid. I want him to suffer, as I suffered; you see, because of his selfishness I lost my son, my wife, I lost everything."

"Your son? Wife? Bernard, I don't understand?"

"Not in this life Trevor, but in that one. In the village you're digging up, my son died from the illness; my wife killed herself because she couldn't bear the thought of our son in Hel alone; and it was all Einaar's fault. If he'd had the courage to follow the true gods ..."

Trevor wheeled his chair closer, "Bernard, I don't understand. You had a son? What was his name?" He quickly glanced at Kathryn who had gone very pale and was shaking.

Bernard leant forward. "His name was Ranulf and I was known as ..."

"Thorlak." Kathryn's voice was barely a whisper.

Chapter Thirty-Two

T he policeman shook his head, "Sad isn't it?"

The nurse stood within the child's room and picked up the girl's chart, "I can't believe it really. The mother looked distraught, who could have thought she would abandon her baby like this? Sometimes, officer, I really hate my job."

"I know what you mean. Seeing this kind of neglect makes my stomach turn. They had me fooled too, but their disappearance has certainly changed my mind." He leant against the doorframe and nodded towards the child, "Any change at all?"

The nurse quickly scanned the chart and replaced it, "No, not really. Her pulse quickens every so often, but she remains in REM state, dreaming. I hope they're nice dreams ... but, no, she hasn't changed, poor lamb." She came to stand next to him, "What do you think will happen if she does come out of this? Will the parents be charged? Will she need a new home? Foster care?"

The police officer shrugged, "Who knows? I would think there would be many questions about their sudden absence. However, there's no evidence of drugs or anything that would explain this and there's no history of neglect or abuse, except we were called out to the house the other night. The mother was frantic, screaming that intruders had taken her daughter. We searched the house and garden and there she was, sleeping peacefully in her little playhouse. Poor darling was a bit chilly, but the doctor gave her the all clear."

"What did the Mum do?"

"She grabbed the child from the police officer who'd found her and clung to her. Charlotte was a bit frightened by it all, but we couldn't prove any negligence at that time. We did wonder if the mother was a user and had either forgotten the child was there, or put her there out of the way? But, her reaction was, we thought, genuine at the time. The doctor was very concerned for the mother's wellbeing, more so than for the child."

"That is odd. She doesn't look like she uses drugs, but, if she's fairly new to it ...?" The nurse shook her head, "No, I'd bet my job she's not a user. She didn't even want a sedative yesterday; we had to get the husband's permission to force it because she was in such a state."

"What do you make of Mr Gunn?"

"Don't know really. The tension between them is obvious and he was highly strung yesterday, pacing the floor, twitching, nervous, if anyone was on drugs, I'd bet it's him."

"You think perhaps he took the kid and put her in the play house and what, forgot about her or to frighten the wife?"

"That would be my guess. He looks dodgy sometimes; I don't like him."

The police officer shrugged, "Hmm, maybe you're right, I'll look into it ..." He suddenly shivered, "Can you feel that?"

The nurse hugged herself and quickly glanced around the small room. "This happens sometimes and I don't know what it is, but it feels horrible."

The policeman rubbed his hands together, "Bloody hell, it's very cold in here. Is it the heating?"

"No, we've had that checked. It feels like something else." She glanced up at him to see if he understood. She saw a flicker of fear before he quickly looked away. "You feel it too, don't you?"

He backed out of the room, his eyes never leaving it. She could see he felt it and was glad, she was beginning to think she was going mad. Seconds later, the room returned to normal and she heaved a loud sigh of relief. She followed him out into the corridor, "Well?"

He looked down at her before returning his attention to the room, "Well what? That was bloody weird."

"What did you feel?"

"I don't know really, but it felt like there was another child in there ... freaky eh?"

The nurse smiled, "Not at all, I'm so glad someone else said it. I have had that feeling half a dozen times since she came in."

The policeman rubbed his eyes briskly and licked his lips, "Well, whatever it was, it's gone now." He stopped and thought for a moment, "This might sound stupid, but I do go to church sometimes and I believe in souls and stuff, it couldn't be her soul floating about, could it?" He watched her reaction, but she wasn't going to tell him he'd lost his mind so he continued. "You know she isn't dead, obviously, but as the doctors have said, she isn't awake; she isn't anything. Her brainwaves are active enough to say she isn't comatose or brain dead, but for whatever reason, she isn't waking up, so what we just felt, could it be her spirit trying to return to her body?"

The nurse stared up at him for a long time, it made him feel uncomfortable and he was glad when she finally looked back into the room. "Well, it's probably the best idea I've heard and if you believe in all that ..."

Embarrassed, he began to walk away, "It was only a thought, stupid really ... don't judge me. After everything I have seen humans do to each other, I don't think anything would surprise me: and don't forget what we both just felt. It was something weird and it was real, whatever it was. I'll see you later."

The nurse watched him leave. She wanted to go after him and assure him she wasn't making fun of him, his idea was possibly the best theory she'd heard all day. She turned back towards the room. It looked slightly darker than it had a moment ago and she wondered if the sun had gone behind some clouds. A slight movement in the far corner caught her attention, but there was nothing to see, only the lone armchair and an old newspaper resting on it.

A cry from another room caught her attention and she walked away; she felt responsible for the little girl and she wasn't even sure if the child was safe. It occurred to her later, what a strange thing to think. Why wouldn't little Charlotte Gunn be safe?

***

The silence in the room stretched on. The April sun blazed into the lounge and it was becoming uncomfortably hot and stifling, but no one moved. The only sounds were the dogs' low warning growls and Kathryn's occasional sniff as she quietly dabbed at her eyes; a sodden tissue pressed against her nose. Tony had his arm around her and gently rubbed her shoulder trying to give her some comfort as her body shook beside his.

Robert was staring at Bernard as if he would tear out his throat, while Helen had a tight hold of the back of his coat. She was reeling from this latest event and was trying very hard to get her thoughts in some kind of order, but it was difficult and judging from the look on everyone's face, they were going through the same thing; everyone that is except Bernard, who was watching her carefully.

She met his stare, hoping her determination showed plainly. He smiled a knowing smile; Robert was right, he was a smug bastard! She gave him her best dirty look and glanced towards Kathryn before turning to Trevor who was vaguely shaking his head in disbelief. "Have you gone mad, Bernard? What's the play here?"

Bernard grinned, "No play, Trevor, I'm not in the mood for games. I have waited long enough for my revenge on that traitor." The last three words spoken with such venom.

"But ... but, this ..." Trevor waved his hand over the room, "What is this? What are you doing? The dogs for God's sake?"

"Ah, yes, I do apologise." Turning to the dogs, he barked a command and they instantly stopped growling and lay down. "They are just for assurance, nothing more."

Robert stepped forward, "Assurance for what? What do you know?"

"Assurance that you'll listen, of course: shall we have some tea? You all look a bit worse for wear ... especially you two ladies."

Something in Helen snapped and she abruptly stood up, "That's it! I've had enough of this bullshit! I want to know about my baby, NOW!"

The Rottweiler immediately stood up, hairs bristling, but she ignored it. "If you do know something and if you really are another spirit returning to this village, tell us how to get my child back or get the fuck out of my way!"

Bernard stared up at her, a smile played on his face, but he sighed loudly and seemed to come to some decision, "Fair enough. Your courage is honourable; you would have been a fine Viking. I will just say, that your little girl was, shall we say, something I didn't see coming. They are not supposed to get any relief from their misery and it would seem that they have fixated on your daughter to relieve their pain. So, for that alone I will help you."

He turned to Trevor, "I am serious about making tea though; you do all look terrible." He returned his attention to Helen, "And you are going to need every last ounce of strength you can muster, if you are to get your child back." The seriousness in his voice was enough to make Helen step back and take a deep breath.

Quarter of an hour later, a tray with a large pot of strong tea and biscuits was placed on the lounge floor and cups were quickly filled. The two dogs remained by Bernard's chair, looking docile again, but no one was going anywhere. Insane or not, Bernard was right, they were all the worse for wear and felt terrible. Exhaustion, fear, anger and desperation were taking their toll. The unexpected shocks, horrors, and subsequent adrenalin over-drive had worn everyone out; only Robert and Helen had a determined look on their faces; Helen looked ready to bolt.

Kathryn had avoided Bernard as much as she could in the confines of the small bungalow. She was very aware of his presence and that he watched her every so often. Darling Tony, her protector, never left her side. She felt dazed, as if she were watching the scene before her in a dream. Her whole body ached with exhaustion, but her head was a whirl of questions.

Thorlak was Bernard. Why hadn't she recognised him? He'd obviously recognised her but why had he kept it secret? Probably the same reason she had kept quiet about her own memories all these years. Did he mean them harm? Two dogs against all of them would do some damage, but not enough to kill surely? No, they wanted to be there, the dogs were just an excuse to stay and hear what Bernard had to say.

She felt such fear and hatred for this man, yet that was irrational. He'd played a part in the deaths of an entire village, but he was still the kind, funny elderly man who came to chat every day. The emotions she felt were not her own now and she tried very hard to distinguish between them. Finally, as she sipped the hot tea, she realised that she now felt let down by him, disappointed; she had liked him.

Bernard was watching her closely as she sipped her tea, it was making her more and more uncomfortable and he knew it. Finally he spoke, "I don't suppose an apology would be enough at this point, Kathryn?" Without waiting for a response he quickly added, "I had no choice if I wanted to live and fight, and by the gods, I wanted to fight, someone, anyone, it didn't matter to me. I had lost everything I cared about and it was my trusted friend who brought that to my door. I was mad with grief knowing I would never see them again. It wasn't until I saw you that first day on the site that I felt something like remorse for you, little Helga."

Kathryn stared open mouthed at him, "Helga? Was that my name?"

"Yes. You don't remember details? I have had quite a few past life regressions over the years with a trusted friend. He helped to fill in the blanks so to speak. I remembered quite a lot on my own and kept a book of everything I saw in my dreams. Your face was one of those I saw most frequently; I was in discussion with your father over a possible match between my son and yourself though I was aware that Einaar had hopes of his own ..." Seeing the look on Kathryn's face, he stopped. "Well, never mind that now."

Kathryn stared at him open-mouthed but it was Robert who jumped in.

"You don't believe in heaven and hell and all that?"

"I'm afraid, Robert, there is more to it than that. You see, I believed that as a Viking we should die in battle, it was an honourable death. Odin would make sure that my soul would be taken to Valhalla or the Goddess Freya would take me to her realm, Folkvangr. There I would wait for my children and wife surrounded by my comrades. But, those who die from illness were not so honoured and they were taken to Hel, so you see, I was never going to see my family again, because of Einaar and his weakness."

He waited to see if everyone understood before continuing, "We were doing what had to be done out of love for our families. We knew it had to be that way to bring honour to our people. Halldor asked each of us if we would do this last request for him once we'd found Einaar and his family and wiped out the source. We knew we were too late, the illness had taken a hold on our village, but perhaps we could stop it spreading to other villages. We believed we were doing good; showing strength and honour instead of weakness, as Einaar had done. We would send our people to Valhalla, together, no more separations, do you see?"

Kathryn barely nodded before he continued, "So, we burnt everything. We left nothing and no one alive to spread the illness. Some fought us, which was good, but others could barely reach for their weapons to defend themselves, they were so weak; we would hand them their sword, axe or dagger before ending their suffering."

"How many of you were involved?" Trevor's voice shook slightly.

"There were eight of us, including Halldor."

"Eight men against how many in the village? How did you do it?"

213

Bernard looked far away, as he recalled that morning. Trevor shuddered as he spoke, "We started quietly, splitting up and beginning at each end of the village, we moved from house to house. We had only been away from the village half a day, but the illness was spreading rapidly; most looked pleased it was over."

"I don't remember being pleased." Kathryn was glaring at him, her fury evident as she fought to control herself.

"No, you did scream, but do you remember what your mother said? She said, 'All will be well in a few breaths of the wind'... And she was right, wasn't she?"

"Was she? I don't remember such details. How do I know you're telling the truth?" Kathryn's throat tightened with emotion. His mention of her mother brought a strong feeling of grief.

Bernard shrugged, "You were so young and dying when your father killed you and then set alight your house. Halldor stood outside, his sword ready to send Agmund, your father into Valhalla after you both."

He watched her face as she took in this new information before continuing, "But I don't see your spirit lost. You found your way to the light and now have returned to live again and I have no doubt that you have lived other lives since, is that not a good thing? From what I have been able to understand through years of research, children were set free, to move into the light, whether it be heaven, Valhalla, Folkvangr or whatever. I now know, it's all the same place, just different names, but back then we believed with our very souls each place was different."

He could see he had everyone's full attention and continued, "Don't you see what happened? When we are alive, we believe whatever we are told, if we are told often enough and live it. We worshipped our Norse gods and believed in them so much, they were real to us and we followed the rituals and the rules to the letter. Then, a priest comes along and people listened to him. He tells stories about a Christian god who is the only god and everything we have believed since birth is false. We had heard rumours for years before the priest appeared but we had always been able to dismiss such nonsense; but then he came and with him, came destruction and chaos."

He leant forward, his voice getting high with excitement, "Some began to question our rituals and beliefs. Halldor forbade it and had the priest killed, but he had already spread his poison into people's minds, causing doubt. Halldor saw it, so did I, when I heard my wife tell Ranulf stories the priest had told about Jesus; the old gods become angry and we were punished."

"You mean, you believe the gods gave your village this illness?" Tony asked quietly.

"Yes, at least that's what Halldor and Ingimund believed, so did many others at the time. When he realised Einaar's child had been the first, but had survived while others were dying, it confirmed his suspicions about Einaar being a secret worshipper of the new God. It made sense, Odin was killing all those who had allowed this priest to talk and spread unrest and hate. The Christian God had spared the child, but no others were being spared."

"Do you know what the illness was?"

Bernard turned to Trevor and smiled, "I do now, and it was a type of flu, perhaps something like Spanish flu. It killed rapidly ..."

Tony pushed his fingers through his hair, "Wow! I feel like I'm on *Outer Limits,* it was a programme; so, you remember all that but, what about the black thing we saw this morning?" He nodded towards Robert and Helen who both looked pale, "And their little girl?"

"Yes, I can see you're not sure whether to believe me or not!" Bernard grinned at Tony. "It is kind of, 'out there' isn't it. Well, let us get even freakier shall we? The black mass of energy is the lost souls who should have crossed over, but realised it wasn't what they had believed in and were too scared or confused to cross over and are stuck. I take it you felt their negative emotions?"

"You mean the anger, rage, all that?"

"Yes, I mean all that, plus loneliness, frustration, fear, confusion, you name it; these people feel it and it has escalated over the years."

"You forgot hopelessness." Helen's voice was barely a whisper, but Bernard nodded.

Robert butted in, "Have you seen it?"

"I have, many times. I feel their energies sometimes and cry for those I tried to help; that's why I live here, to be near them; to relive the memories. We thought we were doing these people a good deed, so they would be together; it seems it wasn't to be, and I feel guilt you cannot imagine."

He sighed and leant back in his chair. He picked up his tea and sipped it. "Then, of course, there's Einaar and his family, they were lost to me. I have searched for them, but they have eluded me, until now. I knew the child would be free; I made my peace with that notion over the years, though at the time, I would not have cared if she had died a thousand deaths, but I wish her no ill now. My son, Ranulf was an innocent and I believe that he is free also." He laughed suddenly, "It sounds strange to me sometimes. I find myself speaking in the first person as Thorlack and have to keep reminding myself that I am Bernard. I am not a wild Viking anymore, but an old man with his own past."

"And what do you believe now?" Trevor's question was curt.

Bernard stopped laughing and replaced his cup, "I am Bernard. An old man who believes that there is energy and everyone calls it whatever they bloody well like so long as it makes them happy and they can use it as an excuse to go to war.

I don't go to church, never have, never will. I believe in what I see and feel every day when I am out walking my two dogs. Nevertheless, I still want Einaar to suffer as those villagers suffer still. He brought it to the village and they are the ones left behind, or so I believed. It would seem otherwise?"

Helen nodded, too shocked to speak for a moment. "They did something to me in the kitchen. I can remember feeling totally helpless as they took her ..." She stopped and put her head in her hands, it was feeling too much, she couldn't stop shaking.

"I don't understand, you said your child touched a rune?"

"Yes, that was the second time ..."

"You mean, they tried it before and failed?" Bernard was suddenly excited.

Helen quickly wiped away her tears, "Yes, they came to the house, in Frankby. Cherry had seen them a few times, but the other evening, I was in the kitchen and I saw a woman ... then, I couldn't move. I blacked out and when I came round, my baby had gone. The police found her at the bottom of the garden, still asleep. You look as though this matters."

"It does." Bernard rose quickly and went to the large bookshelf that covered the far wall. He searched for a moment along two shelves before finding what he wanted and brought the small, battered looking book back to his chair. He held it up so everyone could see, "This, is a treasured book, an old book as you can see. A woman translated it, which was unusual and frowned upon back in the eighteenth century. The woman was a housekeeper, you see, not a woman of learning."

"What's the book, Bernard?" Trevor looked eagerly at the book.

Bernard smiled and handed it to him. He watched as Trevor handled it carefully as most of the pages were loose and yellow with age. The writing looked unfamiliar and he said as much as he gave it back.

"That, my old friend is a lost Norse language. The woman who wrote this was an Irish lady and sadly, once news of this leaked out, the poor woman was tried as a witch and burned. I say, 'tried' in the loosest term, obviously. It was a language no one recognised and so it must have been the devil's work."

"I'm surprised then the book survived, wouldn't they have thrown it into the flames with her?"

"Yes, Trevor, you're right, but somehow, the book was lost and it turned up many years later; about nineteen hundred and ten, I believe. By then society didn't burn interesting books and it was realised what it was."

"And?" Helen and Kathryn spoke in unison.

"It's a book of old rituals, incantations and other information regarding the Goddess, Freya. Women, witches maybe, worshipped her through the ages and this housekeeper was possibly involved with them."

"Very interesting, but what has this got to do with my baby?" Helen was becoming more agitated as time passed. Charlotte had been alone for hours, she could hardly bear it.

Bernard frowned in thought, "My dear Helen, Einaar and Astrid don't have your daughter. They may have tried, but their energy could not take a child away from her mother, the bond is too great. I did wonder how it could have ..."

"Then what is happening to my daughter? Who, if anyone, has my child and how can we get her back?" Helen almost screamed the question.

Bernard shrugged, "Well, I'm not sure why, but it would seem that the Goddess Freya has taken her and the answers to getting her back are in this book."

Chapter Thirty-Three

The policeman climbed back into his car but left the door open. The air was clean and fresh and besides the low murmur of cars on the main road a few hundred yards away and the twitter of birds, there was no other noise, which was wonderful, compared to his usual areas. He much preferred it and wished he were here more often, but crime wasn't that common out here. He chuckled to himself, 'out here!' As if this was the country! A few miles in any direction and it was swamped by people, cars, buses and businesses all desperately trying to live together, and hating it.

He liked this time of the day, especially when he'd been on an early shift. He felt more involved with the day because he'd been up and about before the rising sun; he felt connected. By the end of his shift, his body could feel quite exhausted, having got up and become immersed in his job so early, but overall, he preferred the early shifts. Criminals rarely got up before lunchtime so he could enjoy the morning, the rising of the sun, the feel of its strength as it rose higher in the sky. The world slowly coming to life; it was a magical time of day ... NOT that he would ever tell his colleagues; they'd have a right laugh at his expense.

He quickly glanced at his watch: nearly teatime, his shift ended in an hour and then he could go home to a house of bedlam, which would consist of the kids screaming at each other, while his darling wife, Jackie, would be screaming at them to stop arguing while she cooked the Sunday roast. Then maybe the two of them would walk the dog, if she hadn't done so already, an hour away from the kids. On returning there would be more shouting and complaining and panic over uniforms ready for school and finding forgotten homework, before finally collapsing into bed to get up to peace and quiet; he smiled, life was fairly good.

He leant against the car, looked at the archaeological site, and wondered what it would be like to dig all day looking for rubbish people had thrown away and forgotten. His wife liked 'Time Team' and he had watched it with some degree of interest once or twice, but doing it every day didn't really appeal.

The students were not due to arrive today, so he'd been asked to check the area. Someone might come later in the day to check the site, but no one would be digging today. Apart from the fact that it was Sunday, apparently everyone felt it was wrong to dig after what happened to Charlotte Gunn. Besides, the Health and Safety officer wanted a full report from somebody; but so far, everyone involved had disappeared; which was weird.

His colleagues had already questioned the archaeologists, the volunteers and the students but none of them had had any answers that helped the puzzle. In his experience, what did students know anyway, besides drugs, porn and drinking?

His gaze roamed around the area and stopped at the big tent; movement caught his attention and he stiffened. He was sure he could see someone standing, watching him, but every time he tried to focus, the person faded away. He shielded his eyes against the glare of the sun and looked again. Yes, a young man with long hair ... No, he'd gone. No, there he was again just standing, staring. He began to walk towards the tent, every muscle on stand-by.

They'd been told the parents weren't a danger, but you never could be too careful. If these parents were potential child killers, then maybe they weren't as nice as first thought? Maybe they were mad? Mad people were unpredictable and dangerous. He unclipped his mace.

"Hey, you there!" He quickly unlocked the gate and chastised himself for not doing it earlier. He'd given whoever it was the advantage now, but no, he hadn't moved, had he? He walked closer, all the time watching the man who was half turned away, looking towards the trench on the policeman's right. "Hey, stay there. Who are you?"

The man did not acknowledge his presence in any way. Then, he just wasn't there anymore. The policeman stopped in his tracks and surveyed the area. "What the ...?" He glanced around the site, walking up to the exact place the man had stood, nothing. He checked inside the tent, behind gorse bushes, nothing, there wasn't a soul anywhere; it was deathly silent.

He started to feel a bit queer. He looked up at the surrounding trees, no birds sang as he was sure they had only minutes ago. No rustling of small animals; nothing. He looked towards the road, which felt like a long way away and walked briskly back to his car locking the gate behind him. He'd heard stories over the years about this place. People seeing mists moving about, ghostly sounds of some kind of battle, the smell of burning, and he'd always dismissed them as drunken tales or over active imaginations; but now? He got back into his car and slammed the door shut. Then thought about it and locked it. He glanced at his watch, forty-three minutes until he could sign off, it couldn't come quick enough.

***

Kathryn stood by the back door while Tony poured the hot water into the teapot. He placed it on the large tray and picked it up, the cups rattled and the spoons moved. The smell of fresh tea, coffee and hot toast filled the narrow kitchen. Tony breathed it in and quickly rubbed his hands over his face to wake up. Sensing her mood, he winked at her, "Fancy something stronger to help make this moment weirder?"

She couldn't smile, her face felt numb, and followed him back down the hallway into the lounge. Someone had opened the windows and the room felt a little less oppressive, but the tension had certainly not diminished. In fact, the atmosphere between Robert, Helen and Bernard was almost electric as all three bent over the small book ignoring everyone else.

Kathryn sat furthest away from Bernard and watched him as he flipped through the book. She was trying to remember what it was like to be Viking; of course she couldn't remember properly; images, fleeting thoughts and feelings and she was jealous of his passion to remember. The thought of past life regression had crossed her mind on many occasions, but she'd never had the courage to act on it. There was a small part of her that understood his belief that he was saving the village from Hel. If the illness were going to kill them anyway, which would the villagers have preferred? Valhalla with their families or Hel, where they would be alone?

Bernard had relaxed somewhat in his manner towards them. He wasn't keeping them prisoner with his dogs anymore, he didn't need to; he had their full attention. The dogs now lay by the gas fire watching the proceedings. They looked so innocent, nothing more than a pair of large salivating pets she'd seen and stroked over the last week or so.

She closed her eyes and tried to visualise her past life better. It was strange; since telling the others about her dreams, they'd become easier to think about. She was still frightened by the notion of it all, but the terror of the unknown had gone, replaced by a deep sadness, and anger towards the injustice of their deaths.

She had been about twelve when she'd died, maybe a bit more, she couldn't be sure. A young girl teetering on the edge of womanhood; and they had taken it all away. Granted, she had the illness and the chances of living had been extremely thin, but they had taken that possibility away.

She knew she'd had a family, but couldn't quite remember their faces. Her memories of that time were so sporadic, so many chunks missing. She could remember another child, a younger child, a boy, was it her brother? What had happened to him? She looked across the room and knew the answer, Thorlak had happened.

***

"If I understand this properly, the Goddess will take those she feels necessary." Bernard sat back in his chair and sipped his tea. "For whatever reason, she felt it necessary to take your daughter and I am presuming it was out of harm's way."

220

Helen looked down at the page he had been reading and back to him, "Harm? From what? Or whom?"

"That I don't know, but I believe it all ties in with this village, with Einaar and Astrid, with Halldor and I think the priest. What I see is total confusion about religion. To believe one thing wholeheartedly, all your life, then to be told it is all bullshit and this is the true way? I think it caused some kind of rift between energies; that's my theory anyway."

"How would that even be possible, I mean, it's not real ..." Robert stood up and walked to the door, "This feels ... so ... unbelievable, so stupid. I just, want my little girl ..." He put his hand over his eyes and wept.

Helen watched him for a moment. The urge to go to him was tremendous, but she didn't move. She turned to Trevor instead, "You've been quiet all this time, what do you think?"

Trevor sighed, "I think Bernard might have a point. Think about it. The amount of energy a single man can produce over something he is passionate about is tremendous. What power men and women have produced through their own will? Telekinesis, stigmata, the power of healing in all religions and beliefs has astounded doctors throughout time.

"The problem is that each one claims that they are the real one and all other beliefs are wrong, and they believe it completely. Christians against Muslims, Jews against Christians. Christians against Christians. At the end of the day, it's people against people and it must take a lot of energy and passion to behave in such absolute ways. Burning, torturing, imprisonment, and for what? The power that person can feel would be incredible and believing it with every ounce of his soul. It has gone on for centuries and will continue until people learn that it doesn't matter."

"So, you're saying, a person can believe something so much that it creates energy?"

"I am, Helen. You've heard of the miracles that have happened? Take stigmata. Was this created by believing in it so much, they caused it themselves? Moreover, what about healing? Reiki? People 'feel' the power flowing through them and it heals them. They feel a connection to something greater than themselves; is that a god or goddess or just energy?"

Trevor leant forward and took her hand, "So much energy is created in our emotions; you feel it now, your fear and frustration at what has happened to your daughter, it feels so strong you could almost touch it, right? It courses through your veins causing a reaction. I wonder what your aura looks like at this precise moment, Helen. What colours, what energy have you produced?"

He let go of her hand and sat back, "Men through the ages have felt that so strongly, they have been willing to die for their beliefs in wars, conflicts; allowing themselves to be killed and mutilated in their belief. So, who's to say, their energy doesn't manifest into something tangible? Something they and others can feel

221

physically, as well as mentally believe? Is this how gods and goddesses are created? Or even kept alive? If no one believes in them anymore, do they just fade away and become nothing as the energy dies?"

"I think you might have a point." Tony placed his empty cup back onto the tray. "It's something I've often considered, especially when I talk to people who follow a Pagan path. When they pray to their gods and goddesses, they use their names a lot of the time. It's as if they are making a connection to that particular deity. Some say, 'Lord and Lady' but many focus on specific ones from the Celtic era, Norse, Greek or Roman; they make it personal."

"What, they keep the dream alive, so to speak?"

Tony looked at Helen and smiled, "You could say that, yes. And, if my knowledge is any good, the Goddess Freya was a kind and loving deity who was the Norse Goddess of love and fertility and beauty."

Bernard jumped in, "Yes, you're right, but she was also the goddess of war, wealth and death. She could have half the souls from the battlefield and take them to her realm called Folkvangr. Her sexuality was legendary and she was mistress to many gods and men ..."

Robert interrupted impatiently, "All very interesting, but why take our child?"

Bernard stood up and faced Robert who hadn't moved from the doorway, "I think it has a lot to do with it. Your child touched the rune stone belonging to Freya. Freya would only take those that have requested help. Freya is the granter of magic, a healer, she protects the weak. She is love and peace; she would not do such a thing out of malice."

"Great, the bitch is a fuckin' hippie, so what? I don't care if she's done this out of love, I want my daughter back."

"Tomorrow night your daughter will have been gone for three days and we will lose her forever; a body without its soul can't live beyond three days."

Helen groaned loudly and began to sob, "NO! NO! You've got to get her back, she's mine ..."

Robert came to her immediately and held her tightly, "We will, we will." He looked up at Bernard who watched Helen thoughtfully, "Won't we?"

Bernard didn't answer straight away; he thought for a moment then sat down in his chair, "It'll have to be tonight. We can't wait; besides it's a full moon, perfect conditions to contact Freya if memory serves me well; but I'll need to prepare. Tell me, do you own a cat?"

Robert looked at him stunned, "Why ...? Yes, we have a bloody cat ..."

Helen wiped her face, "We always have, ever since Cherry was born, why?"

Bernard nodded and smiled, "You see, Freya had two blue cats to pull her chariot, so cats were sacred to Freya. We might need it ..."

Helen stared at him at the implications of his unspoken words, but it was Trevor who said it aloud. "To sacrifice you mean?"

Bernard merely looked across at him and nodded once. "We have a lot of preparations to do. I need to read up on a specific ritual that should tell us who your daughter was ..."

"Who my daughter 'was'?" Helen looked panicked, "She hasn't gone anywhere; why are you talking past tense?"

Bernard reached out and touched her hand reassuringly, "No, I mean, who she was in my village. I've got a good idea from what you've told me, but I'd like to be sure."

"Your village? You mean my child is another reincarnation?" Helen shook her head, "That can't be. We lived in York; everyone associated with this place lives near here."

"You can be re-born anywhere in the world, Helen, at any time, but by coincidence, where do you live now Helen?"

"Well, yes, but we moved here, I mean, it can't be ..."

"Nothing happens by chance, everything happens for a reason, and might I add that York has a strong connection with the Norse period. Your move was necessary for all of this to happen. What's your second name?"

"Gunn. Helen, Rose, Gunn. Why?"

"Gunn is an old Norse word meaning 'battle'."

"So what? I don't care what my name means. You said you thought you knew who my daughter had been?"

Bernard shook his head and smiled, "Yes, I think it's the only explanation that makes sense. The runes were made by Rafarta. She spoke with the Goddess Freya regularly and worshipped her above all other deities if I remember correctly. Rafarta knew something bad was coming. She could see things we couldn't. She saw our battles, our eviction from Ireland and she saw the illness coming and what would happen to the village; I'm sure of it."

Bernard sat back and crossed his legs, "She made these rune stones and then she hid them. What if she saw the future this far ahead and asked to be saved from the darkness that has consumed the others? What if she asked Freya to take her soul to her kingdom safely until it was her time to walk on the earth again? What if she asked to be kept safe from the blackness so intensely that when she saw her village site again and touched her old magic, Freya took what Rafarta had asked her to take; her soul. I think Freya is keeping her promise made a thousand years ago."

Chapter Thirty-Four

The doctor rushed into the room ahead of the nurse and clasped the child's limp wrist. "She's getting weaker by the minute. I'm surprised she's still breathing on her own. What was her blood pressure on the last check?"

The nurse picked up the chart and read it quickly, "It's still stable, but her temperature has risen." She gently placed the thermometer in the child's ear and waited a moment. "It's risen another degree; it's not looking good, is it?"

The doctor met her stare for a brief moment before returning his attention to the girl. "Everything has come back negative. I just can't understand it." He took the child's chart and looked at the scans, "There's nothing here, no lesions, no scars, no lumps, nothing to explain this. If anything, everything points to the child just being asleep, but nothing has woken her or stimulated the brain waves. There's no sign of any drugs, or abuse in any way, it's as if her little body just gave up and fell asleep! I'm at a loss with this one."

The nurse reached out and gently touched his arm, seeing he needed to off-load.

"Do you know Derek Morgan came in to have a look? I called him on the off chance he would give me some clues and he's the specialist for sleep problems but even he was stumped. He double checked everything, sat there, in that chair, and scratched his head! Do you know his suggestion? 'Have you tried gently shaking the girl?'" He sighed loudly, "I just don't know what's wrong!"

The nurse reached over and squeezed his shoulder, "You've done everything possible for this child, don't beat yourself up. If you want to blame anyone, blame those so called parents of hers."

"Still no sign of them eh?"

"No, the police have asked us to inform them if they come back, but they've disappeared; a bit weird if you ask me. They looked so genuine when they came in with her, they had me fooled anyway."

"Fooled? You mean you think they had something to do with this?" He looked down at the little girl. "I have to be honest, if they were involved, I can't see how, there's nothing showing up anywhere, toxicology was completely clear, her blood, her urine, everything is clear. But as you say, looks a bit suspect doesn't it, to leave their child here."

The nurse checked the drip, "Well, all I know for certain is that loving parents don't leave their seriously ill child without a damned good reason, don't you think?"

The doctor shrugged as he looked down at the child. Poor little Charlotte, he thought, she looked so peaceful and small in the hospital bed. He reached down and gently took one of her hands in his own. Her skin was so pale, like ivory, he could see the blood pumping through her vein in her small wrist and felt a wave of sadness for this little girl. She shouldn't be alone; where were her parents?

He suddenly glanced up as a shiver ran through his body. The room had grown very cold in only seconds and he could see his breath in the air as he breathed out. He looked across at the nurse and saw she had felt it too. She was rubbing her hands together and staring around the small room. She looked nervous and he quickly placed Charlotte's hand beneath the covers to keep warm "This room is cold, what's happened to the heating, is it broken?" He rubbed his eyes, "And why does it look darker than usual, have the lights gone?"

The nurse hugged herself, "I don't know, we've had it checked a few times, but they don't find anything. To be honest, it feels creepy; I don't like it, none of the nurses do."

"Creepy? That's just imagination and the circumstances getting the better of you, it's just the heating gone mad and maybe they use those special bulbs now to save electricity or something? I'll make a request to have it checked again. In the meantime, keep an eye on her. I want ten-minute checks to make sure she doesn't catch a chill if the heating is getting this bad so quickly. Better get her another blanket for now, and ..." He turned to leave and stiffened. He stared into the corner farthest from the door. It was darker than the rest of the room but he could have sworn he'd seen a young girl.

"What is it?" The nurse quickly looked around and shivered.

He took a step towards the bed to make sure Charlotte was still breathing. The monitors all registered normal as they had only minutes before, but something had changed; something so subtle he couldn't see what it was, but he felt it. He'd read the theories about spirits who supposedly stayed near the body after death or hung around confused when the person is in a coma.

He'd had long debates with his fellow doctors about ghosts and the possibility of them. He'd listened to and spoken with so many patients over the years who'd seen strange phenomena that he couldn't believe they were all kidding themselves, but he found it difficult to believe. He looked towards the corner again, there was nothing there. In fact, the room felt quite normal again. He glanced down at his watch. He needed to go home and sleep, of that he was absolutely sure. His shift ended an hour ago. He was over tired. Most likely explanation.

He gave the nurse a brief smile, aware that she was watching him intently, walked quickly out into the corridor, and welcomed the familiar warmth and smell of it. The familiarity comforted him; brought him back to the real world with a jolt. He glanced back at Charlotte Gunn and sighed, he must be feeling anxiety about his patient, that was all, doubled with extreme tiredness. He'd had some kind of hallucination surely.

The nurse silently followed him out into the busy corridor and watched him as he waved goodbye to another doctor and said something to a passing nurse who smiled at his comment. She stood watching until he disappeared through the double doors on his way out. He'd felt it, she was sure of it, but had he seen it? Perhaps, but she knew he would never admit to seeing it, at least, not to her. Would he admit it to himself in the comfort of his own home? She hoped so. It would be nice to talk to someone about what she was experiencing, to share and offload her suspicions without fear of ridicule. She briefly glanced back into the quiet room and shivered; it was still there, she knew without a doubt and she quickly walked in the opposite direction, hating herself with every step.

***

"We have to get your child from the hospital." Bernard stood before the window and glanced quickly around the room. "Her body has to be with her mother as you make your statement to the goddess Freya."

"Jesus fuckin' Christ!" Robert ran his hand through his hair, "How the hell are we supposed to do that? I have no doubt both of us are under arrest the second we are spotted by the police. Our disappearance under the circumstances will have made us suspects; they'll believe we had something to do with our baby's ..." His voice broke and he shook his head.

Tony jumped in, "He's right you know. We expected to be stopped at any minute; I can't imagine they'd make the same mistake again. I don't doubt for a second the police will think these two are responsible for Cherry's condition, it's too ... oh, what's the word ...?"

"Wrong. The word is wrong; we should never have left her." Helen's voice was raw with emotion, "What kind of mother am I to leave her alone? Maybe Freya does deserve her ..."

Robert jumped up and grabbed her by the shoulders, "Don't you ever say that again. She is ours; she is ours, yours, mine, ours! Is that understood?"

Helen nodded and bowed her head, fresh tears escaped down her pale cheeks, "I'm sorry, I just ... I just don't know!"

Bernard remained standing. He watched the parents silently for a long time before finally saying, "Well, you'll need to be a lot more positive than that. You're fighting a deity for your daughter's soul, getting her out of hospital is a piss in the wind compared, so, go and get her and bring her back here; I should be ready by then ... Good luck."

They all stood in the dusk light shocked, fatigued and confused. Nobody spoke for a long time; what was there to say? Like zombies, they headed for the parked cars and climbed in, but no one started the engines. Each person sat staring into space, their minds racing with all the information that had passed over the last couple of hours. Helen seemed to shrink within herself and sat huddled in the back seat of Kathryn's car, staring through the window. Robert, Tony and Trevor were in Robert's car; both cars had the doors open so they formed a cocoon.

"So, the hospital?" Kathryn broke the silence, but for a few minutes, nobody answered her.

"Do you believe all of that?" Robert wasn't sure if he was asking himself or everyone, but he waited for any replies while he watched Helen; it was Kathryn who finally answered.

"Yeah, I think I do. I mean, I have all of these memories and feelings, you know, as he was talking, I could picture how it was, I could see the people and I remembered them. How about you?"

Robert shrugged, "I have no idea. I can't decide whether that man's a psycho, an escaped head case or a saviour. One thing's for sure though, we do need to get our daughter; I don't believe the hospital can help her." He stretched out and could just reach Helen's arm, he gently stroked it until she turned to look at him, "You were right, we should never have left our baby, but we still have time. She's still alive and she's strong."

Helen nodded, "I know Robert and I want her in my arms." She turned to Kathryn, "Let's go."

***

Bernard sat down heavily in his chair after they had gone and tried to think logically. How the hell were they supposed to do this ritual? He'd never seen it performed, but he did believe it could work, if, and the big word here was 'if', the mother was strong enough and Freya had not become attached to the child.

He considered it a bit longer then slowly stood up; there were preparations to do. The mother looked strong enough and he had no doubt of her love for her child, but could she sacrifice everything for her? He hoped it wouldn't come to that. Not because he particularly liked them, but he could do without the police snooping around his premises and dead bodies did tend to bring the police out of the woodwork.

Clicking the dogs to heel, he went into his small study and began rooting around for any information that might help them. He quickly glanced at the clock on the wall and sighed, everything had to be ready by the time they got back … IF they got back; they were taking one hell of a risk.

It was slowly getting dark; he had to meditate first, clear his head and ask for guidance; he could do that before they came back; he didn't expect them to do anything straight away; they'd have to plan the extraction of their daughter from a secure hospital very carefully.

He glanced down at the two dogs who watched him lovingly. "Well, this is something I didn't expect, eh!" The German shepherd licked his hand and he patted him. He sighed loudly; it felt good to reconnect with his past life again and to be part of this dangerous ritual was invigorating, though he had mixed feelings about where Einaar fitted in; but time would tell.

A thought struck him and he dived towards the old book he had placed on the desk. A few minutes later, he smiled and nodded to himself. "Of course, she chose half the battle-field." He was thinking quickly and began sifting through old pictures. Finding the one he wanted, he slowly sat down and stared at it. "'There is no shame in being chosen by Freya,'" he read and sighed loudly. He could remember how it felt to hope for a deity to choose you in battle. He looked at the two dogs sitting beside him, "Would she send the Valkyries to collect their souls?"

The two dogs lifted their ears to the sound of their master's voice. The Rottweiler placed his nose onto Bernard's knee and sighed loudly; Bernard ignored him and the sliver of saliva that ran down his trouser leg. He was staring into space, lost in a world of possibilities that might save his village.

He had believed wholeheartedly that the gods had turned their backs on him and his village. His soul had flown into Valhalla as he'd died fighting Halldor to the death, as had the other men; it was their reward for following him and carrying out his last orders. But, the gods had betrayed them; or so he'd thought.

Now, as a twenty-first century man, he still believed in the energies, he saw it, felt it and remembered it. He saw now that perhaps the gods hadn't betrayed the villagers, but they had become fearful and confused about which energy to follow. That damned priest had caused this. Why couldn't people believe what they wanted to believe? Why did priests always interfere instead of leaving everyone else alone?

He saw it in this time too. People spreading their beliefs in the street, knocking on his door, all convinced that their way is the correct way and you must come and follow it or you will be doomed. He slammed the book shut; he believed in energy, call it whatever you liked. He had to find a way to call it and then maybe, he could truly save his village from torment …

***

The nurse gently picked up the limp wrist and sighed, poor lamb, they were losing her, they were sure of that, but from what? She had watched various doctors and consultants go in and out of the child's room for days and each one had had that same lost look on their face. The readings didn't add up. The scans showed nothing abnormal, neither did the blood, the x-rays, everyone who entered the room felt utterly helpless in saving the girl's life and it was affecting the entire ward.

She carefully replaced the arm onto the bed and patted the child's hand. She was shocked at her reaction as the emotion rose in her throat and she attempted to choke down the sensation of a golf ball lodged in her neck. She swallowed hard and quickly moved around the small room, checking the drip, tucking in non- existent loose covers and moving the lone chair and small round table to the corner for visitors to use.

She was just straightening up from the table when she froze. She could see the small figure standing beside her as clear as day and every cell in her body became alert. She moved slowly and turned towards it. For the briefest second she thought it was Charlotte Gunn, but she was younger, smaller than Charlotte. She wore a pale brown dress that almost reached her ankles, her feet were bare. Her long pale yellow hair was loose, reaching her thin shoulders. She had pale blue eyes, a small mouth and nose.

Her mouth opened again, unsure what would happen, but she quickly closed it as the figure moved towards the bed and vanished. She would swear she hadn't seen her walk. One second she was beside her, the next, she had moved five feet. She stared at the empty air where she had stood and finally collapsed into the chair. She was shaking so violently, she tried to hug herself but it took a few tries before she could grasp herself.

She became aware of the noises from the corridor. People walking past, talking in hushed tones, someone was pushing a trolley; she heard it rattling along the passageway; all normal activities. She quickly checked her watch and found only a minute or so had passed, but it felt much longer.

Raising herself onto shaky legs, she walked slowly towards Charlotte's bed. Her nurse's training kicked in and she quickly checked everything; nothing had changed. Whatever she'd seen had been no threat to either herself or Charlotte. How she was sure of that, she refused to question right now, but it had felt as if the child was there to protect Charlotte Gunn and for that, she was grateful.

"Thank you." Her voice sounded strange and she cleared her throat as she walked to the open door. Turning back to face the room she smiled and took a deep breath to calm the last of the shakes, "Whatever you are, please help this little girl live." Turning away, she didn't see the slight movement in the dark corner or hear the whimper of a lost child.

Chapter Thirty-Five

They parked the cars a few roads away, switched off the engines and gathered around Robert's car; Trevor remained sitting in the front seat.

"I think we'll have to split up, they'll be looking for both of us." Robert reached out and held Helen's hand in both of his, "We have to believe that the gods, or whoever, are watching over her and if it's meant to happen, we'll get her out ... and then, who knows what could happen ..."

Helen didn't look convinced, but she nodded once and pulled her hand away. Robert let go, "Right then, we'll meet back here. If anything goes wrong ..." He let the sentence hang in the air as everyone mumbled some incoherent answer as they walked away. Helen went with Tony and Kathryn walked quickly beside Robert; Trevor waited in the car.

Helen changed her hairstyle as she walked by plaiting it and put on Tony's hat; she had a wrap-around scarf in the car and put up her collar. There wasn't anything else she could do in such a short space of time. Robert put on Trevor's old granddad cap and kept his head down. They had already discussed how to behave.

"Keep your head down" Kathryn had said, "And keep a tissue over your nose, as if you are upset or something."

Robert nodded, "That's a good idea." He'd fished around in his coat pocket before Kathryn handed him a wet wipe from her glove compartment. "Well, it will have to do. Sorry it's wet."

Robert grinned sheepishly, "I really don't care, I'm not good at this cloak and dagger thing; never been a wanted man before."

Helen and Tony headed off first, arms linked, Helen had found a clean tissue and was dabbing at her eyes. Robert watched her go feeling so many emotions he just wanted to scream, as fear, anger, fatigue and love rushed through him. It had to go right, it just had too.

Tony felt Helen stiffen as they neared the entrance to the main hospital. "Don't worry, we'll get her back. If you see anyone from the ward or security, just act as if you are distraught or something; put your face into my shoulder."

"I can't believe this is happening Tony. I feel like I'm walking in a nightmare. Spirits, reincarnation, a bloody Goddess for Christ's sake! Now this. Having to sneak into a hospital to steal my own child! It is unbelievable isn't it?"

Tony squeezed her arm tight as they entered the main entrance. She kept wiping her eyes and pretending to blow her nose, aware of the cameras that dotted the walls. Suddenly Tony quickly but smoothly turned her towards him as two doctors walked past. He recognised one of them from the intensive care unit; thankfully, they were engrossed in their own conversation and ignored them as they hurried past with their charts; Tony hurried in the opposite direction. Reaching the lifts, he almost stopped and turned when he saw a security guard talking to a nurse nearby, but the doors opened and he escorted Helen into the empty lift and with a hammering heart, closed the doors and pressed the button for the fourth floor.

Helen tried to move her face, but he held her securely against his chest. As if he was whispering sweet endearments, he bent close to her ear, keeping his own face turned away from the camera he'd spotted. Helen froze on hearing his barely audible word "Camera," and tried to behave as if she were crying uncontrollably which wasn't hard to do. They reached the fourth floor and stepped out onto the almost empty corridor. The nurse's station was directly opposite, but the only nurse there was on the phone and barely gave them a glance. Moving to the right, they stopped at the water fountain and pretended to drink as a doctor strode out of a room, before moving further along the corridor.

They were ten feet from her daughter's room when the nurse she had spoken to many times about her child's condition stepped out in front of them. Their eyes met, it was inevitable as she almost knocked into Helen and she stopped mid-sentence, "I'm terribly sor ..." For a moment, she just stared, as if she couldn't quite place the woman before her and then Helen and Tony saw the recognition. "You!"

"Yes, it's me. God, please don't say anything. I can't explain it, I truly can't, but I have to have my child. Please, I beg you, don't say anything, please, don't ..." Helen gushed, her heart hammered in her chest and she felt sick with fear as she saw the nurse about to ruin everything.

"Please, nurse ... Gail isn't it?" Tony butted in, "She just needs her baby. You can't save her, but her mother can."

At this, the nurse pulled her attention to Tony, as did Helen. "This woman can't save her child. She abandoned her."

"Do you truly believe that? This woman has been through hell to get back her child, and it isn't over. I swear to you now, if you stop us, her child is dead." He spat the words at her and felt the tears form behind his eyes as he spoke aloud the words no one wanted to hear. He felt Helen sag against him and gripped her harder as he kept eye contact with the nurse. "Please ..."

The nurse looked away first. She looked Helen over and seemed to notice for the first time how bad she looked.

Tony saw her indecision and stepped forward, "Please Gail, let a Mother save her baby ..."

She glanced behind them down the corridor and took a long deep breath. "The very second you take your child, the machines will give off an alarm. I doubt you'll get very far. You, can't save her here?" Seeing Helen's slight shake of her head, she continued, "I see. I don't really know why, but I believe you. Someone is watching out for your daughter, even if you weren't here ..."

"A child?" Helen stepped forward, "You've seen her too?"

The nurse slowly blew the air out of her mouth and found that she was shaking, "You know about her? I'll give you as much time as I can, which isn't much."

She was about to walk around them when Helen stopped her, "Thank you."

"Don't thank me until you bring that little girl back alive and healthy. Then, you can explain to me why I've put my job on the line and who the little girl is."

She briskly walked away and Tony pulled Helen towards Charlotte's room. The nurse's words echoed around her head, but she firmly pushed them away as she fell onto her daughter, soaking her pale skin with her tears as she hugged her close. To feel her child's heartbeat next to her own was a sensation she could never express to another person. The fear she felt overpowered her very being, but that small movement of life was like a beacon of light in her dark and terrifying world.

Tony watched her for a moment, before moving to the opposite side of the bed. He looked at the various machines and followed the wires down to the wall, and the plug. He looked back at Helen who was carefully wrapping Charlotte in a blanket and as one, they both looked down at the drip attached to her thin arm. "How the hell do we take that out?" Tony rubbed his chin, "I don't have a clue, do you?"

Helen nodded, "I'm a nurse, didn't Robert tell you?"

"The stairs are just around the corner, it's how I got Robert away. They will use them though once the alarms go off, unless ..." He looked down at the wall again, "If everything is unplugged, surely the alarms won't work?"

Helen shrugged, "I think that's what she's giving us. Unplug the machine, we'll have about five minutes before she'll come back and raise the alarm." She then turned her attention to her child again. "Not long now, baby girl. You'll come home with Mummy. I hope this won't hurt too much, but I will kiss it better I promise."

Tony watched as she gently eased out the needle and pressed a wad of cotton wool to the exposed hole. At the same time, he unplugged the machines, while Helen gently pulled off the patches on Cherry's chest that attached her to the heart monitor. She gave him a quick nod as she lifted Charlotte and headed for the door. He said a silent prayer, letting out the breath he had been holding as silence filled the room.

Helen was already out in the corridor and moving fast towards the stairs. He prayed again for help as he quickly caught her up and held open the door to the stairway.

***

Nick fought against the rope and knew screaming was hopeless but couldn't stop the noise from escaping his swollen lips. He'd heard a lot of movement coming from upstairs and it had slowly risen in its intensity. He'd heard shouting, screaming, objects being thrown and rambling words he didn't understand; it sounded foreign. Whoever had kidnapped him was losing it.

He'd seen it many times before, when druggies lost the plot over something trivial. He'd watched some go mental over a spoon or a piece of food to the extreme when he saw a heroin addict kick a pensioner to the floor. He beat him senseless just for being in his way on the pavement. He'd heard that the old guy had died from his injuries; he hadn't really given him a second thought, until now.

He was trying to loosen the rope by gently stretching it. Something he'd vaguely remembered seeing on some film once, where a man had been tied up, but had loosened the knots by pulling and releasing the rope which had weakened it. He'd been at it for hours and it was feeling a little loose around his throat, but there was no way he could get out of the bonds. Whoever the man was, he had tied him well. He'd known what he was doing and that terrified him.

It felt like forever since he'd been left in the dark. Covered in his piss, shit, and blood. Dried tears and snot covered his face and neck and his thirst was unbearable, as his throat felt raw. He'd gone through every scenario imaginable to try and guess what this bastard wanted. If he'd wanted to bugger him, he would have done it by now surely? Part of him wished that was all he wanted and would get it over and done with so he could leave. He firmly pushed away the small voice that told him after fucking him, he'd surely kill him. Maybe he could beg for his life? After all, he hadn't seen him. He didn't have a clue where he was. He clung onto that maybe.

***

The man stopped by his window and stared outside. He'd paced for so long, his leg ached and he roughly rubbed the area. The shadows of his villagers had come last night and told him about the child; he hadn't cared, but now, they talked about a bargain; their chance of freedom, of peace. They taunted him. Filled his head with their voices; voices he knew so well. Voices he had commanded. Voices of people that he'd killed out of mercy and of power.

The other chieftains at the Thing had said it plainly enough, no-one was to live. Everything was to burn and the illness sent back to the Christian God. Out of respect for him and his friendship with Ingimund, they had been willing to give him life if the illness did not take him.

After the deed was done, he had been given a lone hut in which to wait and see if the illness struck him; it did not. With each passing day, it became obvious that he had been spared; the illness had been eliminated. Halldor had been allowed to leave his hut and join Ingimund's house, where he helped him plan his attack on Caerleon; he had had the honour of dying in battle.

The voices of his villagers laughed at his rising fury until he had commanded them back to the dark place. What fools they were. He had grieved for his children and his wife, briefly; but he was a warrior, grief was not an emotion that he held onto. He was their leader, he was their chief. He had done what was necessary for their own good; even if it had been a bargain for his own life. Damned if some wench was contemplating undoing that. If he sent them into the dark, then that is where they must stay. No woman would overthrow him.

He stormed out into the hallway and opened the door beneath his stairs. He reached for the secret latch, but stopped. He stared at the back wall that doubled as a door into a secret chamber. He could almost feel the man inside stop and hold his breath. He relished that moment, feeling his fear, his uncertainty. He missed that more than anything. In this time, everyone pretended, smiled and got along. He missed the rawness of life.

If you wanted something back then, you went and got it from either another village raid or negotiation; he had always preferred the raids. Someone pissed you off, you dealt with it. Wanted a slave girl, you got her. A wife to bring forth your sons, you went and found her, wooed her and married her. Life was simpler in many ways. Honour the gods and all would be well.

Stepping back he gently closed the door and leant against the hallway wall. He glanced around at the photographs that hung there. His parents were long dead. His sister and her brood lived the other side of the world so might as well be dead. His eyes rested on the picture of himself in the army; now that had been the life. The urge to kill the enemy was not easy to hide all the time. During the war, he had managed to slaughter many Germans using guns, but in secret, he had used his knives.

Only one man had witnessed his taste for blood as he massacred three Germans in a bombed out house. He'd sneaked up and cut them to pieces, ignoring their screams for mercy. The feel of the blade against skin was a sensation never forgotten; his only regret was not having a sword or an axe to hand. The soldier who had followed him fled when he saw the pieces of human flesh scattered around the room; he had not made it very far.

He gently tapped the closed door with his foot. They would need to do the ritual by tonight and he would be ready.

***

Robert stared at the display window while Kathryn pretended to be talking on her mobile, but all the while, she was checking where the cameras were. She'd handed him a magazine she'd bought and smiled apologetically when he saw it to be a woman's magazine; "Sorry, it was the first thing I grabbed."

He flicked through it as he moved closer to the stairs. Two security men had walked through the reception area and were now engaged in conversation with a nurse only a few feet from him. He turned away and from the corner of his eye, he could see Kathryn staring further inside the hospital towards the elevators, and bit his lip when he saw Helen carrying Cherry while Tony moved in front of her. He glanced across at the security men. Any second now, they would see her. He stepped out into the middle of the corridor and was about to start shouting, when a high pitched scream rang out from the small café as Kathryn started hopping about frantically pointing at the floor, "Mice! Rats!"

The security men ran towards her as Helen and Tony moved around them and with Robert joining them to cover Cherry from view, they walked quickly out of the hospital. Robert took Cherry from Helen once they were outside and rapidly walked out of the car park, towards the cars. They were all aware of people staring at them and Helen tried to smile at a few to assure them they were not stealing a child, but no one stopped them anyway and they arrived out of breath at the cars.

Trevor smiled broadly at them as Helen climbed into the back seat with Cherry while Robert got into the driver's seat. Tony elected to stay behind and wait for Kathryn. "We'll catch you up if they haven't carted her off by now!" He gently reached down and stroked Cherry's cheek, "You tell this little one, I'll see her soon."

Helen nodded and Robert attempted to smile, "You bet we will, thanks mate." Robert was already starting the engine, "OK, let's go."

Tony watched the car for a while until it was gone from view. His heart was hammering against his chest and not just from the exertion; he was very nervous about what would happen. Stealing a child from a hospital was a major offence, regardless of whose she was.

In addition, he didn't trust Bernard one tiny bit, which upset him as he'd thought he was a nice bloke whenever they'd talked at the dig site. Now, he wasn't so sure, but none of them could think of anything else to do. He knew they all felt helpless and would need their wits about them. He had a strong suspicion that Bernard would ask them to do more that would push their beliefs to the limit and he knew he wasn't comfortable with that; but for the possible saving of a child, what could he do but comply?

He looked towards the hospital, he certainly hoped Kathryn had managed to talk her way out before they realised who she was and who had gone. They would need every person with knowledge tonight, especially someone who might have lived with these spirits before. He could barely get his head around the idea of reincarnation and being able to remember a previous life, but if it were true, they would need Kathryn on their side. Why he thought that, he wasn't completely sure, but it felt like they were stepping into a war. A battle, Bernard had said, but he was extremely worried about which side Bernard was on. No, he didn't trust Bernard one little bit.

***

Helen cradled Cherry in her arms; her head bent low over her daughter. Robert watched her, in the rear view mirror, listening to the soft tune she was singing as she held their child. He had a lump in his throat watching the scene and quickly swallowed hard. He caught the eye of Trevor who was watching him and clinging onto the dashboard as Robert lost his concentration on the road ahead. "How is she?"

When Helen didn't answer he reached behind the seat and gently touched Charlotte's hair, "How is our little daughter, Helen?"

She looked up at him then and pulled Cherry closer. "What a stupid question; all things considered!"

The sarcastic tone was not lost on him and he sighed loudly and removed his hand, "Helen, we can get her back, I know it."

"We?" She bent her head, her full attention back on her child. She gently stroked her face, her hair and kissed her cheek lightly. "Baby. Can you hear Mummy?" She spoke in a whisper, her lips brushing Charlotte's ear. The child did not stir, her eyes remained unmoving, her pulse slow and weak. Helen pulled her closer and leant forward again, "Baby, Mummy is coming to get you darling ... hold on for me please ..." Her voice broke with emotion and she swallowed it back. "I love you so much baby, I won't leave you, ever. You belong here with me. Come back to me Charlotte ..."

The lump in Robert's throat burst and tears he had held back cascaded down his cheek as he listened to his wife talk to their lost child; it broke his heart. Glancing across at Trevor, he saw him wipe a tear from his own eyes. It also occurred to him that she never once mentioned him. It was always *she* was coming, and he despised himself for feeling a fleeting pang of jealousy. He could not save his child. He could not save his marriage. Both were lost to him and that realisation broke his heart.

***

Trevor wiped away the lone tear he'd managed to catch as he listened to Helen. He wasn't sure what he was crying about the most; the lost child, Helen's love for her baby or Robert looking utterly shattered by it all. He didn't trust Bernard, and after what he'd heard today, he wasn't sure he trusted his own sanity, but what did they have to lose? The child was going to die, of that he was fairly certain. If they had to go through some charade to help the Mother at least try to believe she had a chance at saving her daughter, then he would do it. He'd seen much worse over the years in his research. Nevertheless, one thing he had noticed also, positive thinking could turn negative circumstances around and it was this that he clung onto.

The other thought that raced through his head and had done since this morning was Bernard. He was the most knowledgeable man on deities and rituals in the country, Norse especially. If believing he was a reincarnation of some man from the tenth century did it for him, then fine, he would go along, anything, to help Helen come to terms with the loss of her child. However, the threatening way he'd behaved had astonished him, and not for the first time since mentioning using Bernard's knowledge did he regret that decision. Bernard had his own agenda and that frightened him more than anything else did.

Chapter Thirty-Six

*T*he shadows walked through the empty house, their sighs unheard in the dark. They were drawn to the small bedroom where the child had slept. The child's energy was still so strong it aroused such pitiful longings deep within them. They knew that she was not nearby, but a compulsion to search nonetheless was overwhelming. They had repeated an action for such an immeasurable amount of time it was impossible to stop, even now, knowing it would lead to failure.

The man stops to listen and the woman watches him before turning her head towards the outer wall and listens too. For the briefest moment, she feels something she has not felt in an eternity, a child long ago, taken, snatched from her arms and murdered most foul. In that second before the blade tore through her, she had been grateful for death, wanted and needed it so that they would be together.

She had asked the Christian God to bring them all together; he had denied them that. His betrayal hurt them deeply and as they searched for their lost daughter, their despair and yearning had turned into a fury so powerful, it enveloped them like a blanket. She moved silently towards the garden, the smallest feeling of hope awakened; before it was gone, only sorrow remained.

***

Bernard opened the back door wide for them as Helen, refusing to give up her child, carried her into his lounge. Robert quickly followed leaving Trevor to be pushed in by Tony who had managed to catch up with them outside Bernard's house; Kathryn followed more cautiously. She'd been escorted off hospital premises with a warning following her outburst. She had convinced the staff that she'd seen a rodent of some kind scurry across the floor and they'd assured her they would investigate it immediately; the security guard had watched her walk away for some time, a grim look on his face.

Kathryn entered the bungalow and softly closed the door behind her. She loitered in the hallway for a moment, needing to keep her distance; amongst other reasons, she needed some quiet time to process what was happening; and it was all happening so fast. The Rottweiler came and licked her hand and she returned the loving gesture by patting his head; he no longer looked menacing, but one word from Bernard and she knew he would bite her. She retreated into the furthest corner of the small room. Bernard clicked his fingers and commanded the dogs to the front door to guard it; they went without question. *Just like us* thought Kathryn and folded her arms protectively.

Bernard's full attention was on Helen who now sat with Charlotte lying on the couch, her head on her mother's lap. She was watching him carefully as he quickly checked Cherry's pulse, gently lifted both her eyelids and listened to her heartbeat. Raising his head slowly, he carefully pushed back a strand of hair off Cherry's forehead and stood up, his eyes never leaving the girl.

He stood staring down at her silently, which was too much for Helen as she saw indecision in his face and she cracked, "Well? What?"

"It has just this very moment occurred to me how cold I have kept my heart all these years. I had forgotten what it was like to love a child so purely. I had shied away from it knowing the pain of separation. But now, seeing your daughter like this I feel shame ... I'm sorry."

He looked at her then and a sob escaped her when she saw the undisguised sorrow he felt, "No! Don't give up on my baby ... Please!"

"I won't give up, Helen, but you need to realise, this is going to be difficult." He fell to his knees and grasped her hand, "I'm just so sorry for this. Somehow, I feel, responsible."

"Responsible? How could you be?"

"Not me now, but Thorlak me. I was so consumed with hate and pain, I did not care who I hurt. When he gave the order to kill everyone, I was glad of it. I remember feeling that release with every person I killed. I wanted them to hurt as I did but also to be free of having to endure such sorrow. These were my people, my village ... my son. I can still feel the pain of his death. Maybe that's why I don't have any children in this life? I could never face the loss again. I have always been alone ..."

Trevor took one look at Helen's face and quickly wheeled himself further into the room. "Bernard, you say you're sorry, I'm not sure if I believe you, you'll have to prove that to us. Show us how we can save her ..."

All eyes watched Bernard as he slowly stood up and sat down heavily in his armchair. He rubbed a hand over his face, he looked very tired with dark circles under his eyes; not unlike everyone else in the room who'd been up for hours without sleep. He picked up the small book. "In here," he spoke in a hushed tone, "are the secrets of the Goddess. Hidden within these pages are numerous rituals and incantations that were passed down secretly by the women of certain families."

He held up the book, "This, my friends, is the biggest secret of all. If you didn't know what you were looking at, it would be no more than a story, a fantasy written by a woman who was burned for being a witch. And because of the story, and because she could write and the words are strange intermingled with symbols; it could only have been witchcraft as far as men were concerned."

"Men can be such bastards!"

Everyone jumped at Helen's venom, but it was Bernard who held her stare as it was directed towards him. "Yes you're right. We are, we have been, but my dear, can we not also be honourable?"

"Honourable!" She stopped herself, he saw her shoulders slump, and she looked down at her child. She drew a deep breath and let it out slowly, then glanced up at Tony, then Trevor and finally Robert, her gaze lingered longer on him before returning her attention to Charlotte, "Yes, some men can be honourable, and take risks for a good cause, even if it is unbelievable ..."

She glanced up again at Bernard and waited. He watched her for a moment, before shifting his position. He opened the book and held it out for her to see. "This here tells of rituals to summon the Goddess in times of danger. It tells of women who have been rescued and taken by Freya to a place of wonder and light. Held there for safety, until such time as they might return, or if that becomes impossible, they are given a place in her realm." He flicked through the small pages until he found a rough drawing, "See, they are brought here, to her realm, Folkvangr which means 'folk's meadow', beautiful eh?"

Helen leant over and stared down at the small drawing. It was beautiful. Images of ethereal people in flowing gowns surrounded by animals and rainbows; the whole picture had a real sense of peace and togetherness. She glanced up at Bernard and back down at her child, "Is that where my daughter is?"

"Perhaps. I have no idea, but that is where legend says her soul would be taken. Freya is the leader of the Valkyries and they will guard her soul."

"I've heard of Valkyries." Tony leant against the doorframe, craning to see the picture. "Women warriors, right? Some pictures have them half-naked, while others have them dressed in armour and helmets with hair flying. Which one is it?"

Bernard flicked through the book and stopped at a pencil drawing. Obviously drawn by the same person, but not finished. There was no colour other than a bit of shading, but the image of a woman with long flowing hair could plainly be seen. She was curvaceous with large, firm breasts. She looked powerful and strong and in charge. The features were kind, but authoritative; she was mother; she was woman. Her left breast showed while her light, translucent garment draped over the right shoulder. She had power, confidence and grace. Her long hair was flying around her while she brandished a large sword in one hand and a dagger in the other.

"Now that is what I call a Valkyrie." Tony grinned. "But I wouldn't want to meet her in battle." He stepped back to let Kathryn see the picture. "Will we see this tonight?"

Bernard shrugged, "I have no idea. For me, it would be an honour, in other circumstances of course." He quickly added seeing Helen about to retaliate, "But, if they are protecting Charlotte and Freya refuses to give her up, then, I guess, maybe, yes, we will have to show our worth and, fight this."

Tony whistled through his teeth, "I really hope Freya is willing to play nice." He turned to Trevor who had been sitting quietly watching the proceedings, "So, what about you, you're the Norse expert?"

Trevor shook his head, "Expert? No, but I have had a genuine interest in all things Norse for a long time and if I am not mistaken, Bernard, the Valkyries are the choosers of the slain. They take the bravest souls to Valhalla or Folkvangr depending, they don't take or keep little girls' souls in my opinion, unless you're going to create some kind of battle, a fight, so a brave soul can be chosen ..." Trevor let the unspoken words sink in. He looked around the room and saw that each person knew the answer; someone had to die, an exchange of souls, if the warrior was brave enough.

The silence dragged on until Kathryn, who'd kept quiet while everyone looked at the pictures, coughed to get their attention. "I'm not comfortable with this plan at all. I don't want anyone to die; I think this is getting out of hand. Nevertheless, there's also the question of that blackness of negative energy, I mean, what the hell do we do about that? Half naked warriors choosing who dies might not be the only problem."

Robert nodded, "She's right, I don't want anyone to die." He looked across at Helen who seemed to be having difficulty comprehending the situation. "You've all done so much for us, but I can't see how we can get Charlotte back. There's too much danger. I know what I am willing to do to get my daughter back, but I have no intention of letting anyone get hurt."

"But you two were also strong when you united; yes?" Bernard held his stare questioningly.

"That's true; I felt that happen in the house and on the site, but ..." Robert glanced across at Helen and licked his dry lips, "But our marriage, well, it isn't ..."

Bernard held up his hand, "Your marriage might not be the best in the world, but you are still parents and you are still connected to your child." Turning to Helen he continued, "A mother's connection is the strongest there is; are you ready to go into battle?"

Helen clung tighter to Charlotte and took a big breath, she looked at each person in the eye, "Damn' right I am. I'll fight warriors, ghosts and a Goddess if I have to. I don't expect anyone else to be involved, we're in big trouble already with taking Charlotte. If you come, I can't describe how I'd appreciate the help, but I won't hold it against anyone who doesn't." Turning back to Bernard, she stuck out her chin, "So, when do we start?"

***

The nurse sat down heavily on the empty bed, the doctor walked around it before sitting on the large chair. The inspector stood in the doorway, his notebook and pen poised to write. "So, you saw her last about an hour ago, is that right? Your four thirty check?"

The nurse slowly nodded, "Charlotte was here, no change, in fact, if truth be told, she was getting worse by the hour, but we couldn't do anything for her however many times we checked her vital signs ..."

He heard the tremor in her voice, "I see, must be hard watching a child die?" He'd asked it hypothetically, not expecting anyone to answer, but she did in a quiet voice.

"It is worse than anything you can imagine. You feel so helpless, but I tried to do my job as efficiently as possible."

"Oh, absolutely, I have no doubt." He glanced through his notes before continuing, "So, her parents haven't tried to come back and see their daughter?"

"No, not that we're aware of." The young doctor answered.

He sounded tired and the policeman wasn't surprised. A child stolen from the hospital under his shift was a terrible thing to happen, even if it was the parents who took her.

He watched the nurse who was older than the doctor was. She obviously had more experience than he did, but not, he noticed in the art of hiding something. She kept her head down and was fiddling with a piece of cotton. A slight blush on her cheek told him she knew something. She seemed glad the doctor had answered the question, so he directed it at her. "We have them on CCTV carrying Charlotte Gunn out of here; looks like they had accomplices. So, you didn't see them up here?"

"I haven't seen the parents, no."

"No? Not the parents ...?" The policeman stepped into the room and sat on the bed beside her, she didn't raise her head. "As you said, must be hard watching a child die. A mother couldn't do that ... could she?"

The nurse shrugged, "I hope not. A child needs her mother." She raised her head then and met his gaze, "I know I wouldn't deny a mother who needs to be with her child."

"You wouldn't? Where are they?"

"I have no idea."

He knew she was telling the truth and sighed, "If the child is so sick, why would they take her away from the hospital?"

"Perhaps, hospitals are not the place for a child to die. Maybe in her mother's arms is preferable, Inspector."

The young doctor had stood up and was pacing the floor, "If you know where Charlotte is, you must tell us, Gail. You know she can't live without the hospital, they might charge you with something ... Yes?" He quickly glanced at the policeman.

"He might be right, you could be charged with aiding a felony, aiding kidnapping and if the child dies, aiding a death."

Gail slowly stood up and froze. The child stood beside the chair on the other side of the room. She swallowed and opened her mouth to speak, her eyes never leaving those of the young girl who smiled. The two men turned to where she was looking; they saw nothing.

"I have nothing to say." Her voice cracked with emotion, "I pray to God that Charlotte will be alright, soon." She turned back to the doctor, "The hospital can do nothing, perhaps her mother can."

***

The darkness wrapped around them as they climbed out of the two cars. Helen still clung to Charlotte; she'd refused to give her up even for a moment as she herself got into the car. Robert had backed off, but remained as close as she would let him. He gently stroked Charlotte's hand as Tony drove and silently prayed to whoever would listen as he touched the tiny, limp hand with his own. Trevor, Kathryn and Bernard were following in the second car.

No one spoke. He'd already had a conversation with Tony as they both watched Bernard filling up Kathryn's car boot with paraphernalia. "What do you make of all that stuff?" He'd elbowed Robert in the arm getting his attention. "Do you think it'll work?"

Robert shrugged and quickly rubbed his eyes, they felt gritty and tired, but his body was alert as adrenalin coursed through his veins. "I have no idea." He eventually answered, "But whatever it all is, it'd better work or I'll lose more than my daughter tonight."

Tony hadn't been sure if he'd heard him properly, but seeing him choking back the emotion, he felt his own throat tighten. He'd been on an LSD trip years before in University and somehow this situation felt like that; real, frightening, but slightly out of place, as if he was watching it from somewhere else.

They decided to drive to the back of Thurstaston Common, the opposite end from the archaeological site where the police might be waiting for them. As it was, they parked as far up the small road as possible in the hope that the police had patrolled the area already and they would have enough time to perform the ceremony.

Walking in a line, Bernard leading, they walked quickly and quietly into the trees. It was completely silent as if the dark was holding its breath. Was the Goddess watching and waiting to see how they would fight for the soul of the child? If she were a Goddess, wouldn't she know already that they wanted Charlotte back? Helen couldn't help but think these thoughts and had verbalised them earlier.

"Yes, she is a Goddess and yes she probably does know we are coming. However, she is energy and it is our beliefs that keep her energy alive. She will wait and see what we do and will decide if we are worthy of Charlotte."

"But I am her mother! Of course I'm worthy!" Helen had blurted out.

Bernard watched her, not without pity, "Of course you're her mother and worthy of your child, but she crossed over, her soul is free and if Freya already had an understanding on your daughter's soul ..."

Now as they moved silently in the dark a thought crossed her mind. "This ghost, this child who Charlotte talked to ... Inga, do you think she's just energy?

"Yes, ghosts are energy, trapped energy that re-enact some event, like a film or their image is projected onto an area because of some reason; usually something has happened that has created a lot of energy; like a murder or another horrible act; the emotions surrounding such an event would be intense."

Bernard stopped to check their bearings before continuing, "A spirit is different. A spirit is a person who still has consciousness. They still have all of their personalities, they still think and feel. Some will be trapped while others will return to give messages to loved ones; like that fella on the television."

"So the blackness we saw, I would say they were definitely conscious, because I could feel their emotions, the same with Einaar and Astrid, but with Inga, it was more peaceful. She wasn't acting out anything, so I wouldn't put her in the 'ghost' category, I felt she had purpose and she pointed to the rune so that tells me she has awareness; but I don't think she's trapped. I think she's come back for her parents."

"Perhaps, and I'm not sure how I feel about that. I hated that man for so long and felt such a deep betrayal that it has stayed with me all this time to re-emerge in this lifetime. I wanted him to suffer. But now that I know he has, I'm not sure what I feel anymore."

"Do you ever wonder where Ranulf went? I mean, maybe he's reincarnated too?"

"I wonder all the time, but not many people can remember past lives; for all I know, you could be my son reincarnated." Seeing Helen begin to protest, he gently touched her arm, "Not that you are. I think I'd know him if I saw him; they say the eyes never change and as lovely as your blue eyes are, they're not his."

He carried on a few steps before saying almost to himself, "Maybe it's my punishment for denying Einaar his last request." Seeing Helen watching and waiting, he shrugged, "I taunted him that no god would want him or his family and refused to allow him to hold his daughter saying she'd already gone to the weak and impotent

God while he could stay in Hel. He wept while he knelt before Halldor and said he would be with his family in heaven, or walk the earth together …"

He shook his head, "To be torn from your child forever must be a terrifying concept. Would you prefer to walk the earth with your loved ones, or go to different worlds and be parted?"

When Helen didn't answer he continued in a low voice, almost to himself. "He cried out her name when he died. He cursed us all and cursed the gods for leaving him, 'I shall walk the earth to avenge this blood …' Halldor cut his head off before he could speak another word."

"Oh my God!"

He slowly shook his head, "Helen, I was a different man, from a different world. The pain you feel for Charlotte, is what I felt for my son. Can you deny that you would take your revenge on anyone if Charlotte dies?"

Helen swallowed hard to control her rising emotion, "My daughter, will not die. I have to believe that. Because if I don't, I might as well give up now … and that is not an option."

Chapter Thirty-Seven

They stopped dead, all alert when Bernard raised his hand as they entered a small clearing. Everyone listened intently, but it was silent and dark, nothing but the trees and whatever was observing them. Everyone could feel it, as if the wood and the very air they breathed was waiting; watching their every move with anticipation.

Kathryn was shaking badly and took a deep breath to try and calm herself as she scanned the darkness for any sign of a threat; they were all doing it, staring into the trees, the bushes, but it was impossible to see; only their instincts told them they weren't alone and everyone moved closer together.

Kathryn stared at Bernard's back as he scanned the trees looking for signs of people. He kept lifting his head to the sky as if he was looking for something; he seemed very aware of their surroundings and knew where he was heading. Every so often, he would stop dead and stare into the darkness as if listening, before continuing. She took another deep breath and let it out slowly and silently thanked the universe for not being trapped with the darkness; she just hoped they knew that they came with good intentions and Bernard could be trusted; how much of Thorlak still remained with him?

The darkness was solid around them, like a blanket. Kathryn glanced upwards but she couldn't see any stars; only a faint glow where the moon shone behind thick cloud. The wood was deathly silent as if every creature had stopped and was waiting to see how it would end. The air though cold and damp had a sense of something else, like it was alive and alert.

It fleetingly crossed her mind that this was all a mass hallucination of some kind. That they had talked themselves into feeling this strangeness somehow and reincarnation was a farce, nothing more. A suggestion, transferred into her brain by Mr Merton perhaps; that would be one way of stopping the dig. Being arrested by the police as she ran around the dark woods screaming about a Goddess and warrior women would probably not surprise a few people in the museum.

Mr Merton; Halldor's reincarnation. Fried her brain if she thought about it for too long. Where had he gone? She hadn't really had time to think about him and his visit since Charlotte's collapse at the site. What did he want from her by exposing who he'd been in her other life? Acceptance for what he had done. No, he had not looked contrite at all, in fact, if anything, he'd looked proud of his murders.

She moved closer to Tony, she didn't want to think about him or who he'd once been. What they were doing now was scary enough without conjuring the devil in the form of Halldor. She would deal with him another time.

Pinching her arm, she did it again, feeling the sharp pain as a reminder that it was real. No more wishful thinking that it was a hallucination; she couldn't deny it anymore. This was it, the moment when she could finally face the horrors that had plagued her life since she could remember; it might mean answers.

Answers about her dig, the village, her dreams, her memories, if they really were that. Answers that terrified her so deeply, she could barely contemplate the outcome of knowing and it made her stomach churn so badly she thought she might throw up at any moment, or piss herself. She looked towards Helen who was standing near her, Cherry in her arms wrapped in a thick blanket. She could not contemplate what she was feeling and hated herself for being such a coward. She swallowed her rising emotion and waited to see what would happen next.

***

Jonah paced the floor for hours, not really seeing his hallway, the kitchen or his lounge, but saw instead the houses and heard the sounds of his village. He breathed deeply, sure that he could smell the wood-smoke, the cold air and the scent of boar stew.

That stupid woman digging where she had no right had compromised the boundary. His human sacrifice had had no effect, but he wasn't surprised; the man had been nothing more than a useless specimen. He should have planned it better, but seeing him violating the area with his bare hands had infuriated him and besides, he'd found the bronze dagger Rafarta had asked the blacksmith to forge for her own magic. He glanced across at his locked wooden cabinet and gently tapped the small key tucked away in his jacket pocket; now it was his for his own pleasure.

He'd known of course the very second he'd first seen her at the dig that she was from the village, but he hadn't been able to place her straight away. She had been an innocent, taken into the light; he had not stopped that; he wasn't a monster. His own children had been accepted into Valhalla, he was sure of it, but he couldn't remember being with them when his own honourable death had taken him to the great hall of Odin. Maybe that was just how it worked, remembering the lives, but not the in-between bits.

Therefore, Kathryn Bailey had been one of the children released from the pain of illness and a lingering death; she should thank him for his love. Perhaps when she sees what she has unleashed she will beg for his help. It was there, now, in the wood, wrapping itself around the trees, the earth, the air, searching for the answers, searching for peace. They were his to command and his alone; he was Halldor, he was chief. Rafarta may have asked for the protection of Freya, but only he, as a warrior, was worthy of her attention.

The decision made, he armed himself with his large hunting knife, a lethal looking club he'd fashioned out of an old cricket bat and nails, and a shotgun, before unlocking the secret door to his cellar. He heard the sharp intake of breath and flinched from the stench of urine, faeces and sweat that filled his nostrils as he stepped inside. He pulled the switch without looking for it and a faint glow showed him what he was already expecting. The man was a dehydrated, terrified, stinking mess, but a man nonetheless and he would be offered to the darkness along with the others and maybe then, Freya would grant him a place in her hall.

***

"The fire might be seen, but there's nothing I can do about that." Bernard set about making a large fire with the help of Tony who, realising what he was doing had begun gathering wood. "The police are looking for her." He nodded towards Charlotte still held tightly in Helen's arms, "And you two, maybe all of you if they have looked at the hospital footage, so we need to be quick. I'm hoping that once it starts, the Goddess will help."

He refused to say more and allowed Tony to take over building the fire and lighting it as he laid out a large black blanket and lay a small red blanket over it so the black could still be seen around the edges. On all sides he placed green candles surrounded by silver ribbons and then generously sprinkled sandalwood oil in a large circle followed by lighting sandalwood incense and placing the small cones in each direction.

Kathryn was watching this with fascination and eventually asked the questions she could see everyone wanted to know. "What does all of that mean?"

Bernard nodded towards Trevor and grinned, "Trevor should know?"

Trevor had remained quiet, watching the proceedings with both interest and horror at what they were attempting to do. He suspected everyone else felt the same as him, overwhelmed, anxious, terrified that it might work and terrified that it wouldn't. He felt like his heart had been in his throat since all this terrible nightmare had begun.

Now, at Bernard's taunt, he wheeled himself a little closer to the growing fire and nodded, "Yes, I think I do." His voice sounded strange and he quickly coughed, "The red and black are the colours of Freya, protection and physical love if I am correct? Not sure about the green and silver, but the sandalwood is to bring her forth into this life and time." He quickly glanced up into the dark sky and frowned, "It is the night of the full moon, but with so much cloud coverage it is hard to see, sadly." He turned to Robert, "One of her symbols. You see, the idea is to have as many if not all of her symbols, her colours, everything that is associated with Freya that will help our call to her, isn't that right?"

"Right." Bernard bent down and picked up a small box he had covered with a bag. Whipping the bag away, he revealed a small cat box. "Freya loves her cats."

Robert gasped as Helen cried out at the same time, "What are you doing?"

A small pathetic mew from within the box stopped everyone in their tracks; it was Robert who found his voice first. "Now hang on a minute, you can't be seriously thinking about hurting an animal ...?"

"Not any old animal, Robert: your daughter's cat." Bernard placed the box beside the fire and turned to another small box that contained a goblet and small stones. "I visited your home this afternoon while you were rescuing your child." Robert knelt down in front of the cat box and put his fingers through the metal grating. Bernard gently touched his shoulder, "I'm sorry, it's necessary ..."

Robert nodded silently as Twinkle sniffed his fingers, meowed loudly and backed further into the cat box.

Robert took a steadying breath and stood up. Glancing around, needing to think about something else, he saw the stones that twinkled in the firelight, "Is that an emerald?"

"It is." Bernard did not look at him, but continued to place the goblet and stones in the centre of the blankets. "Emerald, Jade, Amber and moonstone are all sacred to Freya. Do you have any silver, Helen?"

Helen had been watching the proceedings with a distant look, but now the shock of seeing Twinkle in a box had jolted her out of her melancholy. She quickly glanced from the cat box to Bernard and back again, "I do have a silver bracelet, but what the hell are you going to do to Twinkle?"

Bernard ignored her for a moment as he began scratching markings into the soil around the circle of sandalwood. "I need your bracelet, a personal object will have more power ... and as for the cat, for your child, would you not kill a thousand cats?"

"For my child! Kill cats! Why?" Helen could feel her nerves fraying and killing Twinkle become the last straw for her.

Bernard finished what he was doing before coming to stand before her. She stood trembling and in the growing firelight, he could see the streaks of old tears even as fresh ones made her eyes glisten; she held Charlotte closer and sniffed.

Bernard reached out and touched Charlotte's hair before letting his arm fall by his side. "Freya loves cats, as I said. Freya loves all of these things. It may not be enough to get your daughter's soul back, but would you not sacrifice a thousand cats, for your child? The question will be, are you worthy of Freya's attentions?"

249

Helen let her gaze fall on the blankets, the candles, the fire, before resting on the cat box where Twinkle was attempting to claw her way out. She let out a trembling breath before looking back at Bernard, who waited patiently. "Yes, for my child, my baby girl, I would kill a thousand cats. I would kill anything to have her back."

Bernard shook his head before returning to the fire, "Be careful what you say my dear. It might come to that." He turned to Kathryn, "Now, do you have them?"

She reached into her coat pocket and held out a small cloth bag. Bernard took them carefully and breathed deeply. "They have power, you can still feel it." He tilted the bag and the rune stones fell out into the palm of his hand. He looked at Helen, "And the one Charlotte touched?"

Helen gingerly pulled out the rune, still wrapped in tissue paper and handed it to Bernard. She let out a long, shaky breath as she watched him placing the stones around the blanket with a growing feeling of unease.

***

Jonah moved as silently as he could through the trees, but without a torch, it was difficult. Add to that the body he dragged along behind him was making the going tough and he was soon out of breath. He cursed his weak and feeble body for the thousandth time and let go of the rope and bent over to try to get more air into his lungs.

He felt rather than saw a change in the dark and turned his head towards it. He could remember when his senses had been so heightened he would know all danger instinctively and move towards it without fear, but now, he sighed heavily and picked up the rope, now he was a pathetic old man who only yearned for the man he had once been.

He kicked out at the sound of a groan from his prisoner and knew his foot had found his head when he heard the gasp of pain and then silence. He knew he hadn't killed him, it hadn't been that hard, but he didn't want him making noise that would give him away. He knew they were here, the voices of the dead had told him. He'd heard about the little girl being taken from the hospital on the local news and he knew what they intended to try. That damned woman! She may be a mother, but he was chief, not her; it was his power alone that could release his people.

He'd done his homework over the years and guessed her boss Trevor would be here. He had an interest in Norse culture and history; always had. It had occurred to him that perhaps he was connected to the village, but having met him on a few occasions, he'd come away disappointed. He'd seen enough to know she'd need him for his knowledge; and he'd come.

Trevor had that lust for his old life before the accident had taken away his ability to walk, to move around, to dig; to live as he wanted. He knew and understood that lust. He felt it every moment of his pathetic, new life and knew he would rather die than continue into useless old age. Trevor had that look when he thought no one was watching, and if Kathryn had persuaded him, then he would be here. To feel something is better than feeling nothing at all; fear was the biggest emotion there was and he, Halldor, chieftain of Thurstaston, was ready to embrace it.

***

Bernard had asked them to stand in a circle around the fire. Helen reluctantly allowed him to take Charlotte and he laid her on the blanket surrounded by the rune stones, the gems; Helen's silver bracelet lay beside her as did Tony's silver ring, which he'd donated, and the cat box, where Twinkle meowed pitifully. Helen choked back the sobs as Bernard gently walked around her child sprinkling fresh sage leaves murmuring words no one could quite hear.

All eyes were on Bernard as he carefully walked around the circular altar murmuring. Trevor strained to hear the words; some he recognised, but Bernard spoke so quietly, he missed most of it. He stopped chanting as he reached Charlotte's forehead and placed the rune she had touched against her pale skin.

"What are you doing? What will happen? Will the rune stones hurt her?" Helen stepped forward unable to stay away from her child. Kneeling down she gently touched Charlotte's cold cheek. "She's barely breathing ... Her pulse is so weak ..."

Bernard didn't answer, but stepped back and raised his hands to the dark sky, "I call upon the great Goddess Freya, to come forth and be here with us on this night of the full moon. We demand to be heard. We demand to be seen. We demand to be in her company. We are worthy." He reached into a small brown bag tied to his trousers and withdrew something between his fingers. He threw its contents into the fire that made the air smell sweet.

Robert breathed it in and coughed, as did everyone except Helen who was watching Bernard with a mixture of hope, fear and horror in the centre of the circle. Robert tried to step forward to reach out to her, but he found he could not move. He glanced across the fire at Tony and Trevor, who also seemed unable to move, their arms hanging by their sides. They faced the fire, a strange distant look on their faces.

He could feel the effects of whatever drug Bernard had thrown onto the fire and he tried to hold his breath; but he had no will of his own. He'd smoked weed in University and it felt similar; but much stronger. He sensed Kathryn beside him and tried to look at her but failed.

"I call upon Freya, protector of the weak, healer and granter of magic. Mother of love and peace I call upon you here and now," Bernard continued and threw more herbs into the fire, and again the scent of something sweet filled the air. Robert tried again to hold his breath; but as much as his brain wanted it, his body refused to comply.

"Kaunez, Fehu, Uruz, Tiwaz ..." Bernard had begun chanting the strange words repeatedly and he could feel a strange sensation in the air. The dark around them began to change and feel like solid walls closing in around him. The words grew fuzzy, and slurred, as he repeated them over and over, louder and louder. The words became one, no ending and no beginning, they whirled around his head, feeling as if he were swaying with each word until abruptly, he stopped and he looked up towards the sky.

Helen was watching from the centre of the circle, the fire at once feeling intensely hot then cold. She knew logically that this couldn't be, but her mind couldn't focus on such trivial matters. As Bernard chanted the words, she became aware that the others changed. They were in and out of focus. One moment they seemed to shimmer, yet remain unmoving, as if layers were building up around the circle and she was trapped within it.

Unexpectedly, she felt a strange sense of calm; it didn't seem to matter, they would be safe, they were nothing more than energy, needed for the ritual and she was grateful. She could sense power, the energy that emanated from the others; like a wall of warmth, of love, but they were beginning to fade. From the corner of her vision, Robert and Trevor looked translucent, as if they were becoming ghosts. She knew she should call out, but her mouth did not want to move.

Her head felt muggy and very heavy, but she fought to keep her eyes open as she knelt over her child's body, holding Charlotte's cold hands in her own. Her hands felt displaced, as if they weren't really there, it was someone else's hands and she was watching them move to touch her own face, but her skin was no longer solid, it wasn't real; she wasn't real anymore. They were not translucent; she was!

All of a sudden, there was movement all around her, but no one had moved; they stood perfectly still, except for Trevor who sat like a statue. It took a while before she realised there were other people in the circle. She could see them, vague forms moving closer, fading in and out of her vision; then she was a part of them. Robert, Tony, Kathryn and Trevor, she wasn't moving, yet she was seeing them through other people eyes.

She could only watch as the forms moved around the fire and the circle. Dark shapes that caught the light, becoming solid for an instant, before dissolving into wisps of smoke and shadow once again. She knew they were the dark mass they had encountered before, writhing its way around the living. She felt the anger and hatred, the betrayal and complete hopelessness and misery within each soul and felt her heart snap with emotion for the wretched beings as they yearned to be free; to find their loved ones and be at peace.

Then, they moved as one towards the centre of the circle, towards her and Charlotte. What had been shadows of people now became one black mass of pain that flung itself towards her, coming to an abrupt halt within inches of the blanket. She could hear the screams, crying out for release, cursing the gods who had abandoned them to their wretched existence. Each soul broken and tortured beyond repair, betrayed by their chief and then their gods, all hope had left them, only a fury so powerful it had become twisted in its terror. She heard the agony of mothers and fathers long torn from their beloved children, lost and terribly alone.

Helen tried to cower from this assault on her, but she couldn't. For within all that rage, she understood. Their children had gone to a place filled with light and love and these poor souls had been left behind. She understood their pain.

Her face was sodden from tears unchecked as she stared up at the blackness. Her hand moved in the firelight and managed to grasp her daughter's hand tighter, which was cold and limp, but still there. She tried to convey her understanding but her thoughts were pulled away from her. In her head, she could hear so many voices, calling, screaming, crying, begging and in that chaos, she tried desperately to make herself heard.

The blackness stopped on the edges of the blanket, it now seemed to move, but didn't come any closer. It was separating, becoming less black, less solid. The voices in her head were fading and she found that she was able to move a little bit more. She didn't feel so hemmed in and gently cradled Charlotte in her arms. "Please, please bring her back. Take me instead. I will gladly go with you all, if she can only live."

Chapter Thirty-Eight

Kathryn watched in horror as her villagers swirled around her and the others like smoke, becoming solid ever so briefly before moving again. Her heart wrenched with so many mixed emotions she could hardly bear it. Faces whose names had long since been forgotten filled her senses and she desperately wanted to cry out that she knew them, she was one of them and to let them live.

Then, she saw him, but wasn't sure if he was real until he came further into the circle. He dragged what looked like a sack behind him, but when he let it drop, she saw that it was a man, or at least, what was left of one. Her eyes grew wide as he moved towards Trevor and Tony. He stood silently between them watching the proceedings with interest before stepping closer to the fire. Bernard noticed him too late as the man swiped him with something heavy that knocked him onto his back. Helen looked up at the movement and bent over her child instinctively but the man ignored her. It was at this point that she registered who he was: Jonah Merton, Halldor!

Jonah stared around the circle. Besides Bernard, he ignored the living, for now, his full attention was on the dark shadows that were attempting to form into solid people. People he knew. His damned people! He turned to look down at the man now lying groaning at his feet. How dare he bring his people back! It was his power and his alone for he was chief, not any weakling who could not keep watch.

Furious, he kicked out and listened with satisfaction at the impacting thud of his boot and the following gasp. He'd aimed for his face and heard the smack of contact on the man's nose; he knew without doubt that he had broken it and smiled to himself. For so long he had dampened his urge for violence in his pathetic attempts to live in this world of rules. He'd killed the occasional tramp; sending them on their way to the gods as a gift, getting rid of the undesirables, but in his heart, he knew no one would understand or thank him for it.

He turned angrily, the shotgun in his hand and now looked at each person standing around the circle. It had only just at that moment occurred to him that none of them had attempted to stop him and he carefully stepped towards the archaeologist he knew so well.

"Kathryn."

He watched her eyes grow wide at his approach, but she did not move. He slowly reached out to her and stopped. The air around her felt warm, almost fluid and he gently moved his hand around the area in front of her face. It felt strange, as if he was moving his hand in thick warm water. "Well, this is interesting. Cast a spell, has he?"

He let his hand fall and turned back to the man on the ground, "Who's been a naughty boy? How dare you call forth my people? They are MY people to command, not yours. And what about you lot?" He moved cautiously towards the three men, but knew he did not need to worry as none of them moved, except for their eyes. Walking among them, he shook his head, "Well, well, well, it's a strong one too if he's managed to still you." He moved to the centre of the circle and stood beside the fire on the opposite side to where Helen sat cradling Charlotte. "And, I'm guessing, it's all because of you."

Helen lifted her head, though it felt like lead and looked into his eyes, "Please, I don't know or care who you are, but don't ruin this for us. It's ... my daughter ..." Her voice cracked with emotion and fear, but she kept his gaze.

He watched her for a moment before gesturing with his head, "See them? They were my people. I was their chief, and still am, aren't I, Kathryn? He directed the question to her, but he was watching the growing blackness that formed behind Helen. "These were my people who I had sworn to protect and protect them I did. Because of that damned traitor Einaar, I had to find a way to protect them from Hel. It was my duty to help them find Valhalla with a sword in their hand, fighting for their lives."

"Protect them? You did not protect them. You had us slaughter them because of fear ..."

He jerked at the sound and stepped back aiming the shotgun at Bernard slowly rising to his feet. "What would you know of it?"

"Do you not see me? Thorlak was my name. Einaar is not to blame for this." He looked towards the blackness and saw the faces of people he had known. "Your fear of what was coming is to blame for this and I am to blame for following you. We killed our people in the name of Odin, but Odin did not take them in. We didn't believe in the Christian God, so they couldn't go to him. We left them in the darkness; belonging nowhere and believing nothing; wallowing in fear and anger and despair. Separated from their children because of one man's greed to be all powerful. I am damned for listening to you, Halldor, and I have not been given the grace to be reunited with my son or wife."

"If you are truly Thorlak, my brave warrior, then you would never talk such rubbish ..." Jonah gripped the shotgun tighter, "This is nonsense, it is my power to send them home to Odin and I have a sacrifice to exchange. Would you stop me, Thorlak?"

Bernard wiped a hand across his face, smearing the blood from his nose over his cheek. He sighed loudly and looked from Jonah to Helen to the four people standing motionless and terrified to the large crowd of villagers who moved between translucent and solid. They were using the energy of the living to stay in this world. He could feel their hatred and he tried not to recoil from it; he deserved it. But there was something else too. Hope; and dare he say, forgiveness?

Bernard took a deep breath, ignoring the pain from his injuries, "I am here this night to try to save this child. Help me, Halldor. Is your sacrifice worth a child's life? Perhaps helping this child who I believe was once the soul of Rafarta will help our people to find peace."

Jonah spat on the ground and glared at Charlotte, "Rafarta? That witch lied to me ..."

"Stop! Let the hatred go: for pity's sake, will you help us?" Bernard stepped forward.

Jonah glanced quickly around the circle. He dropped the shotgun and grinned as he raised the heavy club, "I will not. That pathetic body is not to save her, but it is for them, for Odin." He barely missed Bernard's head before swinging it in an arc that would have cloven a man's head in two, but Bernard was quick and dodged again. He muttered something under his breath as he and Jonah began circling each other. Bernard had a knife for use in ritual, sharp, yes, but no match for Jonah's weapon. Thankfully he didn't have too long to wait.

Tony jumped him first and dragged Jonah backwards as Robert made a grab for the club as he punched Jonah in the stomach. He went down under the two men, grunting as he was punched and kicked into submission, until eventually he lay unconscious with Tony and Robert gasping for breath above him; Robert picked up the shotgun.

"What the ... fuck ... did you ... do to ... us...?" Tony gasped between breaths.

Robert fell to his knees as his strength left him, his hands braced on his thighs as he fought for breath glancing at Helen who sat motionless, Charlotte in her arms, "What happens now? And am I seeing things or, what the fuck is that?"

Bernard stepped forward and gave Jonah a prod with his foot. "They are my villagers. My spell has made them take form again. And that ..." he looked down at Jonah, "That is, or should I say was, my chief, a mad man and the man who started all of this so long ago ..." He turned to the crowd of people who stood silently. "It is time to go home." He turned back to the fire.

Tony looked nervously around the circle at the faces of the dead. Pasty white with dead staring eyes, to a man they watched Bernard. Tony was fighting to stay awake as the word 'opium' flitted through his consciousness. "And freezing us?"

Bernard smiled, "I didn't freeze you; the spell stops the air around you and traps you inside. People who see ghosts generally tend to run, scream and shit themselves with fear, I couldn't have you do that. Now, if you please, would you go back to the outer circle?"

"What about him and that other guy?"

Bernard looked to where Tony pointed and saw Kathryn kneeling down beside a body. She glanced up and shook her head, "He's nearly dead. He really needs an ambulance."

"No!" Bernard shook his head. "An ambulance would stop this ritual; it is already growing weak from the intrusion, though he might become useful if ..."

"You can't be serious? We can't kill an innocent man!" Kathryn managed to stand a little unsteadily.

Bernard shrugged, "You need to make a choice, the child or him?"

Kathryn, Tony and Trevor looked at the man on the ground before looking at Helen who stared at them with a look of pain that broke their hearts. "Choose Charlotte, please ..." The pleading in her voice won and they slowly moved away from the body.

Robert moved quickly and came to stand behind Helen. Tony glanced once at Kathryn before moving to his right side. Kathryn whispered "Sorry" to the dying man, before walking to Robert's left so that they and Bernard covered the four directions. Trevor moved his chair as best as he could through the undergrowth and reached out towards the unconscious man. He managed to find his pulse, it was very weak, he didn't have long left, so he kept hold of his hand while he watched the others. If nothing else, he would not be alone when he died.

Bernard resumed his position before the fire standing facing Helen and the others and called once more to the sky. "Come Freya, goddess of love and fertility. Goddess of War and death, come I say, hear our plea; unite this child with her mother. We reclaim her soul from your realm. A promise asked for in one lifetime cannot be taken in another. A mistake has been made. The mother is worthy to fight for her child ..."

"No, not Helen, I will fight ..."

Bernard ignored Robert's interruption and continued, "We demand a battle for her soul, take one that is worthy. Honour your agreement ... so be it ..." As he spoke his voice grew louder and louder and filled the air around them.

Helen felt her heart almost burst from her chest as she felt the change around her. A wall of energy began pushing inward, from all sides, cocooning her from the others. Then it moved her, slowly, she was moving forward towards the fire. She wasn't sure if she screamed out but in her head she screamed "NO! Bring back my baby!" Nevertheless, the force behind her grew stronger.

She heard someone scream and registered dimly that it had been Kathryn but she couldn't turn her head; all her focus was towards Charlotte. The pressure on her back was growing, forcing her forward, ever closer towards the fire. She was on her knees, but now, she was moving, she was on her feet, and Charlotte was in her arms. The fire was only a few feet away. She could hear the shouts, the screams, the chanting but nothing registered. It didn't matter, she would be free.

Voices sounded distant and then suddenly she heard a whispered voice so close to her ear she could feel a cold breath. So quick, she barely heard the words before it was gone, replaced by another voice far away, calling her name, then close by. Was she moving or were they? She had no notion anymore only that she had her baby in her arms.

Her head felt fuzzy, full of whirling images, hot and cold. Voices grew louder, they crowded her head so all thoughts left, only the voices remained, but there were so many she could not hear or understand what they said. A light, pure and golden. Just a glimpse, before black mists floated before her eyes. Shapes of faces, people calling, beckoning, welcoming, she wanted them, but recoiled from them too; then they were gone.

She felt herself become light, no more burden, pain or suffering and she was glad of it. In that same instance, she grew fearful and she cringed from it, not without Charlotte, her baby, her child; she could never have peace without her. The faces returned, reassuring, loving and she welcomed them. Something in her mind gave in to the inevitable; it was always going to be so. She could not live without her darling baby. Life had no meaning, it never could without Charlotte. She felt herself nod, but wasn't sure to whom she had given her consent.

Nothing registered or made sense. Fleeting thoughts and questions ran through her head, but it felt so muddled, she could not place anything. She floated, of that she was absolutely sure. She was unquestionably happy as she turned her head to look down at her hand that was clasped to another, smaller hand, Charlotte!

The emotion that filled her every pore was like static electricity. She felt so alive, there, wherever they were, together. All her worries, fears and pain had disappeared and she smiled. Charlotte smiled too and giggled and then, they were both laughing with such joy; they were together and all was good and right. "I love you Mummy. Where have you been?"

"I don't know darling, but it doesn't matter now ..." And it didn't.

Within that bubble of joy and laughter, she became aware of a growing darkness. Like a rain cloud moving silently towards them. She suddenly remembered everything as memories flooded her brain and she tried to scream, clutching Charlotte to her bosom, her eyes scanning, looking for the source of danger.

"NO! YOU CAN'T HAVE HER!" Her voice sounded strange, like a whisper on the wind.

Helen stared at the dark shapes that appeared before her. She knew them; they had hurt her, taken her baby away ... "You cannot have mine! I will fight you. YOU CANNOT HAVE CHARLOTTE ..." It took every effort she could muster, but she screamed and screamed at the two entities that slowly moved towards her.

They moved closer and Helen tried to move back, but it was impossible. A strong force behind her, an immovable energy and she felt the fear creep up her throat, she was unable to make a sound.

"Don't worry Mummy," Charlotte whispered in her ear, "They don't want us, they want Inga."

Helen squeezed Charlotte closer to her, "Inga? I have seen her ..."

Saying the name aloud changed the atmosphere abruptly. She watched, as the dark shadows became a man and woman, Einaar and Astrid. The anguish in their eyes was so great; she felt a sudden rush of sadness for them. "Your daughter? Inga? Why do you think I have her? This is my child."

It was the man who spoke, "Your child has the essence of another. She may help us find our child. She had the sight once."

"But, she doesn't. This is not Rafarta, this is not the woman you seek. Her soul has chosen my daughter's body, but she cannot do what you ask. Please believe me; I would help you if I could ..."

"Mummy," Charlotte whispered, "it's okay, Inga has been looking after me, she is not lost. She's been with the pretty lady ..."

"Not lost?" The woman stepped closer, her desperation showing clearly on her pale face, "Where is my child? You have seen my daughter?"

"Yes," Helen and Charlotte said together. Helen smiled, "she is peaceful and happy, I think you have to let go of your anger and feelings of betrayal before you can see her. It is this that has kept you lost ..." Helen wasn't really sure why she said such a thing, but as she spoke, it made sense.

"Let go of my anger?" The man moved silently, stopping a few feet away. "I have no anger towards my child, only the gods who betrayed us and left us wandering the earth searching for Inga, my darling daughter. Is this Hell? To be left stranded between worlds and torn from all that I hold dear?"

"No, this is not Hell, this is ..."

"Freya would have you."

Everyone turned to look at Charlotte. She was watching the man and woman with interest.

"What do you know of it, child?"

Charlotte's features changed ever so slightly and she became someone else, an older woman, her voice full of wisdom and kindness, she smiled at the man. "Einaar, you are a brave warrior, yet your fear clouded your judgement. There is only love, Einaar. No Christian, no Norse, only love. It is we who give the loving energy names. They are everywhere, in the earth, in the air, in the water and in the heavens. Loving energy surrounds us, but if hate, anger, and fear fill our souls, we cannot see the love. Inga is waiting for you."

"You lie! How can you say there are no gods?" He stopped abruptly as a sound escaped his wife's lips. He turned to her and froze. A beautiful woman stood before them. Hair like gold reached her waist and eyes like sapphires. She wore a dress of the palest yellow and white that hid nothing, her perfect pale skin could be seen clearly; her feet were bare. An amber necklace adorned her neck and her smile was like the sun melting ice.

"My lady ..." Einaar knelt down, but Astrid remained standing. "We beseech thee, where is our child? Have we not suffered enough?"

Helen stifled a sob as a small child appeared before them. She recognised her immediately and a wave of gratitude swept through her. She clung to Charlotte as the man and woman flung themselves forward, grasping the little girl in their arms. The reunion was the most touching she had ever witnessed or would again. Their cries of joy filled her ears and she felt the tears streaming down her face.

She hadn't noticed at first, but suddenly, the family were moving further away and as they did, they were becoming less solid, until they disappeared completely. She knew they were at peace and it was beautiful. She held Charlotte close and was thankful.

The Goddess Freya was watching her, smiling ... and waiting ... but waiting for what? Helen took a deep breath and licked her salty lips. Hastily wiping away her tears, she stood straight and put Charlotte behind her. "You can't have her. Give her back to me. Her pact with you was made as another. She has another life now ... with me ..."

The woman remained unmoving, but continued to watch. "What are you waiting for?" Helen shouted, feeling the fear creeping back. "I won't let you take her without me. I won't lose her ... I won't! I'll fight you. I don't hate you, I never believed in you, but I have only love in my heart for my child. You can't have her!" Her voice cracked with pain and emotion, she could see shapes of women moving closer, "Please! Take me instead ... let her live. I'll fight you if that's what you want ...? I'll fight your Valkyries and anyone else you want but you can't have my baby ..."

The pain that shot through her body couldn't be described. Every tiny cell exploded into a billion pieces before coming back together, before exploding again. Her bones, muscles, skin, every organ was aflame with pain and she yearned to be gone, away from it. She tried to turn away, to cower from the pain, but something held her down. She heard voices, lots of noise and realised with a thud that she was back in the field.

A woman knelt over her on one side and a man knelt the other side. He held two pads, which he replaced, "Her pulse is back, getting stronger, we can move her ..." Seeing Helen's eyes open, the woman smiled, "It's all right now, you're safe." To the man she spoke sharply, "Come on, let's move."

She felt the rising panic and tried to raise her hand to move the plastic mask over her face. Seeing it the paramedic stopped her and gently replaced her hand by her side. "Try to keep that on love, it'll help you breathe."

Helen shook her head, which took every ounce of effort she had and tried to speak. Her throat felt raw, but she managed, "Char...lotte ..."

"She's right here, don't worry; she's fine."

The woman stepped aside so she could see Charlotte on the other stretcher. Her eyes were open and she was watching Helen, a big smile on her face. "Hello Mummy."

A cry broke from her throat and sobs racked her body. She fought to lean over and reached out to her daughter. They were together. Charlotte was alive ... and so was she. The paramedics eased her back onto the stretcher and lifted them both into the same ambulance that was parked a few feet away. Charlotte was placed next to her. She was aware of many voices, but had no energy left to care about anyone else. Her daughter was alive, her world was complete.

A terrible stench filled her nostrils and she turned her head away from it; registering vaguely that only someone badly hurt could create such a smell. Dimly aware of many ambulances and police, she knew it wouldn't be good news. It would not end well, but she couldn't find the space in her mind to care. Something bad was coming, news she didn't want to hear, but in that instant, seeing Charlotte lying across from her, awake and watching her closely, she couldn't concentrate on it.

Reaching out, ignoring the paramedic who was monitoring her heartbeat, she clasped Charlotte's hand and tickled the inside of her small palm. Charlotte giggled and her heart almost broke with emotion on hearing that sound. Tears ran freely down her face and Charlotte frowned, "Mummy sad?"

Helen moved the mask off her face and smiled, "Oh no darling, Mummy very, very happy. I love you ..."

"I love you too Mummy ..."

As the ambulance raced to the hospital, she allowed herself a silent moment of gratitude to the Goddess who had listened to a mother's prayer. A battle had been fought and a sacrifice had been made. There would be plenty of time to mourn that decision, but for now, they were alive and she had her child.

Epilogue

She knew Christmas was going to be a strange one, but she was thankful that they were having one and that's all that mattered. It had been a long and gruelling few months of inquests and meetings and the charging of Jonah Merton for the murder and kidnapping of one Nick Mathews and the murder of Lee Jones and the kidnapping of Helen and Robert Gunn and threatening of one Charlotte Gunn. Bernard had dropped the charge of grievous bodily harm considering Jonah was eventually considered unfit to stand trial and had been locked up in a secure hospital.

She looked across at her daughter who sat quietly watching a cartoon on the television; they had got away with it. Justice had been served, but at what cost?

The murder of the two men had been an easy thing to prove, as he was undeniably guilty of the crimes. Nick Mathews, the man he'd dragged to the field had died before the paramedics had arrived. The case of his kidnapping her and Robert had been harder to prove, but clever lawyers and evidence from key witnesses had helped them.

Key to the case against Jonah was that he had become focused on Charlotte after seeing her at the dig site; he'd used some kind of drug to place her in that coma state, believing that she was a child from a previous life and belonged to him, forcing Helen and Robert to take Charlotte away from the hospital or he would never give them the antidote and she would die. He had found them making a run for it and had gone mad, killing Robert with his shotgun before attempting to kill her as she protected Charlotte. The artefacts on the ground had been some kind of ritual he had prepared; the others had come to find them and save them from Jonah.

Sceptical at first, the police had finally accepted it and after months of interviews, it was over. The hospital had been harder to convince as no known drug had been found in Charlotte's system; but they had pleaded ignorance; what could the hospital prove?

Poor Robert, his bravery and his love for his family were what saved them. Seeing her moving towards the fire with his child, he'd fought against the energy holding him and had managed to push her so that she fell beside the fire; rolling away instinctively protecting their daughter, her hair and back on fire.

At that moment, Jonah woke and whilst the others were putting out the flames that threatened to kill Helen, he reached for his shotgun and shot Robert who stepped in front of the gun and fell into the flames. On hearing the noise, Bernard whirled around and threw his knife; Jonah would never be able to use that arm properly ever again.

They had managed to pull Robert from the flames, but he was already badly burned and dead. Collapsing on the ground, sobbing and screaming at the horrifying scene unfolded before them, the smell of burnt flesh was, for just a moment, replaced by a warm, scented wind that gently touched every person there and in that warmth, was love and acceptance. It was his love and his sacrifice that allowed the lost souls to reunite with their children.

Kathryn had told her afterwards that it had been the most powerful moment in all her life and one she would revere for the rest of her days. She believed her. Love really was the strongest feeling of all. It had helped the lost spirits of the villagers move into the light and be reunited with their loved ones and it had kept her alive with Charlotte.

She gently traced the scars that littered her right cheek and neck. The worst ones on her shoulder and half of her back were healing nicely. Thankfully, she hadn't lost her eye and her hair had grown back enough to help cover some of the damage. The hospital had given her some special make-up, which she used occasionally, but not today.

She picked up the photograph that sat on the coffee table. It had been taken the day Charlotte was born. She looked exhausted, but happy with her darling girl in her arms with Robert standing next to her looking anxious. She felt the prick of tears and stubbornly blinked them away.

She watched Charlotte for a few minutes before slowly easing herself down on the couch. She never mentioned anything; it was as if she didn't remember. Play therapy hadn't helped or family counselling until finally, the hospital told her to leave it alone. If Charlotte remembered anything, it would come out in its own time, get on with living; so she'd decided to take them up on that good advice.

Charlotte had enrolled in a new school, which she was enjoying immensely and she had just been offered temporary work in the local hospital to start in the New Year. Nurse Gail had given her a reference and spoken on her behalf; they'd become good friends.

Kathryn and Tony had finally finished the dig that had caused quite a stir. Especially when a local group came forward and showed them an old parchment, written in the tenth century that mentioned the monstrosity and murder of an entire village. They were busy organising an exhibition to show what had been discovered. Both Trevor and Bernard had become involved, giving interviews about the history of the village and Bernard had started a 'Friends of Thurstaston' group who were campaigning to keep the site open for visitors to come and see.

She glanced at the mantelpiece where their invitation leant against the clock; it would be her first gathering since Robert's death; Charlotte was very excited but she was extremely nervous. She heard what they were doing from Kathryn and Tony who came for coffee regularly but she hadn't seen the others to talk to since that night; she'd kept her distance and they'd respected it.

She sighed loudly; Charlotte heard and quickly jumped up and ran to her, giving her a quick squeeze, before returning to the floor where Twinkle lay curled up on a cushion. Charlotte tickled her under the chin absentmindedly as she watched her programme.

Emotion stuck in Helen's throat as she considered what might have been and yearned to reach out and hold Charlotte again, never letting go, but her counsellor had warned her about passing on her fears and becoming over-protective. Instead, she went out into the kitchen to prepare their supper.

She switched on the kettle and was about to reach for a plate when she felt the shift and stopped; closing her eyes, a warm breeze touched her face; like the soft caress of a kiss and she smiled, "I love you too Robert. Thank you ..."

The End

"Lo, there do I see my father.

Lo, there do I see my mother,

and my sisters, and my brothers.

Lo, there do I see the line of my people, back to the beginning!

Lo, they do call to me.

They bid me take my place among them,

In the halls of Valhalla!

Where the brave may live forever!"

The Viking Prayer

Notes from the Author

Thurstaston Common, owned by the National Trust, exists and is a lovely spot for a walk. As yet, no archaeological excavations have begun, but who knows? Wirral is renowned for its Viking finds and there are many books on the subject.

Ingimund did indeed land on the Wirral Peninsula having lost a battle against the Irish and then the Welsh, and was granted land, and for a time he was peaceful before attacking Chester city.

Human sacrifice amongst the Norsemen is documented but I have used my own interpretations as to how it might have happened.

Vikings came into contact with Christianity and over the years incorporated it into their own Pagan beliefs; but who's to say they didn't fight against it first?

The 'Thing' at Thingwall can be viewed from the road as it's on private property.

Thank you for taking the time to read Freya's Child. If you enjoyed it, please consider telling your friends or posting a short review. Word of mouth is an author's best friend and much appreciated.